I0572432

Once and Future Cities

by

Allen Ashley

Once and Future Cities
by Allen Ashley

Publication Date: August 2009
Second Edition: August 2015

Cover art by David Rix

ISBN: 978-0-9555268-9-3

The stories listed below have been previously published
in the following print publications.

My thanks and due acknowledgement to all those editors who believed in me.

"Beholders" in "Dark Horizons" (Editor Stephen Theaker);
"Black Forest Manoeuvres" in "New Wave of Speculative Fiction" (Editor Sean Wright,
Crowswing Books);
"Canoe Boy" in "New Horizons" (Editor Andrew Hook);
"Play the Pipes of Pan" in "Sein Und Werden" (Editor Rachel Kendall);
"D-Leb" in "Postscripts" (Editor Peter Crowther, PS Publishing);
"Waving Not Drowning" and "War Haven" both in "Midnight Street" (Editor Trevor De-
nyer);
"Turbulent Times" in "Poe's Progeny" (Editor Gary Fry, Gray Friar Press);
"Petrified" in "Fusing Horizons" (Editor Gary Fry);
"The Accidentalists" in "Here & Now" (Editor Jenny Barber);
"The Spaces in our Lives" in "The British Invasion" (Eds. Christopher Golden, Tim Lebbon
and James A. Moore; Cemetery Dance Books, USA);
"The Slot" in "Roadworks" (Editor Trevor Denyer);
"Murdoch Celeste" in "Dark Horizons (Editors Peter Coleborn and Jan Edwards);
"Nine Views of the Light of the World" in "Axiom" (Editor Michelle Oliver);
"Today We Were Astronauts" in "Houses on the Borderland" (Editor David Sutton, BFS
Books).

"Shirts" is due to appear in "Terror Tales" (Editors John Ford and Paul Kane) late 2009;
"Slow Planes" is due to appear in "New Horizons" (Editor Andrew Hook) in late 2009.

"The Pamela Faction",
"Flat Top",
"Stoners",
"The Short and Long of It" and
"Future Cities"
are all original to this collection.

Allen is a stalwart of the independent press scene and is well known as a writer, editor and commentator. His debut story "Dead to the World" (1982) has been reprinted on six different occasions, including a translation into Spanish. His first novel was the highly acclaimed "The Planet Suite" (TTA Press, 1997), described by Brian w. Aldiss as "The course for the future."

Since the turn of the millennium, Allen has had two previous collections of his shorter fiction published - "Somnambulists" (Elastic Press, 2004), short-listed for the British Fantasy Society award; and "Urban Fantastic" (Crowswing, 2006). "Once and Future Cities" is the third distinct collection of his unique stories.

Allen was short-listed for the BFS award for his non-fiction collection "Days of the Dodo" (Dodo London Press, 2006). As an editor, he won the BFS award for "Best Anthology" with "The Elastic Book Of Numbers" (Elastic Press, 2005). He has also edited "Subtle Edens" for Elastic Press (2008) and is currently compiling "Catastrophia", an anthology of catastrophe fiction due from PS in 2010.

Check out Allen's web site at www.allenashley.com

Contact Allen at allen@allenashley.com

Contents

BEHOLDERS

Did I fall asleep and miss a shift in the national consciousness? Was it imperative, therefore, to catch up and conform? My tastes had always been broadly mainstream and, like all the other office drones and timeservers, I liked to indulge those fantasies of the lottery win, the redundancy windfall, the retirement home overseas. I usually tried to have finished clearing the dishes and any other 'new man' chores before Cheryl and I settled down to *Paradise Homes Abroad*. I judged I had five minutes to spare but my wife was already calling me to the lounge.

Not that any of those foreign properties would ever usurp Elm Plot Manor and the place that magical childhood holiday retained in my heart.

"Has it started already?" I asked.

"Shh, there's a special news report about Baby Hayley."

I screwed my face up, trying to recall something I'd read on the tube that morning. Cheryl had put down her green tea and left it to cool and invigorate the stuffy air whilst she concentrated on the Philips Flat Screen. The news on the media's latest human-interest fixation was not good. Two months old Hayley Watkins, 'Baby Hayley' to the concerned nation, was not expected to last the week. Doctors were working round the clock to save the disfigured infant who somehow survived on one tiny lung, three deformed fingers and a dog-chewed face that barely functioned and, let's be honest, was uncomfortable to look upon. I didn't want to place a higher value on one life over another but... those paediatricians and other specialists might have been better employed *dispersed* to other cases.

"It would be the kindest thing –" I began.

"No, that's not right, Nigel," Cheryl interrupted.

"But last night you said –"

She cut me off again: "I've had second thoughts. The whole country's got to show its support. Get behind the campaign to save Baby Hayley."

What should we do? Make a donation, wear a wristband, light a candle? The kid already had the top brains from Great Ormond Street doing their utmost.

The scheduled programme of pipe dreams of a distant Eden was replaced by graphic, not to say invasive, footage of the dying minor. Those of us who weren't swept up in this emotional tornado would have to consider how to follow William Blake's lead and somehow create the idyll at home. From memories and assumptions of England's green, *peasant* land.

*

I had never really wanted to live anywhere else, despite the dabbling with romantic holiday shows. England was Elysium on Earth. Apart from the weather and the nosy neighbours and the grim school dinners…

The world seemed duller this morning. Maybe I was being too sensitive but even on the way to the station, the Brutalists and Blockists were out in force. A two man crew was lopping the greenery off the pavement trees; an articulated lorry was delaying the traffic at the main junction in order to deliver concrete slabs to pave over the flower beds next to the cab office and the parade of shops. Were we witnessing at first hand the planned uglification of Britain? Our whole environment must be cemented over so that we become like Soviet Russia, a Stalinist gulag encircled by the M25.

No, I was over-reacting. The wild garden next to Chase Taxis had long ago degenerated into an eyesore of weeds, dog shit and mustard coloured burger cartons. Any action would be an improvement.

The newspapers were all carrying 'Cut Out and Wear' Hayley masks as wraparound supplements. I looked for some action photos from last night's game but there was only a report and managerial reaction. Half of the regular TV pages had been given over to a multinational DIY firm's advertising campaign, "Grey is the new Magnolia".

The previously quite attractive women in the Costing section next door had all taken severe haircuts and were dressed unusually dowdily today. Maybe it was due to some hen night or 'sisters' ritual. It had the desired effect of removing all hint of flirtation from my daily dealings with their department. Nobody was actually wearing their Hayley masks but the ubiquitous accessory perched in readiness at every table and workstation. I lunched at my desk on rather bland ham on wholemeal, watching a gang of roofers work their way down the office opposite. They seemed to be painting over the windows in a matt shade, dark and unreflective. On evenings when I'd put in overtime, I'd often looked up and watched the sunset hues sparkle in Cane Co.'s glass façade. No more.

Dwayne had his huge Nike sports bag on his shoulder. I envied him his freedom to attend the gym three nights a week.

"What is all this uglifying stuff, Nige?" he muttered. "I just don't get it."

"I hadn't noticed it was a social movement," I answered.

"Well, I'm against it," he confirmed.

Several people on the busy street had donned their tabloid souvenirs to show solidarity with the poor, hideous baby's plight. However, riding the tube home I got a seat quickly as if a whole host of people had decided not to show themselves today.

Soon, the train was full of sullen teenagers, presumably off to a gig. They were all dressed in nondescript clothes not far removed from bin bags; most were also heavily tattooed and pierced. It was like a neo-punk revival without the lightning streak face paint and the bright peacock Mohicans. As I watched, they drew out penknives and began further scarification. I stayed alert, only skimming the evening paper and its reports of further bombsites and shell craters, but the punks didn't bother me and my overly bright tie. They alighted one stop before me.

The Turkish guys who ran *Family Grocer* were already packing away their pavement spillage of traffic fume fruit and farm fresh potatoes. Seven hours earlier than normal, by my watch. The streets seemed dark. Cheryl told me the council had been round and boxed in the trees and reset the timings on the lampposts. The television was tuned to rolling news. She was wearing the Hayley mask but the string kept slipping and eventually she removed it and acted normally.

We ordered a pizza. The guy arrived thirty minutes later on a black and grey scooter; he kept his helmet on and looked at the floor the whole time.

The local streets were full of uncollected garbage and the tube station itself smelled of faraway but discernible sewage excavations. And I was paying over a thousand pounds a year for the privilege of using these twenty-first century futuristic facilities!

The available newspapers had reverted to the style of *The Times* circa The Crimean War with columns of dense print and barely any photos owing to 'production difficulties'. The supportive masks were still in evidence and had probably multiplied since yesterday.

I got my head down at work and didn't look up until almost one o'clock. Buzzed by my morning achievements, I decided to take a rare full hour for lunch. Everyone else, however, was choosing to stay in their booths for the duration. Even Dwayne, who was shaking his head at something on his screen but wouldn't show me what it was. Probably a sports car... with an unsporting price tag.

The sun was breaking through the patchy clouds but the River remained as grey as dishwater. There was no apparent police or pleasure cruise activity; only the beaten up barges that remembered service at Dunkirk or other evacuations were in evidence upon the ugly swell.

The Tate Modern was hosting an exhibition of the currently fashionable Blockist Art and the queues were... around the block. Many of those in the line were wearing Hayley faceplates and there was even a safe place to check them into, just outside the building. A member of staff dressed rather conspicuously in black and orange was attending to all queries about the popular new movement as well as updates from Great Ormond Street. The food hatches had dispensed with their colourful, multi-flavoured ice creams and instead offered limp sandwiches and curiously odourless coffee. I checked out the second hand bookstall and picked up a pocket guide to astronomy and a reprint of William Blake's *Illuminated Manuscripts*. The guy seemed almost embarrassed to be selling them.

In the afternoon, I followed the lead of my Friday-dreary colleagues and switched off my PC in order to watch the TV news in the staff lounge. Several supposedly unconnected groups of Japanese tourists on jets at Heathrow were refusing to disembark and were instead insisting on being flown straight back home to the neon land of the rising sun.

"Samurai scum!" somebody cursed creatively before being shushed.

American firms had started dis-investing suddenly: without warning and for seemingly spurious reasons. It looked like things would be pretty sticky in the UK for the foreseeable future. Somebody dubbed it 'The New Austerity'. I didn't think the phrase would catch on, but what did I know? Somewhere in the blink of a half-hidden eye, I appeared to have stepped out of the loop.

In our once pleasant suburban street, all the trees had been stripped, the bushes hacked down, and any remaining flowers in front gardens eliminated by secateurs and strewn in piles next to the bin bags. The pace of change was as disturbing as the change itself. The journey home and an editorial in the evening paper had started me theorising about why all this was happening. Was it guilt for the way we were systematically destroying the world? Or was it a reflection of our inner turmoil?

Indeed, had we set up our remaining mission? I'm not beautiful, so why should you be, why should the world be?

Cheryl had her hair in a towel and was wearing a shapeless old dressing gown. She'd been 'between jobs' for six months now. I wasn't so old-fashioned that I expected her to dress up for my return home or shower me with kisses and condiments. A hug or a smile wouldn't have killed her, though.

She was singularly uncommunicative until the news came on that the child I must no longer call 'The Elephant Baby' was close to death.

"We must all try harder," Cheryl asserted.

*

On Saturday, I awoke with renewed purpose.

"Pass me the phone, let's do something spontaneous."

There was a sweet little Bed and Breakfast in Brewstergate where we'd spent a long weekend just a couple of months ago. They had a vacancy.

"Come on, let's get out of this depressing city for a couple of nights, Cheryl. I've got loads of leave left. I can leave an answer phone message and take Monday off, no prob."

She looked sleep-fuddled, girlish again. "What about – you know…?"

"We can keep the radio news on in the car."

It was a bright London morning, throwing the general ugliness of the locality into harsh clarity. The Mondeo was parked right outside. With its bright red paint and once cool yellow flashes, it stood out on the drab street like a wound. I made an appointment with Harry's Garage for early next week to have it re-sprayed a more appropriate shade, preferably matt black.

We were in coastal Kent within an hour and a half. The weather was dull as a drain and there was hardly anybody about apart from a posse of workmen working flat out along the promenade. I couldn't decide whether they were improving the sea defences or hastily constructing a huge wall to block out the view across the English Channel.

We dropped our bags at the guesthouse then I insisted on exploring a little further afield. We still had the gas stove and some tins in the boot from a camping expedition last month – we could find a place to park up and picnic cowboy style on sausage and beans.

Looking for a beauty spot, I somehow wound up on the winding tarmac of a derelict industrial park. The warehouses and factory units were either boarded up or casually vandalised. Many sported the ugly white tag *Draz* repeated endlessly in bright emulsion. Didn't anyone spot him and stop him? The reprobate must have taken hours, even days to accomplish his shoddy masterpiece.

Finally, we found a council car park on the cliff top a few miles out of town. Fallow farmland and tumbledown cottages stretched away in western undulations. I was relieved to spot a group of kids on the foreshore digging in the time-honoured fashion. When they turned, I could see that several of them were wearing the Hayley Mask as a buffer against the briny wind. They seemed to be constructing walls and trenches and I was suddenly desperately nostalgic for my own childhood of co-operative sandcastles decorated with colourful heraldic flags.

A pair of parents hurried the diggers away from their beach improvements. The dull, grey, Great British overcast miraculously gave way to a beautiful sunset. The pink hues over my shoulder coloured the sands golden and gave a wondrous lustre to the topaz, shining sea. I squeezed Cheryl's gloved hand, suspecting that she was studiously failing to watch, instead shielding her gaze behind deeply polarised shades.

I'd hoped we might re-ignite our relationship with a romantic meal out. However, my still lovely but temporarily depressed wife wanted to stay in glued to the news reports on the television. Even *Millionaire* was truncated by hospital updates. I dashed out to the garage to pick up sandwiches and filter coffee. I didn't miss anything important about the dying kid. I decided to cancel our second night and come home on Sunday.

The drive home was quiet but not trouble-free. At almost every motorway bridge we passed there lurked a crowd of youths in hoodies carrying placards which were too small to read in passing. Several of these hooligans lobbed rocks at our vehicle. I guess we were fortunate that cricket still has a low priority in British schools. Cheryl was all for using her mobile to phone the police but I knew the louts would scarper at the first sound of that banshee wail.

The broadband at home was on the blink so I couldn't Google *Draz* successfully. We ate up some of the stuff in the fridge that was close to its 'Sell By' date. I locked the bathroom door and carefully removed the towel Cheryl had wrapped around the wash basin mirror. One glance showed me that the weekend had been far from relaxing.

Monday beckoned like a tired tart. Light drizzle peppered and fizzled against the grimy pavement. I opened the passenger door to collect my umbrella and noticed that the car had been tagged by the ubiquitous signatory. But how? Had he smuggled himself all the way to London in our cramped boot?

The newspapers were running a new, uglier, more realistic Hayley mask. Everybody on public transport was wearing it as a default to hide their own comparative beauty or to show their solidarity. I still wasn't sure how that worked, me and millions of others pretending to be deformed.

Business was slow and tortuous. There was a slight trickle of local dealing but America, mainland Europe, China and Japan had all frozen us out as if we were lepers. At this rate, the company would go belly up within a fortnight.

I called Cheryl and asked her to drop the car into the garage.

"I don't want to leave the house, Nigel," she whispered over the background static. "I'm still too beautiful; people will pick on me."

Once, tongue loosened by white wine and Bacardi breezers, she'd told me about a slight penchant for self-harm during her teenage years. I was glad that I used an electric shaver rather than naked razor blades. Even so, I was concerned and ached to get home.

"Borrow my big overcoat and my baseball cap, if you want to," I muttered. "Or just leave it to me."

I tried to take a lunchtime walk to calm myself down but the path to the Millennium footbridge had been fenced off. On the way back, I spied Dwayne in a doorway dragging on a cigarette despite his avowed New Year resolution.

I told him, "You know, you look the model of cool… apart from that cardboard mask propped against your shoes."

"Everything's in the eye of the beholder, Nige," he joked above the roar of the traffic.

After a lengthy trawl around the corner shop looking for something palatable, I was later getting home than I'd intended to be. Cheryl was slumped on the living room floor, her auburn hair ragged and her face furrowed by recent tears.

"Baby Hayley has died," she announced. "Haven't you heard? Don't you care?"

I put down my thin shopping bag. "Of course, it's sad," I answered, "but it's probably for the best. We didn't know her. Life goes on."

"No it doesn't!" she yelled. "It can't, not like before. Life is truly ugly. As we all are."

I sat down to offer comforting arms. Softly, I stated, "You know you're as gorgeous now – more gorgeous – than when I met you."

"No I'm not. Look at my flabby thighs, the fat on my upper arms."

She was making my shirt and tie wet. I whispered, "Cheryl, I still think you're the loveliest woman on Earth."

She jumped up suddenly, demanding, "What's so great about Earth? It's a shit hole! And have you seen the other planets?"

I stifled a smile but took her fire as a sign of improvement. "We might not be able to breathe their air, but Saturn and Jupiter are undeniably beautiful."

She surprised me with her knowledge. "Yeah? How about Mars? It's just a red dust bowl. Pluto? Dull, frozen rock. Mercury is half burnt to a cinder and Venus, the planet of love, is totally noxious!"

"What about the moon, you always loved that?"

She spat back, "It's shit if no light shines on it."

Later, as I warmed some vegetables in a saucepan, I found myself amused by this strange eulogy for a dead, young stranger.

Cheryl was refusing food and had wrapped herself in a duvet cocoon on the sofa so I ate silently on a stool in the small kitchen.

Long described as cattle trucks, the seats had been ripped out of the tube carriages so that the degenerative transformation was almost complete. *Draz* and his cronies had been busy with paint around the doors and diamond scratching on the thickened windows. Some of the station names had been removed or suffered daubs of black paint across the bright tiling. I had to keep my unsteady balance and count the stops.

The streets around the office had been blocked off. Even those old London alleyways and passages once frequented by minor Dickensian characters were impassable. I tried the main desk but the line simply buzzed. I called Dwayne on his mobile. He texted me ten minutes later, advising, "Go home and monitor it on telly."

All those wish-fulfilment TV makeover shows had drained the colour and vibrancy out of our home life and I felt like I'd fallen down a time tunnel into the grey gloom of the Eastern bloc, circa 1970. I followed the confused, ovine crowd over the bridges and along the embankment, conscious that my head was uncovered against the slight breeze. There didn't seem any point now that the kid had snuffed it but other men were in balaclavas or tightly pulled down baseball caps. The women all wore headscarves as if the Islamists had won by default. Apart from a couple of hideous crones – no, they were simply wearing Halloween masks several weeks way out of season.

It took me hours to walk home. Cheryl was still on the sofa as if she had become a chrysalis. I wondered: Will she get through this stage and emerge as a butterfly? I decided to leave her be for now.

I took the opportunity to sort out some stuff in a box in the hall cupboard, mostly items from my old flat but also a few childhood reminiscences. I found a postcard of Elm Plot Manor and smiled sadly for the lost Eden. There were also some art prints I'd always meant to get framed and put up around the flat. They seemed to have lost most of their lustre now. Maybe I'd just wrap them in the bin bag for the next collection.

The bread in the cupboard was a day too old so I toasted it. Cheryl roused herself from the pupa stage and silently shared this austere nourishment.

The Prime Minister addressed the nation at eight. His wife sported such a thick black veil that she could have been anybody, even his rumoured Cabinet mistress. His children had been through Goth, punk and body piercing crazes and looked phenomenally repulsive. I tried to concentrate on his words, which seemed to boil down to the usual homilies along the lines of, "We must pull together and rediscover the lost heart of England."

Cheryl sat up after the broadcast and announced, "I'm going to Hayley's funeral tomorrow."

"Are you sure you're … well enough?"

"It's my duty," she whispered.

Cheryl was up and out well before dawn in order to get a plum view. Like the rest of the traumatised nation, I sat myself down in front of the goggle box to watch the show. The scale of the ceremony was that usually associated with dead royalty or dearly departed war leaders. Did the fuss made about the deceased infant represent a shift towards a more inclusive democracy?

There was one other item in the bulletins: a rash of attacks on zoos and wildlife parks as masked protestors sought to kill 'cute and pretty animals'. The camera lingered over the butchered corpses of some ring-tailed lemurs. Texas Chainsaw on a zebra crossing…

My mobile rang. It was Dwayne.

"What's going on, man? I can't bring myself to get upset. We need to get out of this crazy city."

"Pack a change of clothes and get round here," I told him. "I'm off to pick up the car from the garage."

There was no one around in Harry's forecourt. I used the spare keys to start the ignition. The graffiti had been covered over and the tank was almost full. Result. I drove back to the flat, threw a few items in an overnight bag, picked up the spare calor gas canister from the cupboard under the sink, and scribbled a quick note to Cheryl:

"There's somewhere I've got to find. I may be a little while."

Dwayne buzzed the door.

"Are you sure about this?" he asked. Then: "Where's C?"

"She's at the Baby Hayley memorial. That kid don't mean shit to us; let her have her priorities."

The streets were remarkably clear. I kept the radio commentary on at low volume, just in case. My mobile rang.

"Can you get that for me, Dwayne, my hands are on the wheel?"

"I think you'd better take it, Nigel, it's your wife."

I pulled over, listened. She sounded frantic but frightened of showing it.

"Darling, I had a moment of epiphany. What was I doing with all those ugly people, those *deliberately* ugly people? If you're leaving, I want to go with you."

"Are the tubes and buses still running?"

"Some, just for the funeral crowd."

"Remember our first date?"

"Sure, but –"

"Meet me at Ally Pally. You've got an hour."

Dwayne looked sheepishly across at me. "Listen, Nige, if we're taking passengers, there's someone I'd like to bring along."

I'd always assumed he was the "love 'em and leave 'em" type. Changed circumstances…

"Sort it. Same rules," I muttered.

We stopped for provisions at one of the few shops in Green Lanes which hadn't been vandalised or boarded up. The fruit and veg were bundled into one corner rather than spreading out onto the pavement in the customary fashion. The labels had all been ripped from the tins, leaving only the dull steel and aluminium cylinders lining the shelves like items in a Stalinist quartermaster's stores. The owner eyed us suspiciously, fiddling with something under the counter, probably a weapon. He took our grubby notes and overly shiny coins then ushered us out.

"Early Closing," he muttered.

Wood Green Shopping City was like a ghost town, not even the usual feckless youths hanging around the bus stops and the shuttered sports wear store. Where was everyone?

The answer soon became clear. A quick check on the car radio informed us that the memorial service for late Baby Hayley was over; and suddenly the streets began to fill with disciples looking to carry out acts as apostles. Several hundred seemed to be intending to converge on the greenery around Alexandra Palace and I silently questioned the wisdom of using this landmark.

I pulled over, told Dwayne to put his Hayley mask on.

"But I can't see," he moaned.

"It's more important not to *be seen*," I answered.

An anxious, honey-skinned hand was banging on the back window. I wanted to yell: "Go away, we're ugly in here!" but Dwayne was already out of the door and ushering his – girlfriend? cousin? – Bernice into the back seat. I was worried about Cheryl and resolved to give it another five minutes. The rabble was still struggling up the hill in a disorganised yet menacing fashion.

At last, in a flurry of brown cowboy boots and a pink overnight bag, Cheryl was clambering into the passenger seat. Her outfit seemed a bit ostentatious and showy, but I said nothing. She had been back to the flat to pick a few things up and had made incredibly good time.

"Let's get out of here," she announced. "They're going to firebomb the palace."

"Why?" I frowned.

"It's a thing of beauty. It must go."

From the rear, Dwayne commented, "We saw some police vans parked up just down the way, won't they stop it?"

"Stop it?" Cheryl laughed, a throwback to her old, attractive self. "They'll probably help it – and dish out a few broken bones and bloody bruises for good measure. Wounds are ugly... and therefore acceptable."

I gunned every red light in a slowly erupting North London. Courteous driving is the first casualty of civil unrest and we avoided prangs and crashes by mere microseconds. Cheryl slumped in her seat, scared of my abrupt transformation into a stock car racer.

"If you want to be useful, check the glove box," I barked, "make sure I stuffed all the information in there."

She began to puzzle over a small package bound with two red elastic bands. At least it kept her mind off the traffic. I had to take a few detours through the suburban mayhem of Muswell Hill, East Finchley and Hampstead Garden Suburb but finally we were on the slip road and then, mercifully, the motorway.

There were plenty more cars now. Some people were driving in masks with eyeholes. Most drivers kept their foot down and ignored the other vehicles, but a few occupants waved hopefully. Should we trust them, these refugees from the dirty old town taking the grey arterial road away… to where?

After about an hour and a quarter, I pulled over onto the hard shoulder for a toilet break. I didn't trust the state of the service stations; we had water, tinned meat, dry pitta bread in the boot along with our bags.

Dwayne wiped his hands against his dark jacket, asked, "Where are we going exactly, Nige?"

"Just somewhere safe I remember as a child. I found a map for it recently."

Cheryl grabbed the bundle from the passenger seat. "You mean this page from a William Blake book?" she demanded. "He probably thought the Earth was flat. How can that help us?"

I smiled thinly as a riposte to her contorted expression. "It's a key," I replied. "Shakespeare knew it as well. The lost heart of England. Human history is a flight from Eden, a sad vector away from beauty. So we're going back to look for what we lost."

Dwayne took a pack of cigarettes from his pocket, offered them round, commented, "I always found this Camelot and Avalon shit a bit too Anglo-Saxon for my tastes."

I resealed my sports bottle, answered: "Science tells us that all the original people were black East Africans, if that helps you any. For the moment, we go where I say."

Bernice took a long drag on her Silk Cut and grinned, "Garden of Eden? Bagsie I'm the snake."

I wondered whether I should have limited the seating capacity to three, or even two, but made no comment for now.

The afternoon wore on and soon I turned off the motorway and began to drive down a succession of back roads and farm tracks. Despite my companions' doubts, I was entirely sure of *where* I was headed; the route there was far from straightforward, however. Cheryl's shaky compass skills saw us take a couple of unintended detours through decrepit one pub villages with defiled greens and the occasional ritualistically burning thatched roof. One group of browbeaten inhabitants lobbed rocks at our car; their bowling skills suggested they didn't practise sufficiently.

At last, I turned off the engine and announced, "Elm Plot Manor: this is the place."

The estate appeared unkempt, slightly wild, muddy, green and English. *Draz* and his artistic adherents had lately enlivened the walls.

"It looks like a theme park," Dwayne commented. "A really crappy one."

"It's a stately home," I replied. "Let's jimmy the lock and kip in the gatehouse then see how we feel in the morning."

Dwayne was pulling at the strings of his Hayley mask, as if reluctant to let it go. Or maybe he was reaching back to something…? Cheryl was turning her nose up at the crumbled bricks and deer droppings encircling the car. The gesture made her look ten years older and destroyed any lingering illusion of feminine beauty. Bernice, Dwayne's too good-looking girlfriend, was smoking again, the last one in the packet. She'd be suffering withdrawal symptoms by the morning. Maybe we all would.

The gatehouse was unheated and uncomfortable. At about ten minutes to midnight, the electrics failed and we were left to scrabble a couple of stub-end candles from an old cupboard before resorting to gazing solemnly at each other in the blue stinky glow of the Primus stove. We made a pretty poor bunch of survivalists and saviours of the old order in this ramshackle excuse of an Eden. I realised that the unanticipated spiritual and psychological adventure of the past few days had drained me deeply.

The gaslight flickered and our faces were further thrown into concealing shadow. Upended chairs, rolled up coats and some stale cushions formed our bed for the bleak night.

The morning brought rain and oppressive clouds. I donned my insufficiently waterproof jacket and searched the back of the car for my baseball cap as further protection against the inclemency. I was so glad that I'd thought to bring a Hayley mask with me. She might be gone but the British populace wasn't ever going to forget the brave little infant. She died for us.

The rest of my party snored on softly, arms and bodies arranged awkwardly on the makeshift bedding, like maggots or crawling insects dropped from an angler's careless hands.

I wandered around the rundown estate for half an awful hour. Why was I still swallowing that land of milk and honey nonsense? The river was just brackish water and the trees were just trunks, branches and millions of identical leaves.

I'd never been a rebel; I'd generally gone with the flow. Keep your head down and stay alive, was my philosophy.

The door to the gatehouse was hanging loose in the biting wind. I had a screwdriver in the glove box but that would only effect a temporary repair. If I could be bothered.

The journey here was a nightmare. But my mind is correct today.

We need to reclaim this place for the changed order. It's time to wake up, boy and girls.

Some of the tins I bought in London contain paint. This so-called "beautiful oasis in the heart of England" is really an absent landlord, rich bastard's tax haven, National Trust subsidised shit hole. He doesn't deserve it. We don't deserve it.

I don't even want it any more, that old paradise model. Better to be black, white and grey. Turn away from so-called beauty; embrace the *Draz*.

Dwayne, Cheryl, Bernice – are you ready?

Come on, let's smash it up, daub it, uglify it.

BLACK FOREST MANOEUVRES

It's time to stop for the night and first we need to make this place safe before we think about pressing on tomorrow. Whilst we humans have fought our territorial and brain map battles, this dark heartland of the European forest has flourished anew, like a dormant virus waiting till our attention lapsed. Most of the rumours and folk tales are simple superstition but, as my grandmother would have said, if enough people believe something, it might as well be true. Ninety percent of the woodland expanse is still officially off-limits, which makes the children's abandonment, adventure and near-death experience all the more disturbing. I've hardly spoken to them; they remain in the secular care of senior social worker Alice Greening and under the spiritual cloak of Father Riley and Abbess Grant. I am more concerned with the distinctly physical threat of tree serpents, pox fungi and wild boar. Our adult band is a cocoon around the young victims – protective but mobile and determined. The combined forces of the civil, the military and the church of The One True Jesus shall know all eventually. Eternally...

The captain is issuing orders to the guards. I wait until he can give me his full attention. We step away from the fire, converse quietly.

"This is a journey of exploration in present time," I venture, "but also a return. This is where the Anglo-Saxons came from."

His dark eyes smile more than his lips and brown bearded face. "And the Celts, too," he agrees after some thought. "The whole of Europe was heavily wooded until Roman times." He smiles, adds, "The General, of course, based many of his precepts on the Caesars."

I lower my voice further, wary of the clergy, and continue, "Many other races trace their ancestry back to the trees. For we were all apes on the edge of the African savannah."

He indicates our holy leaders with a barely discernible nod. "And if you want to swallow their Garden of Eden story, we were expelled the furthest distance from the tree of life for partaking of its knowledge. Our whole purpose is to get back to it. But will we recognise the tree when we finally locate it?"

"I thought we were seeking a house."

"This time, maybe; it's all about perception, Ralph. Agnostics and believers, here we both are under the canopy of leaves, closer than we could ever have guessed."

A sliver of moon is beginning to show between the highest branches. The rain has eased but the firewood still crackles like the devil's frying pan. It's early days in this curious mission. Hot rations tonight, I trust.

*

Alice mostly stays within a few feet or so of the children therefore I have yet to get to know her. When we rest from hiking, she shakes her long, dark hair free from her woollen hat in a most beguiling manner. No doubt she is spoken for but that need not be an insurmountable barrier. Proximity and increased intimacy shadow each other like a pair of canny wolves. My mind splits easily into two concurrent functions: the repetitive trudge and trample of our present progress; and a somewhat sordid fantasy of the maid by whom I've been smitten. She's a senior social worker. Technically below my elevated station, although it's now two years since I gave up my title in order to take junior government service. Where I come from we don't have social workers, just indentured servants.

But such a stunning beauty is above my expectation, too. As we swish and clear, I ponder opening gambits, ways to begin a friendship beyond the confines of our group talk.

I am aware still of movement all around us. We have a veritable menagerie of small woodland creatures accompanying us. Nothing too large as yet. And nothing which doesn't bow down before the rifle or the silver 'J' crucifix. We hope.

The irregularly spaced but ubiquitous tree trunks are like the bars of an erratic, enormous prison. Their grey-brown monotony dulls my eyes and I fear that I may never again gaze comfortably into the middle or far distance. Indeed, one could easily believe that we will never emerge from between these wooden shafts.

"Be wary of your step, Ralph," Captain Ellis advises. "There's pox fungi hereabouts. A heavy tread releases their spores."

So now my attention is focused on the uneven ground with its mixture of soil, leaf litter, animal droppings and occasional clusters of maroon or cherry red berries.

I am at the vanguard of our slightly straggly line, along with the hawk-eyed, authoritative captain. A few steps behind us, the priest and the nun maintain a good pace, only slowed by adjustments to their official clothing – somewhat inappropriate for this journey – which attract burrs and twig fragments. Alice encourages and cajoles the children, Pietr and Rosa, holding them to our meandering path. At the rear, a corporal and a private march with loaded rifles, wary of any danger: animal, vegetable, human or supernatural. The children wandered lost in this forest for several days and nights. They were caught by a witch and survived only through a clever deception. Their torment seems real enough but the details of their route remain understandably sketchy. Not that anything much fazes our confident, experienced captain.

"I went on survival manoeuvres with The General himself during officer training. The skills stay with you."

"I thought all but the forest fringe was out of bounds then."

"That's true, Ralph, but fighting men have to take risks. The General wasn't afraid of contamination."

"Do you mourn his passing?"

"I'm not one of the old guard clinging to his outmoded ideas. Life moves on. We live in interesting times, though. There's a lot of jockeying for position between the church and the state – by which latter I mean the army and the civilian representatives like yourself."

I stagger my step to avoid the edge of a spiky, vastly overgrown holly bush.

"Do you think it will come to conflict?" I ask.

He smiles, spreads his hands in an encompassing gesture reminiscent of my father in prime. "Not on my patch of ground," he assures.

In my first dream, the house was calling to me. Like a palace of fun, with bright lights, jittery music, cakewalk floors and slapstick bells. Soft toys crowned the roof. I was a boy, barely at school but already a little too old for such comforts and yet...

Candyfloss smells. The grass beneath my feet was stained with oil. Entrance was free, just step right up and walk right on in.

The door was one of those crazy mirrors. My head was too big, bursting with thoughts and dreams, but my truncated legs had surely carried me as far as they could. I reached out my hand to knock but the hand was coming towards mine, towards me, grabbing...

And I wake to moonlight and restless owls.

*

"Where is evil?" Father Riley booms.

"Everywhere," we dutifully reply.

"Who has sinned?"

"We have sinned."

"Who will save us?"

"The One True Jesus."

I am aware of my own voice muttering the hollow responses as we break camp on the third morning. We shall soon be on our own, deep in the self-reclaiming forest and far away from the current reach of our surviving telecommunications technology. Which leaves us hanging onto the priest's mechanical rhetoric about hardening our souls against temptation and seeking out the transgressors wherever they may be hiding. My legs are still cramped from yesterday's hike and I shuffle from right foot to left. At last he's finished.

But there's more: Abbess Grant delivers a short soliloquy of her own, something about childhood innocence, intended as uplifting but, in the cold morning air, it only comes across as opaque and puzzling.

A second night's uncomfortable sleep has made me start to wonder what exactly we are doing by dragging these two children back to the site of their life-threatening trauma. Cleansing, purging, punishing… who? Can't they be helped to rebuild their difficult lives without us forcing them to return to the scene of the crime, the "house of horror" as the daily rags have predictably dubbed it? What sort of cathartic effect are we striving for in their interests and on their behalf?

Last night I noticed Alice chaining the two youngsters lightly but definitely to a strong tree. Does she fear their kidnap? Or that they may sleepwalk their way back home? Perhaps I'll ask her – if ever the boy and girl are not in earshot.

"Quite a double act, aren't they?" Captain Ellis quips as I help him lug a fallen log out of our path. Ants and woodlice scurry away – like looking at a bomb strike, seen from the air. It takes me a few moments to work out he means the ecclesiastical couple.

"Good cop, bad cop," I reply.

"You may be more right than you realise, Ralph," he answers.

*

I have read their testimony but I have hardly spoken with the children. The curious trio of Father, Abbess and social worker keep them within a fluctuating triangle of protection and I am charged along with the captain and his men to undertake landlocked navigation and to be the first line of physical defence. Leave the spiritual, emotional and mental wellbeing to the experts, old son.

The boy is slightly older than his sister but has a dullness about his countenance. The cod psychologist in me sees several indicators of abuse; the rationalist realises I'm merely parroting clichés from news reports. The girl, on the other hand, is bright-eyed and busy, hands always touching the trees and bushes, soft voice pestering her surrogate parents with questions and queries.

I notice Alice thoughtfully gazing into her soup, occasionally risking a slight scald by stirring it with her finger. Is she torn with the same doubts as I am? That the children should be rebuilding the normal walls of their lives amid the usual routine of sums, scripture, safe play and three square meals a day.

I approach but all I can offer is, "The captain collected some nourishing roots and fungi for the broth."

She covers her tin cup with a nervous, discovered motion, manages a weak smile to distract my attention, mumbles, "A little meat wouldn't go amiss."

Has she some secret vitamin or energy-boosting store above the regular rations, which she is reluctant to share? Perhaps she is sustaining herself with some substance the church and state would frown upon.

"How are the kids holding up?" I ask.

"Very well. This is tough for them, of course. But necessary."

I stand silent and still for several seconds like a victim of Medusa. A light rain is penetrating the forest canopy and we should strive to make our temporary camp more waterproof. I nod and return to my own belongings and my own thoughts. Whatever doubts I have about the conduct of the mission I should probably save for the debriefing, which will be less than a fortnight hence.

All things being well.

This is our first sustained spell of rain and it renders the ground slippery and the visibility hazardous. I could suffer the soaking more stoically if I had more faith in our sketchy knowledge of the whereabouts of the pain house. For now, I am at the rear of our line of stragglers, skidding in the muddy footprints of our motley band. Captain Ellis does his best to set a cracking pace but the children drag their feet in a most refractory fashion, like reluctant pets or pack animals. Eventually one of them falls over – it is the sullen boy, Pietr – and we all stop for an unplanned meal break. I'm wary of sitting down as the moisture from the damp earth and tree trunks would very quickly soak into and ruin my only decent pair of hiking trousers. Instead I adopt a rather ungainly squat. The Abbess Grant approaches me after a minute or so and I rise somewhat unsteadily.

"Rest awhile, my boy," she states. "The children have brought us to a welcome halt."

I admit silent curiosity as to her age and her uncloaked appearance. I receive few clues from her plain, educated voice. Maybe if the rain persists, she will throw back her veil and reveal golden tresses of maidenly hair and the physique of an Amazon!

"They – seem a little unconvinced about this journey," I answer.

"They are too young to understand the importance of rooting out and destroying all evil. We must be strong in reminding them."

"I just wish the path from the forest wasn't so overgrown."

"The One True Jesus teaches that the road to paradise is itself narrow, fraught with dangers and often barely visible."

But we're not going towards paradise, I think. Are we?

I say, "I'm sure I'll soon become accustomed to the hardship and ardour of zealous missions."

She looks at me for a long time, causing me to again run with contrary fantasies around her hidden femininity and her spiritual fundamentalism. The silver 'J' medallion below her throat is an eye-catching adornment against her plain garb. If I concentrate, I can see myself reflected therein, imprisoned by the lustre.

In the end she merely nods, flicks an irreligious raindrop out of her lashes and goes to offer assistance to Alice and the children.

In the second dream, the house was bright and charming like a cheery seaside cottage offering ice creams on a sunny day. But within lurked my mother and father, both now mysteriously possessed of hooked, ripping claws and slavering canine mouths. I circled around; my parched dry throat an ironic counterpoint to their rabid, anticipatory dribbling. I wanted to go in to quench my thirst and cool my tongue but no safe opportunity presented itself. And so I circled. And they scuffed and shuffled, tracking me…

I am both puzzled and disturbed by this vision. I'd had a mostly contented childhood. My parents could be a little distant, as is often the way amongst the land-owning class, but they were never less than supportive, both financially and emotionally.

The dogs were, then, either figurative metaphors or non-familial characters. When Joseph interpreted for the pharaoh of ancient Egypt, the thin cows eating the fat cows meant famine would follow the years of plenty. Were the secrets of the house going to remain elusive, perhaps protected by a powerful warding spell? Or maybe mother and father were a warped vision of a different pairing? Possibly the children's future shell-shocked selves? Maybe Alice and I – in which case some power was clearly warning me to go no further down Smitten Alley.

Or else, the hellhounds were the abbess and the priest; or even their heavenly counterparts, The Virgin Wife-Mother and The One True Jesus.

All my daytime doubts are spilling into my nocturnal attempts at slumber. I will ask the captain what curative pills he carries.

The children have escaped. I should say, 'fled', 'cracked under the strain' or some other term less obviously loaded with our culpability, but there you have it…

For what seems like an age, the camp is in turmoil. How could they? Why would they? What is our purpose now?

Revealing a streak of cruelty hitherto unexpected, the abbess berates Alice for her dereliction of duty. I want to gallantly step up to her side and repel the taunts and accusations of outraged religion but the damning circumstantial evidence stays my hand and throat. The children seem to have been untied, let loose or at the very least have been held too insecurely.

"Oh what of the poor waifs now? Two sweet babes lost in these evil, oppressive woods?" her holiness rants.

But they survived before and compared to outwitting a cannibalistic crone with demonic powers, getting away from our merry band probably seems like a stroll in the park.

"Hush, my dear," Father Riley consoles. "The One True Jesus will ensure their safe passage home."

"We waste too much time on talk," the captain interrupts. "I'll send my two aides and we'll have them back before lunchtime."

"And us?" I enquire.

The priest relinquishes Abbess Grant's fair hand. "Yes, officer, please despatch your men. They can rendezvous with us later. We must complete this mission with or without the visible victims. We must never deviate from the path of finding, fighting and eradicating evil."

Stirred into bumblebee activity by his words, we skip breakfast and are back on our trek within minutes of the most basic ablutions. My stomach grumbles and I nibble disconsolately on a crust of black rye bread left over from yesterday. When fresh baked and served warm, the food is a nourishing staple; today it is dry and more than a little stale, promising to pass slowly and somewhat achingly through the gut. Does a bear shit in the woods? Does he ever feel like he's swallowed the stone instead of the plum?

"Ah, Ralph, I trust you will assist the captain with guard duties if necessary. Although I'm sure his soldiers will be back soon." I nod vague assent at the priest's ingratiating, gifts for the baby Jesus voice. "Have you ever seen a witch die, Ralph?" he continues.

"Once, when I was a boy. School trip or official function, I forget."

He grabs my arm, firmer than he'd ever dare with the abbess or the captain. "It's important not to forget. When you witness a witch die, all the evil within your own soul writhes in sympathetic pain."

"I really can't remember. I was very young."

I almost add "and innocent" but he's let go of my wrist now and I need profess no more blessed ignorance.

"We're definitely going to see a witch die," he promises.

Did his eyes strain ahead or rest on the luckless Alice?

I must stay alert to all dangers. Sacred and profane.

Stealthily, whilst our attention has been directed elsewhere at our presumed destination, we have been invaded and overrun by woodlice, beetles, worker ants and other creeping abominations. They have eaten the last of our bread and they have colonised the inner linings of our clothes, boots and bedding. I seem to have spent most of the early morning itching, scratching, delving, extricating and finally attempting to crush the chitinous carapaces betwixt the simian pincer of finger and thumb. Devious, pointless mini-monstrosities! I'm firmly with the Bible-bashers on this subject.

Even our stalwart captain grimly shakes his head and checks the seams of his jacket. Now would be a propitious time to turn back. My immediate thoughts are of the suddenly important – sadly absent – comforts of hot, soapy showers and fresh, ozone scented laundry.

"Hold fast, brethren," Father Riley intones. "This is just another minor obstacle."

How lax his domestic routine must be!

We press on.

In my expected third dream, there was no house at all. No evidence of fire damage from the children's brave escape, no sweet stuffs on roof or wall, no duplicitous rabbits and blackbirds guiding our path to the evil heart of the forest. Instead, I saw a rectangular impression in the damp ground where once the witch's cottage must have stood. No tree branches overhung the large, cleared space. For all the world, it appeared as if a gigantic hand – heavenly or diabolical – had reached within and plucked all evidence away skywards.

I realise that this vision is partly an extrapolation of my slight isolation within the group and my barely repressed longing for the companionship of the beautiful, inviolate Alice Greening. She should share the sack with me, allow me to comfort her, keep our mosquito bitten bodies warm in the manner of nomadic peoples since Adam and Eve were expelled from the garden.

We have been careless of our diet and hygiene, plucking unripe fruits from friendly tress and sipping cool, unclouded water from still pools in gentle hollows. That way lies stomach cramps and nightmares.

What are the poet's lines about the end of all our exploring? The middle of this dark wood holds a questioning emptiness. At the ancient centre of our once expanding but now contracting universe there lurks only emptiness.

I wake in the night and am immediately aware of someone or something abroad at the edge of our encampment. I move only my head, peering past the edge of the priest's stick shelter and the dwindling firelight. Reddened eyes, loping walk, a snuffling like an asthmatic – wolves!

The captain is alert and on guard, poised with rifle in hand. He catches my anxious glance in the thin moonlight; he shakes his head and briefly puts a finger to his lips. Then he rises and snaps his rifle bolt open and closed. It is enough and the wary canines scatter for pastures new.

"They can usually smell the gunpowder on my coat," he tells me. "Still, a gentle reminder never goes amiss."

"I'll finish your duty," I say.

Just after dawn, Alice emerges from her solitary cocoon, offers me the barest nod, then retreats into a stretch of trees where late the wolves made circles. I assume she's attending to feminine hygiene but when four and twenty minutes have coldly passed, I decide to go check on her.

Eventually I find her kneeling near a clump of bushes some two hundred yards away. She is collecting poisonous berries and stuffing them into her mouth, their red juice staining her stunning lips into an image of over-ripe orchids.

"I failed them, Ralph. Leave me alone now."

"It wasn't your fault. We all share the blame."

"I'll be crucified by the press and my employers when I get back. Just let me get on with this."

"That's not the whole picture. Don't let them make you a scapegoat."

She resists but fatigue has weakened her. I force her to vomit, knowing I'm breaking the goddess spell forever, reducing her from Eve to Everywoman. Maybe later she'll thank me for saving her life. For now I offer her the last of my fresh water and comfort her through the heaving and the wracking sobs until Abbess Grant comes to cast her beady eye over the suspicious scene.

Alice's attempted suicide – or episode of self-punishment – delays our progress by an hour or more. When we finally set off, I wonder whether I should have interfered at all. Maybe Alice is braver than I've given her credit for. And nobler, in the terms the late General taught. She shouldn't have been charged with the care of Pietr and Rosa on this questionable expedition. She's a caring social worker not a round the clock prison warder. She didn't make the orders; she just did her best to follow them. The children left – and likely died – because we dragged them back out here, not through a dereliction of duty on Alice's part. Yet she took all the blame to her bosom and tried to make amends.

But her sacrifice would not have brought them back. So why indulge the purging desire?

Revelation: this is the house. Real life; not a dream. From this approach, it presents its picture postcard face with a cute little cottage porch embellished with slightly expired climbing roses and vines. The leaded windows are suitably striated and opaque.

Abbess Grant begins a circuit of its outer shell, her firm white hand clasping the written ire of The One True Jesus. At first she asks for a blessing but by her second perambulation she is clearly laying down a curse. Father Riley smirks, allowing the holy sister her moment in the sunshine. Careless of the damp ground and pine needles, Alice has fallen to her knees and is praying devoutly. The captain and I stand slightly awkwardly, waiting for permission to act. I note in passing that the abbess has been careful to ensure she takes a clockwise route.

At the completion of her third progress, she rejoins the priest and bows briefly in order to kiss his ring of power. There is some inaudible whispering between them which hints of a religious conspiracy. At last the father approaches, hands deep in the voluminous pockets of his ceremonial robes. He eventually produces two large silver 'J' pendants on unnecessarily chunky chains.

"May The One True Jesus protect you," he intones.

I am not entirely comfortable about being lumbered with such ostentatious piety.

"Are you not coming inside with us, Father?"

"Not yet, my sons. The abbess and I wish to conduct extended penance some short distance away. We shall seek forgiveness for all the sins associated with this house of evil." – Which is rather unprepossessing. Around the far side, the building is run down and falling into disrepair. Not yet squalid in the tabloid manner of a 'crack house' or 'opium den', but certainly uncared for and uninviting. Unless one had been lost in the woods for several days and a sweetly singing bird called one's tired eyes to gaze only upon the more presentable façade.

Penance? Like they are to blame for what happened here. Maybe that's closer to the truth than I would wish. Momentarily, I picture the priest as the hapless woodcutter father beguiled by the selfishly beautiful abbess / stepmother, obediently abandoning his scared, young flock in the deep, dark forest. Where the stepmother waited in true guise to rid them both of the cumbersome burden of children.

Holy One True Jesus, where did that thought spring from? Has this nondescript cottage cast such a spell over my weary faculties? Or have my eyes been properly opened?

The captain is already inside the main room. I pause to stroke the walls and the supports of the porch. I lick my fingers hesitantly. No sweet taste, just brick dust and flecks of paint. The roof thatching is dry straw with nary a hint of gingerbread.

For all the talk of ridding the area of the fecund smells and foetid seed of the earth mother goddess, we are faced with evidence of the merely mundane. The same holds true within. Four wooden chairs, a dusty fireplace, a rickety table balancing on three legs and a lumpy bed too short for a soldier or the scion of a rich landowner. The knick-knacks on the shelves and in the one cupboard hold no obvious clue to evil intent: floral-patterned plates and cups, porcelain ornaments of woodland creatures and some plain white pebbles of no obvious aesthetic value. The stove in the kitchen area is impressive, if grimy. I try to picture a human cooped up in its belly. The black lead shows no sign of misuse, overwork or flame damage and I abandon the attempted visualisation.

"Where's the cage?" my companion asks. "Where are the ropes and chains?"

"I don't know. She couldn't have removed them; or if she did, there'd still be evidence. Maybe it was a psychological imprisonment."

"Not so loud, Ralph, there's always eager eyes and ears snooping at the windows. But I know what you mean. In the scriptures I read, the sacred message was one of peace and understanding, not homogeneity and submission."

"Do you think this expedition has been hijacked by the brother and sisterhood?"

Barely a whisper: "I think our whole society is headed that way. People say things about The General now he's safely dead but at least he kept the state maintaining the upper hand over the church."

"We're all pawns, aren't we? All part of the harsh Jesusisation of the depths of the forest. How inappropriate."

"I'd use stronger words than that, Ralph. But only amongst friends."

I remember my duty and capture a series of still photographs of the cottage, interior and exterior. My benefactors won't be happy with the complete lack of drama and salacious detail. Whatever – the truth will out.

The corporal and the private have returned. Clearly, they are blessed with tracking skills I don't possess; or else their technology has a greater reach and efficiency than the army admits. Either way, the two soldiers are unaccompanied. Hail fellows, well met! But -

I tend to the morning's fire, heating and decanting pots of brook water into drinkable quality, eyes and ears cocked for the news that seems ever more inevitable. The infantrymen consult with their commanding officer; the captain speaks to the priest; Father Riley calls both the abbess and Alice to hear his counsel. The younger woman erupts then implodes, her tears threatening to wash her away like a river flooding a soft chalk hill.

I am the last to officially know.

"How did the children die?"

"Combined effects of starvation and hypothermia," Captain Ellis answers.

"It's not been *that* cold –" I begin.

"And *we've* not been *that* hungry. Frankly, I'm amazed the boy and his sister survived their first adventure."

"So where are the bodies?"

"We'll pick them up on the way back."

"Won't the wolves…?"

"They're fully wrapped and protected. My men are quite well versed in bush survival. I trust them completely."

To my surprise, I find my own eyes moistening slightly. Must be due to a stray wisp of smoke from the sputtering fire.

"So, do we turn back now?"

"Not at all, Ralph." He nods towards the priest, the nun and the social worker united in an isosceles of grief. "This journey's never been about the children. Not really." Then, as if a mask or visor has suddenly fallen back into place: "Is that water cool yet? I'm sure we could all do with a drink."

The two riflemen find the witch's corpse leaning against an innocuous tree less than a hundred yards from the house. Death robs most of us of our dignity and controlling nature. Even The General looked wizened and shrunken when I filed past his open casket.

Half unrecognisable due to burn scars, this persuasively powerful crone now cuts a pathetic figure with her ironic mix of charred skin and damp rags. Somehow she must have freed herself and fled the apparent flames in the kitchen but it was too late. We place her unceremoniously down among the litter of sharp, pungent green needles and brown cones – these latter semi-petrified since falling freshly two seasons ago.

The priest and the abbess are beside themselves – and beside each other with untamed excitement. Soon they have us organised into an efficient group collecting the driest branches for a huge funeral pyre. I note that Alice tries to ingratiate herself with our spiritual guides by fetching an almost complete silver birch trunk suitable for a stake. Anger and fear multiply her physical fortitude and she resists my efforts to help her lift and lug.

In truth, the witch's carcass slumps rather than stands, despite all the captain's rope trickery. Father Riley ploughs on regardless in his preparations for the inflammatory exorcism.

"We shall kill her anew," he promises. "We shall purge our souls into righteous purity."

From within his pack, he takes out a pillow shaped parcel. He flips it open and removes several wafers of miraculously unbroken communion bread. I also catch sight of a miniature pharmacy of phials and powders: the source of Father Riley's fortitude briefly revealed.

The priest links hands with the abbess as they begin their chant of exorcism. Soon their voices merge into a wordless keening more eerie than any nocturnal yearning ever uttered by beast or fowl. The heat from the pyre is surprisingly intense. I surreptitiously rest one hand against my chest as the witch's brittle bones crackle and snap, hoping to fulfil the promise of something dying within me as well. But when I close my eyes and focus inward I hear only doors slamming, options closing down and a newly inevitable course being set.

I stagger backwards as a wave of hopelessness washes over me. I mask my faux pas as best I can with a heavy cough against the acrid smoke.

She wakes me from slumber but I find it hard to rouse myself to full alertness. I fumble with my boots; eventually I wear them unfastened, doing my best to tread quietly in her footsteps. Every scratch of leaf or soft crack of twig makes me tense my sleep-deprived muscles: a nocturnally disturbed soldier may shoot first and ask questions later.

We stop by a shallow pool formed in a depression amidst an outcrop of young trees. Does Alice intend a biology lesson about the birds, the bees, the frogs and the water boatmen?

Am I even awake?

"They've been making me take their potions but I'm off them now. I need to cast… and I want you to see the future with me."

Her fingers are even whiter than the stones she takes from her pocket. She drops the first into the water and, to my surprise, it fizzes slightly. When the thin, odourless vapour clears, I experience a feeling of vertigo and am drawn almost physically into the conjured vision.

I see the solace and the secrecy of this tucked-away cottage and its earth magic spell broken by the sudden intrusion of a platoon of soldiers, their chests resplendent with the white stake and the dangling 'J' of the fighters for The One True Jesus. And at their head, the priest and the abbess, joined in spiritual, holy matrimony. "Let us make this place safe," they exhort. "Let us reclaim this land for those who still keep faith. Let us resist The General and the wrongfulness he represented. Hail The Holy Kingdom!"

Alice is on to her last few stones now and, knowing the time is short, I peer intently at this vision of the future. The cottage and the woods around it will become a newly consecrated site of pilgrimage and, just a few years down the line, the government will grant The Disciples permission to 'trim down the trees' into cutesy topiary rather than the dark-hearted, almost impenetrable, staggering battalion of trunks currently holding the land and the myths of the soil together. My last premonition is of a paved road bringing penitents by the busload to the newly commercialised shrine.

"What can we do about all this?" I ask.

Alice shakes her dark, resigned hair. "It's the way of the future – what can anyone do?"

Her passive acceptance bothers me. Surely we have free will and what she has revealed is probability rather than certainty? What is that saying about evil triumphing because good men stand by and do nothing? Good women, too.

"We could talk this over a little further in my sleeping bag," I suggest.

Another negative head movement.

"Let's just go back quietly," she answers. "And slightly apart."

Return journeys always seem shorter and less touched by magic. Our serpentine approach to the cottage now appears unnecessarily circuitous as we cut a rapid swathe through a forest becoming increasingly mundane. The obvious conclusion is that the followers of The One True Jesus will easily clear and colonise this once-was wilderness. Just like Alice's conjured vision suggested.

I find myself counting the minutes and hours until we can expect to be home. Out of the nocturnal chill and the diurnal precipitation. Treading familiar concrete and carpet rather than squelching in leaf mulch. Away from the twin strictures of church and state. As if there's an escape from their post-General posturing anywhere.

"They're just round here," the corporal announces.

Astonishing that we should have found our way to this unconsecrated dumping ground. Astonishing that the real powers – the priests, the captains, not the mere citizens and landowners – ever sanctioned dragging the children back into this forest of death.

There is plenty of evidence of wolf and rodent attention around the hastily built shelter even though the soldiers had used several sachets of subcutaneous repellent. Undetectable by human nostrils, of course. Mercifully, the Insu-sacs are undisturbed. Alice makes the formal identification, quietly unzipping the body bags then closing them with an audible sigh and a shake of her black hair to indicate her deep sorrow at two truncated lives.

Captain Ellis's men have already constructed biers from cord and fallen logs. A carrying rota is arranged. It all seems a bit too neat and pre-ordained for my liking. Alice briefly catches my gaze. Her eyes are tearful but clear and intelligent. She mouths the letter 'J' several times at the mirror of my puzzled expression. Finally, I grasp her meaning – and none too soon, either, as Father Riley and Abbess Grant take my co-conspirator by either arm and guide her away towards comfort… control… condemnation.

Two more days pass. Two days of threshing the undergrowth; eating squirrel and fungi served with hastily boiled water; shivering in the drizzle; snoozing despite the hooting owls and the snuffling of nocturnal hunters; and a seemingly endless cycle of hoisting, lifting and transporting the young corpses. All these events are punctuated by fervent but hollow sermons from the Father and the Holy Mother whenever we pause to eat, sit or breathe.

We are almost within communications range and I am looking forward to a grand reception upon our return. Get the coffee brewing, the beers chilled, and the soft bed warming!

Our journey has been arduous and convoluted, an arboreal labyrinth as much as a learning curve. And what have we found out? That the tucked-away cottage in the deep forest heartland may be heaven or hell, a paradise or a torture chamber. Perhaps it is only a matter of interpretation.

I was mistaken: the forest will not easily relinquish its hold on us. Where on the initial journey we faced mere inconveniences of dense woodland and rough undergrowth, now the bushes are speared like barbed wire and the trunks so nigh impenetrable at points that we must squeeze sideways between them, dragging our damaged packs and tragic load with utmost difficulty over the soggy ground.

The wolves have been sniffing around again. The corporal fires regular warning shots to disperse their unwanted attention. The most recent volley injured one of the beasts; its anguish and the sympathetic mourning of its pack mates echo through the tress like a host of spectres.

Now come flocks of voracious birds and bats, zigzagging through the branches, attempting to pluck out our eyes and nip at our fingers before gouging holes in our chests. Begone, winged abominations!

They are too close for rifles so we resort to sharing pistols, fists, elbows, and penknives. The ambush brings temporary unity to our disparate band as we frantically fight off our foes, wounding and murdering from pure survival instincts.

Father Riley stands with feet firmly planted, holding his silver 'J' ahead of him as if such a bauble could create an impassable barrier. The captain is more pragmatic, gathering up a large branch and swinging aerially at the attackers, like an in-form batsman on a field of glory. I follow his lead and heft a solid lump of wood above my head... swivel... connect... repeat.

The unexpected manic activity and the ferocity of the assault leave me momentarily dizzy. I have a few scratches and grazes on my arms and cheeks but these are mere surface annoyances. A sudden movement behind me makes me turn with the face of an angered ogre -

But then I relax as I realise Alice has plunged a blade into a large crow poised close to where my shoulder had been.

"Thank you," I whisper.

"We are all warriors today," she answers.

Even as she speaks, though, the commotion is dying down and the battle is abating. The dead children are mercifully unharmed within their Insu-sacs; we protectors are all still standing. It's time to take stock, dress our wounds, and continue our planned departure from this untamed – but not invincible – forest.

We arrive to silence.

Oddly deserted streets like a ghost town.

The sky to the west is the yellow and red of exploding shells and flares, not that of a placid sunset. I can hear distant gunfire, a staccato dialogue of death.

The corporal conducts a brief conversation on his walkie-talkie. We shuffle nervously, all potential prisoners now.

"It's happened," Captain Ellis states. "The coup by those loyal to the memory of The General."

"And whose side are you on?" I ask.

"Oh, the winning side most definitely."

"And where does that leave me?"

"Listen, I like you, Ralph, even with your privileged background and your preconceptions and your poorly disguised atheism. I suggest you stock up on provisions and ammunition then make yourself scarce for a while."

"And Alice?"

"Take her with you – if you can snap her out of that trance. This is a time for soldiers, not social workers."

I know I only have sixty minutes or so to ready myself for necessary flight. I struggle not to be disabled by panic but instead borrow – all right, loot – assiduously. In the meantime, the captain has ostentatiously broken the barrel and reloaded his pistol in front of the clergyman and the nun. They are politely asked to, "Wait around for a formal debriefing."

I must be quick, though. Think survival rather than fripperies.

"Wake up, Alice, we've got to get away from this place. We've got another trip to make. Be strong. Snap out of your fugue. Wake up."

I believe we are less than a day away from the cottage now. I feel its pull like a ley line, like a magnet. I would make better progress on my own but Alice's memory of the trail is good. When she is fully with me.

It's terribly quiet. Even the animals have crept into their boles and holes. Man the hunter is in the forest. More correctly, Man the seeker.

Leave no trail of breadcrumbs. Nor white shine in the moonlight stones, dear sister. Let them not find us.

They may not have done the actual deed – although such action is clearly within their compass – but Father and Mother surely ordered the slaughter of those two poor innocents. Under the cloak of a perversion of a religion initially founded on love, tolerance and selflessness. The 'J' imprints on the children's chests gave them away. Along with the bruises and the broken ribs.

Let the real true Jesus judge them now.

Keep up, dear companion. The witch's cottage must be only a short walk away by now. Soon there'll be a clearing… a blackbird singing… and the walls will be made of gingerbread and the roof made of cake icing with hints of cherry.

And if it's just brick, timber, slate and thatch, we'll push open the door anyway and make ourselves at home in the heart of the forest… the womb of the wood… where we can be away from the old world and learn to pretend.

Again.

CANOE BOY

During the two years in which I'd lived in a flat whose garden backed onto the canal, I'd made the obvious assumption that the Canoe Boy was a local urban legend. It was only when I took some unscheduled time off work that I uncovered the veracity of this tale.

There wasn't anything specifically wrong with me. A bit of a sniffle, a trace of a throaty cough, some lethargy, a touch of so-called 'yuppie flu'... I just couldn't face the hassle of going in every day for an eight-hour shift of boredom and oscillating screen savers. I hadn't missed a day's toil at any job during the past seven years so I hoped those callous bastards were concerned and missing my sterling efforts. Or else life would just go on as normal with the Philip-shaped hole hardly noticed and soon forgotten or ignored. I'd find out when I returned.

To judge by his facial features, Canoe Boy was from an Eastern European background, possibly even Romany gypsy: the travelling salesman instinct driving his blood as he braved the drizzle that rendered the bare trees a greyer shade of brown. I was standing at the half-glazed back door idly checking for damp patches and flaky putty when I saw him mooring close to the rusty railing bordering next door's garden. I slipped on a worn but dry pair of shoes and a thin jacket, pattered out across the scrubby lawn and overgrown path, with no hat against the rain and yesterday's change from my evening paper still jangling in my trouser pocket.

Edna was there first. Salt of the earth from two doors down, praise the queen, string up the health service strikers, ain't go no time for them UFO stories, sonny. Bloody aliens, they come over here...

In a hurried, almost silent conversation, she passed over some cash and received a thin but bulging carrier bag striped in Manchester City blue and white. I was surprised to see the old racist biddy buying door to door from a foreign looking kid – although, in truth, he had probably been born in the North Middlesex Hospital and counted Green Lanes as his manor.

Canoe Boy turned to me. I didn't want anything other than the satiation of mild curiosity. He nodded at my fist unconsciously holding the handful of coins. I emptied the smash into his grubby palm. He searched briefly in the base of his small kayak, produced a thoroughly ordinary-looking cloth and a mini bottle of cleanser. I trundled back to the ground floor flat thinking that his function was completely redundant – it would be the task of mere minutes to walk around the corner down to one of the Greek or Turkish supermarkets which stayed open till gone midnight and sold everything from jack fruit to Keo lager to Funtime condoms.

I noticed my thumb marks against the door pane. A little wiping wouldn't go amiss.

Now that Becky had gone , I felt legitimised in scouring the files she'd left on my computer. She'd never divulged her Hotmail password but had saved a ton of personal emails into a non-encrypted folder. Most seemed to be confirmation of orders with Next, Amazon and the like; some others were clearly genuine catch-ups with ex-Uni. friends who were now working in Australia and the other former colonies that so appealed to today's adventurers. I shouldn't have been looking; then again, if there was anything too personal, she should have put it onto a memory stick.

There was no evidence of her misdemeanours. Probably all on the Wi-Fi phone… which she had remembered to take.

We were standing in the kitchen and I was sorting out the recycling. The radio was playing some old song of love and loss, although the signal strength was fluctuating in the high winds blowing through the neighbourhood. The coffee pot was bubbling and the scene ought to have felt and smelt as cosy as Eden.

There were too many empty brown bottles in the bag. I didn't get through San Miguel or Budweiser at quite that rate. Even though the fridge was as full as I'd normally expect, a few other puzzling furniture changes and sixth sense premonitions built up in my mind like a slow tsunami.

She was a strictly white wine girl.

I didn't ask who he was. I didn't particularly want to know.

In red knickers, she was hotter than prime time Kylie.

"I think you'd better look to get your own place," I muttered before my voice could dry up completely. "I think you know why."

The water regulations meant that my washing machine was stuck on 'pause' for nearly three hours. During this period I flushed the toilet just the once, knowing that it would not refill until Thames Aquatics gave the say-so. Two houses away – at the address belonging to Jimmy Asbo and his unsporting, sportswear-clad clan – the father of the house was cleaning his car with a mop and bucket whilst the kids teased the mongrel. How come his pipes weren't stalled? And was it the case that if he disagreed vehemently enough with new legislation he could simply ignore it?

The council had posted more leaflets about further pruning of the middle-aged street trees. They drank too many litres that could be used for running dishwashers and hose pipes, apparently. They cluttered up the pavement with trailing branches, falling leaves and dripping sap. In the ongoing war between Bureaucracy and Nature, the pen pushers and keyboard tappers continued to hold the upper hand.

Canoe Boy's loot was rather plain today: biscuits, instant coffee, sliced bread, cheap margarine and, curiously, several packets of icing sugar, their pink and white cardboard sticky with sweet leakage.

The travelling salesman himself seemed distracted and furtive as if worried someone might turn up. I noticed a white cable leading to an in-ear headphone. Maybe he was simply listening to some thrashy speed garage and it was making him a bit jittery.

I bought a jar of Nescafe, reasoning that when the water failed I could simply eat it off the spoon to get the required caffeine high.

"Can I see you?"

"I thought you never wanted to see me again, Philip."

"I'm more mixed-up than ever. I've found a few of your things around the flat."

"Can't you just post them…? Oh, all right, that Italian coffee bar we went on our second date."

Dig the knife in, Becky, why don't you? But I turned up dutifully and braved the ring of chain smokers loitering outside on the inhalation express to Cancer Town.

She was already there; strikingly beautiful with her high blonde ponytail and contact lenses that accentuated the amber shine of her calculating eyes.

"Have you seen these prices?" she moaned. "Everything's a pound dearer than it was last week."

"Water supply problems," I muttered, coaxing my thin coat onto the back of the hard wooden chair that only offered slippery purchase. "Thames Aquatics is holding the whole country to ransom."

"Well, can't they get their water from France or Poland or somewhere? There must be places in the world that still get better than average rainfall."

I shrugged. "I' dunno. I've given up caring lately."

"Dramatic sod." She took my hand. She was wearing a white gold bracelet I'd bought her last Christmas. "So, what have you got for me?" I passed over the bag and she began extracting and examining the contents. Last out was a pair of purple knickers, sheer at the rear and lacy at the front.

"Becky, don't flash them to everyone!" I exclaimed.

She smiled, "I thought you might want to keep these… you know, for those lonely nights. Listen, Phil, I was thinking – why don't you just go and do something hurtful like go off to a massage parlour with Bill and Jeff and we can call it quits and both move on?"

"It's not my style."

"Well, it's not my style to stay in the wrong. Listen, thanks for the cake and coffee but my new man finishes his shift soon so I'd better make tracks."

She took her mobile out of her over-full handbag and as she turned the screen to show me I thought it would be a mug shot of Mr Usurper but instead it was an uploaded photo of her mother's kitten with a ball of white wool.

"Cute," I agreed but she was already away to the nicotine airlock.

An enforcement officer from Thames Aquatics intercepted me as I went to swipe my card at Raft and Rapid Developments Limited. He handed me a half litre water bottle with his company's distinctive wavy logo on the label.

"Make it last, sir," he implored.

I sat at my desk, curiously glad to be back amid the subtle clutter of my workspace and the familiar hive buzz around me. On the way in, breathing in a shallow fashion to negate the sweaty armpits and soot of the tube journey, I'd felt empowered, ready to catch up with the chores I'd let slip. Now, though, I could only think about the plastic container to my immediate left. When should I drink from it and how? Take little sips throughout the day to stave off the worst of any thirst? Timed mouthfuls? Save it all up till lunchtime and polish it off with my sandwich?

I was glad of the distraction of a proposal meeting at ten thirty in Jefferson's office. I noticed that his personal water cooler sat empty by the far window but he'd made a jug of coffee for the middle of the table. I took just one mug, aware of its diuretic properties.

Jefferson had made a fortune a few years back somehow convincing a major betting house to pay up on the mostly circumstantial evidence in favour of his high stakes bet that the aliens really were visiting us. To his credit, he'd soon become bored with life by the Spanish swimming pool and, inspired by interest from a Freeview channel, had formed his own company to encourage other risk takers and venture capitalists. Fleecing the crackpots, Becky had called it from her lofty position in the more sedate financial world of Cohen and Co., but what did her opinion count for now?

Today's proposal was from an investor who sought to turn a large chunk of central London into a canal system inspired by those of Venice and Amsterdam. As a tourist magnet it was first class and as a riposte to Thames Aquatics, with the possibility of our own private reservoir, the appeal was also compelling. But it was a great idea out of its time – London was too criss-crossed with tube tunnels, gas pipes, electric and communication cables to be so easily dug up. Globalisation, immigration, steady birth rate, longer life spans and various other factors had contributed to the city's continuously rising population for the past couple of decades. There just wasn't the building space for this cool project. If only it had come along during the time of Christopher Wren or even as an alternative to the Docklands development.

Jefferson gave it the thumbs down. We all concurred, once for the real world and a second time for the next screening of *Give Me a Quarter for My Bricks and Mortar*. I went back to my desk and my already tepid water bottle. I decided that I should pop out later and purchase some fresh juice, whatever the cost.

I looked for Canoe Boy all day but he never turned up. I was low on a few essentials although I could probably get through till Monday. The peace of the Sabbath had been well and truly broken by the arrival of several vehicles carting heavy machinery to the road bordering the southern outstretch of the canal. I'd never understood why they called this equipment 'plant' as it was far from being either green or organic. The contractors were working under the aegis of Thames Aquatics and seemed to have plans to drain this branch of the Enfield Dig, leaving a bare concrete-lined cutting. I'm sure the skateboarders and graffiti artists couldn't wait.

I'd grown to hate weekends. All the decent sport had decamped to Sky and I'd let my subscription lapse since Becky and cuddly Saturday night movies had departed. These days I found I could read a novel for only an hour before my eyes started drooping.

I texted her to say that one of her favourite films, *A Matter of Life and Death*, was on BBC Four tonight. Over an hour later she finally replied with, "Busy but thanks." No name, no kisses. No future.

I looked for Canoe Boy all day but he never turned up.

*

Becky emailed me to ask if she could pop round tomorrow and pick up an Elemis make up bag she'd left behind. I could have posted it to her long ago but was never at home during post office opening times. So I said.

I'd never actually found out who "the other man" was – she neglected to describe him, didn't openly admit anything at the time, although the circumstantial evidence was conclusive. Perhaps I should quiz her now. Or offer a figurative olive branch.

The council had given the nod to Thames Aquatics for all the current, tall and well-established street trees to be lopped and felled. Their intention was to put in new ones – rowans, mostly – surrounded by wire cages and white wood fencing for protection. It all seemed quite ecologically unsound. Coupled with which, when I arrived home most of the parked cars were covered with fresh yellow wood shavings and the air itself was throat-catchingly dusty. Several of my neighbours were openly flouting the water control laws by chucking buckets over the roof and bonnet to wash away the debris. I was not at all surprised when the supply was cut off for four hours from eight p.m. and I faced the prospect of waiting for my fleeting appearance on *Bricks and Mortar* with an itchy nose and a dry mouth because of the disruption.

To my surprise, I spotted Canoe Boy out on the canal at about ten to nine. He'd fitted a pocket torch to his NY baseball cap with coiled twine; otherwise, it was the usual business – he in the front seat of the flimsy fibreglass structure, smoothly wielding the two-tongued paddle, with a curious range of groceries precariously stacked behind him. Perhaps he'd brought some over-priced Perrier or Highland Spring.

I examined his offerings by flashlight. He had a not-too-battered box of mince pies. Their expiry date was only a couple of weeks away and we were nowhere near Christmas yet.

"Special offer, boss," he promised.

Maybe I could heat them up for Becky tomorrow.

She turned up half an hour later than the appointed time. Some things never change. Her hair was shorter though, and her smart new coat had been modelled by Kate Moss during the advert break on last night's repeat of *Father Ted*.

"Are you coming in, Beck?"

"It's all right, I won't stay for a tea or coffee."

"You've got someone waiting haven't you?"

She paused and I could hear the industrial pump at the far end of the road emptying the Enfield Dig of precious fluids so we could all wash and drink for another couple of days.

"OK, yes. I'm meeting him when he gets off work. Listen, Phil, we are over and done with. I know it hurts but that's the truth."

"Look out for me on the telly on Monday night. There's going to be a long pan around the conference room."

"Phil, I always watch out for you but that Jefferson hogs the show."

"He's hardly there any more," I mumbled. "Neither am I much," I added but she'd already departed for pastures greener.

I took a longer route home so as to swap my library books and pick up some tools and low energy light bulbs from the hardware store. I was sure that Canoe Boy's shop was along the same row although it seemed a little pointless to enter each emporium with its racks of vegetables sprawling onto the pavement. What would I say if the kid were there behind the counter, anyway? Don't call on Thursday because I'm in a meeting about raising money to rebuild the Titanic at one-quarter scale and get Russell Crowe or Charley Boorman to plough it through the last of the Arctic ice sheets? Or should I enquire whether he had a solemn, dark-haired older sister who'd be interested in dating a lapsed Christian with his own flat backing onto the stagnant canal?

It was probably the speed dating evening that had caused me to skip work on and off during the past month. Jefferson thinking about 'Good telly' and increased profits rather than staff morale or, indeed, his sweet wife at home.

Best suit, new £80 shirt, a winning smile even if I am a loser… it should have been a piece of piss. Five minutes each to impress a parade of perfumed and pampered beauties from the ad agency up the road. By their seventh Bacardi breezer I ought to have appeared as hunky as the new James Bond. Not the more accurate list of adjectives, which went: bored, desperate, tongue-tied, still in thrall to a previous girlfriend…

"Treat it as either a team-building exercise or an evening of fun," Jefferson had advised.

Fortunately, it was his fumblings rather than my mumblings which had made the final cut for the TV show.

I was five minutes from home now; the street lights already rendering the visible sky that curious shade of urban brown. This detour took me past the disused railway bridge that the alien spaceship clipped with its tail fin three years ago. If you took a deep breath in its vicinity you could just catch a tang of astral oil above the omnipresent car exhaust and dog shit fumes. It was about time the council or Thames Aquatics or someone made something of this local attraction by putting up a blue plaque or interactive information board. Instead, the place was still cordoned off with red and white tape; although that did nothing anymore to deter the usual graffiti hoodlums: 'Toxic', 'E-Zy2' and the rest. In the early days, someone had painted, 'UFOcker', which at least raised a smile.

I'd downloaded a map of the recorded and verified UFO crash sites. At a one to one hundred thousand scale the red points formed the outline of a curved kayak. Like tracing constellations in a clear night sky.

I missed the feminine presence that would keep me from indulging in such boyish conspiracies. Stuck at home all day since I quit Raft and Rapid, I yearned for the old time punctuation of visits from the milkman, the baker and the ice cream van to break up the monotonous, water-restricted day. But even the postman avoided the building five days out of seven.

Only Canoe Boy was constant. Those robbing bastards at Thames Aquatics had so drained the canal that the kid could slip out of his Reeboks, roll up his jeans and comfortably wade across the channel; holding his craft full of battered goodies to one side like Santa with an odd-shaped sack.

She wouldn't admit it even though I'd accused her straight out. I didn't have proof but I had belief. That spell she'd taken off work recuperating from skiing injuries… the perfect opportunity to hook up with the door to door back door man. She was probably minding his van, his shop or his paddles right now.

"You like these, boss. Alien sweets. Good for cough and chest."

The level was so shallow that he'd virtually walked on water to get here. Trampled on broken hearts, too.

"Just give me the beckies – I mean the biccies."

He shook his lank black hair. He couldn't have been twenty. Fucking toy boy.

"Tomorrow, boss. Maybe. No, promise."

PLAY THE
PIPES OF PAN

She stepped out of the shadows towards him and he easily anticipated the gist of her message, if not her words verbatim. She was just seventeen, bobbed hair dyed henna red, tartan skirt too short and suede boots too long.

"You want a fantasy, darling?" she crooned.

"Chemical or sexual?" he snapped back.

"You know what I'm offering, sonny."

Was the lamplight that poor and her mascara so heavily applied that she didn't recognise her old friend Jack? Or was it all part of the act? Brazen promise twinned with icy defence.

"I don't think so, Ruby," he replied. "The last time I went with one of you slippery ladies I caught a dose of itches. The time before that I got slapped with a paternity suit."

"Jack? Shit, that we've both come to this… Listen, you needn't worry about diseases and stuff. I've got just the thing. Look, it's a thin pink rubber tube you can roll over your william. I call it my red riding hood."

"They ain't invented the sex aid that'd fit me yet, babe. Keep safe. Send my best to your Granny."

The busker in *The Maiden's Virtue* was playing a pan pipes version of The Beatles' song *Revolution*. When the uprising comes, pal, Jack thought, you'll be first up against the wall. Didn't anybody care about sacrilege anymore? Clearly, Dumpy Humpy wasn't bothered – Jack even caught the not so gentle giant tapping his Cumberland sausage fingers on the table top in intricate time to the breathy melody.

"You're a good lad, Jack," the old villain wheezed. "I may have some work for you pretty soon. Starting a protection job, if you know what I mean."

Jack looked ruefully at the mounting pile of empty tankards, their glass sides smothered with fingerprints and DNA kisses. Dumpy Humpy caught his gaze and guffawed. Thick spittle and shreds of tobacco collected on his fat chin.

"It's OK, son," Humpy continued, "I'll stand for these. For old times' sake. How old are you now, anyway?"

"Seventeen. Same as last year. And the years before that."

"Ain't nothing wrong with eternal youth. You should try to be comfortable in your own skin. I've learnt to enjoy the room in mine. Diet? What diet? Nowt ain't never gonna change me."

Humpy took a flick-knife from his waistcoat pocket, began filleting his yellow stained nails like a fastidious fishmonger. Finally, he carved his initials deeper into the mahogany table where he'd made his mark last night. He left the blade point down at the edge of the crossbar on the 'H'.

The busker was circulating *The Maiden's Virtue* with his pleading straw hat. Jack ignored him but Humpy told him to, "Piss off, you foreign bastard." Jack held his tongue. Everybody had to make a living. You gave a coin or you didn't. Insults just sour up the atmosphere.

Still, it would be nice if the ponchoed geezer took his business elsewhere. Jack preferred a bit of indie guitar or a killer beat. But if the pan piper tried to reproduce something by Dizzee Rascal or The Arctic Monkeys he might just have to do violence.

A sudden blast of cold air cut through the warm beery fug of the tavern. Two superheroes, complete with capes and primary coloured costumes, strode in from the cobbles and sauntered up to the bar. Each ordered an energy drink and a side dish of Creatine. The busker, sensing a buck-making opportunity, began blurting out a staccato version of *O Fortuna* from *Carmina Burana*, which Jack felt was a bit over the top.

Humpy caressed his weapon and announced, "This place is really going downhill. They open *The Maiden's Virtue* to any old riffraff these days."

The taller of the superheroes – the one with the yellow cape, purple leotard and leggings topped with yellow *over*-pants – inquired, "Is there a problem here, partner?"

Humpy fetched a couple of innocuous though glowing rocks and a rose gold charm bracelet out of his left trouser pocket. Was he starting to indulge his feminine side?

"There weren't no probs till a minute ago," he announced.

His interlocutor was about to take something out from his utility belt but his shorter companion – natty in scarlet and Lincoln green – tapped his arm, pointed at one of the dangling amulets and said, "Let's drink up and go, Claw. Save our powers for another day."

Humpy was already letting rip with derogatory laughter before the door was fully closed. He finished his pint, ostentatiously took his fob watch from his waistcoat and wondered aloud, "Is that the time? I ain't had sex for over twelve hours now. Let's se if there's any decent looking slags along the Strasse. You coming, Jack?"

"Ah, no, Humpy. I'm gonna get an early night, thanks. See what I can conjure up at the market first thing in the morning."

*

The next day found Jack first in the queue for the revolving window display at Castle Briar job centre. The righteous fingers of the *Green* agenda had now reached as far as Fairy Tale Land, which meant nobody would be doing any wood cutting for the foreseeable future. There were vacancies in the Yorkist marching army. The pay was decent but so were the chances of getting your leg blown off by a landmine when they posted you to the Literary East. The only other openings were for young women – euphemistic opportunities to become a 'hostess', a 'personal chambermaid' or, for the more voluptuous and larger bodied lovelies, a 'jolly strumpet'. Honestly, his home town was going downhill on a coal cart and fast becoming the new sex capital of the known world. Amsterdam without the spliff and coffee; Thailand without the noodles.

"Looks like I'll have to dip into my savings for another week," he muttered.

"You could always become a pimp," said a familiar voice at his shoulder.

Jack turned to see a dishevelled Dumpy Humpy propping himself up against some convenient street furniture. Burger mayonnaise stained his chin and his jeans hung so low that his pubic hair flourished over the waistband like weeds on a kerbside.

"I thought you already had several business interests on the go," Jack replied. "Surely you're not after work, too?"

Humpy licked at a mysterious, slightly pungent red stain on his fingernails and seemed pleased with the result. "With *my* appetite for pleasure? I'm too busy shagging, eating and drinking to knuckle down for the daily grind. Nah –" He stepped closer and last night's ale and whisky chaser was now a sour miasma emanating from his overworked mouth. "I ain't looking for employment, sonny, just checking the response. I placed all them ads meself."

He judged that Ruby Hood would be at home now. If she'd been working all night she'd probably be sleeping it off but perhaps she'd still see him for old times' sake.

Jack's route took him through the so-called *Old Quarter* – yeah, really, this whole place was old, all four quarters circumscribed by the outer ring of hastily constructed temporary accommodation. Still, this was the part the sightseers flocked to with the cobbled courtyards, the dray horses in their narrow stables, the shoemaker's and the milliner's, the old-fashioned dairy and the bakeries selling muffins, blackbird pies and out of season hot cross buns.

"Jack? I'm absolutely knackered. I'm stiff and sore. What d'ya want?"

In truth, she wasn't much of a ringer for either Juliet or Rapunzel but he called up his response to her open window, begging entrance to his lady's abode. She shook her head briefly. He stood his shaky ground as a rag and bone cart trundled by a yard behind him. He could have scaled the wall – its height wasn't even one twentieth that of the beanstalk – but he opted to bide his time chivalrously. At last Ruby relented and tossed a tiny silver key down to his feet. It looked barely large enough to open a tinderbox but it unlocked the downstairs door to her apartment block.

"I suppose you think you've come to save me," she greeted him.

"The thought had crossed my mind."

"Why the sudden interest, Jack? I mean, I know we had a fling a few years back but I thought we were just mates."

"I can't see you living your life like this."

"Well I can't sell eggs in a basket for the rest of my days."

"I've got some savings stashed away. We could get a place by the sea. I could work at the local surfing school. We'd get by."

"What about your mother?"

"We'll find somewhere with a granny annex."

"You've thought this all out, haven't you?" she smiled.

Her eyes were slightly bloodshot but her teeth were bright. All the better to gobble you up… no, that was the wolf in Nan's clothing!

He was distracted by a sound from the street below, a melodious accompaniment to his amorous endeavours. He strode across the boudoir, pushed back the net curtain and spied the annoying pan piper on the opposite pavement. Was the guy shadowing him for some nefarious / hilarious purpose?

"Oi, Mozart!" he yelled. "Push off!"

He picked up a glass perfume bottle from Ruby's dresser. It still retained some residual scent of autumn days and November nights. The missile made a reassuring thud against the busker's right shoulder and the music abruptly ceased.

"Hey," Ruby moaned, "that was my last Fairy Mist. I was saving that."

"It was empty."

"I was going to rinse it out for a few more dabs. Anyhow, I think you'd better go, Jack, before the peelers get here."

*

He sought solace in the spiritual oasis that was the Church of Ambiguous Certainties. The wooden pews were prone to splintering and the stone floor simply exacerbated the cold draughts seeping through the old brick walls but the stained glass windows offered bright choices of Jesus feeding the five thousand peasants or Hansel and Gretel defeating the wicked witch at the Gingerbread House. One could easily indulge in internal contemplation or else tune in and out to the stilted eloquence of Doctor Foster, rotund Rotarian and regular lay preacher. His sermon seemed to be something along the lines of love thy neighbour, welcome the newcomers and watch out for flash floods.

Later there were hymns with the wheezy old 120 key pipe organ its usual half-beat behind. Stirring stuff – preferable to those pansy pan pipes.

Jack said his amen, dropped a couple of passable blazer buttons onto the collection plate and went outside to the town square. It was twenty-four hours till market day but the place was thronged nevertheless. Several superheroes were showing off their powers in that ostentatious fashion which apparently passed for 'cool' in the modern world. Kangaroo Boy was hopping two-footed over the stationary traffic. Laser Man was tossing old cabbages up into the air with one hand and zapping them with his incendiary finger. You're the proper tosser, pal, Jack thought but didn't vocalise.

His belly was rumbling. There was one place to go.

Miss Muffet's Muffin Shop – finest family owned purveyor of croissants and buns this side of sundown – was run by the fabled heroine herself with something approaching military precision. The military precision of the losing side, that is. Mademoiselle Muffet still sported her girlish pigtails and a dress short enough to make the boys blush even though she supplemented her income with a State Retirement Pension and had worn out several Freedom Passes. Her incipient arachnophobia ensured she kept a clean establishment. You could get cheese pancakes out the front and delicious cheesecake round the back. If you tipped generously, the girls would keep their waitress uniforms on while they serviced your erogenous zones. Sex here was always *au naturel* – none of that red rubber riding hood nonsense coming between a man and his venal pleasure here, thank you very much.

Jack was fully aware of the irony of visiting this pastry filled brothel whilst still on a mission to save fair Ruby from a life on the game but… he kinda liked Claudia in her black smock and white apron smelling of baking and talking of dough and icing sugar. Maybe he should try and save her soul as well? Then again, she was a relative newcomer and not old Fairy Tale Land blood like he and Rubes and… not him again! Big boned bastard in a cravat, pimping his way around every back alley and brick wall, his shirt untucked and half his arse and genitalia on view to frighten the chickens.

Dumpy Humpy. What was he up to? Maintaining an empire or heading for a fall?

Jack washed off, zipped up, paid up and quickly sneaked off.

The nocturnal music of Fairy Tale Land was either suitably baroque – a burst of Bach and a pull of Handel – or else fairground and carnie. Jack wasn't entirely happy about the pan piper and his latest affectation – accompanying the macho displays of the town square superheroes with breathy bursts of *Ride of the Valkyries* or *The Eye of the Tiger*. It was like trying to play *Anarchy in the UK* on a plastic pennywhistle.

Today, though, *The Last Post* might be more pertinent as one of the caped crusaders – Hot Coal Guy, the one man crime fighting carbon emission – lay inert in the dirt, his extraordinary powers reduced to mere embers. Jack crouched over the half-hour dead body, wondering if the kiss of life was appropriate or even viable in such cases. Maybe the corpse's residual heat would burn the sensitive skin cells around his mouth. Better safe than lip-less.

Somehow he suspected that this killing might mark a return to the bad old days of gang warfare between the Grimms and the Hansels which had blighted the locality until the reign of King Just. Just about keeping a lid on it. So which side had restarted hostilities this time? And would that make any difference a week or so down the line?

Jack took a shortcut through the recently regenerated commercial district where every second square metre of castle wall was plastered with adverts proclaiming 'Insurance Against Spells and Bad Magic – Competitive Rates' or 'Talk to us if you've been involved in an incantation and it wasn't your fault.'

Ruby was out working her patch in a sparkly silver dress like a retro-futurist Christmas angel. Like a walking magnet: she'd already attracted her first punter. One of the superheroes, no less; his speciality indistinguishable from this distance.

Jack doubled back, fingering the copy key bouncing jauntily in his jerkin pocket.

It was the matter of a minute to sneak up the stairs and secrete his svelte body within Ruby's wardrobe. There was no magical translation to another kingdom but the lingering feminine scents and the brushed silk caress of her hung garments were enough to transport him to a keener mental state. Why had he never made his intentions crystal clear before?

Schooled in stealth, he maintained a viewing crack. Waited… Here she was now with her customer. The guy had lustrous lightning zigzags descending from his shoulder pads and flames decorating his thighs. Was he the fabled Fire Starter? Or another sad manifestation of Wanker Man?

Ruby quickly disrobed down to bra and knickers as red as her Christian name. But no further. The superhero perched on the edge of the narrow bed, still fully clothed in his peculiar fashion. It seemed likely that he was one of those clients who wanted simply either to look or to talk. Jack was not sure whether he cared to listen to the guy's self-pitying spiel. He made ready to interrupt at a convenient point like a character in a domestic farce or in the manner of his jumpy namesake in the press down box.

There was a sudden commotion at the door as Dumpy Humpy burst into the bedroom, vicious flick-knife in hand, and lunged at the terminally surprised superhero.

"Another one bites the dust," Humpy crowed. "Not so super now against the might of troll-forged steel."

"Oh my God!" Ruby screamed. "You've killed him."

"So what, slag? Just give me my percentage."

Amid the mayhem, Jack had emerged seamlessly from the wardrobe.

"Leave her alone, you bloated pimp!" he blurted.

"Stay out of this, Jackie boy, I'm protecting the maid's honour."

Ruby snorted. "What honour? Eh? And anyway, I was never going to shag him. Take a look at his groin. He's a genuine old style superhero; they've all got flat packets."

Jack heard a familiar sound from the street below and chanced a glance out of the half-open window. Yep: unshakeable piper again.

"Humpy, come and have a look at this," he said, all casual and street-smart.

The murderer waddled over to have a gander.

So was unprepared when two peelers and a pair of impressively muscular, possibly celibate, superheroes bounded into the room from the rear, to arrest him.

*

After they'd watched Humpy carted away strapped to a carriage pulled by a quartet of the king's horses, Ruby stated, "You knew this was gonna happen."

Jack pursed his lips. "Not exactly," he replied, "but I realised that the piper might well use some sort of code. More subtle than a policeman's whistle."

Ruby waved her bare arms at the carnage. "I can't stay here tonight. And I can't face clearing up the blood or the body."

"Come with me to my place. Give me eight hours to change your life."

"You can't manage that," she sneered.

Jack took her hand, regaining his gentlemanly swagger as he wrapped a blood red cape about the young woman's shoulders. "Listen," he told her, "I was only six hours in the giant's lair at the top of the beanstalk. Have some faith."

And to the hopeful piper still stationed at the foot of the stairs, he ordered, "Strike up a happy love song, for fuck's sake, Mozart."

THE PAMELA FACTION

Life had been a constant struggle since the gaggle of Pamela dolls had seized control of the rotary washer. Today they'd turned it to bright sunshine, hoping to parch Stevie to pieces with their witchly weather control, but he was not ready to be beaten just yet. Not by a bunch of eleven-inch high animatronic harridans – no matter how numerous and casually evil they were. They could have elected to starve him out – he was pretty close to famished as it was – but their leader, Pamela Ten, was becoming too impatient to indulge in long term solutions. She it was who'd talked Gonzo George into pulling the plug at the far end of the swimming pool, a move which had depleted but not exhausted Stevie's water supply owing to the distinct camber towards his end.

The things we do for lust. Gonzo George had been promised the attentions and ministrations of several of the dolls but had only succeeded in rendering himself almost unserviceable. He lay now on a striped, sodden deckchair being used as either a makeshift stretcher or mortuary slab. As Gonzo George expired in the exhausting heat, he seemed to emit a series of sighs and subdued whirrs. The sound travelled across the rooftop air to Stevie's alert ears, the only indication of his friend's continued stubborn existence.

Stevie had never allowed room in his wholly human heart to bother with the suffering of erstwhile enemies but he wished he had the guts to hasten George's end and put his pal out of his prolonged misery. The lack of closure was doing his head in.

Stevie's only survival hope was to get back to the Catalogue Woman but such a quest courted danger and demanded a strategy. He wished he had one. Apart from throwing the last of his caps at the Pamela Faction and making a mad dash for the maintenance stairs, he was clueless about how to quit the roof without sacrificing his own skin.

He still had a few items stuffed in his pockets including the remnants of a long softened bar of plain chocolate. He licked at the foil wrapper until the metallic after-taste began to spoil the memory of this minuscule repast. He had to learn to think like a big cat these days and judge whether the expended effort in acquiring sustenance was justified by the energy and nourishment to be gained from the kill. Not that he'd actually killed anyone or anything yet. Not knowingly, anyhow.

Against all this speculation was an over-riding thirst and a dawning realisation that if the dolls kept it this hot for much longer the puddle in the pool would evaporate anyway. He looked all about him. Scrabbled. Jumped. Gulped.

*

Stan Tan, the man of the world, was back on this side of the roof. He had a method of ingress and egress that Stevie had never been able to discern, despite attempts to follow his sudden exits.

"We've run out of explosive caps, Stevie. I'll see if I can concoct some weaponry from whatever we've got lying around the office."

"You're useless," Stevie stated, adding, "I hope you've brought some supplies."

The MOTW emptied his pockets in a mock ceremonial manner. "Dried stuff. Soups and stock. Quite nutritious," he elaborated.

"How am I s'posed to eat it?"

"Mix it with a little water from the pool, dummy. It's been filtered. Honestly, you're never satisfied."

"Ain't you got anything immediate, Stan?"

"Just some chewing gum. You want a stick?"

"Sure, though I've never seen the point in it."

"Stimulates the gastric juices. Helps you digest."

"But I haven't eaten all day, Stan!"

"Quit your moaning, the Borg dolls will hear you. Try and put a positive spin on things."

On their daytime setting, the Pamela Faction dolls marched two abreast, their plastic legs kicking forwards with pointed feet in slip-on white slippers. Toes were an innovation too far for this otherwise superficially fetching model in halter-top and combat hot pants. Their hair fell in glossy swathes of horsetail brown, chimney broom black or barnyard blonde. Up close – and Stevie had been up close, perilously close, but fortunately when they'd temporarily laid down their weapons – their beautiful bland faces were dominated by doe like eyes adorned with lustrous lashes which blinked becomingly, s l o w l y, and sometimes with a discernible click.

Stevie's lifetime best friend Gonzo George had become entirely enamoured of their potent mix of sex and death. Long believing himself capable of sweet-talking the birds down out of the trees, he set off on a brave but doomed charm offensive to conquer the mechanical hearts of the manufactured faction.

"Panic's over, girls! Gorgeous George will see to all your romantic needs!" proved to be memorably prescient final words. Amazons to the core, they didn't completely kill him straightaway. Instead, they left him barely alive, tied down by nylon fishing line, more like a Breughel abomination than Gulliver, exposed to the elements, moaning with wordless agony until expiration.

"Hey you," one of the female killers called across the brackish water, her voice like a cloud of drunken mosquitoes, "other man! You're next, you know."

Stan Tan's many, many words had given Stevie much to ponder regarding what his benefactor called 'The Female Principle'. The notion that the fabled, and currently nigh unattainable Catalogue Woman might hold no memory of her earlier life in Stevie's arms was troubling indeed. The radical suggestion, however, that the goose stepping soldiers patrolling the far end of the swimming pool and outdoor lounging area must also be accepted as an aspect of *La Femme de la Reve* was a crushing burden for mere mortal man. Surely it was still imperative for him to somehow bypass these foul-mouthed, binge-drinking hussies and seek domestic solace with his half-glimpsed heartthrob and her glossy choice of furnishings?

He thought he could hear thunderclouds approaching. Clearly, the soldiers' weather control was spatially limited. Something to bear in mind.

The Pamela Faction was active tonight: marching up and down in a storm-trooper pirouette from some mechanically choreographed fascist ballet. Always up and down, back and forth, never gentle swaying or twinkle-toed sugar plum fairy skitters across the water. Maybe, on balance, that was a good thing. And their limited range of responses continued to raucously cut the air like rusty scissors wielded by drunken seamstresses.

"Hey, splash in a bit more vodka, pal!"

"Halt, who goes there? Boyfriend or foe?"

"Come and chat us up if you think you're man enough."

He ought to be used to their nocturnal oration by now but they still disturbed his slumber and made him weak and sluggish during the day. Doubtless that was part of the plan. It was like living across the river from a rowdy hen night every evening.

A few gull-like cries split the air just as he settled down to shallow dreams. The resulting laughter and high-pitched giggles appeared closer than ever but that was an aural illusion amplified by the darkness.

"Hey, Pam!"

"Yes, Pam?"

"I'm bored, Pam. What time's the strippergram get here?"

*

The key was surely to go directly to Pamela Ten, the leader of the demonically deployed platoon. Slightly taller, recognisable by her natty jacket and greater command of common English phrases. How would Stan Tan, the man of the world, put it, in his inimitable, politically incorrect way? Something along the lines of, "Go straight to the chief, ignore the Indians."

There was still a little, slightly crusty black ink left in the biro next to the rubbish chute. The storm and gales of yesterday evening had mostly refilled the rooftop swimming pool, at least temporarily, and had deposited a few items of windblown litter around Stevie's sleeping area. Since the universally Enforced Reduction, many tools and everyday items had proved harder to manipulate. This not too soggy cardboard, for example, was quite awkward to fashion into a suitable raft. Pens had remained the same size so were now comparatively much larger. Stevie wrote as neatly as he could but his old schoolteacher would have dismissed his efforts as a 'scruffy scrawl'. Still, it was the message, not the medium or the execution of the missive that truly mattered.

"I have no quarrel with you. I only want safe passage. Let's agree a truce."

The plea formed the sail of his home-made yacht of goodwill. With a careful push and a following breeze, the peace boat began its unmanned maiden voyage from the deep end to the shallow shore. Stevie watched from the cover of a fast-rusting lounge chair. His ship was making good progress, there was no doubt about that, and all being well was due to dock at the enemy barracks within a half-hour.

Suddenly there was action from the furthest bank as two squaddies scrambled to action, laser rifles at the ready.

A girlish voice screeched, "Halt, who goes there? Boyfriend or man foe?"

Her more impetuous colleague let out a volley of gunfire and the white flag sizzled and crackled briefly before the whole contraption sank beneath the disturbed waters.

Pamela Ten herself appeared. Stevie hoped it was to reprimand the pair of shoot on sight privates. Instead her authoritative tones declared,

"No more Francis Drake tricks, guy. We know your game."

*

Stan Tan, the man of the world, indeed the man *from* the world, was using his superior stature and was towering over Stevie with his hands stretched towards the supplicant's head.

"Stevie," he crooned, "you will only succeed in your mission if you learn to see your objective clearly. Now, visualise!"

After a short spell of the requisite swaying, Stevie began to babble, "Yes, I see her now. Oh Katerina, the Catalogue Woman – you cannot come to me so I shall seek entrance to your consumer goods Eden."

"Oh this is good, Stevie! Where is she now?"

"She's on page 100, relaxing casually on a sofa. Not lying down but comfortable. If only she had a television or a Dolby system to entertain her but they don't start till page 450. Maybe I can help rearrange the layout when I get there."

"You'll get there, Stevie, if you continue to believe. How are the children?"

"They're fine. There's an excellent array of toys from page 610 onwards. I don't mind that someone else fathered them, even out of wedlock; they're good kids. They give no trouble."

"You know we all want you to get there, Stevie. Everybody's rooting for you. One final push and you could be with Katerina tonight. Don't let all your view… supporters down."

"There's a lovely double bed on page 333. Maybe one day we'll share it. For now she's chosen a bunk."

"Top or bottom?"

"Oh she's underneath. I'll be on top."

"Traditionalist!" Stan exclaimed, stepping backwards slightly and accidentally severing the connection.

Stevie's spiky hair looked wilder than usual, his cheeks drained of colour but his eyes red from assisted dreaming.

"I need to rest now, Stan," he mumbled. "The effort…"

"Sure. For the big push later."

*

Even at this late stage of human development, Stevie was still very much a creature governed by the weather. The occasional smoggy mist brought confusion; bright sunshine caused amnesia regarding his previous life and even his purpose in this. Cold, clear spells thankfully encouraged similar levels of thinking. However, in a typical military change of strategy, the Pamela Faction now required heavy rainfall to permanently refill the pool for their own nefarious purposes.

From his hidey-hole at the masculine end of the bath, he could eavesdrop on several of Ten's orders and observe the mostly meek acquiescence of her charges. Two of the dolls were deployed to replace the plunge plug, six were on technical duty and just one remained on guard against a potential Stevie incursion. How insulting! But then again perhaps it was a good moment to take advantage of their stretched numbers.

Whether the rotary washer actually needed half a dozen technicians plus a military supervisor was a moot point. He was surprised they hadn't elected to deploy this local cloud controller more frequently since they'd seized it. Must be really complicated to operate or maybe the manual was in Mandarin or something…

The first few drops cooled his troubled brow. Soon the drizzle turned to stronger precipitation and he judged this an opportune moment to break cover. The squally shower would confuse his enemies' laser sightings and he might just make it past them unscathed.

Come on, legs, keep moving across the slippery tiles –

There was a sudden commotion in the shallow end. One of the Borgs had slipped on a stair rung and got her leg entangled at an awkward angle. Errant raindrops caused sparks as she short-circuited. Her companion was several steps above her, half-turning to see the problem then screaming blue Mayday. The remaining dolls deserted their task of steadying the webbed arms of the rotary washer and rushed to assist. One of them caught sight of Stevie sneaking along by the high edge of the pool. She hissed and reached for a hand weapon.

Ten strove to reassert command as the sky darkened and the droplets fast turned to hailstones. Stevie knew this melee presented a great chance to escape but suddenly felt as if he was at the bottom of a chute in a pebble quarry. The hard balls of ice bounced off his head and his body like round, white bullets. It hurt like crazy.

He must go on.

He couldn't go on.

He took shelter back in his hastily constructed den. The neo-Biblical plague lasted fully fifteen minutes before the clouds were exhausted.

The girl soldiers began a surreal keening which eventually resolved itself into intelligible words as they placed their damaged colleague upside down on the top of the rotary washer:

"Wash them, rinse them, hang them out to dry!"

There was no fixing the dead doll. One down, nine to go, Stevie thought with grim determination.

After ten minutes of ear-splitting wailing, the platoon leader hefted the corpse over the parapet and into the void.

Just as ruthless with their own… Stevie pondered.

Stevie was undergoing a nightmare. This fairly regular occurrence was a consequence of the Enforced Reduction, which had taken him and so many others down to a mere thirty centimetres. He'd never suffered bad dreams as a child – and he'd been bigger then!

To his left he could see the late Gonzo George, to his right was Stan Tan. This latter apparition might have been actually present, one could never tell during sleep, except that both figures were hovering in mid-air above and slightly beyond the parapet.

"Turn back, oh Stephen!" his lifelong pal Gonzo George proclaimed. "This mission is not thine own."

Even in the midst of befuddled slumber, Stevie recalled that his friend had never spoken with such Victorian pantomime portents whilst alive. Dreams, eh – who needs 'em?

"You must go on," shiny Stan Tan insisted. "Every hope is riding on you now, Stevie boy."

"Pah!" – George speaking out of character again –"Who's to say this Catalogue Woman even exists? Who's to say her catalogue home is real? Everything is virtual these days, even buying furniture and appliances."

"That's nonsense," Stan Tan countered. "She so exists: Katerina the goddess of the domestic bible, home shopping version. We must reaffirm our faith and belief in something – *someone* – solid and substantial that we can pick up in our arms, turn over with our hands –"

"Picture in our fantasies, more like," George interrupted. "Listen, Stevie, hark to some advice from beyond the grave: You can get down from this rooftop killing ground with your head held high and find a purpose elsewhere. Don't feel obliged to turn kamikaze for this snake and his CCTV viewers."

Stan Tan, the man of the world, stretched himself to his full height as he turned both a dismissive sneer in dead George's direction and a placatory smile towards the still silent Stevie. A two-faced media mogul oozing invisible charm oils, he finally offered, "The choice is clear, Stephen. Be left wondering, left with unfulfilled desires, left behind with the ordinary multitude; or else, go right ahead, set yourself on the correct path, do what's right for you and everyone who truly cares for you."

Stevie's lips wouldn't move. He managed to shift an index finger and, for want of the lucidity and logic he might demonstrate when awake, began an extended mental childish chant of, "Ip dip, do, the cat's got the flu…" He was on the verge of a decision when his slumber was shattered by laser fire and falling masonry He blinked away his spectral visitors and brushed brick dust out of his hair.

A harsh female voice called from across the water, "Hey, hand job! Keep the noise down over there."

But I never said a word, he pondered briefly before falling asleep again.

Every time Stan Tan departed there was a moment when he appeared to literally *melt* away. As producer of a top-rated reality TV show, he doubtless had some tricks up his smarmy sleeve; or else, he had several special effects minions, with their worn-out sensible shoes and skewed baseball caps, primed to do his bidding at any moment. His was the world beyond the secret stairs; Stevie's was currently limited to these few square metres of concrete, mouldy grouting and stagnant rainwater. The only way was onwards. To the twenty-first century Camelot, the laminated pages of Avalon.

"But, Stan, what am I going to eat there?"

"You remember those Christmas hampers on page 872? They're all full. There's cases of wine nearby."

"I'll be drunk all the time."

"Nonsense. That water cooler on 903 will see you all right. There's a high definition TV on 452. You might even catch yourself on repeat."

"You make it sound so easy. I wish you'd make it so, Stan."

"Not allowed to, pal. Rules of engagement and all that. Still, I can give you these."

Quite what use he could make of a manila envelope stuffed full of multicoloured elastic bands, Stevie was left to guess.

His stomach rumbled again. Stan Tan had neglected to bring any victuals on his latest visit. Maybe that was "rules of conflict" too. Or perhaps his killing hunger would finally spur Stevie into going over the top across no man's land to the promised country of milk creamers and honey decanters.

The Pamela Faction didn't seem bothered by lack of food. Despite the cruel desiccation they'd performed on the luckless Gonzo George, it was likely that they didn't need to eat at all. Just the occasional dry Martini or Smirnoff ice to look cool.

Did he have to sit out this war of attrition until either he starved to death or the girls' batteries ran down? He flicked a band across the scummy surface of the swimming pool, surprised to see it veer off and trouble an abandoned pair of sandals over to the left. Perhaps his puny, underfed arms could yet mount one more sortie against the mechanical encampment...

For George, who only wanted to get to know you!

In revenge for your cruel dismembering ministrations of a guy who just had so much love to offer!

For Katerina, the Catalogue Woman, in the sincere hope that she will remember me after these cruel years since we parted!

For the survival of the fittest!

For the watching millions!

Stevie had hoped that he might yet receive some form of last minute encouragement from Stan Tan, but it didn't pan out that way. You're on your own now, boy, against the laser guided miniature female army.

The dolls were busy again with the weather-controlling rotary washer. Just another weapon they would try to use against him... although maybe he should seek to strike first.

Katerina, his ex and all-time love who had done quite well for herself by setting up home inside a consumer goods and interiors catalogue, probably had access to a rotary washer. He thought there might be one in the seven seventies. But it would be merely the pedestrian sort. For drying washing, not corralling clouds.

He was using the biro to help catapult his stack of elastic bands. He'd tried a few practice shots on the morning pigeons; without notable success, but still…

Aim for the joints. Disable rather than attempt and fail to kill. Take out those marble eyes with the horsehair lashes. If they don't see you, Stevie – if they're crying real tears of pain or frustration – you've got a chance.

He was flicking to an inner rhythm now. Two of the guards were already down with contusions and he'd yet to pass the pool's halfway point. With a large slice of luck he could finish the job before he had to get up close and resort to hand-to-hand combat.

Another one down with a possible hip fracture. Result.

The Borgs were torn between returning fire and swivelling the weather control to murderous hailstones.

They were retreating. Or perhaps regrouping by the sun lounger and coffee table over in the corner by the stairs. Their last holdout. He flicked more bands, striking one of the callous assassins hard on the forehead.

They knew where he was headed.

Their casualty list was mounting.

But, hang on, he couldn't count all their number. Which meant –

Ow!

A nick to his neck sent him sprawling.

He rolled away from the roof edge and fired off a shot, like he'd seen cops and secret agents do back in the old TV days.

He was nowhere near as accurate as he wished to be. His projectile completely missed the Pamela target but winged an arm of the rotary washer. As he watched in horror from behind a half-deflated beach ball, the apparatus began to spin. Slowly at first and then with a greater and greater velocity as if caught in – as if *making* – a sudden hurricane.

At the far end of the pool, Pamela Ten had risen to her full height and was displaying in her animatronic hands a glossy covered holy book. Indeed, it was *the* holy book and her sacrilegious fingers were about to dump the catalogue into a watery grave at the well-defended shallow end. Stevie shouted at her to stop, to leave the innocent out of this conflict, to not destroy the only Eden he might ever know.

Perhaps she heard him. At the very least, P Ten paused with her arms upraised.

The strengthening gale loosened her grip.

The deluxe edition of *Shadwell Interiors and Consumer Desirables* plunged into the murky water.

With an unbecoming scream, Stevie followed it.

The closest soldiers piled in on top of him and the surface frothed like sharks attacking a walrus saving a baby seal pup.

Mayhem.

A watery wipe out.

Pamela Ten was pleased that the line had held firm and that order, of a sort, had been restored. She had lost six of her crew, though, to malfunction or battery cell deterioration. A high price to pay.

And here were the culprits: soggy pages of shopping dreams littering the brackish water of the rooftop pool. And a lone, impetuous warrior captured, killed and displayed for all passing aircraft and CCTV cameras to see.

Her surviving underlings had made a great show of pinning Stevie upside down on the rotary washer and yelling their traditional chant of:

"Wash him! Rinse him! Hang him out to dry!

Catch him! Kill him! Hang him up to die!"

Pamela Ten had made sure she joined in this celebratory song but somehow, for some peculiar, scarily *human* reason, her heart wasn't really in it.

D-LEB

As my personal life continues to splutter like damp blue touch paper, I keep thinking back to Oliver and wishing things had worked out with him. Of course, he was typically commitment-phobic but, to my knowledge, he was always faithful. And he had the excuse that we were both in our early twenties so why the need to settle down or 'get glued' as he charmingly put it? I could have saved myself a stack of false dawns if I'd persevered. He cast my need for proximity as possessiveness; my desire as desperation. Twelve years on from our first meeting and five years since we split, he remains the high water mark of a feeble tide. If only I'd known.

I was thinking about Oliver purely because from my cramped position by the tube carriage doors all I could see clearly was an advert for some men's health supplement and the guy's face was vaguely similar. I'd bought a copy of *Heat* on my way in. Standing on the grey platform, I flicked through the contents and was annoyed to notice several of the pages were either blank or unprinted. It was too late to go back for an exchange. The station started filling up. The indicator board froze on the 'next train one minute' announcement. By the time it actually arrived, the vehicle was seriously over capacity. A one-metre surge of desperate commuters at least got me aboard for the half-hour hell ride to Kings Cross Sans Pancreas, where I could gratefully change lines. And if that suit with the laptop and the half-folded *FT* poked me in the tits once more I swear I'll take my stiletto and rupture his cruciates.

If I could lift my foot. If I could breathe enough regurgitated air to oxygenate my flabby muscles sufficiently.

Why had we stopped again? There had been no trains ahead of ours within ten minutes so what could possibly be the hold-up down the line?

Looking askance over my left shoulder, I could see that the tunnel wall with its trunks of wiring was no longer visible, which meant we were close to one of the innumerable sidings and access tunnels which were attached to the main tube lines like barnacles to a cetacean. An old boyfriend had once conjectured a story in which a computer glitch causes points failure and all the trains are re-routed down these dead ends. *Passenger Peril*, he called it. I think it even got published somewhere.

The boyfriend was Oliver. Why was I suddenly obsessing? For the first eighteen months after we split, I was still hurting. An Internet trawl through the Electoral Register and a carefully worded plea on *Friends Reunited* had yielded zilch. Let it go, girl.

But then he'd started his own web site a couple of years back, just after his first (and so far only) novel hit the shops. I logged on to look… but resisted contacting him. Let him go, Claire! Read the book again if you want to, but otherwise…

Let us move. Please. I'm already sweaty and late.

Technically, I was in charge at the office this morning. Joyce was at a midweek media awareness conference in Leicester and Nasreen was due to escort our major patron, the Earl of Tetchley, through a meet and greet at the Park Lane Hilton. I'd held down better jobs in my life but this was the first place I'd ever worked in which the top three posts down the chain of command were all filled by women. That ought to be worth something. A twenty-five per cent pay rise or a huge hike in my tax-free clothing allowance would be worth even more.

I decided to let a few items rest easy in my Inbox and make myself available for the junior members of staff. They might need a gee-up or a comforting big sisterly walk through a complex procedure.

In truth, it was remarkably quiet for the first couple of hours. Darren and Andrew – our recently appointed trainees – seemed to be diligently absorbed at their monitors but I could detect a faint susurrus every time I wandered away. They were probably just gossiping football tittle-tattle like the majority of males below the age of ninety. I couldn't see them sticking it here more than six months.

Janie had the company TV running in the rest room. The smell from her herbal infusion tea reminded me of past diets and health kicks. These days it was caffeine all the way on a regular two-hourly schedule.

"Is there a big news story?" I asked.

"Nah, I was just catching a bit of *Celebrity Airship*, except it's stopped transmitting."

"The first series was all right," I responded. "I used to go to school with Annie Clarke."

"She shoulda won it. What's she doing now?"

"I don't know, actually. I'll have to call her some time."

I'd let Janie wrong-foot me and felt I couldn't now boss her back to the empty desk.

The day ticked over. At half past twelve, Nasreen returned with her green jade earrings mysteriously steamed over and her usually immaculate black hair sticking out like she'd had a fight with a crow.

"Bloody English nobility!" she blurted out. "Useless toffee-nosed toff. Wants to be our president but can't get off his fat white arse to attend any functions."

"Needs a bit of the Indian work ethic," I told her.

"Absolutely. My grandparents kept grafting into their seventies. I tell you, Claire, come the revolution, that Tetchley prick will be the first up against the wall."

"Right on, sister," I smiled.

So how does it feel to have one of the most instantly recognisable faces on the planet?

– It's not something I'm entirely comfortable about but I've learnt to live with it.

Do you find there are other unexpected benefits from being so well known?

– I suppose I have a certain amount of influence. How much is open to conjecture. Politicians come calling from time to time wanting to get me 'on board' or 'singing from the same hymn sheet' or some such jargon. I don't want to be allied to some party line, especially when it inevitably all goes tits up. But if there's a cause I believe in, my attitude's different. If I can, for example, get people behind an irrigation project in Central Africa just by pledging my own support, that's a fair use of celebrity status, I'd say.

Any regrets?

– Bundles. I'd love to be spontaneous and inconspicuous again. It would be nice to just pop out to the local café for a cappuccino without the need for bodyguards or minders or people 'setting it up'. I mean, how much setting up should it take just to put some beans in the grinder and heat the milk up?

Cancellations crowded the tubes beyond their usual sweaty capacity. I couldn't force my way to the exit door and had to wait a couple of stops and make a different connection. This had me coming in to Finsbury Park on the Victoria Line. Just as we reached the station, the tunnels merged and the Piccadilly train briefly curved towards us with its cargo of commuters like a subterranean apparition, then veered smoothly onto its own platform. Somehow I manoeuvred my way on to a vacant blue seat with red armrest. The guy opposite was poring over the *Evening Standard* which sported the headline, "Why is the government on holiday?" Lucky sods! I didn't have any leave available for a couple of months yet.

I didn't recognise the newsreader on TV and I had the sound down anyway. Without any captions. Oliver would have accused me of practising my lip-reading skills and I would have smiled. The accusations grew much worse prior to the break-up. Occasionally I logged onto his web site… just to check that he was still OK. There was rarely anything of any import happening.

I was on a tube train one day and they did that typical thing of giving you 30 seconds warning that they'd decided for no acceptable reason to terminate the service at Wood Green. So we all shuffled onto the platform and the driver closed the doors. But there was one passenger in the next to last carriage who had failed to heed the call and we all chuckled in a nervously macabre fashion as he was shunted off into the dark sidings. Of course, eventually, he would have been released by the negligent driver from the mysterious staff only tunnel. It brightened up the journey home no end for the rest of us.

I was leafing through old copies of *Grazia* and *Prima* wondering if I could bear to send the dreams of designer lifestyles and diet couture to the recycling bin. I was failing to eat properly most evenings and sometimes it made me a little light-headed. It was certainly cheaper than binge drinking with the girls from my old office.

My stomach hurt, anyway. I could feel my period coming on. I bet Britney and Angelina didn't suffer like me.

The tube was unusually roomy this morning as if the government had declared a public holiday but forgotten to tell me. Maybe it had been announced during the ad break punctuating *Tynesiders* or *Celebrity Airship*. I thought I spied my old friend Annie Clarke beyond the double plated glass at the end of the adjoining carriage. I couldn't be certain – her face was half-covered by an unseasonable woollen shawl as if she'd recently crossed the Gap from Gucci chic to Islamic haute couture. She didn't look up and I was left with a five per cent doubt.

Nasreen and Joyce were busy at their desks but the junior staff members were gathered in the rest room. Janie was manipulating the TV remote like she was a Playstation hotshot. Had we given up charitable fund raising and simply become a social club?

"Here comes the news again," Darren muttered.

The screen held only the latest BBC logo, not even a studio shot.

"Westminster sources have ruled out foul play in the recent celebrity disappearances and people are urged to get on with their regular lives. A minister has insisted that we should simply carry on as normal."

"Why's there no newsreader?" I asked.

"That's the whole point," Janie answered. "No one wants to be seen. No one wants to be famous."

"They're all vanishing," Darren added.

"You're having a laugh," I told them as they channel flicked again. "And why won't they send the Home Secretary or someone to make a statement?"

I left them to their conspiracy theorising and made myself a much-needed coffee. It wasn't the best drink of the week but it was the timeliest.

My period was kicking in with a vengeance and I had that low, dull ache I associated with the left ovary. Sinister sister. My vision was getting just a tiny bit blurry, too. The headache couldn't be too far behind despite the best efforts of copious reinforcements from Planet Paracetamol and Mount Nurofen.

Nasreen was waiting for me as I stepped gingerly out of the washroom. Surely I hadn't been *that* long?

"We're sending everybody home, Claire," she informed me.

"Is there some sort of national emergency, Nas?"

"Not exactly. This disappearing celebrity business has got everybody right shitted up, though. Can't stand them but can't live without them in the charity business."

"We'll cope."

"I'm not sure we will, Claire. People don't dig in their pocket for spare change or use a swipe card because they feel sorry for a starving African child or some AIDS victim on life support – they do it because Sir Bob or Her Ladyship does it and they want to ape their lifestyle –"

I wasn't entirely convinced by her logic but the prospect of snuggling up under a duvet with a couple of slabs of Galaxy chocolate and a hot water bottle was suddenly a mere hour away and no sick leave allowance to use up. Count me *out*.

*

When I got home, I bedded down on the sofa, strategically placed between television and computer screens. I had never got around to having the whole electronic caboodle in one package so now I suffered double eyestrain to go along with the dull ache in my legs and the throbbing in my womb.

If I'd expected the country to have already descended into apocalyptic meltdown, I was disappointed. The news stories were cannily read off-camera or by on the spot reporters who appeared only briefly in the shots. A little of the Blitz spirit still survived, it seemed, along with some Churchillian chicanery. No one was offering a holistic view, everything was disparate: a sneering little item about a drug-addicted pop star missing yet another festival gig; concern is growing for a raft of Hollywood 'A' Listers, the so-called *Ocean's Fifteen*, believed lost or stranded on exotic location; or the tongue in cheek amusement of, "If senior government ministers are still on holiday and the country is running itself quite adequately, should we bar them at customs upon their return?"

The Internet was no more helpful. The long arms of Microsoft / Google / AOL and the other usual suspects and linked limbs across the ether had imposed a Soviet style clampdown on the possible 'real' stories. Out of habit, I had Oliver's home page up and some of his links to other fantasists and conspiracy nutters were still active.

At last I found *WIES*. Short for *Warhol in Extremis Syndrome*. The gist of this seemed to be a sudden limitation imposed upon celebrity – but how? By whom? – which meant that if you'd already had your proverbial fifteen minutes then your time was quite literally up.

Don't you always find that these end of the world freaks concoct the most ridiculous theories and yet somehow there's a tiny irritating nugget that tempts you into believing them?

I went back to Oliver's web page but the welcome had changed to, 'This site is being discontinued. Please remove it from your address book.' He'd probably defaulted on the payment. Clearly the market for science fiction stories was being squeezed by true-life technological advances and W W W wild rumours dot com.

I couldn't take any more painkillers for at least another hour so sleep was the only curative action. I was tempted to pop a couple more. After all, I'm quite a big girl; not some 'size zero' bimbo. Surely I could stand a higher dosage?

The Day of Judgement might have to wait until I'd bled a whole lot drier.

*

You had a full five years at the very top of your profession. You had all the success you'd craved since you were a child. You had accrued all the trappings and benefits concomitant with fame: wealth, influence, access. Any car you wanted, any building or food you required, any woman who took your fancy, any stimulants or sedatives to keep your mood cool and on task. You could walk into any shop or restaurant in the Western Hemisphere and have a gaggle of obsequious staff instantly attend to your every whim. Yet you gave it up. Why?

– That's just it, everything was all too easy. I was getting bored with the facility of my life. And it was all so unreal. I was a product. I was a snivelling little creature behind a gigantic, powerful public mask. It wasn't me everyone was celebrating and clamouring over, it was a dream. And not even my dream, anymore.

Some would say that what followed, when you abandoned the dream, constituted a nightmare.

– I went through… some changes. A personality breakdown of sorts. It was important for me to withdraw from the public gaze for a while. In therapy speak: I went to some strange places during this journey.

We're not adding any visuals to this piece but I have to say how different you look now to the abiding poster image that adorned so many student walls.

– I'm keeping a much lower profile nowadays. It's the only way to survive.

"You again!" he sneered. "What do you want?"

"I was just a bit worried about you, Oliver, that's all."

"Well, after five years apart, I'm no different. Still broke and living in a poky flat. You've changed, though. Fuller figured."

"You mean I'm fat."

"No, not at all. Curvier, sexier… you always were sexy, of course…but, hey, Claire, we've put all that baggage behind us."

"Can I come in? I need to change my tampon."

"My new girlfriend wouldn't like it, Claire."

"You haven't got a new girlfriend. I've read your web log for the past hundred weeks. Come on!"

I pushed past him, desperate for the bathroom. A few minutes later, a scene of domestic destruction greeted me in the living room.

"What are you doing, Olly? Why are you destroying all your books?"

"Don't you know what's been happening? Everybody remotely famous is dying or disappearing. I've got to go incognito."

I took a deep breath, surveyed the wreckage again, finally stated, "Oliver, I don't want to stride back into your life and puncture your balloon like some evil harpy, but you're not actually that famous."

"I can't take the risk, Claire. Nice mixed metaphor, by the way. And you should be worried, too."

"Me? Why on earth?"

"That spot you did on *Blue Peter* when you were eleven. It's always on the box in some *I Heart TV Cock-ups* type show. BBC3 had it on the other night."

"I'm totally different now. I was a little madam then but nowadays I just want to keep a low profile. We're neither us in danger from this… whatever this celeb killing plague is."

"Then why did you come all the way over here on a rescue mission?" He had me there. The boyish smile signalled his small victory. He continued, "Who knows what's happening? Divine judgement? Some government or terrorist inspired form of biological warfare? An anti-fame virus? It's already sent the currency and shares market through the trapdoor. Property values are plummeting. All my savings have been wiped out. But that's not the worst of it."

"OK," I muttered, "go on: what is the worst of it?"

"Well, suppose this disease is retroactive."

"Meaning?"

"Suppose it works backwards, into the past. No Shakespeare, no Dickens, no Queen Victoria."

"No Hitler, Stalin or Pol Pot. Doesn't sound such a bad idea."

"But history is what shapes us, Claire. It's the bedrock of our whole civilisation."

It was good to see him animated again, and not simply with anger over some minuscule domestic tiff. I hadn't filled the gap; he hadn't filled the gap. We could still…

"But nobody knows who tamed fire or invented the wheel," I told him, "so just how much do we stand to lose?"

"You're right – up to a point. But so much progress has been initiated by individuals. Thomas Jefferson, Emmeline Pankhurst, various Ancient Greeks, James Logie Baird. Robert Louis Stephenson."

"Who?"

"Steam trains. Liverpool to Manchester."

I had a sudden thought, a half-crazy memory. Or maybe a clear route out of the killing maze.

"Olly," I whispered, "I've just developed a theory."

I could feel our whole society just about keeping things together but teetering on the brink. No one needed celebrities and stars for anything of productive value – the factories and schools could still operate, the buses run and the shops open their usual hours. After a few cold turkey days with literally nothing worth watching on the TV, perhaps we'd all start relating better to each other in a face to face way.

The few channels still running were thin on news. The announcements came from off-screen voices lightly disguised by vocoder effects. Did anyone honestly expect the populace to take such cyber bulletins seriously?

A recorded message at my office announced that we were 'on hiatus'. Displaying a foolhardiness I hadn't shown since my teenage years, I took the tube into town anyway. The big department stores had armed guards. A looting spree was surely imminent. I phoned Oliver and told him to bring the plan forward. The reception was really crappy.

A shrewish woman in a hoodie gave me a lingering look and asked, "Dun I know you?"

I suspected it was the prequel to a mugging. "Nah, sister, I ain't nobody," I answered, heading for the stone steps and then the stalled escalator. I ran down it, ignoring the wobbly leg feeling when the gaps became uneven. Fortunately, she didn't pursue me.

Even my friendly local Turkish shopkeeper was acting nervous. I bought double quantities of a few essentials. He gave me my change hurriedly, pressed the button that activated the metal shutters as I exited the store.

One of the TV stations was broadcasting only old black and white films with Humphrey Bogart, John Wayne, Ava Gardner and their ilk. Too long dead to be affected by this… virus, syndrome, decimation, removal, plague or whatever it was.

So we lose all our celebrities? Big deal. They're just leeches and parasites and over-inflated, hyped-up egotists, all of them.

The old Soviet Union had survived pretty well without such abundance of luminaries: Stalin, Yuri Gagarin… uh, that was your lot.

But were we also losing a sense of direction, our aspirations and dreams, even if they only amounted to a shallow desire for fame and fortune?

Plucked from obscurity into instant stardom.

Culled by an unknown hand as Britain descended overnight into a grey gulag of scared non-entities.

"You're late," was his greeting.

For a moment, I had the worst sense of deja vu. And why not? We were re-activating a dormant, close to extinct relationship. The old behaviour patterns and petty squabbles were all likely to re-ignite into pyroclastic flow.

"I'm not cut out for this Mulder and Scully business," I muttered. "Can't we get somebody else to save the world?"

"Just get this safety jacket on," he ordered. It was bright orange and didn't flatter either my figure or complexion.

"What about ID?" I asked.

"Sorted. The hackers and spooks have still preserved their secret identities. So I printed some stuff off the Internet and got it laminated this morning. Let's move."

I was sure his confidence was all bluster. I'd seen him go full speed ahead before like the captain of the *Titanic*. Then I'd watched him crash and splinter into emotional pieces. I didn't relish the prospect of sinking into the icy waters with him. SOS should be SYS – Save Your Self. Or *Sauve Qui Peut*, as the French have it.

The nocturnal travellers were as self-contained and reticent as ever. Nobody wanted to be looked at lately; nobody wanted to be recognised. My throat was unbearably dry and I wished I'd thought to bring a bottle of water. We were laughably under-prepared.

The supervisor at Wood Green underground station spent so long poring over our security passes that I was certain Oliver's handiwork had been rumbled.

"Where's Obafemi and Chantelle?" the boss asked eventually.

Ollie executed a cool shrug. "We just go where we're told. We did Hammersmith last night."

"All right. Cupboard's open for anything you need. No slacking."

I wanted to say we haven't even started so quit the discipline, but I held my tongue. Ollie fetched gloves, bin bags, brushes, a bucket and two slightly manky mouth and nose masks. Like using someone else's discarded tissues...

"Are you sure the power's off?" I said for the third time.

"It's safe, Claire. Promise."

It was hard, physical work clearing the tracks of accumulated litter beneath the emergency lighting. I'd never complain about a tough day of meetings and phone calls ever again. Despite all the precautions, the dirt and grime gagged the back of my throat and collected under my inappropriately long fingernails. The soot accumulating on my face and itching my tied-back hair made me feel like an over-aged Victorian chimney sweep.

At the second toilet break, Oliver whispered, "I think I've found what we're looking for. But I don't quite understand it."

"What? Where?"

"Down the sidings, like you said. Give me a minute then follow me."

I can see you but I can't touch you.

You're there and yet somehow not there.

No longer fully here.

Carriage after stacked carriage of the recently famous and more recently disappeared. Actors, politicians, pop stars, athletes and footballers, media-faced captains of industry. All trapped together with no apparent rhyme or reason. Like a subterranean *Sergeant Pepper* sleeve.

And here before me: Annie Clarke; the cool guy from the toothpaste ad; some love rat who plays for Chelsea; that topless bimbo who made a million after shagging the washed-up singer on *Love Island*; and also… Nasreen? How did she get taken? How long does the recognition thermometer register its crucial setting?

We're all at risk. I told you so. Oliver talking again.

I can see them but can they see me? Their shocked, vacant faces suggest not. When I reach my hand forward I pass right through both the window glass and human flesh. They are apparitions. Or they are out of kilter with this reality. Oliver again with his theories of parallel worlds and his early manuscript which posited travel between them.

No wonder he's worried.

I can still see you. And you. And all you others. But I can't touch you. And I can't help you.

It's eating me up.

You're no longer fully here.

I can't bring you back.

It may be all I can do to prevent my non-celebrity soul joining you in this limbo.

This hell.

Nothing works any more.

Not the telephones, not the traffic lights, not the holes in the wall. I feel I may yet need some cash to smooth over a few transitions and transactions, although money is only a promise to pay the bearer upon demand. We're moving not into a cash-less society but a cash-free society. Wealth has become a fatal encumbrance. Society itself is crumbling, dissipating.

The Internet still functions occasionally. The American soldiers may be on their way to liberate us… although both their president and deputy commander in chief have gone mysteriously AWOL. My Wi-Fi connection now defaults to a server calling itself *The Radical Nobodies*. Better be careful, boys, word gets around...

There's a guy has stationed himself atop a nearby tower block with some sort of rifle. He's challenging everybody who walks by to identify themselves. But either response is dangerous, potentially fatal…

Oliver is desperately trying to post some theories on the Web before the whole thing crashes. Before he disappears, too.

We're all so media literate nowadays. Our knowledge is remarkably wide and yet scandalously shallow. We know names, faces, and remember one trivial fact about each personality. We attach equal importance to all those we casually recognise.

There are more famous people alive today than have existed throughout the whole of human history. We recognise every character from *Eastenders* and contestant off *Big Brother* but know not the philosophers and philanthropists of yesteryear.

I never wanted fame of any sort. That disastrous appearance on *Blue Peter* as a child prodigy has been an albatross for the rest of my non-entity life.

Some religions have it that Humankind's purpose is to list all the names of God. We have spent most of our history simply shouting our own names and 'qualities' at the tops of our voices.

Look at me. Recognise me. Celebrate me.

*

It's dark and cold now. There's no light or gas for the boiler. The batteries on these laptops won't last much longer. We're sitting wrapped in blankets and safety jackets against the cold of the universe. Soon I will stop tapping and reach out to touch Ollie's hand, to know he's there, to feel him, until one of us is taken…

When we came staggering out of the tube station, the maintenance crew had vanished and the steel trellis gates were pulled together but, fortunately, not fastened.

Even more of the world has vanished overnight. So much more of our influence, our habitation, our *conquest* has disappeared since… Was it just a week or so ago I was worried about Lord Edgar not turning up to lead the fund raising for our charity?

Oliver is fond of saying, "Charity begins at home." He always was a selfish git.

Look at me.
Look, don't touch.
Don't look any more.
Forget all you knew me for.
No face, no name, no number.
We're holding out here. Just. We have provisions, bottled water, First Aid kits and rudimentary weapons. I'm low on a few necessities such as Nurofen and sanitary towels. I'm dreading my next period.

Claire. There is no Claire. It's an assumed name to protect my true identity. If you knew my real name, you might remember me. And we can't allow that to happen.

Oliver, also, is a nom de plume. Nasreen, Joyce, Janie, Darren, Andrew, even Annie Clarke and the Earl of Tetchley – all fictitious monikers to muddy our trail, to cloak and disguise, keep us out of the *slime* light for a little bit longer.

If you see me on what's left of the street, don't say hello, don't even acknowledge me. Look away. Recognition is fatal.

Celebrity is death.

WAVING NOT DROWNING

For my first seven nights here in Yareport, I suffered worse insomnia than Einstein on a caffeine drip. Eventually, I learned to ignore and even take some comfort from the waves crashing on the shingle and the sound of the sirens on the seafront. Once or twice I even dressed again and took a stroll down to Jeff's All Night Broccoli Stall to chew the cud with the friendly geezer. The rich ozone in the sea spray made me tired to my bones. I was a city boy, not a coastal townie, and adjustment took quite a while before I was able to draw consolation from the omnipresent nocturnal noises.

Which left me with the 24-hour task of adjusting to the electronic tag around my left leg. Rumour had it that the heavy metallic presence left a permanently indented impression of the patrician profile of the PM King – something like a concave tattoo. The future would reveal that prophecy's veracity. For now, I had to try not to drag my manacled limb behind me like some bit part zombie in a straight to DVD horror flick. At first, I kept my trousers long to cover my shame but it was such a hot summer and such a sweaty job in the pleasure gardens that eventually I reverted to shorts and wore my clasp like a badge of honour.

The mark of my misdemeanour fascinated my nonagenarian landlady Mrs Duffy. Somehow she kept charge of three guest rooms in her Edwardian terrace conversion. I could barely imagine there had ever been a Mister Duffy – maybe Noah or one of the scriptwriters plotting character development in the Old Testament – and yet… And yet she had a fascination for my manly ankle that bordered on the perverse and hinted at the young girl she might once have been back in the long lost land of milk and honey. Blimey, even Queen Victoria was a goer back in her very young days!

So I wore thick socks indoors beneath disguising blue flannel tracksuit bottoms. I resented her pinch nosed attention for all the expected reasons. But mostly because I was being shamed and punished when I was patently not guilty.

I know, I know, they all say that. Except in my case, it's true.

*

At breakfast, the TV was playing a news magazine featuring royal correspondent Barbara O'Sequious. Some men I know worship her but I've never been able to see the attraction myself. She reminds me of someone my ex-headmaster might have secretly fancied at his bridge or polo clubs.

" …And with this initiative, His Right Honourable Royal Highness is appealing both to the educated palate and, crucially for the emancipated serfs and other riffraff, directly to the pocket. A tax break on the five fruits and veg," she concluded. "It's pure genius! Heaven bless the PM King."

Mrs Duffy's morning choice of cold croissants, sugar-saturated jams and 'Full English by prior appointment' suggested that government initiatives hadn't yet filtered through to every corner of this newly health-conscious kingdom. Still, at least her coffee was caffeinated.

The 'other' Jeff was doing the day shift down at the broccoli stall. Some people claimed the plant came from outer space but I believed local clay soil allotments provided strongest proof of its traceable origin. I went for the regular standby – three florets in soft white pitta – which I ate in situ while we chewed over the latest sports gossip. As traffic fumes wafted and mingled with green veggie taste on my tongue, I wondered briefly if a roadside health food kiosk was somewhat self-defeating.

The sky promised a fine, brisk day. The idiosyncratic mini weather systems common to seaside towns meant things could change in the blink of an oyster shell but I began work in shorts and T-shirt.

We had some bushes to re-plant and I had soon worked up a manly sweat to go with my red tan and labourer's muscles. I knew that the admin girls liked to sneak through the park on their way to the office and I savoured the feel of their feminine gaze as it lingered over my back and buttocks. I knew most returned their attention to forthcoming phone calls and emergency faxes when they spotted the tag on my ankle. But what are you scared of, ladies? I would never hurt you. And my crime wasn't such a big deal, you know. So I was declared responsible for a few young idiots dying? Even the crooked judge could only slap me with manslaughter, not pre-med. Don't shed any tears for those louts – the world won't miss them.

*

Harry had done his penance for a still unspecified crime against the kingdom. At the end of his stint, he'd somehow insinuated himself into a senior role with the local steam railway attraction and settled into the ways of Yareport. Essentially, he was where I wanted to be in three months time… with remission for good behaviour. He was into all the usual blokey things – football, pub rock, films featuring big explosions – but surprised me with an abiding obsession with astrology. The reason only became clear on the night of his beach barbecue.

"The girls should be on the closer rocks tonight," he whispered to me as we stood like bushmen at the griddle.

"There's girls here already," I answered. "Friends of Julia's, mostly, but they seem all right."

"I'm talking about the sirens, you dummy. Real women. Goddesses, not town fluff. I've done all the lunar calculations on my laptop."

"I thought they came all the way onto the beach some evenings."

"Not since the partial occlusion. We have to swim out to them. So go easy on the burgers and hotdogs. Lager you can piss away, but –"

"Sure."

My tag had been giving me gyp for the last half-hour. Maybe I should have opted for sonic instead of vibrate; the ear can eventually assimilate most annoyances into the general white noise of existence.

An angry yellow flame shot skywards from a skin-ruptured sausage and our raggle taggle revellers raised an ironic cheer above the bass-heavy music and the lapping of the waves. Jeff Number Two was explaining the offside rule or the intricacies of the constitution to Julia Number One and her female friend. I thought I'd wander over and interpret as necessary.

The television was turned low: Barbara O'Sequious, reverential and hushed yet still headmistressy as she offered a précis of the PM King's latest plans to restore our country to lost or illusory greatness. It would be somebody else's turn to borrow the portable tomorrow night. I only put my name down for the rota to improve my sense of belonging. Jeff shuffled the cards nervously; Harry counted his matchsticks. A knock on the door sent us all scurrying for apparent innocence.

"I've told you, Mr White, No female visitors allowed."

I spread my right arm in an expansive gesture copied from TV shots of our glorious ruler. "It's just me and a couple of the lads, Mrs D. You probably know Jeff from the broccoli stall; and this is my work mate –"

"Harry Leicester. It's an honour to meet you in your lovely abode, Mrs Duffy."

She fixed Harry with her entomologist eyes. "You got one of them tags as well?" she enquired.

"Briefly did I sadly stray from the straight and narrow, ma'am. I shall not trouble his right honourable majesty in future."

She sniffed, conducted a lightning sonar sweep of the room. "Just as long as you ain't smoking or drinking," she concurred.

When we were assured of her graceless descent back to her hidey-hole, Jeff said, "I'd really better be going – my shift starts soon."

"Can't have the punters missing their veg and vitamins," Harry agreed. "Talking of which, you still up for the beach barbecue on Friday?"

"Will there be any, uh, single women there?" Jeff asked.

"I'm doing my best on that score."

"It's just – Julia doesn't like me going out on my own."

"But I thought Julia was going out with –" Harry began before I shushed him.

"That's a different Julia," I stated. Then: "Bring her along so she can keep an eye on you."

Jeff nodded, left. Harry turned his puzzled gaze towards me, pondered, "Is every Jeff in a relationship with a Julia?"

"Just like they run the greens trolley."

"God, I can't wait to find out who they've got lined up for me."

"Probably Catherine of Aragon," I assured him.

"As long as it ain't Anne of Cleves."

I'd now been at the barbecue for so long that I'd lost all track of time. Not so my desperate tag team mate.

"Leave your stuff behind these rocks," Harry insisted.

"But what if –"

"So somebody might nick your T-shirt or your stinky old trainers? Trust me, it'll be worth it. There's no one around, anyway."

He was right. The first visit by the police squad car had halved our number and lowered the sound system to acceptable decibels. The second had caused us to douse our yellow fires and let the moonlight bathe the hard sand and shingle in its silver effluence. Jeff had gone off to take over the late shift, the doting Julia meekly in tow. Her teeth would be green by next month. She would bear him many children: a new species, the Broco-saurians –

"Jesus Christ and the PM King!" I shouted into the empty night air. "This water's freezing."

"Get swimming before your circulation gives up. Come on."

I thrashed a few dozen flailing front crawl strokes to get my heart rate up before settling into a more sedate, sustainable breaststroke. Yesterday evening I'd borrowed Harry's binoculars and espied the beautiful sirens lounging on the rocks; tonight I was dragging my full bladder and slightly bloated belly towards their sweet indulgence.

"Don't they ever come ashore?" I'd asked him.

"That's just a myth put about by some of the local girls making themselves out to be something they're not."

An unexpected swell had me swallowing salt water, gagging, losing my rhythm momentarily. As I blinked brine from my eyes, the constellations seemed to re-form into celestial question marks. How pathetically penis-driven was this whole escapade? Shouldn't I have grown out of such lust-fuelled jaunts? And wasn't the whole siren business a huge hoax in any case?

I could hear their sweet voices clearly on the gentle breeze, a soft caress like the combined soothing whispers of Kate Bush, Bjork and Hope Sandoval. To my right, I saw a fishing boat carrying a thwarted stag party; their vessel caught in a slow whirlpool conjured by the maidens. Best to turn tail, lads.

My kicking feet touched stones and I walked the final two yards. Harry, for all his athletic prowess, arrived ten seconds behind me.

"Hello, boys."

She was taller than I'd expected, veering towards the Amazonian. She was draped in those strands of chiffon so beloved of Renaissance painters circumventing censorship. The nocturnal exertion had left me breathless, open-mouthed. Her skin held the lustre of the interior of the oyster shell; her wavy hair tumbled past her shoulders in a cascade resembling a freeze-frame avalanche. I would never look upon such splendour again.

"What have you brought for us?" she whispered.

At that point, shivering like a half-drowned puppy with my half-frozen genitals barely conspicuous – in fact, noticeably absent – beneath my damp shorts, I suddenly understood the full fallibility of our mission.

Harry was less fazed than I and piped up with, "Plenty in the bedroom department."

Venus had by now been joined by Athena or Persephone or Demeter. She turned to her sister and in the broadest South Hampshire accent stated, "No trinkets."

"Nah trinkets?" gasped the crag-bound goddess. "Cheapskate landlubbers. Sling their 'ooks!"

I tried to move, to remonstrate or plead in some way, but as the body-enveloping chill was starting to abate so I became more acutely aware of the pain in my left shin as the restraining device pulsed against my leg like the jaws of Cerberus. As if I needed a sharp focus against the women's hazy aura of languid dreams!

Aphrodite advanced with her fingers poised like talons as Harry and I retreated.

"Another time, Ladies," my companion promised.

"Don't call us, needledick," she hissed, "and we won't call you."

Somehow I found the energy to swim back against the outgoing tide; even losing my bearings once as a cloud obscured Luna. My calf muscles felt like they were on fire whilst the rest of me froze like the berg by the 'Titanic'. At last there was only wet gravel beneath my chest and I let my eyes rest in the dear knowledge that modern electronics had triumphed over the pull of mythical physiology.

It was dawn. A stray dog was sniffing the back of my knees. I would catch hell from Mrs D for staying out so late. And I was due at work in two hours.

Which didn't stop me taking an overlong refreshment break during the afternoon, having retrieved Harry's binoculars from my works locker, and climbing to the highest spot on the cliffs in order to spy again on the sorority of sirens. The moral minority had often questioned, "Why doesn't the government do something about them?" But the ending of the Bland Age had encouraged a new wave of hands-off liberalism to sweep across the country – even though a hand was firmly clamped around my left ankle, aggravating an old football injury and playing havoc with my shin pads on the couple of occasions I played again. The creed was "Modern Laissez Faire" and we had a parliamentary monarchy benevolently ruled by the PM King. Apologists such as Barbara O'Sequious proclaimed this as 'a Golden Age to rank alongside Camelot'. The apotheosis of hyperbole, more like.

My concentration was broken by the buzzing of the Air-Sea Rescue helicopter overhead. The pilot completed an arced mini descent, which took his craft on a fly past of the fabulous island. The women waved excitedly; my mournful gaze lingered lust-crazed on their jiggling bare breasts. The crew of the chopper stood to attention at the open door of the yellow vehicle, saluted against their helmets, then flew off in search of drowning rubber dinghies.

I had regularly experienced problems with those old padlocks. The thick brass mechanism would have been an acceptable deterrent to intruders, except that it had a tendency to spring open unannounced. A copy of the requisition order for a new one was on my desk. Recently faxed, this was a repeat order – the company had told me six months ago to wait a while, till the new financial year. Maybe I could have popped to a local hardware shop and spent my own cash but I had a few other matters on my mind. Besides, there were signs up everywhere reminding riders and paddlers regarding safety rules.

Now the rain was gradually soaking through my uniform but it was not yet heavy enough for the super to call off work for the day. So I kept digging, uprooting, making space for the next tourist-pleasing shrubs and flowers. I couldn't see the sea from where I laboured but the sky loomed ominous with the threat of an approaching storm. Oh the great old British seaside!

I had loved that job. I loved the bright, excited faces of the kids at the end of a school session when they'd been soaked, scared but exhilarated. So our security set-up wasn't state of the art. So the people in the canoe didn't wear helmets and lifejackets. How is that *MY* fault? They broke in and stole the boat. I was on duty – yes – but they should be responsible for their actions, not me.

But the judge wanted somebody to blame and as both of the drunken yobs had perished in a flurry of dropped oars, tipped kayaks and beer swilling, his honour decided to slap me on the wrist and ankles. Blame culture prefers to shame the survivors.

Mrs Duffy was at the window, incongruous in tatty mauve velour dressing gown and expensive gold high heels. She turned to lick me with her scorching yet rheumy eyeballs; the wooden rolling pin in her none too steady grip kept a jazz buff's counterpoint to her inquisitive words.

"Where are you going so early?" she snarled.

"Got to see my new probation officer," I answered.

"New? What happened to the old one?"

"Got arrested for pimping," I muttered, dodging ill-held cylindrical wood.

I knocked several times on the rough-hewn outer door of the office on Glebe Street. I was about to give up and phone in my confession when Harry opened the door from the inside.

"Admit to everything, Jerry," he advised. "Every sordid little detail. It's the only way."

I acquainted myself with an out of date though still fascinating music magazine whilst I waited my turn. I hadn't realised before that Cliff Richard's *Summer Holiday* and Helen Shapiro's *Walking Back to Happiness* held such depths and layers of politically coded meaning –

"Jerry White? I'm Claire Bull. I hear you've got a little story to tell about a midnight dip. What is it with you men and those sluts on the rocks?"

She was dark-haired and pretty in that 'dressed formally for the office' way popularised by ubiquitous Barbara O'Sequious. She let her spectacles perch on her nose in an unmistakably coquettish manner. I judged her to be maybe a year or two older than me. The certificates and diplomas plastered on the back wall added to her assumption of superiority but I'd played bass in a band on *Top Of The Pops* and I'd been shot by a Cyberman in the new *Doctor Who*, so why should I be intimidated?

"That's just it," I mumbled. "The apparent ease. But it's all illusion. Usually, I'd see the person. Yet I don't even know myself properly anymore."

"You know I've got to invoke the extra month on your sentence, don't you?"

"It was just a skinny dip! I didn't hurt anyone."

"There are electronic records. My hands are tied. It's not the end of the world, Jerry."

"It feels like it."

She raised her feet up onto the wooden table, kicked off her black court shoes. I began kissing her toes in the show of obeisance Barbara and the PM King had lately demonstrated. She tasted of body lotion, not at all sweaty. A thin silver ankle chain didn't disguise the lingering indentation left by a recently removed tag.

"What did they get you for?" I asked.

"Misdemeanours. Me and my ex-boyfriend Jerry."

"*Ex*? *Jerry*? Hey, I'm developing a theory about names that go together."

"I'd like to hear it over dinner some time. But not one of those green veg places – I've got vitamins and minerals coming out of my ears."

Claire. Like the French *Clair de la Lune*. What did that mean? A moonlit sky or too much feminine lunacy? I couldn't wait to find out.

"Look at this," said Jeff.

For a moment, I wasn't sure what or where he meant until, eventually, I focused on his hands waving like sea anemones in the incoming tide.

"Green fingers," he confirmed. "Hazard of the job. Like working in a fishmonger's or a chippie – you can never lose the smell."

It didn't seem so bad to me – proper paid employment without electronic restraint – but Jeff was a mate so I simply murmured agreement.

The broccoli stall on every corner was a phenomenon of our time, just like the solar flares and comet debris that had set the telecommunications industry back fifteen years. Sometimes the veg would be steamed with a little low fat margarine and an airline style wet wipe for your greasy fingers afterwards. Many people like it stewed, although my worry is that it has been in the saucepan so long that all the goodness will have leaked out. A better idea might be to drink a mug of the juice. Of course, the Raw Vegetable Movement, who held a 5% share of the popular vote but more importantly had the cauliflower ear of the PM King, recommended florets be eaten uncooked and for the best effect *in situ*. All very well for those who'd turned over their manicured lawns and patio decking to grow-bag allotments. One of the supermarkets had enterprisingly incorporated it with a roll mop of fish and 25g of rice into 'P M King's Sushi'. This had taken over from Cheese Ploughman's and Tuna Mayo triangular packed sandwiches as the refrigerated lunch snack of choice in offices across the kingdom.

Jeff was waving his stained digits again. "Is this all there is – for now and the foreseeable future?"

"It's not so bad," I answered. "There's less Saturday night fighting than in most seaside towns. And you've got Julia."

"She's so insipid, just like this shit I have to cook all day. I want excitement… danger…dodgy women. But that's neither my fate nor my nature. I'm just as bland as she is."

"Cheer up, Jeff, you're spoiling the sunset. You sound just like an old girlfriend of mine – whenever she had PMT."

"Get outta here!" he chided.

I wiped my thumb on my overalls, grinned, departed.

*

Seaside rain is more sudden and stentorian than the meagre dribbles one suffers inland. What the waves can't reach, their airborne grey cousins soon extinguish. All the colourful lights above the amusement arcade, the brightly painted ceramic souvenir stalls, the parents and kids in their red, green or blue cagoules – everyone driven indoors or blanketed by the darkening downpour. I shivered by the window of the keepers' hut, wishing my work clothes stretched to long trousers and a thick crew neck pullover. The click of the raised latch brought my attention back round.

"You got a towel?" Claire asked.

Strands of hair were plastered to her head in crazy 'S' shapes. Medusa *softened* but still irresistible. My hands rested on her waist, aching to reach higher; her fingers danced over the stretched elastic of my shorts, desperate to descend.

"We mustn't," she whispered eventually. "I'll lose my job."

"You'll find another one."

"Not in Yareport."

"Come back to London with me when my time's up."

She'd removed her glasses to wipe away the moisture. Still her hazel eyes twinkled bewitchingly. "You're not going back to London," she stated. "I'm keeping you here."

I chanced one more glance out of the window at the soggy rosebushes and the rain-soaked lawns.

"You could sit on my lap," I suggested. "The park's empty and we won't be disturbed. You wouldn't even have to take off your wet dress."

I loved the acrid taste of perfume on the back of her neck and the girlish boniness of her thin shoulders. I smiled at the way she folded her white knickers ever so neatly into a pocket of her handbag.

Later, I watched the downpour abating beyond the glass. I wondered briefly whether the sirens on the rocks had any shelter from this unpredictable and inclement weather. Claire would tell me not to overly concern myself with their welfare. "Let the bitches freeze and drown!" was her succinct opinion.

She was at my side, arms warm around my navel, murmuring, "Hey, lover boy, any chance a girl might get some hot chocolate to warm her up?"

*

Claire was busy with arrangements for a 'VIP visit'. The rumour mill had been working overtime – a cabinet minister, a raw vegetable powered sporting hero, maybe even the PM King himself? She was remaining resolutely tight-lipped, a curious counterpoint to the frisson and openness of our suddenly intimate relationship.

My landlady was certain of the visitor's identity and applied geological layers of lipstick in preparation.

"Barbara O'Sequious," she crooned. "Imagine!"

"Imagine is all I'll be able to do – I'm on shift all day."

"No rest for the wicked," Mrs Duffy smiled. "Quite right too."

The weather had picked up again and I saw several parked cars with surfboards and kayaks strapped to their roof racks. I walked on enviously, detouring when the containment cordon and striped tape and bunting required it. I sweated several hours in the sun, my tag chafing against the fast tanning skin on my leg. I took a late lunch break. Unusually, the broccoli stall was boarded up. Security reasons, I assumed.

By the end of the day, I had a magnificent white silhouette on my left arm representing the ghost of my wristwatch. I tried Claire's office and home numbers from a call box; hanging on until the line buzzed its annoyance and the machine gobbled up my precious change. It crossed my mind once every hundred and twenty seconds that Claire would soon get cold feet over the blissful blurring of her professional and private life. Back at the guest house, I even summoned the nerve to use Mrs D's phone: still no answer. I showered, changed, hit the seafront.

The sirens were particularly loud tonight and I wished I'd brought the binoculars to ascertain what had disturbed them so.

Then I discerned a figure… male… floundering…

I didn't have time to think about my smart shoes and trousers and the few pounds in my pockets. Strewing attire behind me like onion layers, I raced into the icy evening water on my mercy mission. The catcalls echoed off the swelling waves and my quarry bobbed helplessly, still more than a hundred yards away. I admit that it crossed my mind that, if successful, I could expect at least praise, perhaps a reward, even early release… No, it was altruism that drove me forward through the waves even though my electronic tag was half killing me and the pain was pulling me back like a giant magnet.

Nearly there now. Hang on, pal, just keep your head above the surface if you can. And you sirens can give it a rest, too.

"Hey, landlubber, lover boy! We told you afore, we don't want you. You ain't up to it."

"Call that a six-pack, man? It ain't even a punnet of raspberries!"

I wanted to answer – oh, God, I wanted to give them a piece of my mind, these slags that lay around on rocks all day, useless to all and sundry. Get a proper job and give something back to society. I certainly have. And my muscles have got me here and will get me home, so meditate on that, sisters!

A rogue wave caught me up in its choking, saltwater struggle but I recovered enough to swim carefully onwards. The seaweed-infested water close to the rocks was uncomfortably similar to broccoli broth. Of the semi-frozen variety.

I could see the guy's face now. It was Jeff. Silly sod, chasing mythical fantasies. Didn't know when he was well off.

Don't listen to them, let the water block your ears – but not your mouth and nostrils.

Come on, mate, and give us your arm. Now, hold on, not too tight, kick your legs if you can, it's a long way back to shore and no sign of a rescue helicopter.

It's just you and me, friend, hindered by the restless brine and the shrill catcalls and the water swirled by the sirens' pointed talons; hampered by tiredness and lethargy and broken dreams and distance.

So much distance.

The worst thing about it was that I didn't even make the front page of the local newspaper. That dubious honour befell the photogenic matriarch Barbara O'Sequious, who lately graced Yareport with her neo-regal presence.

In fact, there was a whole host of downsides to my marine adventure. Like coughing my guts out for several hours afterwards. Like having Claire confront me with a heady mixture of concern and annoyance.

"You've violated the conditions of your parole – again, Jerry! The tag will stay on even longer now."

"It means I'll remain here in Yareport – with you."

"Maybe I want a free man who puts others first."

"I *was* putting other people first, Claire."

"You weren't thinking about me. You were swimming out to those floozies again. I give up!"

At least I'd seen the SOS and saved a soul. Or maybe not so.

A bedraggled Jeff still insisted, "I was waving, not drowning."

"Stop being the macho fool, Jeff, you were floundering and going under."

"Possibly, but it was my choice. The sirens had called me. They hadn't called you, I'm sure they're sick of you poking your nose into their business. This was my moment but the chance has gone now, they won't ever call me again. You think I want to boil pallid green vegetables all my days?"

Life is a 3D flow chart with regular box stops involving decisions. It seemed I'd messed up at some crucial point, picking the wrong option on whether to interfere or to stay put. All with the best motives, but...

The PM King claims the green plant that looks like algae and tastes like rattan is debris from a previous comet. This vegetable from outer space apparently adds four years to your life expectancy. I've made one more decision, in solitude and in repose:

The hell with another 1500 days of hardship; I'm never eating broccoli again.

FLAT TOP

I didn't think I'd miss having Duncan as an upstairs neighbour but that was before Laurence moved in. Duncan I'd grown used to: heavy-footed like the proverbial herd of elephants stomping meaningfully over the bare wooden floorboards; sunbathing until late in September in his half of the miniature garden, his genitals and slight paunch barely contained by a pair of blue Speedos; or cooking up exotic dishes in the manner of currently fashionable TV chefs. These latter appealed more to the sensitive smoke alarm than the modern cosmopolitan palate.

Janie had commented on all these matters and sometimes I wondered if her dismissive remarks actually cloaked a well of feminine curiosity. But Duncan was history now. Neither had I seen enough of Janie lately.

The first indication of the new state of affairs came with Laurence's positioning of his audio-visual equipment. His lounge was directly above mine and his television would have plugged into the socket for the shared aerial. He'd indulged in that bane of modern urban living: the home cinema speakers. They never came packaged with an obligatory soundproofing system for one's put-upon neighbours. On a couple of occasions I was assailed by the stereophonic explosions requisite to the terrorist-foiling action of some Bruce Willis or Tom Cruise film. Mostly, though, it was *Newsnight*, *Sky Hourly Update* and the like. I could silence my own set and still be up to date on world affairs: freakish weather in Colorado; slipping share prices in Tokyo; political upheaval in the Philippines.

He had a DAB radio in his bathroom and portables in both kitchen and back bedroom. A finger on the pulse: distorted voices straining for the consensus of immediate history in every audible corner.

He has a newspaper delivered daily. I didn't think anybody did this anymore: we all pick up the *Sun*, the *Mail* or the *Independent* on the way to the station, not wait in for some spotty teenager to ram the fragile pages into the letterbox. We get a free local paper, of course, crammed with stories of street robberies and education crises; funded by adverts for stock clearance warehouses and massage parlours.

I quite like the idea of a leisurely breakfast of tea, toast and a tabloid. There's something of the hotel life about it. Should I set off for work an hour or so later so that I can indulge in this relaxing morning ritual?

*

We share some plumbing. I have a small hot water tank sitting like an eyeball from the Cyclops just below the ceiling in the hall. All the cold water, however, flows through the same copper pipes. I hear the flushing of his toilet, the tap rushing as he rinses his hands or brushes his teeth, the staccato intake and rumble that signals the operation of his washing machine. Sometimes I have been waiting for my cistern to re-fill to rid the bowl of a particularly difficult shit and a tower of toilet paper but he's used his loo at the same time and we're in competition and the delay is endless. I hear his footsteps and guess his intentions so jump out of my chair and try to beat him to it. That's the only way to stay ahead.

When his girlfriend's over she always takes at least one shower every day. She's a pretty, petite thing with dark ringlets, a prominent nose and a slightly Turkish aspect to her skin colouring. Miriam or Meriam or something. On the few occasions when Janie's been around I've encouraged her to mirror the woman's activities but she's been resistant.

"I bathed before I came over." / "I'm not that dirty." / "Are you after shower sex or something, Billy?"

In our early days we would often soap each other up in the bath, illuminated by scented candles at the non-tap end. Then I developed an allergy to evening primrose oil and some of the other perfumes. Or we ceased being so interested in each other's bodies.

I wish I could watch Meriam bathing.

To do so I would need to become Laurence.

He's had his hair cut. It looks like something of a modern variant on the flat top, which I thought was well outmoded. But hang on: the hard man on *Eastenders*, a couple of prominent Premiership footballers and even the reporters on the local news broadcast are bringing it back into fashion.

There's a cheap barber's in the parade of shops by the railway station. I need a new style. Helps the male swagger.

*

I was reading something in the press about the growth of CCTV over the past couple of decades when I spied Laurence leaving the building. Every railway station, office entrance, high street pavement, supermarket and corner shop has sprouted cameras and recording equipment, tracking our movements more than a hundred times a day. Laurence was wearing a nondescript jacket a little too short for the season but a really well-cut pair of trousers: stone grey chinos that hung casually perfect as he paused to open the front gate. I wanted to look as effortlessly cool. Maybe I needed to expand my range beyond a perfunctory browse through Next, Topman, Gap, Burton and, lately, M & S.

As luck would have it, the communal postbox had plenty of mail for my upstairs neighbour, including a catalogue of menswear and other accessories such as shavers and executive toys. It was badly packaged in some sort of ill-fitting plastic shrinkwrap liable to tear accidentally, especially across the space for addressee… The hallway was the almost last public space in London not prone to 24-hour surveillance.

It was the matter of barely ten minutes to access the credit account with Direct Male Postal Services and order some new strides. They promised delivery within three to five working days. I would have to ensure that I was not actually working during that period so I could be ready for any possible confrontation.

"But I always order my clothes from this company."

"But it's my address on the package."

"Easy to mistake 'B' and 'C'."

"It's my name, too. Stop trying to steal my stuff, Laurence."

He surprised me, lurking just behind the front door as I arrived back from the shops. Up close, he needed a fresh dab of deodorant. Still, I could talk.

"You see this?" he asked, fluttering a sheet of glossy paper in front of my face. It took me ten seconds to ascertain that it was an estate agent's flyer. "They've just sold a flat up the road for two-ninety," he continued. "That's ten thousand more than I paid. In a month!"

"I don't know how people keep up," I muttered.

I was acutely aware of the contents of my shopping bag: Value brand potatoes; sausages not fillet steaks; a packet of salad a little too wet inside the bag as it reached its 'Use By' date.

"You ever think of selling up?" he asked.

"Not yet."

A shake of the head, two keys in locks and I was safe again.

When I was younger, I was all for 'Live and let live'; but now…? Most of the world's population seems to equate liberty with licence. The right to assert their own lifestyle over everybody else's. Western capitalism, Islamic terrorism, noise culture – they're all at it, the bastards!

I'm waving the latest estate agent's bumf around like a raving politician. "Quiet residential street" / "Pleasantly tree-lined" / "A mixture of well-appointed flats and terraced houses". They don't mention the Sunday afternoon alfresco car mechanics convention. Or the kids either bombing up and down on motorised scooters or booting footballs from one pavement to another whilst they project the racket from their MP3 players to all and sundry.

I can't stand it tonight, I want to go out and confront them. I take a step to my door and then into the hallway and as far as the shared outer door, angry fingers poised over the latch, pausing…

It's not a class thing. That's simplistic shit to claim that because someone is working class, whatever that means these days, one is prone to anti-social behaviour. My mother was a dinner lady – doesn't that make my background proletarian?

I'm outside now, sorting something out in the recycling bin, counting the crowd of miscreants just down the street. The police don't want to know. The local council probably gave them the hovel in the first place. Except it wasn't a hovel then.

I can't deal with them on my own. They'll stone my windows, piss in my front yard, stab me in the guts without a second thought.

Laurence is at his window gazing at the annoying mayhem. Come down and give us a hand here, you cowardly bastard.

But he doesn't and he won't and I snivel back to my cramped lounge and switch the TV on to some crime drama that I'm not really interested in but creates sufficient volume to mostly drown out the shouts and revving motors.

Later I hear sounds close to my window. A parting of the curtains reveals Laurence putting out some rubbish and taking a peek at the street. Is he echoing my every action now?

*

The lovely Meriam had arrived with a shopping bag containing two bottles of wine and a box that probably held a cake. So now Laurence was an expert chef and was doing Sunday roast for himself and the skinny minx who provided the fripperies! Would he forsake the ream of newspapers for once or let them form the basis of an enlightened dinner party conversation?

"Did you hear about the constitutional crisis in Turkey?"

"What's your opinion on the National's Beckett revival?"

"It says here that fifteen percent of couples under thirty are open to experimenting with multi-partners. I think we need to talk about this, Laurence."

They are a few courtship stages ahead of me but I'm on the phone now to Janie.

"It would be so nice if you came over."

"I thought you used Sundays for silent contemplation. Anyhow, I've arranged to see my parents."

"Make an excuse. I'm doing a cold meat salad."

"Well, if you put it like that, Billy…"

Upstairs they were listening to Classic FM. I whizzed through the downloads on my MP3, found some Mozart and *Nessum Dorma* style light opera, plugged a jack into the hi-fi speakers. We're all disc jockeys nowadays.

Later, toying with some ham a little too close to its 'Sell By' date, Janie says, "This is all I've asked from you, Billy, just a bit of commitment. Putting us first for once."

"Let's go and talk in the bedroom," I suggest.

My timing is superb because I can hear they're already onto the main course upstairs. The bed is creaking as the wooden feet slip and resettle against the increasingly persuasive rhythm of their lovemaking. I haven't indulged in pansy stuff like scented candles but did have a hoover round earlier. Use your ears and a little of your imagination –

"Sounds like they're busy upstairs," Janie smiles.

I can hear her – the girl above – begin a breathless ululation – as the humping gains momentum.

"We could do something ourselves," I whisper, trying to keep the tension out of my voice, the desire not for Janie as such but to find my own space within the ritual, to be parallel or a mirror or a delayed display… to match up to my neighbour and the lead he's setting.

*

Strange knockings from above. What is he planning now? What is he constructing now? Some sort of further espionage to undermine my position. Undermine? In a literal manner, I am under him but I shall turn this hierarchy upon its head with the application of stealth technology and wariness.

As a youngster I was quite handy with the saw, the scissors, the vice and the craft knife. I made myself a cool periscope with mirrors and tubing and I shall consider again – in the absence of opportunities to gain physical access to his property – how best to observe his plans and machinations.

Where to lay my spying devices? How to arrange my optical traps and snares? Knowledge is power. Observation is everything.

I am first to the post again. He has a communication from his bank detailing ways in which he can guard against identity theft. *Ten Steps to Protect Yourself on the Internet.* Never open attachments from senders you do not know. Never reveal your password.

Open your neighbour's mail before he can get to it.

Learn what he's planning and what he's saying about you.

Never reveal anything.

At last he's left the building.

I know he's been spying on me and my hope is that he will be careless in how he disposes of the evidence.

So I casually stroll out to the bin bag he placed in the container not ten minutes ago. If someone asks – and why should they, it's not their business? – my reply will be that I forgot to recycle some empty bottles.

I gash my fingers on a badly opened can in the depths of the sack. I want to suck the blood away but the smell of tinned fish makes me nervous of picking up a secondary salmonella infection, so I wipe my bleeding hand cautiously against the leg of my trousers.

At last I find what I seek – the slim, metallic SIM card that is the oracle of our age.

But when I plug it into my own electronics, I get only a snow storm of white noise punctuated by a smattering of out of focus shots taken at an office Christmas party some ten years ago to judge by the fashions. I'm not in any of the photos and neither is Laurence although he maintains the excuse of having wielded the camera.

It's still early enough in the day for me to change my outfit and go off to the shallow pretence at which I earn my daily crust. No one speaks to me at work although the wound has closed up and I've washed thoroughly so I can't be physically *that* repulsive.

I drift through a series of chores, a blind lab rat in a closed warren lit by fluorescent tubes and eerily blue PC monitors.

Signal failures delay my return and Laurence is already by the window watching for me. I don't wave. I pull my coat tighter around my neck as if his gaze is a blizzard.

I've largely stopped using the far end room, keeping its door closed and radiator shut to save on heating bills. There are a couple of old packing cases full of stuff I once thought to sell but now ought to simply throw out. I was in there seeking some old T-shirt as an extra underlayer against the domestic chill when I caught a glimpse of myself in a free-standing mirror propped against the back door and took a step of amazement backwards just like a character in a cheap cartoon.

It wasn't simply the flat top hairstyle or the shabby indoor clothing, even my skin tone was unfamiliar and a curious foreshortening effect had robbed me of at least four inches of height. Or maybe I was weighed down by cares: old man Sisyphus with a bent back from endlessly pushing metaphorical stones.

I was down to the bare bones in the adjacent kitchen: tea leaves that had lost their aroma and mostly quit the imprisoning bag for a life in the corner of the cardboard box; a rancid scrape of cheap margarine that turned my stomach even as it touched my tongue. I'd been remiss in my commitment to survivalism. Where were the stacks of baked beans, tinned meat and vegetable soups sure to see me through the apocalypse?

I had little piles of silver and copper change stashed in sock drawers and back pockets of unwashed jeans. Enough to fill a couple of cheap bags from the local convenience store.

I was dubious about quitting the flat even for the ten minutes or so required for the urgent task. My adversary had already imposed much of his inimical influence onto my immediate environment and, subtly, onto my own physical appearance; what if he took the opportunity of my temporary absence to make his final push for conquest?

They'd known me in the corner shop for a few years and usually offered some comment about sport or the weather. Today they treated me like a stranger. I was annoyed yet also grateful.

I was back in situ within a thousand seconds. I was too smart for that bastard upstairs.

Laurence is outside in the front hall. I can't smell his after-shave but I'm sure it's him. He uses Paco Rabanne, same as I do. His footfalls are heavier than mine, though, and all his lion pacing the cage activity can only lead to one conclusion… and so it does. He's at my brass letterbox now, rattling it, tapping his knuckles against the wooden door, demanding let me in or I'll blow your house down.

He couches it in modern parlance, the veneer of friendliness, the cloaking device of we're all friends and this has been a misunderstanding and why don't we sit down over a drink and sort it all out?

No poisoned chalice with you, pal, thank you very much.

He's raising his shoulder for a run and thump against the door. I can't see him doing so but I know that's his next manoeuvre. I brace myself for the impact, the shudder and crumble…

Which never comes.

Clearly he can't get the run-up to achieve the required power and, displaying unusual intelligence, has decided to not even try.

Impasse. Lasting… how long? Thirty seconds – yet it feels like thirty minutes. Now he and his sweat and his heavy feet have returned upstairs.

This is my opportunity if only I could seize it. Classic tactics – take the fight back to the enemy's territory with a thrilling counter-attack.

I plead exhaustion.

My moment of triumph shall come. But later.

*

He's made my flat smaller. The ceiling is much lower, the rooms boxy and claustrophobic, the shared hall space entirely his territory now. The front yard has been colonised and the street beyond rendered unobtainable. The siege continues.

He's made my life smaller.

Listen to his taps. Wait for the casual overfill of his bathtub and the ensuing flood in my bathroom which will short out all my electrics. Hark to his loud phone calls, his booming voice proclaiming to his friends and allies in high finance and global advertising that he is now king of this urban jungle. His footsteps beat out the rhythm of the prison warder.

I've given up on books, CDs and the TV. Like a rebel hiding deep in the cellar, I choose my moment to employ the radio at the lowest audible volume. I heard something just yesterday, a thrilling boys' own war story from way back when of how the inhabitants of a town enclosed by the enemy had refused to be starved and beaten but instead had broken through the blockade and taken the surrounding soldiers by surprise by unexpectedly carrying the fight to them.

I want to regain my self-belief, my assertiveness, my individuality. But even if I push back Laurence and his noise and his encroachment, I shall surely be a mere Canute failing to stem an unstoppable tide.

Widescreen TVs; home cinema systems; Bose speakers; in-car stereos; talking tube trains and buses; garbled station announcements at an uncomfortable volume; polyphonic mobile phone ringtones; I'm on the train, I'll be home in ten; close that deal with Harber's, it's our best prize; yeah, what she's doing, right, she's dissing you, man; the endless roar of traffic, a background wash from the encircling M25 supplemented and supplanted by the engines of London's capillary roads; the passing aeroplanes, especially at night when the clouds briefly hold and echo their boom; police sirens, ambulance sirens, ear-bursting screeches; construction work; destruction work...

We are all on top of each other, screaming and yelling the cacophony of our existence. I need to make my voice heard.

There's no future in silence. There's no silence in future.

STONERS

Work was a diabolical drag. Martha was lucky enough to be out at a sales call but Angie was stuck in the office until clocking off time. She couldn't wait to get away. It was that old cliché of having to work so many grey and tediously indistinguishable days in order to light up the hedonistic hours of her free time. But, Angie reasoned, clichés make the world go round. We flow from watching the clock and wishing to escape to worrying that the good times pass so quickly and that Monday morning will soon inexorably rise above the horizon.

Hark at me, she thought, I'm starting to sound just like my older brother.

She took advantage of her supervisor preparing his notes for his Friday closing address entitled, *What have we sold This Week? / Let's set an Even Tougher Target for Next Week* and printed out some funnies from her favourite web site. Doubtless the manager's pep talk would also include the familiar lines, "Remember that at all times you should uphold the good name of Cane Co and use your time away from here for rest and reflection."

At some future date, the intensely old-fashioned, not to mention ancient, Homerton would call it a day and the new boss would have them all in on a Saturday and Sunday shift system, so be grateful for small mercies. Until then, stick your quiet weekend crap up your backside, Mr Homerton, sir!

She phoned Martha's mobile while the sucker's door was still closed.

"Where we going tonight? Jazzles? Balearica?"

"Club Nesta. They've got some new DJ with hot new sounds."

"Heard that before... OK, no prob. What's in the kitty?"

"Forty pounds."

"Is that all? Shit!"

"Forty pounds each, Ange. Anyway, Paul's going and he's got a mate so we won't have to buy a drink all night. I'm getting a bite to eat first on the way back to the flat."

"Sorted. Catch you at ten?"

"Half nine – I may want to borrow your lippy."

All the talk was of quotas, market shares, upward projections; all the thought was of body jewellery and transfer tattoos, halter top or skinny black dress.

Five-thirty. At last.

*

I don't understand why my parents called me Tom. 'Thomas' means 'twin' and my sister Angela – no angel, by the way – is five and a half years younger. No matter – it's plain and everyday enough to never have caused me major problems. Back in the Middle Ages, there were only just over half a dozen names available for men: James, Henry/Harold, John, William, Thomas, Edward, Paul, Christopher, that's it. Perhaps this explains my continued post-school and graduation interest in history. Or else, I was at a loose end on a Tuesday evening since they cut my hours at The Royal Oak to take on cheap trainees who are barely old enough to open their own bags of crisps let alone pull pints.

The venue was my local library's function and study room. I'd become a born again library user of late with free hours on the Internet and DVDs on offer a tad cheaper than at Blockbuster. This weekly run of history lectures – snazzily titled, *The Past – An Undiscovered Country* – promised a modicum more mental stimulation than the soapy operatic screaming matches cluttering up the evening's TV schedules.

Do you ever do that thing where you have one important task only and all day to get somewhere but you still arrive with only a minute to spare? Such a strange human habit! I'd expected the audience to consist of five or six self-improving pensioners but instead the space was packed, with the premium seats in the back row occupied by a large gathering of people my age and younger. Eventually, I discerned a vacant chair right at the front next to a grey-haired senior citizen who looked like the archetypal maiden aunt and needed only a slice of sponge to complete the tableau. As I sat down, she smiled and offered me her spare biro. I declined and dutifully took a notebook out of my jacket pocket.

Technology advances incessantly and I'd been to presentations which were like *Son Et Lumiere* shows; this guy eschewed Power Point and didn't even use a flipchart. Instead he rattled on like an old gramophone on his subject: *There were no winners in World War One*. After twenty minutes I noticed that Auntie Ivy next to me was busying herself with a moderately difficult sudoku puzzle. A commotion at the rear some five minutes later alerted me to the departure of the younger crew. I wondered if they were headed for The Royal Oak. I hoped not: the service was shit when I wasn't on duty.

In an extraordinary piece of programming which echoed the mayfly gadding of the National Curriculum, next week's lecture promised, *Local Findings from the Neolithic*. Maybe there would be some Champions League on telly or else I'd get back to that book about *The Titanic Conspiracy*. My notepad was bare and I felt cheated by the iniquitous Treaty of Versailles.

*

"Aren't you cold in that get-up?"

Angie turned to the lecherous male voice, ready to give the guy a vituperative stab of invective, but-

"Oh, hi, James! How hangs it?"

"Rod-straight as ever. What about you answer my question, Ange?"

"Easier to wipe the sweat off when I'm chilling."

"Ladies don't sweat."

"I ain't a lady, James, as you might remember. What's in your hand?"

"Throat sweets. Flow sweets, you know? S'posed to be a new, stronger mixture but they gave me the same moderate high as the last lot."

"I'll take a handful."

"You'd better swallow them now: Black Adolf and Mrs Hitler are on security tonight. Nothing gets past them. Where's Martha?"

"Stupid cow swapped purses at the last minute. She's at the cash point."

"Sounds like my sort of woman."

"A girl could get jealous, you know… oh, wow, this is good gear! Let me on that dance floor, I'm gonna kick some serious arse."

"Just don't let them see your pupils dilating like a kid at Christmas time. Talking of which, why don't I see your brother around any more?"

"He's gone square. Given up clubbing. Proper job and all that."

"Another loyal customer bites the dust. Just hope there's more fish in the sea. And at such great prices. Call it twenty quid, Ange. Next lot'll be thirty."

Waiting for this week's library lecture reminded me of queuing for one of those free BBC Radio comedy shows: the same odd mix of bargain-hunting matrons and feckless-seeming students. One of the latter group – their leader, in fact – seemed familiar so I felt OK about approaching him.

"Name's Kenneth. You took me on a tour of your university when I was still at school."

"It's amazing you can remember something like that," I commented.

He grinned, "It's the recent stuff that's hard to recall!"

I warmed to him straight away. Habit had me inviting his ragtag group to The Royal Oak even though they'd stopped offering me work lately. In a world where my self-improvement ethic seemed out of step with the hedonistic urges of my sister and her pals, I was intrigued by this group's dedication to the history classes. I should have realised earlier that it wasn't all that it seemed.

Is it just me, or are all jobs these days part time and temporary? Companies don't want to commit – to seating arrangements, personal extensions and paid holiday, never mind the so-called pensions timebomb. Maybe it was merely a reflection of the sort of work I was seeking. I was hovering uncomfortably close to thirty, and companions and peers are well into their first, even second, career by that age. There were things I still wanted to do – and decisions I hadn't yet finalised. Perhaps I was as commitment-phobic as British employers – by which logic, I should probably start up my own business! In the meantime, I was picking up crumbs here and there – a bit of delivery and removals work, teaching guitar a couple of times a week, and technically still the Entertainment Manager for The Royal Oak, although I hadn't so much as shuffled a quiz question or plugged in a karaoke mike in weeks.

I was hoping to revisit my old glory and stage another weekend of *Superstar Doppelgangers*. The pubs of Brightport have an honourable history of supporting up and coming bands but these earlyish years of the new millennium have been characterised locally by a great deal of looking *back*. Rock 'n' roll is well over fifty now and even the fifteen year olds sneaking in with their adenoids and bum fluff know as much about The Beatles and Elvis as they do grime and garage. Shite like Westlife and shows like *The X Factor* have made even these callow schoolkids apparent experts on the tunes my mother likes to call 'Golden oldies'. So, what the gassy lager and vodka slammer drinkers want from the musicians is a familiar song done in the expected style. I'd put on a whole rash of covers bands – technically competent but faceless and interchangeable. Sure, they could all do *Desperado* and *Sultans of Swing* and get the beer glasses and mobile phones waving in the air for an encore of Robbie Williams' *Angels*, but they were strumming down a dead end. The Sixties didn't happen until Lennon and McCartney started singing their own shit instead of copying Gene Vincent or Little Richard. It said as much every month in *Mojo* and I was a true convert to that lost golden age of musical experimentalism.

More interesting to me than wedding reception bands were the acts who were so in thrall to classic pop that they sought vainly to ape their heroes. This was what my hugely successful nights of *Superstar Doppelgangers* were about. Of course, I didn't have the finance or facilities to book the top imitators such as Bjorn Again, The Bootleg Beatles or The Australian Pink Floyd. Some carefully placed publicity and word of mouth ripples, however, brought a deluge of CDs, tapes and five-minute auditions.

Among the acts I squeezed onto the early part of Friday's bill was Me Dread Zeppelin. Page and Plant took the Chicago and Mississippi blues, sprinkled some Celtic fairy dust and psyched the whole thing up; these streetwise kids from an edge of town estate reclaimed and reconfigured the music through a third generation West Indian sensibility. Their demo of *Whole Lotta Love* bubbled for half an hour; unfortunately, I could only offer them fifteen minutes.

I soon had a stellar line-up for Saturday, including Drier States, No Way Sis and Michael Jack's Son. Friday was designed to be a little more leftfield. It was my gig so we opened with Robert Zimmer Frame. This guy was seventy-five if he was a day. His take off of Bob Dylan was extraordinarily accurate. When I went to see the man himself at Brixton Academy a few weeks later I had to squint and pinch to tell them apart. Dylan spat out lines like an ancient cobra and revisited songs in a manner that was often unrecognisable for several minutes. Zimmer Frame, clearly a Bobcat of some standing, aped his pained performance perfectly, even down to the white cowboy hat and the string tie.

The Royal Oak crowd hated him. Even a verse from the all-conquering *Like a Rolling Stone* was greeted with jeers and empty fag packets. I had to rush on Flabber – an overweight spoof of the Swedish supergroup – just to calm things down.

I heard that Robert Zimmer Frame – real name Frank Dobbs – passed away from complications following a urinary infection a mere week later. How did it feel to be all alone with no direction back to the old folks' home? Did he die for his art or did his art die with him? We may never know.

"History," the lecturer continued, "is not about 'his story' or, indeed, 'her story'. That's all an unfortunate Anglicisation of the Greek. In truth, it's about 'our story'."

The young woman with the hennaed hair and the pretty eyes passed a scribbled message to the young white guy with the dreadlocks and the thoughtful stare. He smiled, showed it to me.

"I heard the pub opens in five minutes," I whispered.

I tried to use all my fancy footwork and twinkle-toed wing play to make a quiet exit and thus impress my companions, particularly the girl with the nose piercing, but still ended up scraping a chair and drawing a sussurrus of hushes from the library crowd.

Bottled lager in hand, the rebellious Kenneth said, "We usually enjoy old Coote's lectures but he should stick to his forte and not try to branch out."

"Too much focus on the Victorian era and bricks and mortar," Rosa confirmed. "What we want is cave men."

I suppressed a chuckle and swigged my drink, letting the fizz subside in both the bottle's neck and my oesophagus before adding, "History's such a huge subject, who knows where to start?"

Rosa grinned. Her teeth seemed tiny, the canines pointed and child-like, yet she was surely in her twenties. "The obvious answer – Tom, is it? – is to stretch back beyond what's catalogued and recorded. So-called prehistory has more to teach us than the doings of kings and queens and bellicose bridge builders."

I nodded assent as Kenneth took up the baton. "That's where we come in. We're having a little weekend fact-finding jaunt the Friday after next. Wenlea Cove – do you know it?"

"Heard of it. Isn't it restricted – MOD land or something?"

Rosa laid her right hand on mine. She had bands of metal around every finger. Celtic designs, my untrained eyes assumed. "Ignore the New Age accoutrements," she ordered as if reading these thoughts, "we're serious researchers."

"If you're up for it, ring this number on Monday," Kenneth confirmed.

Yet for all his young, free thinking swagger, Kenneth's views seemed almost wholly cribbed from the lecturer they all referred to as 'Old Coote'.

"The thing is," Kenneth pontificated, "the life priorities for Neolithic Joe weren't so different to those of modern man. You know: get a bit of grub, a roof over his head, some action beneath the moonbeams, and not let his neighbours boss him around."

The smoke in my nostrils and the solid mass of beans in my belly was slowing my thought processes, but I answered eventually: "That's all a bit reductive... and not quite the way you put it before."

His viper's tongue flicked a crumb of food out of a gap in his teeth. "What we're studying, Tom," he drawled, "is the... gap between, uh, the... I mean, *our* proximity and estrangement."

He sat back with a satisfied smile and looked like he might nod off or even disappear completely, Cheshire Cat style. Ken was good-hearted enough but not quite the stimulating company I'd first judged him to be. His little gang was just another bunch of "It was better in the old days/ Get back to the agrarian idyll" revisionists: the sort who'd driven Western culture since the expulsion from the Garden of Eden. A bit of hippie philosophy, some Eastern mysticism and a sprig of Ancient Briton paganism. From William Blake to William Morris and Dante Gabriel Rossetti… all the way through to Page and Plant. Seekers of the lost English paradise. But was I any different with my tastes in art, poetry and psychedelic music?

An owl hooted dramatically, the leaves rustled in the breeze and the corny atmospherics chased away my momentary ill humour. I took a long drag and believed I could clearly see the minute ridges denoting the applied layers of Rosa's fetching lilac makeup, even though it was dark and shadowy where she sat.

"So," I continued, "tell me about Neolithic music."

I was trying hard to concentrate on her words but my main preoccupations were the fog in my forehead and the yawning chasm where my stomach should have been.

"It's not about banging sticks or stones together," Rosa stated. "And, of course, they'd yet to develop the skills to properly work metal or catgut. I suppose the word is shamanism. But it needs the right conjunction and the rocks are key."

"The rocks are key?" I repeated.

"It can happen there under the right circumstances. It's not going to happen in the local park or your vegetable allotment. Wait and see."

"Talking of vegetables," I stated, "I've got a really bad case of the munchies. Is there any more of that stew or bread left?"

"Sure. You shouldn't eat so late, you know. It will disturb your rest."

"I'll walk it off on the way home. I'm a light sleeper anyway."

Time to squirm onto the dance floor. There's a good space there. The lights pulse on off on/off
ononoffonoffononnononoffffffonnn.
Move in time, move in time,
give yourself up to the beat,
the pulse,
the lights pulse off and on,
offonononononon.

You're feeling the rush, your feet aren't your own, they move in a rush, in a blur across the floor, your hands are in the air, we're raising a ragged cheer before we go on again. Here we go again, so fast you're a blur and everybody else is motionless. Why can't they keep up with you? Why can't they go with the Flow?

Why can't they go with the Flow?

A keyboard swell and we pause and cheer.

This time faster, as fast as you've ever moved, you're dodging the debris of the tornado, you're outrunning the crashing wave of the tsunami which is the rise and fall of the music, the stylised breaks in the beat which don't allow any time for your heart rate to slow in between the super sprint that forces you on into new insights and an altered state of time perception. You're dancing so hard. You go with the Flow. I want you to know. I want you to know right now. The Flow pushes you on, gives you the will and the strength to keep pushing harder, you keep pushing harder, knowing young but ultimately useless limbs can still find greater energy and speed... Why call it the Flow? It's hardly gentle, this is Friday night, the hardest night, you can't just chill because it's imperative to party hard and celebrate the end of another shit week. Sure it takes you over but this is no river cruise, ooh-ee baby, let me take you on a river cruise and by this I mean the red salt river, the bloodstream, I'm into your metabolism, you've never felt so fast, quicker than those coiling tongues on jungle frogs and chameleons, so why is everybody else so static?

Even the lights have slowed so that now you're aware of their changing, the flick from off to on, which takes the best part of a quarter minute, just as if somebody's fucked with the dimmer switch. But you shouldn't be able to see all this. That *Twilight Zone* experience nonsense is just for gawping Odeon audiences and Trekkie nerds. How can you? How can we not go with the Flow?

You somehow hold your head steady for long enough to realise that so many around you are all dancing but their movement is so rapid that they seem to be still. Persistence of vision keeps them in one arced place, one sacred place... and even suggests they are slipping backwards through time... we are heading so quickly into the future that our only possible course is backwards and we are reverting. The modern, the futuristic, the primitive, it's you and me and us and them, it's all the same. Impossible to stop. Impossible to stop. IMPOSSIBLETO

At last, the release of the tidal wave crashing onto a terrace of black and white pebbles arranged in five octave formation and the keyboard chords become actual cords that restrain you and pull you back so that the movements are the normal ones of heart beating and blood coursing and oxygen transfer and regular eye blinks to clear the dust and the visions… and a final ragged cheer signals the temporary end.

I received an excited phone call from Kenneth. I couldn't remember giving him my mobile number; it had been one of those saloon bar/ carry on at your place nights.

"Tom, our hero Professor Coote, is giving another lecture at the old town hall. It's only a fiver."

"He was a bit slow last time."

"He's back to his speciality: *Magic and Transformation in Neolithic Society*. We're having a drink-up afterwards. Come on, you know you want to go."

I was possessed of no such knowledge, but… I was dutifully there two nights later, trying not to clink the beer bottles in the carrier bag beneath my feet. Everyone else would be stocking up later at the local Costcutter so I felt a bit premature.

Coote had some interesting theories about primitive rituals involving chanting, sacred herbs and animal skins. Stuff about honouring and absorbing the spirit of the departed, acquiring the power traits of the slain, and then becoming one with the earth. These propositions were backed up with several slides and animations on a Smart Board to the rear. Much of it sounded like wild conjecture to my cynical, modern ears but the event met with huge approval from the Young Person's History Club who set up a brief chorus of, "You're so Coote it's unbelievable!" to the master's obvious embarrassment.

We ended up at the flat Rosa was sharing with one of the other women. She sat herself next to Kenneth and I remained convinced that they were or at least had been a couple; still, she turned her attention to the slightly awkward newcomer enough times to keep my hopes alive.

"I hope you're coming to Wenlea Cove," she stated above the din of the stoner music from the speaker behind her.

I smiled, answered, "I haven't been to a beach party in years. Some Stone Age rituals of drugs, dance and cave paintings certainly offer a different slant."

She pulled a face, spat back, "Don't be so dismissive, it's going to be awesome. And not interrupted by Plod this time."

"What do you mean?"

She hurried off to get the group's press cuttings. Kenneth took a long draw on his cigarette before seizing the opportunity to re-establish his position as alpha male.

"You think we're just a bunch of crusties, don't you, Tom? Listen, I worked as an estate agent for eight years till I got sick of ripping people off when all they wanted was to put a roof over their heads. But I kept all my commission. I was living at my mother's, so I tied most of it up in savings – Peps and the like. Jason over there is a trained barrister. We're not averse to invoking the might of English law when it suits us. And look at this mobile phone. I can access the Internet, text message my brother in Thailand, find out whether Juventus beat Inter Milan last weekend, even send a picture of myself to www.druids.com. We're not entirely stuck in the past, you know. Do we want to have our cake and eat it? Maybe; we're just humans."

I was calculating in my head to see how his maths added up because I'd lately suspected Ken was older than he let on. Maybe it was *he* who had guided *me* on a tour round campus.

Rosa returned with a tatty folder, pointing out their run-ins with provincial police and English Heritage during the group's younger, more clichéd days. Her pretty face emanated pride and I got the feeling that, in her mid or late twenties, she was already looking back to a perceived Golden Age.

Kenneth butted in again with: "So many people are dropping out. Giving up Business Studies degrees. Falling off the Electoral Register and planning their route round the ley lines of Britain from one festival to another. Living off the land. Refusing the wage slave compromise and conformity of modern life. As globalisation shaves off the so-called deadwood through re-restructuring and downsizing, the disenfranchised are re-grouping. Not so much fighting back as refusing to be part of the capitalist concept."

It was a stirring speech, especially after four beers and two joints.

"Is there going to be trouble on your next trip?" I asked.

"Nah," Rosa laughed above her lip ring, "we keep a nice low profile these days."

"And this could be the one," Kenneth added, "where we make the transformation. Coote's given me a few more pointers."

"I don't have a tent," I answered.

"Just get your own sleeping bag," Rosa replied, "and we'll see if we can squeeze you in."

Angela was wearing a woolly hat pulled low over her forehead, a Topshop jacket over her H & M business attire, and a pair of 'knock off' sunglasses from the market trader near the station. She knew she didn't look her best but at least she was here on time for the fifth day in a row.

"Has it suddenly gone sunny outside?" Piers quipped from his desk by the door.

"Got shampoo in my eyes this morning," Angela snarled. "None of your beeswax anyway."

Martha was more sympathetic, offering a consoling hand and a suitably lukewarm tea with two sugars.

"I'm in such a state," Angela whispered. "What time did we crash last night?"

"No idea. That ambulance business disrupted the evening for me. Maybe we'll try somewhere else tonight – where the punters ain't dropping dead by the dozen just because the music speeds up. I thought you'd sleep in this morning."

"Can't afford any more time off. An' I thought you had a sales call."

"Got cancelled. Message on my old mobile, forgot to check it yesterday."

"How about we have a girls' night in with a DVD and a pizza tonight?"

"Shit, Angie, are we getting old or what? Why don't we try that pub where your brother works?"

"He's not working there at the moment. Most of the time he seems to be doing evening classes or going to the theatre. How poncy is that? Hey, you still like him, don't you?"

"I'd like him more if he could keep up the pace these days. Hey, look lively, Homerton's on the prowl."

I'd been pretty sure of my crowd-pleasing line-up for the Saturday *Night of Superstar Doppelgangers*. On Friday, following the unfairly unpopular Robert Zimmer Frame, I was also somewhat let down by the Neil Young tribute outfit, Lazy Horse. In a gesture no doubt deliberately intended to ape their grizzled hero and his cohorts, they objected to the manager using a camcorder during their performance of *Cortez the Killer* and stormed off. Still, *Cinnamon Girl* had been a hit with the punters. I was almost tempted to ring up the weirdest of the auditions, the psychedelic band who came complete with a cod-Austro-Germanic psychiatrist narrating over the top of their soundscapes. They weren't right for my event but I had been so taken with them I'd even bought one of their art college T-shirts: Shrink Freud.

Almost. We brought the raffle forward, handing out a few budget CDs and beer tokens as prizes. The house PA kicked in. The local post-ironic, slightly pissed hipsters seemed to be enjoying the show, especially the shambolic moments.

I was called out to attend to our top attraction: Kabushka, who'd already given me earache about the facilities and the lack of a rider.

"This is a pub, not the Palladium," I'd told her, hearing my late father's tones permeating my firm words. "I can get you a beer or a vodka and ask the chef in the lounge bar to microwave a burger and chips. We don't have shower facilities and you'll have to get changed in the portacabin. You get a flat fee of twenty quid but we can do you a deal with a local cab firm."

Welcome to the bottom end of the market, dear.

She was wearing a strapless, slightly conical bra, high-waisted knickers and an auburn wig. The room smelled of nervous cigarettes. She jumped up, gave me a good luck hug and pressed her curves a little too close for propriety.

"Now then, Tom," she purred, "can you lay your hands on a sewing kit? My hus- my manager usually packs one but he's off with another act tonight."

Seeing her disrobed, I had the curious impression I'd met her before. But where? She was a good looking woman but close up you could tell she was probably fifty; then again, so is Kate Bush herself these days. I didn't want to seem ageist as I was already pushing thirty but, once the costume was out of the way and the soft spot lights had given way to bare light bulb, it would have felt like shagging one of my mothers' friends or an ex-schoolteacher.

One of the barmaids gave me some needle and thread she'd pocketed on a hen night at a Travel Inn. Kabushka took it gratefully from me, stroked my right leg coquettishly and asked for the third time, "Do I get paid after the gig?"

"Sure," I grunted.

"Cash," she hissed. "Don't want that snake getting hold of it."

She delivered a knockout fifteen-minute Kate Bush tribute. She started with a version of *Wuthering Heights* which was close to being note perfect. Although this was clearly not the elfin sprite everyone would recognise from that iconic video, if you closed your eyes and opened your ears, you could almost be back in the late seventies.

She did a couple of quick changes behind the speaker cabinet. I had to hold back an attempted mini stage invasion during these brief interludes. I still couldn't quite place my apparent earlier memory of this goddess with the swirling hair and Xena clothing. Did it matter? Martha would have said, "Seize the moment" and meant it wholeheartedly.

She should have stuck to warbling and let an expert do the darning. An important part of her costume came apart during her final number, revealing sweaty white skin and a small swathe of pubic hair. Predictably, this received the biggest cheer of the evening. I stepped up to the mike and thanked the crowd, reminding them that the bar would remain open for another sixty minutes. As I rushed out to the car park, they were still baying the "uh-ooh" parts from *Hounds of Love*.

Away from the spotlights and back under the bare bulb of the portacabin, Kabushka – real name Helen – looked fragile and curiously girlish in her half-dressed despondency. I put my arms around her. I didn't let go when she fumbled for my zip. I gently eased her lips away but bade her finish off the hand job.

It's not that Martha and I were even an item. We were just seeing how far we could take it.

"You were brilliant," I mumbled.

"You've got my mobile," Kabushka smiled as I left her to pack up.

"Sit down, Angela," Homerton ordered. "How are you today?"

Loaded question, she thought, but replied brightly, "Ready to crack on with the job of making Cane Co a top one hundred company."

His owlish gaze gave away his doubts and all but burst her forced sincerity. He scratched at non-existent fluff on the starched cuff of his striped shirt. "Not partying too hard, I hope," he beamed. "You know what they say: Early to bed, early to rise…"

"It was only the man who got wealthy in that saying," she responded.

He smiled. "Well, your wit's not dampened any, so that's good. Let me cut to the chase. I'd like you to handle some of my computer correspondence, including one or two personal items."

She frowned: briefly, because it made her headache even worse. "Are you sure about that?"

"Oh, one hundred per cent so. My great talent is an intuitive feel for the right business venture. I let the under- the, uh, support staff – handle the day to day details. I'm sure Payroll will recognise your extra duties."

"That's good," she muttered. She realised he was only partway through the morning lecture and attempted to relax against the blue hessian fabric of his guest chair.

With his eyes on the clouds gathering beyond the flat roof of the offices opposite – a local division of fierce rivals Salt Mine Securities – Homerton continued, "We're all slaves to technology these days. When I was younger, you wrote to other companies requesting services. When you used the phone, you might have to go through an internal switchboard and an overseas operator and then you'd still find the person you wanted to talk to was unavailable. So you'd try again or leave a message. And wait. Now everything's got to be so instantaneous.

E-mails are the bane of my life. I'm getting a hundred a day!" He jabbed a nicotine stained finger at his flickering screen, moaned, "Look at this. I can't be bothered to open them, let alone reply. What's so bloody urgent? Have they uncovered the true nature of God? Are they going to press the nuclear destruct button if I don't get back in two minutes?"

It took Angela a few seconds to realise that Homerton's pained outburst had subsided. The volcano had spewed and was temporarily dormant. "Give me your password and I'll deal with them," Angela smiled.

"Thank you. And when you sign off to my granddaughter, remember to say, 'Bye bye Bunnikins'."

"I still feel too fucked to eat," Martha complained. "I'll share a ciggie with you by the door, though."

The pavement was wet but the cool air felt refreshing. In small doses. Angela flipped open her Motorola. "Tom's texted me again," she announced. "Going on about an archaeological dig next weekend, how he's trying to broaden his mind. Must be some posh new floozy in wellingtons he's got a crush on!"

"Hey, that's my ex you're dissing," Martha grinned.

"Has to be done. I love my brother to pieces but – hell, two or three years ago all he wanted was to go out with us and get bladdered. I don't understand the change in him. After a working week – after even a day! – all I want is to get totally shit-faced. Like they used to say, fuck art, let's dance."

Martha stubbed out the dog end. "It was a great concept, best friend and boyfriend from the same bosom," she began, "but… I dunno, it got to the point where he wanted to listen to the *music* and all I wanted to hear was the *beat*."

"That's men for you, I'm afraid. Always trying to educate us or reprimand us. Like fucking Homerton and his homilies about the weekend being for relaxing and recharging. I'm here to make him millions and earn a crust for myself along the way. This ain't convent school."

"Was he all right with you this morning, Ange?"

"Oh, you know… I flash him a bit of leg where I waxed it the other night… just enough to keep him thinking that one day… Hey, what's that stuff they use to stick in window panes?"

"Putty?"

"Yeah, you got it in one."

*

We'd taken the precaution of approaching Wenlea Cove from different directions. Anything resembling a convoy might just alert Plod to our technically illegal presence. Now we were safely here though – in a small clearing next to the pine wood and overlooking the too-dark-to-see-at-the-moment beach – our party had relaxed. A portable CD player was laying down a stoner groove: maybe something by Hendrix or Neil Young and Crazy Horse circa 1975. The roots and herbs Rosa had sprinkled into our drinks were really starting to have an effect and I could no longer remember whether I preferred *Sergeant Pepper* or *Abbey Road*. I was standing but felt laid back and receptive.

The music faded and Kenneth began to drone. The deep rumble became a prehistoric premonition of an aeroplane engine revving; maybe the rocks themselves were slow motion exploding. The vibration was a physical presence, all encompassing, and I realised my own vocal cords had joined the chant. Proper words were almost discernible above the wall of sound, but of an ancient, hand me down Celtic / Ancient Briton language or its skewed interpretation.

"Hold to the circle and the holes will appear. Believe in the transformation and you will ready yourself. Open your throat and your heart and you will surely free your soul.

"Oh Earth Mother, we give of our life essence in this imperfect union. Accept the offering of our blood, flesh and life force. Ensure we are absorbed.

"… But not yet. This we hope will be our final night as separate entities. We have readied ourselves for the morning. We are open. Receive us in the dawn's light when Sister Moon has departed your cloaking gown.

"We rest."

Below the lights and above the music, Martha cupped her narrow hands around Angela's right ear and said, "I'm bursting for the toilet."

Only one cubicle was free. Angie let her friend go first, waited. One of the wooden doors jarred open and a young woman with blonde highlights and Manolo heels emerged. Angela smiled, brushed at her nostrils to alert the woman to the white powder still evident.

"Things are pretty cool here, but one or two of the security staff might object," Angela muttered.

"Cheers, nice one. This Charlie's so shit, I don't know why I bother."

"We're more into Flow," Martha interjected, striding to the wash basin for a cursory rinse of her fingers.

"Done some of that, too," Blondie answered. "Must be my incredible metabolism. I can eat cake all day and not put on any weight."

"Lucky you!" the friends chorused.

Then they were back in the throng. Perfumed bodies, deodorised pits, sharp shoes, bright shirts, short skirts, knickers and boxer shorts apparent above hipster length trousers and skirts, the strobes and UV rays pulsing in tune with the frantic beat, revealing garish, discoloured details of tattoos and piercings. Hands in the air, catch your breath then feel the rush, we're taking it down and faster. It's the dance Olympics but no *Bolero* soundtrack. We're moving so quickly we can hardly see ourselves, we become a blur, all these girls and boys, remixed for the years beyond the noughties, all you teens and twenties, don't stop moving, stillness is death...

A visible wave of gestalt emotion passed across the crowd, peaking and crashing in a corner of concern. What was it? The usual dehydration or low blood sugar? Guy down there says it was an epileptic fit. No, just some blonde bird going at it too hard. Did you see it then? No, but I heard... Fuck, I didn't see nothing, though, 'cause I was giving it so much that I was almost off this plane... Wow, man, that's freaked...

Slimboy Delroy – the whitest guy with a faux West Indian accent in clubland – was on the decks tonight. He had chatted up Martha in Tesco's two months ago. "Wants to be a gangsta but is really just a wanker!" was her terse opinion.

Now his studied patois came over the speakers:

"Right den, you crazy loons, this be him Delroy telling you dat if any of you have dem troubling medical conditions, you done go take a break now because we is gonna whip it wild in here like you've never seen before. We go call dis hide and seek. If you can't hold the beat, that's cool, you've got to me count of ten to clear the floor for those who are here till death do us PARTEE!"

...The subsequent cheers were half an hour gone. Martha felt like she was moving at an incredible speed and would never, ever stop. Lift-off, we have lift-off. Escape velocity reached now. To the planets, to the stars...

They were splashing water over her and gently rubbing her face because they thought she wasn't moving, was maybe even unconscious. She was just on a different time line. Like almost everything in this purgatory of a life, it was all about perception.

*

I awoke with some ancient song by a nonagenarian blues singer nagging at my back brain. I'd picked it up as a free CD with last month's *Uncut* and had even considered bussing up to London to see the guy in concert this weekend before he croaked it. Speaking of which – the shamanistic mantra was audibly under way and it appeared that I'd been left out.

Somebody was keeping up a regular, pattering beat outside. Amidst the neo-Celtic, Pan-worshipping gibberish, I could discern the occasional recognisable, modern English phrase along the lines of, "Oh spirit of these woods and caverns, assist us in our holy transformation."

If I couldn't be part of the actual ritual, at least I should be a witness.

One barefoot step outside alerted me to the fact that the rhythm was that of rain. Kenneth, muddy and almost naked, was performing a few metres way. The rest of the New Stone Agers stood about in disconsolate pairs or threes, shielding their sleep deprived heads with blankets or shabby cagoules. The potential for Ken to dance himself into a state of higher consciousness or oblivion seemed remote at best.

"The dawn time has long past," Rosa intoned from over to my right and our glorious leader broke off his performance almost instantly.

"It isn't happening!" he ranted. "We're stoners, man, all we wanna do is get stoned but... those BBC bastards, all that money, all that equipment, those fucking satellites orbiting round our head and they still can't forecast the weather properly!"

Kenneth stormed out of camp and, although I wasn't yet dressed for the inclemency, I set off after him to ensure he didn't come to grief. We ended up halfway down the cliff with the wannabe druid deflecting his anger by slapping the unyielding rock. I offered him a helping hand back up the slippery limestone.

Everyone was already breaking camp. Some had shop or bar jobs to get to later in the day. I'd hoped we might stay and explore a little more of the recesses and seagull holes Kenneth had once described as, "In their depiction of Neolithic culture, the potential English equivalent of the caves at Lascaux." But the choice was a lift back now or a five-mile hike along the coast so I acquiesced.

Rosa remained chirpy about it all. "Let's reconvene next Friday," she suggested. "The moon will be waning, but it's still auspicious. This is the month of changes."

*

I scrolled through the menu on my Nokia, expecting – and getting – a message about some van and light removal work tomorrow. Things were looking up. There was a text from Angie telling me that Martha was, "Maybe interested again… if you're paying." That was OK but I didn't really think it was going to happen. Except perhaps when we're both twenty years older, wiser and probably poorer. For now, she put too much into every leisure minute and I couldn't keep up with her and hold down a series of part time jobs and stay focused on my studies.

God, I'm getting so pipe and slippers lately! Even a night with Kenneth and the Young Person's History Club – or the New Age Stoners as they lately styled themselves – left me knackered the following morning.

Maybe there is no shying away from apparent maturity and changed values and we're all doomed to turn into a slightly taller version of our parents.

If Martha ever fancied another night down The Royal Oak to watch the tribute bands, she only had to text. What can I say about her? Physically, she was the best looking woman I've ever been with. She had a body to match any girl in the *High Street Honeys* section of the lads' mags. She was like a gorgeous girl band member in her short skirt and boots: K. T. Tunstall dress style yet matched with a Page 3 face. She was sharper than a needle, intelligent and witty but, of course, when gazing upon the goddess the worshippers and supplicants only notice the surface. She got chatted up every time she went anywhere, even when we were clearly together.

I had brought her along to the Saturday *Superstar Doppelgangers* night. I was frazzled, still a little confused by Friday's events, and desperately trying to keep the bill running smoothly. No doubt I should have paid her more attention, but I was working. At one point I went to talk to her and she'd got headphones on from her I-pod.

"Don't you want to listen to the bands?" I asked.

"It's old music. I only go for modern beats," she sneered. Then: "Hey, do you want one of these?"

"What are they?"

"It's Flow. A new substance – pills or take on your tongue like sherbet," she smiled.

"No thanks, I'm on duty tonight, gotta keep my head clear."

"I'll have yours, then," she replied and wandered off to the toilet.

Later I found her shaking and… not exactly whimpering, but making a strange, low, continuous noise. Angela was with her.

"What the fuck's going on?" I demanded.

"I'll get her home in a cab, Tom. She's done this before, she'll be fine."

"We should get her to hospital – the hell with this gig."

"Stop freaking out. I've done this stuff – it's out of your system by Monday."

I acquiesced and let Angela take control of the situation, but I was deeply concerned – for both of them. Why were they doing this shit? Where does mood enhancement end and medical damage and potential psychosis kick in?

I phoned Martha on Sunday afternoon. She sounded sleepy and I could hear a male voice in the background.

On Monday morning she texted me to say, "Let's go to Jazzles tonight" but I was working for the rest of the week, so I let it ride.

Maybe she's the one I'm going to be chasing towards and retreating from for the rest of our lives. If the drugs don't kill her first.

Kenneth took another slice of pizza and a drag on an expiring joint then stated carefully, "This time we're really gonna do it, Tom. I promise you."

Meaning what? Make fools of themselves on a windblown beach conducting some ludicrous neo-pagan ritualistic nonsense when sensible Englanders were still abed? I'd had enough of his admittedly well-intentioned peace offerings and I put down my glass of beer and refused a toke on the cigarette.

"The transmogrification you're proposing not only defies the laws of physics but," I added, "amounts to little more than an extremely expressed death wish."

"You've got it all wrong, man. Take a break from your literalism. We're all about getting back to the land. Imprinting empowers us."

"And if it doesn't work?"

"We'll find a new way. What's that old saying about the journey being more important than the arrival? So, be part of the New Stone Age quest."

"My sleeping bag got ripped last week."

"Rosa will give you a spare or share with you. I know you're keen."

I smiled. "I bet you were a preacher in a previous life."

He chuckled. "Tom, man," he replied, "I was a druid high priest back in the day. So – see you at the van on Friday."

I tried to neither nod assent nor shake dissent. I walked carefully down the stairs out of his flat. The nocturnal breeze hit me like the passing of an express train. I steadied myself then meandered towards the bus stop.

*

Wenlea Cove, take two, and I had tagged along again. One of the hippie girls had cooked up a vegetable stew laced with sacred herbs and some curious hallucinogenic known as ardlah roots. I hoped they didn't give you ergot poisoning like fly agaric and several other forest products. They provided a slightly bitter after-taste to the evening's repast. I was secretly glad that New Age labour still seemed to be divided along traditional gender lines: I was better at collecting firewood or lugging a calor gas canister than rustling up a meal for ten people.

Once more, someone had brought along a portable CD/cassette player. The earlier trance and chill-out sounds had given way to a stoner selection: Hendrix, Jefferson Airplane and a load of other 1960s stuff I ought to have recognised. The evening was unseasonably warm but the emerging constellations beyond the tree line promised plummeting temperatures later.

I couldn't quite work out the situation between Kenneth and Rosa. For the second time he'd suggested I share a tent with her and, although I found her extremely attractive, there seemed little prospect of reciprocation. The pair of them certainly had shared history and I suspected Kenneth was toying with me – the king lion pretending to loan out his favoured female.

"It's happening this time, Tom," he intoned over his hash pipe.

"And am I included?"

"Tetchy! Listen, you'll know if you hear the call. If not... they also serve who only stand as witness. You can borrow the van to get back to town."

"I've only got a provisional licence."

"The vehicle's only held together with gaffer tape and string. Not much more than a go-kart really."

I smiled and took another swig from the bottle of full-bodied red wine. It had grown warm by the stick fire, but not unpleasantly so.

"You're an unusual bunch of people..." I muttered.

"Yet you can't help liking us," Ken added.

"I'm here, aren't I? I know you've got a fixation on history but... things like the music you listen to – none of you were even born when this stuff was recorded. I'm not slagging it, just asking questions like any proper historian does."

He laughed. "We're all *Mojo* readers here, Tom, you included. The vibe takes us on our groove, helps us with our trip. Hey, you ever hear of a band called Spirit? That's one bunch of dudes I'd like to have seen in the flesh. And the original Doors, of course. Not forgetting Jimi... Janis..."

Later, as I rather inexpertly undressed within the confines of Rosa's tent, I tried to draw her attention away from the goose bumps on my thighs by suggesting, "You should rename yourselves *The 60's Music Club*."

"Oh, that's just a passing phase with Ken, our leader. He'll be back on his trance and leftfield dance soon."

"And you all follow?"

"Sure, why not, it's just sounds, innit?

Angela wiped sleep remnants from her eyes and whispered, "You know, even for a smoker like me, it was pretty clogged last night. What happened to their no cigarettes policy?"

"They just don't police it," Martha answered. "Look lively, Homerton's been let out of his cage."

She picked up her telephone with her left hand, began scrolling down her screen menu with the mouse in her right, her green eyes and Rimmel lips a study in employee concentration.

When the coast was clear, she whispered to Angela, "Well, the weekend starts once we get that twat's pep talk out of the way. Are you going tonight?"

"I don't know. Maybe I'll give it a swerve."

"Lightweight! When did you turn forty?"

"Oh yeah, Martha? When will you stop being sixteen?"

Martha tapped her nails against the controls, maximised her eBay page and then minimised it again. "Hey, come on," she whispered. "You've got the rest of your life to stay at home watching repeats of *Friends* with a bag of Doritos on your lap. This is the time of life to feel invincible. Just go with the flow. Just go with a little more Flow."

Angela smiled, playfully punched her mate's arm. "You ought to be the one giving the Friday pep talk, girl," she commented.

"You warm enough?" a soft female voice asked.

"Not too bad," I replied to the semi-darkness, racking my brain to bring the sureties of her remembered face back into focus. Pink highlights in stringy black hair, a nose stud and an eyebrow ring, a pleasant smile and a petite body. If we get out of this alive, Rosa…

"We could push the sleeping bags together," she continued. "Shared warmth and all that."

"Sounds sensible," I agreed, "and you're probably more experienced in these matters."

"Hardly! Fingers of one hand, you know."

"Are the police or... the coastline patrol likely to bother us?"

"No. And there isn't such a thing."

"There, what did I say, you are more experienced than me."

I could hear her giggle, almost see her smile and certainly now feel her feminine heat next to my tired body. Her small fingers squeezed my arm for a moment and she planted an affectionate kiss on my shaven cheek.

Later, I suggested, "Would you like to...? I mean, we could snuggle up a bit more..."

She braved the cold air again, rested her am across my chest, answered, "You're a nice guy, Tom, and I'd really like to get to know you better but, well, we're not here to shag. It's a more spiritual thing. Maybe some other time, though. Some different lifetime. Sleep well."

Which was easier said than achieved. I lay a long while trying to count the number of stars I could see through the loose fastening of the tent flaps. I wasn't desperately disappointed: it had been an opportunist request. I was glad of her company even when she began to snore lightly and even when the sleepless hours dragged and later an unexpected light rain shower sprinkled itself onto the tent canopy, arhythmically but persistently, like the oddly comforting white noise of the universe...

We all start by listening to our mother's heart beat, but, as a species, for so long the drum was everything. Smash that femur against a tree or the mammoth's skull. Groove to the Piltdown stomp.

Extroverts of the bland savannah, we next discover the power that comes with control and careful deployment of the voice.

So we approach in time with the bugle calls to arms and the steady funereal pulse that led the Assyrians, the Trojans, the Spartans and Romans into battle. And there he is, the archer turned piper or timekeeper for the Saxons and Normans and those who argued over the relative merits of red and white roses. Music to make you feel brave, boys. Music to inspire on the way to expiring. Music that leads to death.

But we're branching out, oh look at us go! Better still, cop an ear to all this: The classical, the gentle three steps of *The Blue Danube Waltz* and the grand canvases of sound that only a hundred piece orchestra could achieve. Sit yourself down, dearie, and 'ave a cuppa or a pint to the singalong, swingalong of Music Hall… yet already the Charleston is coming to speed things up. Oh lawdy mama, I've got the trad jazz blues. Daddy, why has that Caucasian painted his face black, his lips white and put on an unnecessary voice? Still, the big bands and the crooners keep it smooth for a while until Awopbop and rock n roll, let's speed it up, let's jive. And through the simple harmonies and the stoned peace messages of the 1960s we work our way towards progressive rock and heavy metal, but when everything became too bombastic or else too disco clockwork, punk came along and speeded us up and when that tide had ebbed away, leaving its detritus of spikes and safety pins, we had techno and rave and pumping house and jungle and Ibiza, all pushing us faster and faster. Current heart rate: 124 per minute. 130, 150, come on let's hit 3 a second or even 200 every 60. As the pace of technology-dominated life gets faster so must we. Ending where?

Lost in the music that is our greatest, most beautifully human creation. Yet everything that's created is doomed with mortality. Listen a little closer and you'll know the secret. Told you once before but it bears repeating.

Music is death.

Dawn brought a slow, warm tingle to exacerbate my slight dehydration. The usual urge to urinate gradually overcame the pleasure of the sunlight bathing and baking me in my sleeping bag and I rose, exited the tent, and sought a friendly tree. There was not a soul around within the small cluster of breeze-charmed khaki tents. Rip Van Winkle awoke after twenty years; I checked that I hadn't sprouted a mysterious, long white beard. No, I was the newcomer and they'd left me to sleep in again.

There was a little activity in the grass and tree tops: rabbits scuttling down warrens, seagulls and wagtails attending to their needs. I called names, softly then more urgently as replies failed to materialise. Yet instinctively, I knew where I would find all my erstwhile companions.

Careless of the slowly burning sunlight and the carcinogenic ultraviolet rays, Kenneth was naked, pressed against the bare cliff some two metres up from the tide line. I was pleased to note that he was nothing special in the penis department, but as a shaman and an alchemist of change…

Already he was beginning to be absorbed into the rock. Wind blown sand grains formed a light sheath over his unmoving form. It wasn't death as such but the longed for, long-planned mystical imprinting into calcite existence... or at least a convincing illusion thereof. I had sniffed at and refused to swallow his crackpot New Age *Necronomicon* and yet here was evidence of a strange change brought about by chemicals, rituals, and the power of faith.

The other members of the group were all close by among the nooks and shallow caverns that dotted the beach area. Their bodies were still, as if temporally frozen and spatially immobilised in sand-frosted, instantly setting cement. They had yet to be so fully absorbed as their great leader had been in this extreme mission to use their transformed spirits to protect this ancient holy site.

It was like the aftermath of Pompeii but without the expressions of agony. Instead, their faces bore a yearning for happiness... completion.

Rosa was clothed in her usual attire and was still breathing. I could even detect a slight, slow pulse in her neck. But when I reached out to touch her skin, it was cold and smooth as if she had become a statue of herself.

I fought against the urge to shake her back to consciousness. I remembered something I'd heard on a First Aid awareness course about not moving anyone in a coma or subsequent to motorcycle crashes and the like. I thought about phoning 999 but couldn't get a signal on my mobile. Besides which... wouldn't the whole effect wear off soon enough and they'd all emerge like sleepers on the spaceship just come into orbit around a new world?

Suppose they were all *actually* dying, at least in the accepted sense of leaving this particular mortal plane? If someone truly wants to jump from a high building or stuff themselves full of hallucinogenics or truly become "at one with this ancient land", did I have the right to prevent them?

I was out of my depth, I admit it.

So I made that human decision that is the most obvious course of action in these circumstances: abandon the area, pretend you weren't anywhere in the vicinity. Save your own skin... even while others are transfiguring their own epidermis into modern day cave paintings, life size.

I stuffed my tatty bedroll and spare clothes into an ungainly pack and strode down to the coast road, intending to hitchhike back to town. I didn't want to risk my befuddled, unqualified hands behind the wheel of their rusty van.

As I waited for a friendly response to my outstretched thumb, I mentally ran through my options. I wanted to avoid reporting the incident to the police. At the very least, they would round them all up on some trespassing and soft drugs possession charges, and who needs that? Plus, I knew from past experience that such incidents have a nasty habit of rebounding back upon the concerned citizen.

Maybe I should come back that evening and see if they'd all returned from their stoned trip. Today would be warm but the night would bring chill and exposure.

Or return tomorrow. Or never. They'd iced me out; I wasn't part of their gang, I should leave them to their self-imposed fate.

Hey, didn't that white Ford Transit belong to Tony, who I'd helped with some second hand furniture delivery a few years back?

He was slowing down.

Result.

Sunday. Hung-over. Already close to noon. Get a face ready, find some clothes and prepare to dash for the hourly bus.

"Family duty calls," Angie murmured to her slack-eyed flatmate. "Come along if you want – there'll be extra portions."

"What's your mum roasting today – lamb or chicken?"

"Lamb."

"I ain't got the energy to chew it, thanks, Ange," Martha mumbled.

Angela alighted one stop early to pick up some tatty flowers and non-alcoholic grape juice at the 24-hour convenience store. Her brother opened the door.

"Wasn't expecting you here," she stated. "How you been?"

"Been studying," I told her. "Local history, the jobs market, the racing form."

"Martha will wish she'd attended."

"You won't let that go, will you, Ange?"

"I like to tie everything up neatly. You know where we go and how to find us."

The potatoes were crisp but the gravy was too thin. Mother offered a choice between a game of cards or a *Midsomer* on DVD. It beat talking. It beat trying to explain to everyone that I'd been deserted by people I'd adopted as friends; that Kenneth's flat was dark and empty day and night; that I'd borrowed Tony's old bike – the one where the gears didn't work – and cycled back to Wenlea Cove but there were no signs of abandoned tents or personalised cave decorations.

*

The local library was closed for a week while they upgraded the computer terminals but I had a leaflet for another enlightening lecture by Professor Coote. Be there, Rosa! Turn up, Ken and the gang! Market Hall, Friday, seven-thirty, my scrappy bit of paper said.

Seventeen-thirty, the notice on the door informed me. I thought I saw a couple of pairs of Doc Martens, some army fatigue jackets and a flash of pink hair scurrying away from the municipal building just as I turned the corner of Coronation Road.

I must have wandered around the town centre for hours. The chip shops and burger bars were warm places in which to mull over a coke or a bag of chips. Soon, the party animals were out in force and their regular hangers-on: the mini cab dodgem drivers, the small time drug dealers and the kids in anoraks with their flyers for clubs that always vainly promised to be better than the one you were queuing for tonight.

I didn't want to go home. Ever.

I mislaid or lost my watch somewhere along the way. I knew instinctively that it was well after midnight; in fact, more like three or four a.m. There were ambulances moronically whining outside Balearica. In the confusion, I slipped inside, taken by some vague notion of seeking out old acquaintances. Whatever the medical emergency was, it seemed now to have passed as the crowd moved frenetically, like a multi-headed monster, to the huge pulsing sound emanating from the speakers. I experienced the usual sense of sudden extreme disorientation as I stepped into the main arena. I felt my senses assailed by illegal cigarette haze, the erratic lighting from the intermittent strobe lights, the rapidly pounding bass and hi hat soundtrack to our destinies, the slippery patches of spilt alcohol on the thin carpeted slope leading from the bar, but more than anything else the overpowering aroma of human sweat poorly masked by cheap perfumes and failing deodorants. Damp fabric, dripping foreheads, wet underarm hair and soaking shirtfronts.

It was all too much. Another party that had started without me and at which I wasn't really needed or even welcome.

But at Club Nesta half an hour later the scene was markedly different.

The doors were wide open and the psychopathic bouncers were nowhere to be seen. There was a ragtag group of people in the lobby, Angela amongst them. Her eyes were closed, her head resting on her bare arms, her lips flecked with remnants of fruit from some fancy cocktail. Maybe it was vomit. Sleep, dear sister.

"She's all right, mate," some wide-eyed E-head announced near my elbow. "But there's possible fatalities in there. Get on the dance floor if you wanna help any."

He was in no fit state to assist me. His forehead was a Niagara of perspiration and his palms held the whitish residue of a hit of Flow.

I could hear a humming like an amp left on… and yet, no, it was more like a swarm of bees because there was movement within it, very fast movement…

What had been a parade ground of joy and celebration now resembled the aftermath of a battlefield of bleeding-eared corpses, violently shaken and discarded dolls.

This is the new kicking tune, the sweet flowing music guaranteed to make the heart beat faster. Move every part of your body into a blur. If it's too fast, you're too old.

But once you've begun this frantic, epileptic, Parkinson's motion it's very hard to actually stop it.

My first thought was that Martha was rooted to the spot. As I drew closer, however, I realised that I could not see her constantly, that she was in a state of such rapid continuous movement that at times she was almost beyond vision. I stood statue still a while. I fought against the urge to shake her back to consciousness.

I was out of my depth yet again. Maybe the best I could do was to leave her to her fate, return to the lobby and try to offer a little comfort to the survivors.

That hoary old mantra about "taking it to another level" had finally come to pass: she and many around her had passed through to another stage. A chemically and musically assisted evolutionary step that rendered my own existence flat, that offered the release the Stoners and the clubbers and the nihilists and the hedonists and everyone alive except conventional, boring, under-employed me seemed to be seeking.

The promise one might call death.

The Pied Piper called with his beautiful tune but one child was left behind to mourn the loss as the mountain closed behind the revellers.

TURBULENT TIMES

Having a noose around one's neck is not necessarily a bad thing. There's a certain comfort in its heavy solidity. After a while it even starts to feel familiar, normal…

"OK, Chris," Gina called, "that's it on the close-ups."

Dean came over to help me lift the rope up and over my head. "Pardoned at the last minute," he quipped.

I slipped out of my Confederate greatcoat and performed a couple of stretches to restore circulation.

We were filming Ambrose Bierce's *An Occurrence At Owl Creek Bridge* on the sort of shoestring budget which wouldn't keep Tom Cruise in café latte. If we delivered the ten-minute epic on schedule we *might* get a screening at a local film festival. But so what? I'd loved the story since my dad read it to me when I was seven. I'd dreamed myself into the role of Peyton Farquhar at least a dozen times and now I was actually playing him. Let Hollywood chuck millions of dollars at CGI overkill blockbusters; we had a gripping plot. Surely –

"All right, folks," Gina announced, "public baths at eight-fifteen tonight on the dot."

"Public baths?" Dean scoffed. "How quaint!"

He could afford to take the piss: he was shagging the gorgeous Gina every night while me and the sound guy sat in our separate homes dozing with the DVD and reminiscing on past girlfriends.

Like Cassie B: the older sister and, I suspected, subtle manipulator of pop siren turned civil war generalissima Amber B. It was almost a year now since I'd last seen Cassie and eleven months since a taut, crackly conversation on our mobiles. Perhaps the problem was less to do with poor reception and more about MI6 surveillance, interference…

I had a pile of work to complete before the evening's rendezvous: post-grad research on Bierce and his contemporaries, my column and a couple of reviews for *Accolade* magazine, a bit of advertising copy for the *Death Arcade* Playstation tie-in. I tried having the radio on in the background as aural encouragement but the hourly news bulletins – riots and stabbings at home, mortar attacks and car bombs abroad – proved too distracting.

Shit, was that the time?

*

I would have to keep my eyes open under water for some time. As my legs sought to stabilise my sub-aquatic floating, my hands grabbed at the gunmetal shells with the grace of a swan. In a Confederate uniform. Computer whizz-kid Dean – I love that old-fashioned term! – was going to work in more of the spent, ineffective bullets slowly sinking past my head. We hoped the end result might have the quality of a Radiohead promo video.

The civil unrest dubbed The Turbulence had yet to really take hold of this comparatively safe corner of the British Isles. The only problems for the local police came from the usual Saturday night pissheads. Which meant there was still an opportunity to indulge in fiction rather than being forced to engage with reality. Although I still had to concentrate on the quotidian necessities of delivering a dissertation and supplementing my student loan with time-consuming journalism.

The newspapers tended to characterise The Turbulence as a race war, a class war or a hybrid of both. The truth was, as ever, more complicated and awkwardly variable. Whatever – I was careful in my choice of reading matter, especially on campus, and took my news updates and analysis from the generally reliable Radio 4 bulletins.

Gina had called in several favours to obtain hire of the municipal baths for a few quiet evening hours. The hanging rope breaks and Peyton Farquhar plunges into Owl Creek. This marks the start of a freestyle splash for safety.

I was intrigued to see how the director and her special effects genius were going to mask the tell-tale blue tiling and spectral light of a public pool and substitute the rush and murkiness of a deep, fast-flowing river. Such trickery was beyond me. That might yet be the least of their worries, though. I'd swum indoor lengths like a shark as well as putting in plenty of hours in the North Sea, with the odd bit of wobbly board surfing along the way. However, I hadn't swum in proper clothes since going for Challenge One back at primary school.

Happily, my underwater floundering and frog-faced, bug-eyed gasping for air must have looked pretty convincing as they gave me several hearty, though squishy, backslaps at the end of the shoot, along with the usual jibes about Oscars and Baftas. Dean produced a large holdall and relieved me of my sodden costume. What would the local dry cleaners make of that?

Later, home, changed and showered – like I needed to get wet again! – I slept like the corpse of General Ulysses Grant.

In the morning, Amber B was on the television again. She had somehow emerged as a spokesperson on what the media called The Turbulence. The things she said were pretty right-on and she had a winning personality that had taken her high up the pop charts but some of her confederates were more questionable – tooled up, hard-line black and white rappers whose every utterance was Oedipal. The outside broadcast lights glinted off their pistols and neck chains and their proclamations of peace bounced hollowly back from the brightly tagged walls.

The other channels were showing the usual range of home improvement programmes or yet another spin on the quit the rat race / colonise the Costas dream. Memo to Middle England: fortify now or quit the sinking ship while you still can.

On Wednesday, I had a seminar at ten so I set the alarm for eight. Showered and breakfasted, I collected the notes and quotes I needed then gave myself half an hour to finish and polish a couple of pieces for *Accolade*, the new high street film / DVD / PC gamer mag I'd written for since its inception just nine months ago. Lately, I'd been trusted with a commentary column and had even melded some of my own pithy observations to Bierce's outpourings, creating *The 21st Century Devil's Dictionary*. The country was going to hell in a hand basket but somehow I was scraping by. Being mostly tucked away on a campus that put the 'okie' into parochial certainly helped.

After abortive careers in journalism and even teaching, I was glad to be back studying for a while: courtesy of savings, loan, overdraft, freelancing and a generous bequest from late Uncle Bert. The role of widely read cynic chose me, not I it. Thus:

"A mysterious and controversial death does wonders for the reputation of any significant creative or culturally important person. Might Princess Diana's star have eventually faded into low candle glow but for that fateful Paris car crash? Might angst-driven Kurt Cobain have ultimately turned his left hand to muzak and cheesy listening? The truly significant difference with Bierce's mysterious disappearance and likely demise is that he was over seventy when he went missing: hardly the poster adorning, too early-departed blond modern society sanctifies…"

I hadn't told anyone of my tangential involvement with The Turbulence. It felt odd to be slightly complicit and yet so distant. Like I'd made some ludicrous, offhanded suggestion for a Reality TV show and, extraordinarily, the company was implementing it. And people were getting hurt.

Cassie B was Amber B's much older sister. A tornado; a honeypot; a flame never to be extinguished. My aptitude for sports got me past the first hurdle of her protective, equally volatile brother Delroy. But maybe I lacked the stamina for the cross-country decathlon of Cassie's emotional demands.

Bristol. Two, three, four years ago. Bierce's story – a hundred and ten or more years ago. "Too much looking back when there ain't no future for the looking forward." One of Amber's lyrics. She seemed to me just a kid back then and I took little notice, but now… Delroy still gets into the camera shot as part of the entourage but though I strain my eyes at every newscast, I never catch sight of Cassie.

Sport. What would Lucifer's lexicographer have to say about it?

Maybe: "Mindless pastime imbued with unwarranted meaning by the male species. A miasma of team co-operation cloaks the true, selfish, egotistical intent of participants."

I'd save that for my next column.

Even though I'd written twenty per cent of it, including the cover feature on-set interview with Hugh Bontempi, I had to admit the latest issue of *Accolade* looked really good. Like any other writer, I went through firstly to see where I'd been cut. There was a little re-sequencing of my piece on *Cahiers Du Cinema* but otherwise Mat had kept faith with my work. I'd cribbed some stuff from Bierce and then dropped in my own pontificating for *21st Century Devil's Dictionary*. These were hailed as part of a regular new series.

A genuine independent, Mat couldn't afford to give away a blockbuster or PC game but had somehow obtained rights for some obscure post-revolutionary Soviet documentaries. Maybe next year I'd have time to enjoy this particular free DVD.

Even *Accolade* – a film magazine devoted to the escapist fantasies of Hollywood and the dream factories in general – had made direct reference to The Turbulence with a lengthy piece by Charles Lizz on *Films Against Social Cohesion*. The usual suspects: *Rebel Without A Cause, If, La Haine*… This well-researched, slightly polemical piece made me think I should have stuck at full-time journalism and become a Civil War correspondent just like Bierce, rather than skulking away in the Arts and Culture department of Moxon University. Better still, I should have taken a side, become engaged, be a voice standing up to the implacable, sometimes intangible enemy.

We move on to the dream sequence tomorrow. Peyton Farquhar – my character – emerges on the riverbank, sodden but free, and travels in hope of reviving the brief domestic idyll he shared with his wife, played by Gina. This will test my acting ability, as the thirty-six months I spent on and off with Cassie B were never exactly blissful.

I check myself in the mirror. I could easily pass for a Confederate officer from a hundred and forty years ago: straggly blond hair, droopy moustache and slight air of fading grandeur. Cassie would never have approved of this unkempt look.

The phone bleeped me out of a DVD reverie. Gina, Cassie, please… No, it was Mat, my editor – source of funds, fount of wise compromises.

"Chris? Wasn't sure I'd catch you in. Listen, matey, loved the new dictionary stuff but we can't run your review of *Ballyhoo Brothers Two*."

"You mean you've actually found some merit in this money-grabbing sequel?"

"No, but the company's taken out several pages of advertising and we only want to tread lightly on their toes, not cave their heads in with a blunt instrument."

"You should leave the metaphors to me, Mat."

"Shut up a minute. Look, can't you write two hundred and fifty words along the lines of, 'Not for everyone but a fine example of its type'?"

"And get misquoted on the posters again?"

"You weren't misquoted… they just trimmed it to fit. And if we're ever going to compete with 'Empire' we want to be on as many posters as possible. By the way, are you done with that Amicus retrospective?"

"In the middle of it now."

"Deadline's Friday. Ciao."

Shit, Amicus retrospective – I'd completely forgotten! And I had a tutorial tomorrow to expound my overview of *Literature Of and During the American Civil War*. Then there was the betrayal scene, which we were re-shooting tonight.

Betrayed? Not exactly. Dumped in the water and floundering? Definitely.

Like all editors, Mat was a bubble-bursting bastard. But I really should get on the case, pronto!

*

Ambrose Bierce defined a day as "a period of twenty-four hours, mostly misspent." To which I offer: "Wednesday. The fulcrum of the week when, having finally recovered from the excesses of the previous weekend, one starts to crave and savour in anticipation those soon to come."

When the doorbell sounded, I rushed to answer it, thinking it must be Dean or Gina, and discounting the likelihood of charity collectors or gadget salesmen.

"Shit, Cassie!"

"Hey, guy, is that any way to greet me after all this time?"

"But – how did you… and why…?"

"You developed Tourette's or something, boy? Let me in, there's too many eyes out here."

Settled and yet slightly unnerved, I sat on the hard chair opposite the sofa and asked, "Can I get you anything?"

"I'm fine, thanks. But you can do something for me, Chris. I want you to start speaking and writing for our side."

I shook my head, hiding a disbelieving smile. "How can I, Cass? All I'm doing is stupid film reviews."

"You've got that column."

"It's just satire. It's not going to hurt anyone or change anything."

She reached across and grabbed my right hand with hers. She sported even more white gold and diamante rings on her elegant brown fingers than I remembered… but how trustworthy is memory, anyway?

"It's happening, Chris," she stated. "The civil war, the clash of cultures. I guess you could say I'm on a recruitment drive."

Images from recent TV documentaries and a newspaper exposé on 'Amber B's Evil Massive' flooded my brain and I floundered like I had once or twice during the swimming pool shoot.

Before better judgement could reassert control, I blurted, "So, you've run out of muggers and crack dealers."

She jumped up, pushed past me, called over her shoulder, "I can't believe you're buying into that racial stereotype!"

"I never mentioned race. You did. Half your army's white, anyhow."

170

I reopened the slammed door, watched her clamber into the back of a silver car and speed away.

The settee still retained the impression of her womanly curves. I let my hands describe the arcs of memory.

How had I lost her again?

For Bierce, Radicalism was: "The conservatism of tomorrow injected into the affairs of today". And Revolution? "In politics, an abrupt change in the form of misgovernment". But maybe, were he alive today, he might class Revolution as "an act of folly committed by the young and cloudy-eyed".

It was the final day's filming. Just after dawn – the perfect time for a hanging. Dean and his brother Sean pranced up and down in their blue uniforms, rifles smartly shouldered. I stroked the hemp rope around my neck. I was getting quite used to it. Born to the role. Soon to die in it.

Gina had located a railway bridge where the branch line ran on diesel – so, no anachronistic overhead cables to worry about. Dean spoke his line; I said mine. I prepared myself for the abrupt lurch.

The banshee wail of a police siren pierced my reverie like a Sioux tomahawk. Suddenly there were people emerging from the woods over to my left. Illegal ravers, seditious rioters or unhappy campers, I couldn't tell. A dozen cops with batons and riot shields chased after them like a co-ordinated swarm. In the confusion, Dean struggled to untie me whilst Gina and Sean sought to stow all our audio-visual equipment back in the van.

I hadn't moved or protested but I still took a heavy truncheon blow to my right arm as I instinctively shielded my face. I heard a female voice warning not to damage the college's equipment then I was thrown forcefully to the floor.

At the station, they confiscated our antique weapons and state of the art camera as they held us on a charge of 'criminal trespass'. Dean didn't reckon they'd make it stick but computers and carpentry were his thing, not emergency

Home Office legislation. They offered us digestive biscuits and weak Nescafe in chipped utilitarian white mugs. It was rush hour at our convenient local Cop Shop and the woodland folk had rapidly filled all the holding cells. The desk sergeant sat us in their mess lounge, guarded by a twitchy cadet with a distressing case of shaving rash. The morning news played brashly on BBC television.

The army – the army! – had arrested Amber B and the other prominent figures in her posse on a charge of 'general sedition'. Cassie's handcuffs glinted silver as the paparazzi flashguns popped. I glanced at the eighteen-year-old standing sentry by the door and wondered whether I was now a combatant or still merely an observer.

The Prime Minister was on screen promising to push through all the necessary restrictions on civil liberties to keep us safe in our beds at night. My arm ached horribly. Beyond that pain, I could still feel the noose around my neck. Doubtless many others – comrades and lovers – were experiencing a similar sensation.

Maybe I was going to feel its presence forever.

PETRIFIED

Quite often, I still walked down Charlotte's road, even though we'd acrimoniously broken up several months ago. It was the most direct route to Bethnal Green tube station and, if I wanted to get anywhere, the sixty foot escalators were the best place to start. Dave told me that my demeanour might be interpreted as provocative, a defiant posturing in the ongoing secret war of the sexes.

"Since when did you start fancying Germaine Greer?" I asked him.

"It's Amy, my new girlfriend," he answered, with the satisfied air of the recently fellated. "I'm a reconstructed man now," he affirmed, sipping his Belgian lager.

By sheer coincidence, I bumped into Charlotte, my ex, the very next day. She nodded coldly, thought better of it, ceased the clatter of her square heeled boots on the way to the number '8' bus stop and announced, "I'm looking for work in Manchester so I've put the flat up for sale."

There was a CD I'd left behind which I now had maybe eight weeks left to retrieve... or just let go.

"I hope things work out for you," I muttered.

And I did. Charlotte was history because my main concern now was Shelley. Long black hair like a waterfall at twilight. Skin smoother than any kitchen surface you care to name. Habits at once acceptably modern and yet quaintly archaic. I'd meet her for lunch and she would write me a letter that afternoon or evening, often posting it by hand rather than trust the Royal Mail vagaries of pearly kings and postmen. Phones were generally anathema to her. Since the Mast Disaster of last year, instant telecommunication, especially on the hoof, had become problematic for all of us but for Shelley it was sometimes like the last two decades had never happened. Maybe she'd been frozen in time and released from the temporal bubble just a few days before our paths so righteously crossed...

Which meant I was surprised when she called me at work for the first time ever.

"I can't talk now," I informed her, mindful of my line manager's open door.

"I don't want to talk," she whispered. "You suggested Friday. Friday's fine."

It took me several minutes to be able to return full attention to my flickering screen. The inconstancy of the image – battling as it was with the persistence of vision – didn't help my brain to settle or my concentration to fixate. The artificial wrestled the seemingly natural and I was slipping off-task again...

but masking it well, I hoped. A learnt habit: nurture, if you will, the other vertex of the indissoluble behavioural triangle.

I still saw some people fiddling with their mobile phones, vainly hoping the generation was not dead but merely dormant. There had been a few burnt ears and twisted thumbs when that whole line of technology had melted down, I can tell you! Muscle memory still dragged digits across defunct keypads although a new craze was lately in evidence. Seats had never been plentiful on the Central Line but now many of them were taken up with hutches and small cages. I wanted to politely enquire, "Have you purchased a travelcard for that pet, madam?" but I was too English and accommodating. Live and let live? More like tremble and let trample.

They were odd-looking creatures in the main. Genetically modified fashion accessories with unnatural plumage, iridescent fur or pleading, eerily human expressions on their wan faces. Even when a well-heeled owner – or *carrier*, as they ironically termed themselves – deigned to move this urban accoutrement and its posh domicile off the nylon cushioning so that paying passengers could sit down, one still felt just a little reluctant to become so proximate. Who knew what weird, man-made viruses these ungodly pets might be unwittingly unleashing down here in the London Underground catacombs.

When I arrived home there was a hand-written note pushed through my letterbox. It simply read, "I'll meet you at the time and place we agreed" and was signed, "Love Shelley". I thought of phoning her but was wary of further muddying the waters.

Not that we went out all that much. Evenings when we met, I would shave and lather before taking the twenty minute stroll to the oxymoronic Cul De Sac Close. Number 12. The warm night would slip by in a gently caffeine-fuelled, Chateau Le Fils Rouge lubricated haze until I thought it was probably best to return home even at this late hour because that's where my clean shirts and boxer shorts still lived.

"I've got some food on," she announced, the touch of her lips as fleeting as rice paper butterflies.

Most of Shelley's surprisingly hearty meals began with a heap of tomatoes either tinned or chopped. Mince, soya, green and yellow vegetables, roast potatoes, cheese topping – a whole smorgasbord of delights often ended up in the pot. I wondered how Shelley kept so thin. Maybe she only ate when I came around. Would she therefore starve and waste away in a lonely garret should we ever part?

I strummed a few songs on her battered Spanish acoustic: simplified versions of Dylan or Lennon and McCartney which I knew from memory. I liked her large kitchen-dining room. I had to: we spent most of our together time there. She'd made one of her pleasingly periodic spring cleaning efforts and everything was either in its designated spot or out of harm's way behind the Laura Ashley curtain covering several sets of mismatched shelves. On a couple of occasions I believed I'd heard scratching noises from this part of the room. Shelley allayed my rodent worries with assurances that it was just some stray cats scrapping in the paved back yard.

"I feed them occasionally," she elaborated. "I don't know what they do the rest of the time."

I loved the way puzzlement wrinkled her nose and gave her a deliciously girlish air. Before long we had our hands inside each other's clothes and were soon having sex half-standing against a stucco wall. We hardly ever seemed to make it as far as her slightly lumpy double bed. Afterwards we let the smell of cafetiere coffee freshen us and picked up the threads of an ongoing conversation about childhood, ambitions, how you need to love yourself before you can have regard for anyone else and a sprawling analysis of life's purpose in general. Happy moments.

Dave was scrolling through something on his screen which wasn't entirely pertinent to our employment.

"Simpson's out till lunchtime," he informed me.

Dave was looking remarkably fashionable these days. Doubtless, it was Amy who had encouraged him to finally drape himself in attire appropriate to the twenty-first century and to let a fastidious barber tame his naturally unruly locks.

"You look tired," he said. "Did you spend the night at Shelley's?"

"Nah. Walked home at about three."

"Maybe she looks really bad first thing in the morning, mate. Or probably she doesn't want to face your awful dawn countenance."

"What's on your screen, Dave?"

"It's an exhibition that's on next month. *New Finds At Pompeii.*"

"I had you down as more of a pubs, pizza and football bloke."

"Yeah, but this is Pompeii. It's cool."

"Or pyroclastically hot," I answered, immediately hating my smartness.

"Whatever. Amy wants to go."

"Book a couple of tickets for me, too. We'll make a day of it."

I realised – or rather, remembered – that Shelley and I hardly ever ventured out together. I knew she didn't have much spare cash but was always offering to treat her to nights on the town. She expressed requisite interest in the films and shows just a few tube stops away but somehow we never got much further than spaghetti bolognese and *Blowing in the Wind*. Perhaps the best approach was to present a fait accompli.

I worked late, completing a batch of processing I should have finished by last Monday. Dave was up for a drink but I wanted a quiet(ish) night in with my CD player. The tubes were slightly less crowded at this hour although at Chancery Lane the carriers and their charges took the opportunity to colonise the carriage. I was trapped between a portly, middle-aged woman with a pet somewhat reminiscent of a spider monkey and an overly made-up Japanese girl whose accompanying hand luggage shone with gold and moonstone. I could not see the occupant of this expensive hutch but heard its several plaintive mews and detected a scent reminiscent of incense and joss sticks. Maybe the animal had a habit of pooping in public and his owner had taken preventive measures for good manners.

I noticed that all the other passengers were female. By their quietly confident demeanour and occasional utterances, I formed the impression that they all knew each other and were a branch of some great society. I alighted at Bethnal Green; the well-to-do ladies were staying on until the Essex borders at least.

There was another letter from Shelley.

"It was nice to see you yesterday. You are looking much healthier than before. I wanted to have the opportunity to say something but it did not present itself."

We'd talked for hours. If she'd had something of import to impart last night, surely she should have just come out with it?

"I'm trying to formulate what I want to say to you. It matters to me very much that I get it right otherwise I experience regret. I feel a burden of responsibility in many directions – as I'm sure you do. You will think I lack so much perception about my own life until now. I never realised how little freedom I have: it is virtually nothing. Honestly, sometimes I could go mad. I feel trapped and often it seems to me that my only course of action is to deny everything." Then, lastly, before the sign-off, "You probably won't even believe me but I love you and treasure every minute with you."

I couldn't completely unravel the apparent contradictions in this unexpected literary outburst. Was she seeking to end our relationship –"dumping me", as the vernacular terms it? Did she have someone else on the go? Was this all a paean to late-lost virginity? Or, conversely, was she in some roundabout way requiring more commitment from me, maybe a moving-in together? That would certainly suit my agenda… just as long as she wasn't completely Mrs Rochester.

The urge to phone Shelley or hurry over to her Georgian terrace was almost overwhelming but I resisted it, busying myself instead with rescuing my football kit from its hiding place in the dark, dank corners of the laundry basket. I hadn't played for nearly three weeks and should have dealt with this compost heap of shirt, shorts, socks and knee support much sooner but the washer-drier would have them all ready for tomorrow. Ah, the thrill and excitement of the single masculine life!

I realised, of course, that I was indulging in a displacement activity but I rationalised that I was actually waiting to see how things unfolded rather than attempt to force any issues. I remembered some footage I'd seen of Michel Platini (great player; autocratically out-of-touch, anti-English administrator) showing remarkable presence of mind during an extra time scramble. Instead of just lashing at the ball he waited a split-second whilst defenders shifted their body weight into their proper slots… then he rifled home the winning goal. I wanted to show such Gallic cool.

Which left me warming up in a desultory fashion at a half-empty North London sports complex at eight o'clock the following evening. I hadn't heard from Shelley all day. I'd even taken a slight detour down her street on my way to work but it was, as I've stated, a cul de sac so I retraced my errant steps away from her door and back towards the Central Line station.

By half past, I was still on my own. I sipped some more water through the sports cap, began searching through my bag for the scrap of paper with Martin's mobile – and, more importantly, *home* – number scrawled upon it. Nokias still weren't working reliably so I trudged in my astro turf boots along a residential street towards the nearest public phone-box. The interior was covered with obscure sexist graffiti but at least the handset hummed when I picked it up.

"Hi Martin. Where is everyone?"

"Sorry, Al, meant to ring you. We've had a few people drop out. Carlos and Ray have to work nights now. And Jimmy and Deano are getting themselves petrified."

"You what? Turned to stone?"

"No, not that. Look, I can't talk at the moment. I'll send you something about it through the post. What's your address?"

*

The next morning I tried *petrification* on my console. Lots of calcified bodies from ancient Herculaneum and Pompeii; some fragile black and white forest in Arizona which looked more like a film set for the Brothers Grimm; then flicker as the still only intermittent Internet crashed once again. Just in time, as it turned out, for Simpson was undertaking his time and motion study an hour earlier this morning and it behoved all employees to distil our temporal shifts into an appearance of perpetual motion.

At Shelley's door more than half the day later, laden with red wine and yellow flowers, I paced awkwardly from foot to leaden foot as she took an age to answer the doorbell.

"Something's come up," she muttered, hands as busy as insects, hair like a windswept crow's nest. "I can't see you tonight. I'm… not feeling all that well, actually."

"What about the exhibition?"

"I should be fine. Oh, flowers! That's really sweet. Thank you."

"Twelve-thirty at the tube station,
Sunday. Call me tomorrow if you can."

A cheek peck and I was gone. I was burning up with curiosity but reining in all the enquiries as best I could. Clearly, Shelley didn't want me around tonight. Her words were plain enough; on this occasion. Also, I'd been wary of pressing too hard because I'd been burned once before. Charlotte had been griping about going away to a conference in Bath as part of her management training and, tiring of her prevarication, I'd insisted, "I'm cool about it so what is the real problem here, Charl?"

"The *real* problem," she spat back, "is that, at the last soiree in Peterborough, I slept with that creep Michaelson and I'm sure he's expecting a repeat performance in the West Country!"

We went downhill so fast after that little outburst that I sometimes suspected I'd strapped myself to an invisible snowboard.

Martin's mailing duly arrived. It consisted of a couple of pages from one of those quasi-newspapers originating in America but lately available in supermarkets throughout the UK. You know the sort of thing: *Elvis Lands On The Moon – Official* or *Sixty Year Old Grandmother Gives Birth To Goose Girl – With Three*

Heads. I was surprised he'd given this fabulation any house room what with him being a down-to-earth geography teacher.

I also had half a dozen letters from Shelley. The gist of their content seemed to be an externalised monologue about whether she could or could not see me tomorrow. They were unnumbered so I read them in several different sequences to try to ascertain her concluding decision. I remained unsure. I can see now that these mixed-up missives may have constituted a cry for help; at the time, I interpreted them as an annoyance and resolved to wait and see how the counters fell.

So that several CDs, a decent takeaway and a Saturday night's highlights package later, I was semi-conscious on the Sabbath and it took several insistent buzzes to rouse me from slumber. Bare-chested but barely a bronzed Adonis, I staggered to the front door. Shelley in tight jeans and a new, patterned jumper.

"I thought I said Bethnal Green. Shit, is that the time? You'd better come in; I won't be long."

She took my hand as we crossed over the road before the bus stop. I couldn't remember the last time we'd been out together. Despite our different domiciles, ours was a very domestic relationship.

I saw Charlotte emerging from the newsagent's on the corner with a thick tabloid and a pint of milk clutched precariously in her slippery fingers. She looked at me longer than was decent but remained silent. Clearly, the Trafford Centre and the Ship Canal still awaited her gracious presence.

Dave's girlfriend Amy was even shorter than he was. On balance, this was probably a good thing. As if in compensation, she spent a lot of time straightening his jacket or patting his hair – even going so far as to answer direct questions on his behalf. He didn't seem to mind at all so neither did I.

The exhibition was crowded and it was hard to get a sense of the grandeur and importance of these new Pompeiian finds. The mosaics were stunning in their proximity to perfection. The mummified corpses were at once de-humanised and yet fragile, vulnerable and quite empathic if one switched off the audio commentary and the hubbub all around. There you are one minute stuffing your face with grapes, moaning about the emperor's one denarius tax on new sandals, planning your next Roman bath and orgy, when suddenly the earth and sky literally collapse from under and on top of you. Then nearly two thousand years later the Celts, the Angles and a multihued assortment of unconquered tribes have come to gawp at your misfortune. Oh Ozymandias!

Shelley was still talking about the exhibition on Monday night when I came round to call. The wine sat unopened on the kitchen table but the flowers were in vivid bloom like flames above a volcano.

"There's loads more things I'd like to take you to," I told her.

"You can't keep spending your money on me," she countered. "Really-"

Her speech was interrupted by the shrill screeching of the landline, inconveniently plugged into a socket below the stairs. By her prolonged absence, I ascertained that the sea cables or the satellites were functioning adequately and that the caller was her garrulous sister from Sydney.

The scratching from behind the Laura Ashley curtain was more apparent than ever. I tiptoed across.

The little creature in its ornate cage scuttled into a corner at my inquisitiveness. I grabbed a biscuit from the sideboard and tried to coax him forwards. Ever so slowly, I gained a modicum of trust.

The pet was neither fur nor fowl, but an odd amalgam of mammalian and avian characteristics. Clawed feet, lightly haired legs topped by a kittenish body to which were attached... not wings exactly, more like feathered arms. God's creation given way to man's abomination. And the face: so appealing, so desperately mewling, so annoyingly cute and yet also so *human*!

I could still hear Shelley's merry chatter from the hallway. I scrabbled around like an incompetent bank robber, uncovering and speed-reading documents and disclaimers. There was the same press cutting as the one Martin had sent me; also, advertising literature and contracts signed by both partners in this skewed test of self-sacrifice and fidelity.

"Petrification. Take a year out and have her lavish her little girl love upon you. And at the same time show your devotion to the marital bond."

You poor misguided sod! As if such an imbalance could ever right a teetering relationship.

"All the rage in American households. Now available here. Guaranteed fully reversible or your money back."

I couldn't bear to look at him / it any longer. Shelley was winding up her pan-hemispheric phone conversation. I took a slug of red wine, coughed dramatically, picked up the guitar and began a lacklustre version of *Don't Look Back In Anger*. Later we talked about religion, spirituality, premonitions and intimations of the afterlife. Home-made lasagne had never tasted so good. When we finally went upstairs to fumble and rut like teenage wildebeest I tried to absorb and imprint every moment and sensation on the deepest possible level for endless lonely replay.

I arrived home at three in the morning, left a 'sickie' message on the company answer-phone, pulled the set out from the wall, locked and bolted the front door and tried to sleep.

With surprising success.

*

I thought of staying out of sight at Dave's for a while but even his sofa was deemed out of bounds because Amy was moving in at the weekend to gently take control of his domestic life. An end to our occasional Stella strewn nights but otherwise I was pleased for him. Them.

"Listen, Al," he said, "you're the one who always says not to believe everything you read on the Internet."

"Meaning?"

"It's some gene modification technique that the Japs are up to. They're breeding these mongrel monkeys with human faces. It should be outlawed, if you ask me."

"I'm asking you about Simpson."

"He thinks you've got the flu. But I wouldn't stay off more than a week."

As I put the phone down, I heard my letterbox rattle. A hand-delivered bundle but no sign on the pavement of my elfin postmistress. Again, the missives were unnumbered and contradictory.

"What have I done to upset you?"

"Yes, I am a married woman but that's all over with and shouldn't come between us."

"It's not an issue of feminism, it's an issue of commitment."

"Look, lover, it was a present. I didn't really want to accept it."

"I feel invaded and on trial. You shouldn't go looking and delving."

I left the multicoloured but unscented pages on a work surface next to the kettle. I switched on the radio and they were playing some Goth rock epic that I hadn't heard in years. It was a bit doomy and overblown, of course, but I'd always liked the lyrics: "You will know when the last days begin / Because every urban myth / Will come to exist." I was dancing around the kitchen singing along and my mood lightened considerably.

The option existed to just get back on with my life. I could even go back to the office this afternoon – I didn't have to walk down Cul De Sac Close to reach the tube.

At last, I composed a reply to Shelley's many letters telling her that it was a matter of trust because she'd withheld things from me. If she wanted more commitment then *she* had to show more commitment.

I didn't have any stamps. Probably I'd walk it round there this evening. Wait on the doorstep with a bottle of Jacob's Creek.

Maybe I should have felt sorry for that abomination hidden behind her curtain. What was Shelley hoping to achieve by confining it so? Husband or household pet, her treatment of the creature seemed pretty heartless.

I read an article in the *Evening Standard* about how modern reconstructed men are secretly scared of the new power women seem to have. Get shrunk and spend a year as your sweetheart's pet then pick up from where you left off… but with her somehow in your debt. What weird stuff had I been swallowing?

I had certainly been somewhat overwrought recently. I just hoped Shelley would understand and accept my apologies.

…Sometimes, though, I worry that in any cage there's always room for two.

THE ACCIDENTALISTS

Coming into the more developed parts of the city, Jim saw up ahead a crowd on fire. His first inclination was to rush forwards although his medical and pyrotechnic knowledge was scant at best. His next urge was to consider flight. Who knew, the victims could stumble into a chemical factory or, more likely, a petrol station.

The bus had dropped him and his last day's cash in the snobby outskirts and the two mile walk plus three weeks toil picking spoolberries by the kilo had taken their toll. He decided to walk slowly towards the conflagration. Towards the gesticulating and panicking figures half-engulfed by yellow flames and grey smoke, acrid even at this distance. Souls in torment in an urban hell.

Such a contrast to his back-breaking days in the sun picking up a tan for his aching white man's muscles which might get him a little closer to being the bronzed Adonis his ex-girlfriend seemed to prefer. Working in fields and hillsides too uneven for machinery then relaxing in the Rec. Room every evening to play cards or watch the one channel state television, he'd experienced something akin to the kibbutz lifestyle. And a tantalising, tentative sense of community. How many people did you need to hold that feeling together? And how many before excess destroyed it?

He wanted to help although he wasn't entirely sure what he could do. Wrap a blanket round someone, maybe? The best he could offer was a thick jumper and that was stuffed at the bottom of his grip bag. Find a water supply, start a bucket chain? Where and how exactly? There was now a small crowd watching the human flambeaux. Hadn't anybody called the emergency services? Oh yes, to the left, hard by a couple of blackened corpses – a solitary ambulance and, at last, a troop of firemen, hoses extended.

Absence and second-hand news of the late Summer scams sweeping the city – The Car Stereo Stand-Offs, The Accidentalists, The Overnight Parking Meter Planters – had made his home seem a fantastical, untamed land. Thus through urban myths of old provenance one might revisit the childhood world of grim fairy tale -

"Step back, please!" a strong male voice ordered. A firm arm blocked Jim's progress and he responded automatically to the authoritative tone and the spanking new uniform. On further inspection, however, the fire chief was unconvincingly long-haired and youthful. Perhaps this was a video shoot – some pouting boy band or dollar crazy blockbuster full of explosions and hyperactive actors.

Bored and stymied, he set off again for The Star And Garter pub where some of his old cronies might be taking an early lager or two on this Friday evening. Dry weather and late sunset would surely bring most people out of their hovels and apartments to lap up a little pavement culture and bar repartee.

His regular haunt was in the old part of town near the railway terminus. Already the pulsing bulbs and strip lights were busy imploring consumers to drink this, watch this, drive home in that. The prevalence of artificial illumination made it suddenly feel like night time and the new craze for diagonally tilted billboards – designed for a greater degree of impact – gave Jim the uncomfortable feeling of being trapped inside a gigantic pinball game.

He re-adjusted his shoulder strap and pushed the door open onto a fug of smoke, hot bodies and conversation competing with the blare of a sports round-up programme on the giant screen in the far corner. It took him five minutes to locate his erstwhile friends; another fifteen minutes of nervous sipping at a bottle of Becks elapsed before they even acknowledged his presence.

"Ah, Jim," began Steve, "how's life? Not as we know it, eh?"

Over the guffaw, Jim answered, "If I had a pound for every time someone's said that I'd be a Euro millionaire."

Danny interrupted, "If you had ten bob's worth of old sovereigns you'd be a Euro millionaire."

Jim sipped his beer, deciding not to correct the fiscal misconception.

"So," Steve continued, "why ain't we seen you for a while?"

"I've been out west picking spoolberries for cash and credit."

"Yeah, you always were the manual labour sort," Danny commented.

"Spoolberries?" asked Eric. "Have you seen how much they cost?"

"Don't!" Danny agreed. "Nearly a day's wages for a puny punnet. I wouldn't bother except the wife likes 'em and what with her expecting and everything –"

"I had some the other day," said Eric, "that were as sour as shit. Not ripe at all. Shop caused such a fuss about a refund I told 'em to shove 'em up their arses."

"I blame the pickers," Steve suggested with a smile. "So, Jim, now you've built up a bit of muscle you could manage to get a round in, I reckon."

By the time he came back with a tray full of gleaming cold lagers, the conversation had moved onto a recent refereeing controversy in a supposedly friendly international match. The game had been screened by one of the satellite channels so Jim felt too ill-informed to comment.

He'd been looking forward to being back with the lads but was still rather on the edge of things. Maybe he should drink up and try to get in touch with Alison. Tell her he'd still got her picture, crumpled and kiss-stained, in his trouser pocket. She might yet forgive him and consider taking him back. During a warm spell back in the Spring, she had taken to constantly wearing a dark blue dress patterned with overlarge daisy petals and leaves. It really hadn't suited her and in his opinion was the sort of attire a middle-aged woman would wear thinking she was being fashionable. He knew silence and a bitten lip was the best policy but one night when she'd reeled out the regular items on her nagging list – his cluttered living room, his clapped-out car, his primitive sexual technique – he'd unwittingly let his honest opinion slip out and thus precipitated their seemingly final parting.

After a further fifteen minutes of miserable marginality, Jim became aware of a lull in the general pub hubbub. Even the beeping till and the nudge machines had temporarily subsided so that everyone heard the sudden screeching cacophony of crunched metal outside. The saloon door burst open and a red-faced, breathless man with a striking ginger beard rushed in to tell the crowd about the accident outside.

"You must come and help!" he implored. "If you know any First Aid or can just help move some of the wreckage... come on, people are dying!"

Jim shook his head, stated, "Don't go, it's a trick. I heard all about this at Yasger's Farm."

But already the pub was emptying. Even the Australians behind the bar had clicked the cash registers closed and joined the rush. Fearing the worst, Jim kept his legs firmly clamped over his grip bag containing half a ton of dirty washing and a battered MP3 player with drained batteries.

A side door opened and half a dozen sportswear sporting teenage tearaways burst into the almost deserted room and with the facility of locusts scooped up the abandoned valuables from handbags and jackets – wallets, purses, mobile phones and other paraphernalia. One lanky black kid pulled out a craft knife, cut the electrical cords and tucked the two tills under his arms. The sneak thieves looked menacingly in Jim's direction from beneath baseball caps and hooded tops but said nothing. He was reminded briefly of an old comedy sketch in which a dubious character in a sheepskin jacket warned the viewer not to mention having seen him. There was one gassy mouthful left in the beer bottle. Jim drained it down the back of his nervously dry throat, shouldered his belongings and followed the last of the robbers as they legged it away out of a side door.

He wandered around in a daze for a while. Was it his curse to always be on the edge of things or had he, in fact, unwittingly been suddenly catapulted into the centre of the action?

It was still quite early for a Friday evening, the weather was clement and the atmosphere on the streets seemed celebratory rather than manic. It would be a shame to go home just yet. When he felt the need to urinate, he found a half-full burger joint. Alcohol had made him hungry and he ordered a cheap meal and a coke. He sat toying with his stick-like regulation fries for three-quarters of an hour, wondering why he'd neglected to mention the burning people to the boys down the pub. He was surprised when nothing untoward happened at the Flame Grill. They didn't even run out of cheap tomato ketchup.

At the corner of Chenery Street, one of Jim's erstwhile drinking pals spotted him and shouted something incoherent. Fearing a haranguing match, Jim bolted in a northerly direction. No doubt his pursuer would assume flight equalled guilt. Whatever, the crime victim soon gave up the chase and Jim eased to a more manageable walking pace. They weren't friends he was desperate to hang on to and he was glad none of them knew his flat number.

His old banger of a car was still parked outside, complete with hubcaps, radio aerial and almost empty petrol tank. He wondered whether, during his absence, the seemingly sentient mechanical beast had taken the opportunity to reconsider its decision to refuse coaxing, coaching, cussing and the simple everyday act of ignition.

There were no answer-phone messages from his girlfriend. There were no answer-phone messages at all. Three weeks of minimal electricity keeping the machine connected and the miniature red bulb alight. His jolly outgoing recording along the lines of, "I can't talk to you right now but I'd love to get back to you really soon." The hope that time might have healed things. All a vain waste of time and energy.

The telly was full of comedy programmes, imported and home-grown, but Jim found himself unable to laugh. The radio was in party mood with a persistent offering of a hundred and thirty beats of music but he felt too physically tired to dance along with its Balearic hedonism. His bookshelves groaned with best-sellers purchased in the supermarket. Did everyone bar Jim have a glittering career in media marketing these days? Had that been the root of his ostracism in the pub?

There was a loud knocking at his door. He promised himself that he wouldn't answer unless it was Alison bare breasted and penitent. He tried to picture her semi-naked. Such occasions had been so rare that he was forced to give her the imaginary body of a trashy film starlet.

He peered through the spy-hole. It was just some ordinary guy who had now taken it upon himself to rattle the letterbox as well. What was the fuss?

A throaty, male voice called out, "Can you help? There's been an accident. Is there anyone knows any First Aid?"

Jim double-locked and bolted the door as quietly as he could. Then he placed a chair against it. Through a tear in threadbare curtains, he chanced a look down onto the street below. There was a crowd gathered on the pavement. Some of them might have been his neighbours, it was hard to tell in the sodium light. They were gathered round his battered old Ford Archaic. He wanted to go down and order them to stop leaning on the vehicle, the body-work won't stand the pressure, but he dared not leave his flat. Would the insurance cover the damage? Was he still insured at all?

He slept fitfully on the sofa. Nothing was stolen, no one tried to gain illicit entry and eventually the kerfuffle outside became the usual muted roar of distant traffic and, later, birdsong. Just the normal urban noise pollution.

All his cheese had gone mouldy and the icebox had iced over. He decided to beat the crowds and drive to the nearest Savermart. If he could cajole his car into one more local ride...

Descending to street level, he found the vehicle unscathed by last night's shenanigans. The pavement, however, had been ripped up to make way for a parking meter painted in ominous dark green. A yellow demand on the front windscreen screamed 'Fixed Penalty Notice' at him. Jim checked the cash in his pocket. He was 70p short of the charge.

THE SPACES IN OUR LIVES

It was fast becoming the year of all the natural disasters. The European earthquakes, the second tsunami, the hurricanes and tornadoes, the volcanic blast in Guatemala which was set to shroud the sky for three years and block out the sunlight but keep all the pollution in. Oh but the women all looked fabulous with their brown boots and their dyed blonde hair and their gypsy skirts swirling. Even Claire had made an effort to shuck off her usual unisex uniform of ripped jeans and nondescript T-shirt and instead indulge the feminine fashions of autumn. No doubt I should have been more appreciative; but I had other problems on my mind, such as the new *luxury* flats being built within gobbing distance of my bedroom window, soon to block out the daylight as effectively as ash from an erupting cone. The legal fight with the private developers had already wiped out my holiday budget for the next two summers.

"Sell up," was Claire's succinct advice. But she didn't add, "And move in with me" so I didn't press her on the issue.

"I can't afford to," I answered. "House prices have rocketed everywhere but here. And who's going to want a room with no view?"

"Maybe David Blunkett or Stevie Wonder. Shit, this phone's gone dead again."

Earth's changing atmospherics and several satellites crashing out of unstable orbits were playing havoc with all telecommunications. Yet another inconvenience when you wanted to buy onscreen or order a pizza.

"This thong's killing me," she stated. "I'm going to the bathroom to put some proper knickers on. And don't get any funny ideas."

As if.

Claire's Diary, 27ᵗʰ September:

Things are becoming difficult again with Andy. I don't know what he wants from our relationship. It's not as simple as the cod psychology notion that he wants a replacement for the mother who died when he was fourteen. How awful that must have been, to see her knocked over and killed by a bunch of small-time crooks in a stolen car. In some ways he's recovered really well, not that I can be absolutely certain, as I didn't meet him till nearly fifteen years later. In deeper, hidden ways, he'll likely never recover. But is feeling desperately sorry for someone enough of a basis for a serious, long-term commitment?

Commitment? That's not really his style. And maybe not mine at this moment, either. There are unfathomable distances between men and women. I need my own space just as much as he does. I need to reassure him about this.

Sometimes he's so typically male. He's one of the cleverest people I know but he's wasted in his job. He told me when I first met him that he only took an art history degree as a way of meeting girls! I know he hates the clients he has to deal with at the gallery – the buyers and the artists – and he could create better work himself. He's right. Blocks of blue and swathes of primary arcs on otherwise untouched white canvas – most children could produce that rainbow effect on a wet Friday afternoon.

I'm writing too much about Andy. Why is my diary not simply about me?

The next entry will be all Claire Smith. Promise.

Space exploration began in the mountains of Equatoria when Ugg the Cave Man saw a hole in the ceiling that held a watery sparkle of the night sky. Blessed with the comforting notions of 'As above, so below', the first astronauts mistakenly took a nocturnal dive into an unusually deep drinking hole. If the whirlpools and the tangled weeds didn't get them then the patient crocodiles certainly did. These tearing-toothed log impersonators had already survived one extinctive holocaust, so having to play crafty to catch prey was merely a minor hardship. For the primitive hominids, it was another sad lesson to be carried forwards and held as a buried memory to be expressed much later as jungle-trashing, rainforest-burning revenge.

From Icarus to the Apollo missions, the question has not been the reaching out but the bringing back. Space? Been there, done that, got the souvenir moon rock and NASA T-shirt to prove it. Shame we all got a bit burned up on re-entry.

I'd never cared for Ranulph Whitemeat's canvases either aesthetically or technically but it was still my job to publicise and sell them. Claire was even more dismissive: "Great huge swathes of nothingness. In colour." She didn't accompany me on this latest jaunt. As our London-dressed group shivered in the fierce wind off the North Sea, I felt the full sense behind her decision.

"A seascape," Whitemeat pontificated. "A series of seascapes. In grey, of course. Showing the space we don't own."

One of his corporate sponsors, a suit from Food Co or Flexi-Build, smiled shark-friendly behind his Ray Bans. "Perhaps you'd consider something more futuristic. Something indicative of our development plans."

"I don't do science fiction book covers!" Whitemeat hissed, stomping back to the minibus.

The company director, Mr Slater-Williams I now recalled, mumbled, "Ah, the artistic temperament. What an indulgence! The guy's a Turner prize winner but thinks he's actually Turner."

I smiled despite my role. On the drive back I pressed the guy about his company's vision.

"Available land is almost full or subject to too much planning red tape. The future is marine."

"Above or below?" I asked.

"The former. Cities like giant oil rigs stretching over thousand of square miles, I mean kilometres."

I was thinking by the seat of my pants. "What about the weather systems – water evaporation, tides, the Gulf Stream, the lunar cycle, storms and so forth?"

He took an object from his smooth jacket pocket. "Look at this. If our guys can manufacture the perfect heart-shaped tomato, they can overcome a few local difficulties."

Claire was typically dismissive when I told her the story that evening. "Local difficulties?" she scoffed. "Pie in the sky, more like! Two thirds of the world's surface is covered by water but there's going to be no rainfall."

"They're going to build desalination plants."

"More like de-sanity," she answered. "Still, you always wanted to live by the sea. I suppose now you'll be picturing yourself living *on* the sea."

I loved her when she was animated like this. The dull times receded and our shared landscape became vivid and filled with life.

I read in the paper at coffee break that the planet is shrinking. Imperceptibly, of course, but measurable nonetheless. Maybe it's because of all the ejecta – the satellites, the space probes, the lunar landers left to freeze at minus 200 hundred degrees Kelvin; thus, with no recent comets to replenish our mineral supplies the Earth's mass is slightly diminished. Then again, perhaps it's just a matter of perception: people are larger and more numerous than ever before, dwarfing the short-arsed cave dwellers and Roman legionnaires, so the available space is much smaller. Even the natural disasters or so-called acts of God only thin out our infestation by a few thousand here and there.

What would my father say? "It's all down to the enforced change from imperial to metric. They don't know nothing, these boffins!"

Claire's diary, 6th October:
There was another feature on the Jane Wylie Solar System Theorem, the one that postulates an impermeable barrier protecting and enclosing our little bubble some several million miles beyond the orbit of Pluto. All those radio telescope images of distant galaxies and nebulous stars are merely distortions on the inner lining. Honestly, science is the new rock 'n' roll!

The beauty of the hypothesis is that no one is ever likely to travel far enough to prove or disprove it. And, of course, every Internet conspiracy crank and religious freak on the planet has found something to latch onto in this crazy supposition. And talking of beauty – Jane fucking Wylie herself is photogenic in that black tresses, smooth Caucasian skinned, subtly made-up not flashy, thirty-something way that makes her the new 'thinking man's crumpet'.

Brains and beauty, the bitch! I know Andy has got a picture of her hidden in his sock drawer. I'm sure I'm still number one in his affections; I just hope that astro-tart never goes blonde!

Doodles and painting programs on the PC. Thoughts about quitting my job of selling and curating other people's creations and taking up my own brush and pencils once more. Yes, it was a quiet day at work again. I hated those: action and business kept me grounded in the present and helped me to side-step the pain of the past and avoid the void of the future.

After two decades, more than half my lifetime, the police had decided to reopen their inquiries into my mother's death. The third man in the car had never been identified. His accomplices had never squealed. From the other side of the street, I'd watched the getaway car screech its brakes, collide with her shocked-into-stillness body, then speed away on burning rubber. I had nothing more to offer as a witness. The guy was half-crouched in the back, what can I say? How could I pick him out in an ID parade?

I've had the therapy; I've undergone the hypnosis. Shit, I still don't know how I had the presence of mind to scribble down the number plate before rushing across to Mother. The key piece of evidence, as it turned out. Excuse me if I don't feel heroic about it.

I remember the two nights at the hospital and how difficult my behaviour at school was for the succeeding few months. My mind's erased so much since then, filled up the gaps with TV dramas and nights down the pub. What is that saying about how air, no matter how mediocre or unpalatable, will rush to fill a vacuum?

Eventually my father let me go and took up a job offer abroad. Found a sympathetic new woman. Christmas cards, birthday phone calls, and male avoidance of emotional issues: he copes in his own way. I did what I could with the compensation money and when the petty criminal passenger was due for release, I moved a hundred and sixty miles down the country so our paths were less likely to cross.

I knew that I'd lumbered Claire with the memories and the emotions and the trauma and the guilt that always accompanies sudden loss. She'd stuck it for longer than I could have expected. Surely soon she'll have had enough, though, and I wouldn't blame her.

Now the Old Bill wanted to restore all the wounds and scars to their original freshness. For what? So that some youth – now in his thirties! – who watched his mates steal a cash till from an off licence and was then party to a hit and run gets an eighteen-month stretch for conspiracy? There was no justice that would bring my dead parent back. The emptiness, the space in my life remains forever and I lived around it every day and tried not to burden Claire too much with a memory she didn't share but doubtless felt she did.

My only other coping mechanism was that typical masculine strategy of filling up the absence with work and activity.

Claire's Diary, 31ˢᵗ October:
The female part of me wishes I could walk past a building site or into a wine bar and turn all those antlered heads. The feminist part of me wants a fulfilling life and career that isn't contingent on pleasing any men or man, no matter how close he is.

I wish I didn't but I still remember gym class at St Petrifa's. Watching all those bitches suddenly develop breasts like grapefruits, film star cheekbones, waxed long legs draped along the wooden benches or crying off class because of their periods. When would it be my turn? And when it all came late to me, like

Sissy Spacek in *Carrie*, I bloomed a little from a runty caterpillar but only got as far as moth. I remained tomboyish – which was OK to the extent that my opinions were taken more seriously in seminars and tutorials, but I wanted to be the butterfly. Not for the boys, but for myself.

Andy loves me, in his rather non-committal way. I wish he took more notice and didn't have to be prompted on things. I've grown my hair longer and gradually highlighted it to a subtle blonde instead of its natural mouse brown. I've bought a couple of skirts at the market to go with my new caring, sharing, soft-centred, make a donation to the disaster fund, hippie chick idealism.

No, I'm not convinced, either. I look in the mirror and I still see my hard-faced, hard-life self. I look at the two of us together and we're drifting – in interconnecting, Venn diagram circles – but for how long?

Humankind has sought to explore and conquer space throughout assumed and documented history.

The indigenous people of Payguya province in Central America farmed the fertile slopes around their local volcano, which sported an unusually wide though shallow nose cone. Advanced to the state of monotheism, they believed in a god of emptiness, Payguya, whose name could be spoken or invoked but never written. Occasionally it was demarcated in their recorded tales as a space, which Victorian ethnologists originally misinterpreted as an omission.

Payguya may once have dwelt within the hole-y mountain although, in living memory, no one had ever seen, heard or indeed smelt his presence. In desperation, they called upon this wise being to send weapons and reinforcements as the tide of plunder swept across the New World. Help was not forthcoming and so they ultimately put up no resistance to the conquistadors.

Space exploration continued during the years of deforestation as the cows ate their way across the increasingly arid plains. All stories about the outer reaches are really stories about Earth.

Meanwhile, the worshippers' graves lay dormant and unmarked until the temporally challenged god Payguya got back from his coffee break and took note of their memo. He took a long drag on his magma cigar, exhaled a puff of smoke, and sent a polluting blanket over the whole of the misbehaving planet. Crop failure and summer starvation beckoned but Payguya was replete, relaxed, considering his full response…

*

Claire and I went to a Bonfire Night display. It was chilly up on the hill and we should have snuggled together under my big coat but she was in one of her stand-offish moods.

We haven't had sex for at least four weeks.

Fifteen minutes of rocket launches got me thinking about how it might be if there was actually an atmosphere in deep space. A contradiction in terms, I know, but just imagine how it might all smell, sound and feel as well as look. Suppose Wylie is wrong and the old structures are correct. What if you could take a whiff on the fiery exploding nebula, let your ears hear the fizz of the celestial fireworks, but keep your fingers away from the searing flame, it's not all simply a November the fifth treat for the eyes.

But for now we poor humans remain trapped on this crumbling rock.

I wasn't feeling at my best, having been woken by drilling and cement mixing at five-thirty this morning. They're already three months into the job with little visible progress, but they're so far behind schedule that now they're starting work in the dark. I spoke to – all right, shouted at – the Polish foreman.

"Not me, boss. You phone council mobile, boss."

"Don't worry, mate, I will."

And I did. But it was one of those multiple choice, press this button, say 'yes' now, which service do you require labyrinths, so I gave up.

Ranulph Whitemeat, great British art hope, had upset another of our key sponsors at a meet and greet. At some point that over-rated twit has to learn that being an interesting painter is ultimately about the work not the coked-up, celebrity-shagging, media-dissing lifestyle that accompanies it.

All of which was not very good preparation for my private meeting with Inspector Blatch of Derbyshire CID.

"You know there have been some possible developments, Andy," he stated.

"I'm going to be a disappointment to you, inspector," I answered. "I gave everything I could at the time. There are some people who claim they can remember everything but the rest of us – even with a clean record as regards alcohol and drug use – retain just a few edited highlights. And, if we accept the idea of constant file updating and reclassification, we remember less and less, fewer and fewer details, over time. My mother died twenty years ago and the shock still hits hard but I can no longer retain all the ins and outs of the crash, the hospital drama and the funeral. Christ, I can't even remember who passed me the ball for my first goal last night. So *you* may want to pick up these inquiries after all this time but no matter how disturbing, deeply scarring and life-changing Mum's death was, I can't retain the vivid impression from every minute. There are bound to be spaces. Even under hypnosis."

He finished his coffee, looked in his jacket for a cigarette to light once he was outside again. "Just keep your details on file with us, please, Mr Green."

"Are you going to question me again?" I asked.

He smiled thinly, replied, "That thing they say about art is true of my work, too. A criminal investigation is never concluded, it's simply abandoned."

Claire's diary, 12th November:
I was thinking today, at a quiet moment before the Middle Management meeting, that during our lives we must meet thousands of people, but the choices we make and how our paths – our orbits if you like – can, in retrospect, seem very narrow and predetermined. Alternate futures die like unplucked leaves on the vine. The great vistas beckon but we can't always reach them, we don't have the money or "Captain, I dinna have the power!"

How different things might be if... It's a game we all play when we feel like life is passing us by.

Maybe it's just that as the universe expands, my brain is shrinking. Cheryl asked me today, "Where did you holiday last year?" and for at least ten minutes I honestly couldn't remember. What did I do last Tuesday? What was my Infant School teacher's name?

I was awake at ten to seven this morning. Five minutes in the bathroom, another five to put on the clothes I placed so carefully on the chair last night. A quick cup of tea and a scan of the news on Ceefax but suddenly it was twenty-five past and I'd lost all that time and even though I got hot and sweaty running for the train I still missed my connection. Where did I drift off to during those missing moments?

How many times have I ridden or driven somewhere and reached my destination with no memory of the journey?

Long ago, I recognised how damaged Andy still is and how our relationship will always involve a certain level of care from me. While it lasts.

We passed our anniversary quietly. Things are drifting between us, by which I mean it's an experience we both share, this feeling that we are floating away from each other.

I've been stressed at work plus I've just had a particularly bad period. We haven't made love for twenty-two days.

Space – it's not a frontier at all but a subtle barrier that bends inwards then repels back again. All those Hubble pictures are simply distortions. No one and no thing has ever left this solar system because nothing can. We're trapped inside this billion-mile sphere – God's thought bubble or the extent of existence? This whole Jane Wylie Theorem is causing the hugest controversy of the 21st century so far as, if it's true, it speaks to the very roots of and reasons for our sorry existence.

People talk about the spaces between notes in music. Sometimes I can hear it – that aching expectant moment before the guitar or the drums kick back in, but mostly it's just poncy theorists making themselves sound cleverer than they are. That John Cage piece was a joke. Likewise so much of what passes for modern art. I'm not saying it should all be representational but huge swathes of one colour or canvases that are mostly empty white… they are the emperor's new clothes – the ultimate empty space trickery.

There had to be more to life than selling huge compositions filled with paint. There were countries I'd like to visit before the whole world became an environmental disaster zone.

But things were starting to look up. *The Daily Mail*, bless them, had followed the lead of the *Evening Standard* in running a two-page centre spread unfavourably comparing Whitemeat's work with that of a chimp. The TV companies were queuing up to film inside the gallery and even Ranulph's studio. That was when I knew we'd attract the visitors and, more importantly, buyers. Everyone's favourite art is something they can slag off, something where they say give me a brush, I can do better than that. I was ready to enjoy the ride and reap the bonuses…

Claire's diary, 3rd December:
The world is going to hell in a sandstorm. We've got all these theories about the nature of the universe but we can't keep a lid on our own excesses. It's not a case of "Live now, pay later" because the likelihood is there will be no later. Or else, with every day bringing televised news of another flooding, another landslide,

another hurricane or monsoon wreaking devastation, the pay-up time of 'later' is already here.

I want to believe in a future worth living for. I want personal fulfilment and I want to progress in my career. The only maternal feelings I ever have are when Andy wants some comforting for past traumas. I want to remain true to myself but I'll put on the business suit five times a week if I have to. I want this promotion more than almost anything. I know I need a holiday but Christmas is meaningless to me: just an empty round of slurred hymns and filial duties.

Come on; give me the promotion, you bastards! You know you want to.

Space exploration ended in Xangsang territory when the last available unit was taken by a socially housed pair of newlyweds. Ordered to produce no children until ten years hence, they fill their evenings with TV listings and scandalously difficult bouts of Sudoku. All stories about the future are truly tales of now.

The planet was going into meltdown as Gaea sought revenge on her human parasites, but I was on a roll. Monuments, flats and factories were falling into the fissures across the Richter ripped continent and the government couldn't decide whether the main priority was the casualties or the refugees. On a socially conscious level, I was disturbed and concerned, but on a local level I was made up because the local council had finally accepted my objections to the planning application. Property developers, nil; real residents, one.

Wow, all this a couple of days before Christmas! It was enough to renew anyone's faith.

The nocturnal builders simply left the half-completed building and the scaffolding so there was still some chasing up and clearing up to do. Then again, I'd looked out on worse scenes from a first floor window.

In fact, I was quite inspired and was seriously considering buying some paints and canvas to use this vista as a pitch for a science fiction book cover while it lasted. Entropic civilisations. The spaces between the bricks, the gaps around the steel…

*

Claire's diary, 31ˢᵗ December:
Another year goes by and here we are at New Year still together through habit more than love. The space between increases exponentially. Isn't it about time one of us either reached out a steadying, unifying hand? Or else cut the umbilical?

THE SLOT

Author's Note:
My thanks to D. F. Lewis for the loan of one of his ideas.

I remembered careering along tram-lines or what seemed to be a purpose-built trench. I was riding a tricycle; possibly a go-kart. I must have been five or so. It's my strongest childhood memory and yet still tantalisingly impressionistic.

I left it in the 'fond recollection' drawer for over twenty years until gradually it became important for me to pin down the image with a 'where' as well as a 'when'. It wasn't somewhere we'd lived, I was certain of that much. A special holiday, then?

It took a little nerve to put the question to my mother. She had spent the past several years in genteel denial in a ground floor apartment close to the museum district. Her stock response to everything other than meteorological or gastronomic chit-chat was, "No perturbances, please, Harry dear."

"We didn't holiday for years when you were a young boy," she answered after a thoughtful sip of lemon tea. "Your father was too mean and stingy. You must have dreamt it, dear heart."

My estranged father – still active but terribly embittered – finally granted me an audience at an inconvenient venue one wet Thursday afternoon. I knew he would set out to deliberately contradict Mother. Maybe I could sieve the truth grains out of their combined testimony.

"I was an important man back then," he reminded me. "Briefly up to ambassador level, don't you know? We travelled to every European city imaginable and some beyond. Beyond imagination, that is. How am I expected to remember all the times and places, eh? I'd still be going to them now if it wasn't for your mother filing for a messy divorce. I lost standing, old boy. People stopped respecting me."

Soon after, I saw an article in a Sunday supplement and I was suddenly convinced I'd found the right place. The concrete channel I'd remembered was known as The Slot and marked a chasm where a wall had once stood. The magazine editor – an acquaintance from media college – assured me that the brick structure had only been removed ten or so years ago. I'm twenty-eight now; which meant that I must have been rattling along its length on a tin trike at the tender age of... eighteen!

The World Wide Web proved unusually scant on information and historical detail about the city, the wall and the resultant Slot. I suspected a deliberate block. Mostly, all I could access were glowing biographies of the city's mayor, Councillor Smalls.

I was more intrigued than ever. I had no current assignments or even assignations to attend to at home. I asked my sweetly ancient, semi-retired secretary, Rosa, to make the arrangements. I was on my way within twenty-four hours.

Some twenty-four years late.

The areas surrounding the airport, my hotel and the commercial district were as predictably mundane as any other major European city; instead, I sought out the old quarter. This proved to be the demesne of several gangs of slouching, beetle-browed youths wordlessly disputing the cobbled turf in front of the funeral parlours, pawnbrokers and dusty cross-stitch shops. I ought to have been scared, I suppose, but when you've made documentaries about religious fundamentalists and gun-runners, teenage layabouts are rather small beer. The video game and slot machine arcade at the corner of Padgett Street seemed positively out of place, however, and I was secretly pleased when I later learned it had closed due to recurrent vandalism.

At one end of Madge Road, a mangy cat played with an intestinal length of string whilst the horses from the rag and bone carts ate and shat simultaneously. At the further corner, next to a dilapidated office offering *Wills, Pension Plans and Marital Endowments*, stood a rambling old curio shop – *Des's Morte Au Monde*. This was the sort of place, I assumed, where I would be able to begin my surreptitious probing into the history of The Slot and, indeed, the city itself.

The proprietor was a tall gentleman affecting square-lensed glasses above a Shake 'n' Vac beard. He was blessed with a dome-like head, indicating apparent grand mastery.

"Are you an antiquarian?" I enquired.

"My dear fellow, I'm not quite that old yet," he replied with a smile.

There was one other customer – a pretty young woman busying herself amongst the Wade, Delft and Clarice Cliff ceramics. I wanted to ask the obvious question about girls like you and places like this but I refrained. Just. I did, though, get a glance at the name on her credit card –"G. Petty" – and a twinkling glance upon her pleased departure.

"I would have expected ancient coinage or bartering to be the order of the day in an establishment such as this," I informed the owner.

"Or a pact with the devil, perhaps?" he replied. "No, young sir, Uncle Des has moved with the times and I've got all the modern cons in the store now. Seen anything you fancy?"

"I was quite taken with the limited edition goatskin Dickens and the signed Lovecraft," I answered, "but they're not...er...?"

"Genuine? Far as I know, they are. Wasn't actually around at the time so can't be one hundred per cent, of course. They're slow sellers so chew it over for a few days, if you like. In the meantime, we're doing a special promotion on jigsaws. Would you like one?"

"Jigsaws? I'm not Mrs Citizen Kane stuck in her mansion, you know!"

"Don't be so dismissive. I know you're working on a puzzle; else, why would you be here? A bit of lateral thinking never hurt anyone. Here, have this box. On account or gratis, I don't really care."

I waved a few local notes under his nose but he shooed them away. "This shop's just a hobby," he confessed. "I make my money in underwriting, fortune telling and other such worthy stuff. Squirrel farming's my biggest earner."

"Are you sure this is going to help me?"

"Come back if it doesn't. I'm always open. Except on days when I'm not here, of course."

I was in the right city – the holiday destination recalled from childhood – of that there was no doubt. I was still finding it a little hard to come to terms with everyone's extreme reluctance to discuss daily life prior to the inauguration of The Slot. Things can't have been that bad, surely? And if they had been, wouldn't it be therapeutic to speak about them now?

I'd learned to quickly recognise the facial signs and body language which meant: probe no further. It seemed certain that my research was going to be a mostly solo investigation. Commencing with Monsieur Monde's thousand piece jigsaw, whose plain box bore only the legend 'Another world mystery unravels.'

I made quite a good start that very afternoon, identifying and joining together much of the border. Mentally tired, I decided after an hour or so to pay another visit to the cultural museum to see if history really only took us up to one hundred years ago and to have my aching eyes further strained by a collection of the psychedelic hodge-splotches which passed for a modern art exhibition. Upon returning, I was dismayed to find that Elsa, the over-efficient chambermaid, had changed the sheets and neatly scooped all the puzzle parts back into the box. I would have complained to the management but she was quite attractive – in an athletic, East European sort of way – so, I'm afraid, inherent sexism prevailed.

Instead, I went back to the old curio shop. Pretty Ms Petty was again in attendance sifting through the urns and vases. Today the proprietor was as taciturn and guarded as everybody else; maybe he was merely distracted or overwhelmed by his weekly voluntary stock-check.

Just before I exited, I noticed Des's store sporting a scaled-down version of the political poster proliferating like a paper plague throughout every neighbourhood:

"For One

For All

It's Gotta Be

SMALLS."

I chuckled with a mixture of surprise and embarrassment. Back in my home town, Councillor Smalls had the reputation of being, as some journalistic wag put it, "A tin-pot despot piss-pot." Yet his local popularity seemed unassailable.

"You want I should vote for some upstart, sandal-wearing, champagne socialist instead?" Des asked over my shoulder. "I know which side of the scone gets the butter and sometimes jam. Yes, sometimes jam. Don't knock our democracy, Mr Wood. We believe in 'one man, one vote'. Councillor Smalls is the one man we always vote for."

"I'm a film director," I told her.

For a moment I could see her eyes go all casting couch misty. As she recovered her composure and a firmer grip on her virtue, she enquired, "Oh really? What was your last movie called?"

"It was called *Lost Tribes of the Diggory*," I answered. "It was an anthropological piece. All my stuff is, I suppose. I won a couple of festival awards."

"Oh, you're a documentary film-maker," she smiled. "So what brings you here?"

"The Slot. The wall that must have existed previously. Childhood memories. The charisma or otherwise of Councillor Smalls. Er, the interesting inhabitants of your wonderful city," I added hurriedly.

"Childhood memories? But you're not from here originally. Not with that accent."

"No, I'm just re-tracing a journey I believe I made when I was much younger."

"How interesting. I'd really like to talk to you about this but I'm due back at work any minute. No luxurious self-employment pour moi, I'm afraid. Perhaps tomorrow...?"

"Certainly. I can't wait."

*

I had made some serious money from my latest filmic venture. I'd achieved some notoriety as well, which made my extended absence from my homeland somewhat easier to bear.

It appeared that the long-lasting primitive lifestyle I'd so carefully documented was about to be engulfed by back-pack tourism. I ought to have felt terribly guilty but somehow I couldn't bring myself to express more than a few minor qualms. The tribes had had their chance. They could easily have slung me in the cooking pot on the first night, no questions asked and no reprisals taken. Except they were mostly vegetarian and insectivorous. God keep me from ever having to spend another six months feasting on roots, berries and hard-shelled tree beetles!

Maybe I should have set up some sort of trust fund and worked with some concerned charity in order to preserve The Diggory's heritage.

In the meantime...

Her name was Gill. "With a 'Juh' not a 'Guh'. I don't breathe underwater, you know. I don't swim, actually."

There was, to be fair, nothing at all fishy about her. Much of the summer, though, with her clean fresh smell, blonde hair and bright blue eyes. I'd met her on each of my first three visits to *Des's 'Morte au Monde' Old Curio Shop* but we spoke profusely on the third visit, as if already established friends.

As we left together, I stated, "I'd just assumed you were family. Desmond's daughter, maybe."

She giggled. "That would make him a teenage father, the randy old coot! I'm thirty-five, you know."

"Never! There's not a line or grey fleck anywhere."

"And you're remarkably short-sighted. And, I would guess, a little younger than I. Is that going to be a problem?"

I stopped in the middle of the street. I realised I had my left foot deep within The Slot bordering Des's eastern side. My other foot remained on more common ground. Either way, I was still a full head taller than my companion.

"I'm hoping," I replied, "that most of my problems have now come to an abrupt, happy end."

She slapped my arm playfully. "You big bloody charmer!" she exclaimed.

"Keep your hand there," I requested.

We bought filled croissants and take-away coffee, sat with them on the traffic filled but still indomitably romantic Old Roman Bridge. She'd done a little bit of waitressing, nannying, even supply teaching. Currently, she was temping... and "whiling away the years till retirement." She was not spoken for.

"And you?" she enquired.

"I'm between girlfriends at present."

"Between? When are you expecting the next one to come along...? Oh no, don't tell me... if you get any smoother, I'll slide off you and into the river!"

I took several short taxi jaunts to significant nodes and junctures along The Slot's extent. I discovered that all the city's taxi drivers were mutes who communicated with their passengers by a combination of florid gestures and liquid display screens. It was the sort of equal opportunities stunt meant to endear Councillor Smalls to the inquisitive outside world. I couldn't help suspecting deeper motives in his employment policies. Certainly these cabbies possessed The Knowledge; deprived of speech, they were less likely to inadvertently spill their secrets.

"The thing is," Gill stated plainly, "people count their lives as beginning from The Slot Year Zero. The time before then is looked on without nostalgia or affection. Many citizens won't talk about it at all. Some will... but only under the influence of copious amounts of alcohol, close friendship or hard currency. Preferably all three."

"I see."

"No, Harry, I'm not sure you do. Your first act before I can even begin to help you must be to lose that awful accent! We welcome tourists and outsiders here... but we don't trust them with state secret information."

She was seated on the edge of my hotel bed, wearing one of my dark blue long-sleeved shirts, her smooth, pale legs a promise temporarily deferred.

"Let's sort out a few basics," she began. "Firstly the short 'u' sound..."

*

Gill knew someone who knew someone... so that I was able to secure a berth on a helicopter flight over the metropolis with a cowboy operation styling itself, *Fitzworth Airways – Entrepreneurs and Aviators.* I'd been airborne in jerkier buckets but not for a couple of years. I hefted my camcorder on my right shoulder and rigidly held a brown paper sick bag in my left hand.

From the air, the jagged scar left by the removal of the wall was far from regular and right-angled. The two old stone bridges conclusively formed continuations of The Slot as would the politically sensitive Hunger House Crossing currently under construction at the eastern bend of the river. Rumour had it that Councillor Smalls was cutting corners by re-using bricks from the old wall, although this had neither been officially confirmed or denied. Certainly there had been several well-documented superstitious ceremonies conducted prior to the commencement of foundation laying – another example of the population's mass phobia against bad karma?

My pilot seemed to have no such fears or inhibitions, however, swooping low and 'buzzing' the navvies who responded with cheerful catcalls and hand gestures. I hoped my heavy breakfast wouldn't make a similarly sudden descent.

Eventually, we banked high enough for me to attempt a long shot of The Slot's entire length. From distance, it resembled some ancient form of writing, an indecipherable hieroglyph vaguely Semitic or Arabic. I hoped to fax it home and run it through my computer, checking both for meaning and a definite measurement of its entire length, interruptions included.

Perhaps the well-to-do citizens were contained within an ancient blessing.

Perhaps it was a curse.

Some of my early suppositions had not been entirely correct, for it seemed that the majority of the citizens were not only accustomed to living within or around the compass of The Slot but, indeed, mostly celebrated its existence. It was a much sought after address, with consequent rent hikes for property bordering its twisted lengths. Certain junctures had become places of pilgrimage as if famous poets, pop stars or minor royalty were buried there. Multifarious bunches of redolent flowers would appear magically overnight and provide a blaze and a rush for eyes and nostrils for the subsequent two days or so until the tolerant city watch officers removed the fading, dehydrated blooms. On the surface, it was all so life-affirming and I began to wonder what it was within me that made me always seek out the dark side of situations. There were several incidents of neat piles of bricks, often up to hip height, being carefully arranged as a re-constituted barrier within the vacant Slot. Responsibility for these terrorist atrocities was claimed by the self-styled *Art Installers*. I never, to my knowledge, spoke directly with any members of this shady organisation but as I penetrated the facade of jollity promoted by Councillor Smalls and his lapdog Tourist Board, I became aware that many inhabitants were ambivalent at best about the new social order and the denial of whole chunks of the past.

Forgive the cod psychology, but, it seemed to me that at one and the same time people tried to embrace and enjoy the apparent benefits brought about by the wall's removal and yet a part of them wished also for the cast-iron certainties which would be signified and re-affirmed by its return.

"You knew where you were back then," one sozzled old fogey confessed over a schnapps and gin in a seedy bar called *The Blue Angle*.

These conflicting wishes were a paradoxical dialectic common to the mind-set of most modern European states. I recognised similarities with a debate over trolley buses back in my hometown. I was aware also of such rosy past versus glitzy present arguments occurring continually within my own mind. There was no clear solution.

That wouldn't stop me seeking one.

Gill had to go back to work. She wouldn't tell me where and what beyond, "Something in administration – yawn, yawn."

Confused but not overly worried by her reticence, I returned again to the quarter of The Slot close by *Des's 'Morte Au Monde' Curio Shop*. This time, however, I approached from the southern edge, passing through the dregs of the red light district with its washed-out daytime whores clustered sullenly around the TV lounges and Laundromats. The area also boasted several fringe theatres and cabaret bars. I was intrigued to read a poster for "A new musical version of *The Mousetrap*, starring Josephine the Singer: 'The finest, most distinctive voice to come out of the ghettos.'" I made a mental note to book a pair of tickets whilst I was in town.

"And how are you progressing with the jigsaw, Mr Wood?"

"To be honest, Monsieur Monde, I'm completely stuck. Are you sure the box and the pieces haven't become inextricably muddled?"

He scratched his bearded chin and smiled. "It's funny you should say that because I was going to suggest to you that you may need to discover one or two pieces beyond the box, so to speak. On completion, things may get very interesting or," and here his voice reduced to barely a whisper, "may even cease to be altogether!"

"That's as may be," I harrumphed. "I've come to talk about other things. There are questions I think you could answer."

"I see. Would you mind if we took a little walk? The...uh, air conditioning's not working properly today and we might be more comfortable outside."

There was and never had been any air conditioning within his stuffy junk shop. Outside in the busy market area, dodging the various scallywags and horse-drawn tourist carts from *Falada Enterprises*, he explained, "I can't always speak freely in my own shop. CCTV, you know. Installed by Councillor Smalls Senior. Even more of a tyrant than the current one in many ways."

"But isn't there also...?"

"Only at certain stretches. Now, Mr Wood – Harry – I have to ask you plainly – are you seeking to restore the old wall?"

"No, not consciously. Would it be so bad if I did?"

"You might not get out alive, but... Some people preferred life back then. And in any case, the wall wasn't as mythically oppressive as the Berlin Wall or The Great Wall of China. It was quite decorative, in fact. At most points it didn't even reach to eye level so you could easily see, or, indeed, climb over it. There were also countless attractively filigreed gates which, to my knowledge, were never locked. In my opinion, the city is more compartmentalised now than it ever was before."

"I see."

"I'm sure you do. All this rhetoric of freedom... such a state is, of course, more psychological than physical. Ah, look, the silhouette artists are out already. I'm sure your young lady would appreciate such a souvenir."

He left me then. I stood stock still whilst a fleet-fingered young man punched out the edges of a large piece of black card, leaving me with a life-size profile emphasising my prominent proboscis. I paid handsomely.

On the way back to the hotel, I paused briefly outside a traditional toy store. The window display was full of train sets, Lego and Duplo bricks and even kiddie jigsaws. I was reminded again of how many elements in our lives are incomplete until slotted together.

*

There was so much denial and refusal floating about. The bisecting river did nothing to carry the citizens' cares away and the ninety year gap in the museum exhibits was like a yawning chasm asking to be filled, or else threatening to collapse in upon itself. I wondered whether the populace had become fearful and reticent because they were waiting for the wall to suddenly fall back into place at any moment.

Alternatively, it occurred to me that maybe the wall hadn't ever actually been removed: it was simply being studiously ignored. Still there, but everyone indulged in the pretence of its non-existence. Me included.

The third alternative was that there never actually had been a wall... at least not yet. What I think of as past time is, in fact, in some strange Einsteinian way the city's future, or a premonition thereof. The Slot is in place and soon enough the full barrier will go up. By constant denial, the populace is perhaps successfully postponing that doom-laden day.

I wanted to make my own recording of the official opening of Hunger House River Crossing. I got as far as the early ice cream vans, hot dog stalls and shady blokes in leather jackets selling black market brickwork. Had I been unencumbered I would have detoured awhile to investigate this latter.

"You can't come in here with that camera, pal," said the burlier of the two uniformed security guards. His eyes were obscured behind mirror shades. His similarly attired comrade studiously flexed and cracked his dark brown knuckles.

"I'm a foreign journalist," I stated. "Here's my press pass."

"Not valid. Councillor Smalls' orders. Invited dignitaries and state TV only."

The finger athlete briefly ceased his exercises and added, "You'll have to go watch it on the box at home, like everybody else. Now push off!"

I was a little out of practice at guerrilla raids and unarmed combat; I took their unsolicited advice and retired to my hotel room. Every available station was covering the event, even the German porn channel. I settled down with a room service cappuccino and cup cake.

The production was the usual job: long shots of the preparations, snippet interviews with dignitaries, computer simulations detailing the history and construction of this post-modernist splendour. The commentator had that syrupy sycophancy generally reserved for royal occasions: "And there is Mrs Smalls, alongside her husband, looking resplendent in a three-quarter length brocade dress... how proud she must be and how proud we all are..." The glorious leader himself looked a touch well-padded around the midriff. Unless it was a bullet-proof vest. Not quite the universally popular figurehead he styled himself then -

I was jolted back to full attention as the camera panned over "the friends and family of our great Mayor" and its electronic eye briefly alighted on Gill! My jaw dropped straight to the plain brown carpet as she stepped forward and hugged the cretinous ogre, her bright eyes and teeth flashing as she exchanged inaudible amusing small talk with him.

"Duplicitous witch!" was the most printable of the epithets that poured from my mouth as I regained traction. I was appalled but horribly fascinated. I realised just what a sucker I'd been made into. Petty? Petit? French for... Small.

"Look where lechery leads you," I muttered.

I could watch no more. I went down to the almost deserted street. There were no taxis to be had anywhere. I decided to walk to Des's shop, hoping he wasn't also in on the deception. But I thought I might stop at one or two bars on the way and drown my sexual sorrows.

The waitress service at *Daisy Dietrich's* was as shambolic as most other places in the world but they had an extensive snack menu and Des's recommendation of the rather fizzy local brew proved potent enough.

"I'm sorry, I thought you knew," he said for the twenty-first time. "I thought you were being clever-clever; you know, double agent, hush hush and all that."

"Whose round is it?" I asked.

"I dunno, Harry, but we'd better steer clear of the fried egg sandwiches!"

This had become our unifying catchphrase for the evening, so much so that we both regularly repeated it in over-loud voices in the vague direction of the barmaid before collapsing into beer-fuelled guffaws. If there'd been more customers we'd have been asked to leave. If I'd gone easier on the booze I might have chanced my arm with the dark-haired lovely pulling the pints. Just as a rebound, of course. Just out of anger and a sense of betrayal...

Finally, my belly and bladder could take no more punishment and I bade a bear-hug goodnight to my shopkeeper chum. I used up a lot of small change trying to book a taxi but I must have been slurring my words like a butter-coated video tape because I failed to make myself understood. The night was cool but pleasantly dry and I felt confident of walking myself back to base, no problem. The occasional totter here, some uncomfortably wide sideways strides there... just the usual tipsy ride on Shanks' pony until I stumbled across a segment of The Slot I had not previously explored.

When I managed to clamber to my feet again, I had a not unpleasant flashback to my childhood recollection and there I was again, playing choo-choo trains along this narrow, almost purpose-built chasm. Was this where I wished to abide?

Eventually, I staggered back to my hotel and, after several attempts, managed to press the correct buttons for the lift and successfully slot the key into the lock. I opened a bottle of carbonated mineral water from the mini bar and slumped down on the bed. My right hand punched digits on the remote and the wall TV flickered into life.

What I saw almost shocked me back into sobriety. A black-bordered caption read, *New Bridge Tragedy – Full Report To Follow.* I waited an anxious minute, debating whether or not to change channels. At last, the bulletin board was replaced by a sombre newscaster. My still blurry brain couldn't concentrate on his every word but I recognised the tone well enough:

"It began as a day of celebration and civic achievement. It has ended as a day of grim tragedy. Unsturdy supports and a freak tidal wave are thought to have caused the almost immediate collapse of the Hunger House River Crossing. So far, police divers have recovered ten bodies from the stretch of water around Lime Dock Reach. Councillor Smalls has been treated for shock but is otherwise unharmed..."

Unharmed? Maybe he was physically safe, but politically...?

The Mayor was not my concern. I turned my left ear red-hot as I began a frantic series of phone calls to hospitals, news agencies and all-night undertakers; frequently interspersed with Gill's home number. Blanks all round. A good sign or bad? I tried again. And again. And then: a voice so soft that I thought I'd somehow activated an answering service.

"Hello, this is Gill Petty speaking."

"Gill? Gill! Is that you? Are you OK?"

"I'm alive and in one piece, Harry. I've been helping with the bridge casualties all night. I'm exhausted. Can it wait?"

It couldn't. Not really. I wanted it to be resolved now. But –

"Sure. Call me tomorrow. I'll be in my hotel room."

*

"How could you? Honestly, Gill, how could you?"

"Don't you understand, Harry? I was trying to protect you."

"Protect me? Keep me away from the truth, you mean."

"No, not exactly. I was guiding you towards what you could discover and keeping you away from sensitive areas."

"You mean you were in league with Smalls."

"I work for him, yes. But I ploughed my own furrow in this, Harry. He wanted you eliminated. Completely."

"That would have sparked a major international incident. At the very least."

"Nothing scares him, Harry. I know."

"Ten deaths in the river is going to finish him."

"No, it won't. He'll survive. He always does. He's much tougher than Uncle ever was."

"Uncle?"

"Councillor Smalls Senior. The man who removed the wall."

"Which makes you and the Mayor kissing cousins!"

"Oh, you're just impossible! I've tried to help you –"

"Help me? Deflect me, more like!"

"I've tried to help you. I've come to feel a great affection for you. Don't let your ego get too inflated, but you're the best shag I've had in a couple of years."

"So what? All this hasn't stopped you betraying me."

"Betraying you? I think, actually, you need to examine your own motives for being here. What exactly are you trying to achieve? Nobody wants the wall replaced even if it's just some stunt for a film or a pop concert. So what's in it for you, specifically?"

"I don't know. I'm just trying to get back to somewhere I was in the past."

"Really? When exactly, Harry? I'd certainly like to know."

"I'm not sure. Maybe when I was seventeen and full of the flush of youth: quick on the ball and popular with the nubile girls."

"Typical!"

"OK, maybe much earlier than that. Perhaps when I was six or seven and still just in touch with the magic, imaginary world of childhood. Possibly I want to return to the womb."

She snorted. "I'm not convinced by all this amniotic Eden stuff. I suggest you give it some further thought, Harry. I mean, I'm sure you love and honour your mother despite the break-up with your father, but would you genuinely want to be absorbed back into that? Come off it!"

I laughed and took hold of her hand for the first time in two days. "You're taking it all too literally, Gill," I told her. "I don't exactly want to return to that conjoined innocent state. The notion of a return to the womb is essentially an image rather than an actual desire: it's an expression of a yearning for comfort, safety and removal from the rat race and other responsibilities."

She squeezed my fingers. "And have you thought you might achieve all that here? In this city? With me?"

"It had crossed my mind, until..."

"Harry," she stated, pert and direct on the edge of the bed, "there's a little bit of my womb you might want to investigate."

"I don't know what you mean."

"Oh, I think you do. It's an image. And a desire."

If I were to stay in the city for a while, I would need my bank at home to release more funds into my travelling account. I phoned my secretary, Rosa, asking her to make the necessary arrangements. She had served my family for the majority of her seventy-odd years: cook, nursemaid, child-minder, chaperone, general office dogsbody... Her arthritic fingers were still nimble enough to cope with a little light admin in my absence.

"There's something else, young Mr Wood," she stated. "The Diggory Tribe send their ancestral regards. They want you to represent them in their application to become a United Nations protectorate. And they've sent you a gift."

Unreconstructed racist visions of poisoned darts and shrunken heads briefly flashed through my brain as I asked, "What sort of gift, Rosa?"

"It appears to be a hardwood box but I haven't been able to open it yet. There's lots of markings and match-stick sized grooves carved into it. Maybe it's some form of writing: an instruction or message. One of them must spring the lid though, surely?"

"Scan it for me, please, Rosa. Then fax the images through to the hotel. Thanks."

Grooves? Slots, more like. Maybe the friendly tribesmen would airmail a set of keys in the next post.

I flicked on the TV for a while. Councillor Smalls was face to camera with his *Am Ex* credit card in one hand. His sizeable donation was about to kick-start the Bridge Disaster Memorial Fund. I wondered idly whether my hotel ran a video facility. If I freeze-framed the Mayor's image for long enough, I could copy down his card number, phone a few facilities, leave him over-drawn and quartered...

I switched off the box. The Mayor's forced grin reminded me that Gill wouldn't be off work for an hour or so yet. I was looking forward to surprising her with flowers and theatre tickets outside her office.

I still had Des's large scale jigsaw puzzle left to finish. He'd suggested that some of the pieces might need to be discovered 'beyond the box'. Upon completion, Des had promised, "Things may get very interesting or may even cease to be altogether." Talk about salesmanship!

Unseen by security cameras – I hoped! – I'd played the part of an urban archaeologist and made a point of collecting likely looking debris from the nooks and crannies of The Slot. Once I'd used up all the cardboard cut-outs I'd started with, I turned my full attention to this detritus, looking for indentations, deckle edges, straight sides, rounded nodules and U-shaped slots...

The jigsaw picture was of a stone bridge over a nondescript river. Typical. The sweepings from the street proved surprisingly pliant. Once in place, I could no longer detect what was original and what was additional.

Finally, I had one more piece which would fit and complete the puzzle so obviously that, with a moment's trepidation, I arrested the movement of my hand. I waited. Oh well, this was it. I slotted it into place and -

Nothing happened. On closer inspection, I noticed that a piece in the opposite corner had popped out of place. Maybe it had expanded due to heat or water seepage; whatever, it resisted all efforts to make the jigsaw complete and pristine. My thousand-part masterpiece would always be slightly imperfect.

Just like everything else in this life.

I checked my watch, grabbed my jacket and went off to meet Gill for a night of romance and passion.

MURDOCH CELESTE

Trevor had lived at the flat for four days before anybody knocked on his door.

"Hello, I'm your local councillor and leader of Neighbourhood Patrol. You'll be interested in joining, of course?"

Trevor nodded without conscious direction. The visitor was somewhere between muscled and paunchy, tilted on the further end of the seesaw from the fulcrum of middle aged towards later years.

"You from London?" the guest continued.

"Yes, but not round here exactly."

"Thought as much. Name's Murdoch Celeste, but most people call me Murdoch 'cause, well, the surname's a bit effeminate."

"French, isn't it?"

"Nah, I don't 'ave nuffink to do with them ponces. You seen their toilets?"

Trevor remembered a Paris café with Susanne and had to admit that, on the latter issue only, Murdoch had a point. "I'm forgetting my manners," he muttered, "do you want to come in for a cup of tea or something?"

"Bit busy, son. So, what work do you do?"

"I'm in financial services. Yourself?"

"This and that. Actually, we're trying to get a local TV channel off the ground at the moment."

The walk home from the station, the view from the bedroom and a catty aside from the estate agent suddenly crystallised and brought enlightenment. "Oh, is that your house with the six dishes?" Trevor asked.

"Yeah, got it in one. Signed up for cable and webcasts, too. Don't know why I bother: it's all rubbish. Game shows and celebrity movie star wankers, but, you know... Anyway, we want to do a more local focus. Real stories for real people, like. Course, if you could see your way to sponsoring us or making a small donation..."

Trevor mentally rifled through his wallet and recent bank and credit card statements. He shook his head. "Sorry, mate, I'm flat broke what with the deposit on this flat."

Murdoch snake-smiled, "Yeah, well, another time maybe. Financial services, huh?" he added during departure.

*

But that night, Trevor dreamed that he was on a quiz show, something like *The Weakest Link* except offering three wrong answers equalled a trap door.

The Medusa turned her stony gaze upon him and he tried not to let the swivelling stone snakes distract his considered reply.

"When," she hissed, "was the Battle of Waterloo?"

He wanted to respond with, "Uh, 1815," but somehow it came out as, "I live to dream," and he felt himself falling, that down from a mountain moment when you know that impending impact with the ground means certain death…

He forced himself awake. It was already dawn and only twenty minutes ahead of his regular alarm. He rose and pulled back the curtain. In the cool early urban light he could see the side of Murdoch's flat and registered that one of the satellite dishes was pointing straight at his window. Receiving or transmitting? No, the latter suggestion was nonsense.

Trevor suffered a poor day at work, almost losing the important Kapok account through his distraction and inattentiveness. At four o'clock, with an extra two shots of filter coffee filling his pressured bladder, he saw the figures and customer details on his screen swirl into an image of himself under the fiery red lights of a TV studio, struggling to answer a hellishly difficult quiz question. Tired and troubled, he resisted Dave's offer of a beer on the way to the tube and instead snatched a kip as soon as he reached home. Paracetamol cleared his head a little and, gazing out of the back window, he realised that almost every household sported dishes and they were all pointing towards the closest transmitter or booster rather than the more fanciful sci-fi notion of the morning.

There was a pile of letters on the doormat. So far Susanne had failed to phone, text or email him; he clung to the romantic fancy that she might resort to an old-fashioned letter of reconciliation.

But it was all junk mail. Amazingly, several were already addressed to him by name rather than simply as *The Occupier*. Would he like a subscription to a gardening magazine even though he lived on the first floor? How about various home entertainment packages? In truth, after looking at a screen all day and spending much of the time wearing headphones when required to take a turn on the customer info line, Trevor was actually looking for some peace and quiet at home. A good book, a glass of wine, a hot shower.

When the bell rang at some time after ten he assumed it was just some kids messing about. Already in leisure bottoms and dressing gown, he grabbed his house keys and padded cautiously downstairs.

It was Murdoch.

"Did I wake you up or something? Listen, I forgot to tell you about little Kelly. She's a four year old who lives down the street and she needs a spinal op but she can't get it on the National Health, so we're clubbing together to send her to the U.S."

"There's a fiver in my jacket pocket, I think," Trevor answered. "Just hold on there." He hurried back upstairs, aware that Murdoch had waited a few seconds then begun puffing up the steps behind him. The councillor was strong-willed, pushy, if a little out of condition. This was something they neglected to tell you at the lettings office.

Still, Murdoch's heart seemed to be in the right place and money made the guy vanish, at least temporarily.

A domestic dish was designed to receive encoded sounds and images rather than *project* them. Therefore, bad dreams were due to work worries, blocked sinuses or a Dickensian piece of cheese turning acidic in the gut.

When Trevor accepted Murdoch's invitation to 'pop round' that evening, he recognised it as the opportunity to allay all irrational fears.

"This is my lovely wife, Maureen, the power behind the throne," his host suggested.

"And don't you forget it," the woman agreed, taking Trevor's coat and stepping out to the kitchen to boil a kettle.

Even to Trevor's untrained eyes, the décor and furnishings seemed dated. The shelves and windowsill were full of porcelain ornaments: cutesy woodland creatures and souvenirs from Spain and Paris that would struggle to fetch a decent price at a car boot sale. The house smelled of extinguished cigarettes and stale cooking. Maybe Murdoch, or more likely Maureen, could recommend a dry cleaners' for his jacket and his suit trousers.

"Now, where's my manners?" the lady of the house beamed. "Let me give you the grand tour."

Trevor put down his PG Tips – already sugared and not entirely to his taste – and followed his hostess up the stairs.

"This is the spare room for when our daughter Janine comes to stay, she's twenty-six this year; this is Murdoch's study – more of a junk room if you ask me, he really ought to tidy it; and this is the master bedroom."

Trevor realised this was the correct location for a reverse view of his own flat and lingered. Unsurprisingly, a wide-screen television dominated the area below the window. The headboard was pink and the duvet covering the double bed held more roses than Kew Gardens. There was a confusion of mirrors – wall-mounted, attached to wardrobe doors – and Trevor gained the impression that tuning in to *Coronation Street* or *Champions League* could be a little like being inside a kaleidoscope. Which screen to concentrate on: which was real and which reflection? Were Arsenal kicking left to right or right to left this half…?

"Is there a Mrs Trevor?" Maureen repeated.

"Ah, no… my girlfriend's busy working away at the moment. Germany, I think."

She offered him a maternal smile beneath the paint and peroxide. Her stone-laden fingers patted his left arm. "I won't pry," she promised. "My Janine's married but her feller leads her a dog's life. Perhaps… well, there's always another fish in the pond, or whatever the saying is."

They returned downstairs. The drink was mercifully cold and safe to ignore.

"Did I tell you I've started a local TV company?" Murdoch beamed. "The studio's a few streets away. We're doing a share option soon."

"I'm a bit stumped for cash right now," Trevor began, wondering if this was to become his regular mantra.

"Sure, everything's so expensive these days. Look at this package from Hamlets Telecom. They want twenty-nine ninety-nine a month for your basic satellite package. I can arrange a better deal for ten pounds all in – Sky Movie, Premier League, the lot. Are you interested?"

"Well… I could just get a Digibox."

"Mediocre choice. Seriously, Trev, give us your spare house keys and we'll run up a subsidiary cable tomorrow while you're at work. Go on, you won't regret it." Salt of the earth or busybodies with insidious claws? Murdoch turned towards Maureen and said, "What about we get a takeaway tonight, girl?" Then: "How about you, Trev, you eaten yet?"

"I think there's some quiche left in the fridge."

"Quiche! Come on, I'll show you the best chippy in town. My treat."

Despite the recent health scares, Trevor felt obliged to order a chicken burger he didn't really fancy. Murdoch ordered two large doner kebabs with chilli sauce. As he walked back down the road strewing bits of off-green lettuce behind him, he grumbled, "Shit, I've told Hamid a hundred and ten times: 'No salidd'."

*

There was a little time left to put on a load of washing, iron a shirt for the morning and check through his post. Oh, the exciting existence of the single urban male! There was a consumer questionnaire with a small sachet of filter coffee attached and the promise of a free gift – maybe a watch, a gold cigarette lighter or even a Florida holiday for two, worth £1500 – for all respondents. Putting some mid-tempo, not overly experimental jazz on the CD, Trevor began to fill bits in: "On a scale of one to seven do you consider yourself financially secure?"; "Are you likely within the next month to purchase any of these brands of malt whisky?"; "Which of these retroviral potions would you recommend to a partner for the treatment of sexually transmitted diseases?". The 'No', 'None' and 'Not Applicable' options were notable for their absence or some such eleven o'clock at night apparent paradox. Besides which, Trevor decided, there were already enough people and organisations who held a lot of personal information about him so why give them more ammunition? Even a sunshine state holiday wouldn't necessarily win Susanne back.

After a surprisingly peaceful sleep, he felt rested and comfortable, at last, in his new flat, enabling him to perform well at work the following day. When he arrived home in the evening, everything seemed much the same. There was a large brown envelope pushed through his door containing his spare house keys and a rather battered looking, second hand, remote control with no accompanying instructions. He tried out the more obvious buttons on his slightly rundown Panasonic. The programmes were all in English but didn't seem to correspond to the listings in his evening paper and he couldn't locate the button to bring up *Channel Ident*. There were a couple of game shows, a hyperactive shopping channel selling mountain bikes for knockdown prices, some sort of reality TV series set on a boat which he watched for a time, and a music programme with two personable singers, one black and one white, taking it in turns to rhythmically bemoan the 'global conspiracy and police brutality'. They were cool and lyrically ingenious but surrounded themselves with gyrating nubile girls exposing a lot of smooth buttock and even, occasionally, a glimpse of brown nipple so that Trevor got slightly distracted from their important social message.

He was about to switch off when he stumbled upon a talk show with minimum production value – three chairs and a plain light blue background – in which a bespectacled younger man was interviewing Murdoch Celeste, who was partway through saying, "Well, the future will see a complete merging of televisual communications."

"How so?"

"VR helmets are a complete dead end. The big computer companies have already developed and are refining mini TV / computer screens that click down in front of the eyes like sci-fi glasses. But the next stage is implants accompanied by receivers in the ear or just behind. You can stay in touch: never miss anything. Chat to the person next to you whilst keeping up with *Eastenders*. Straight into the brain, you see."

The signal faded and was eventually replaced with a caption *Murdoch Neighbourhood Television – The Final Solution in TV*. There followed a cartoon shot of angels rescuing a baby girl from what appeared to be a montage of broken hearts.

Trevor switched the monitor off. There was a strong moon tonight and a wind that brought sirens, caterwauling and revved engines. As he looked nervously out of his bedroom window, he expected to see that new dishes had sprouted like wild mushrooms on Murdoch's walls and roof. The immediate vista, however, was the same as before. He'd allowed himself to become unnecessarily paranoid. Didn't we all believe in free enterprise and the can-do entrepreneur these days, whichever party we voted for?

At last he heard from Susanne. Her message read, "Trevor, I don't think there's any point raking over old ground. We shd both move on. S." He wouldn't delete it just yet. It was a microcosmic affirmation of the changed mores of the early twenty-first century: he'd been dumped by text. At least she hadn't used many abbreviations.

There was also a missed call. Trevor dialled it.

"How's your new TV channels?" Murdoch asked.

"Not quite what I expected," Trevor replied cautiously.

"Teething troubles, that's all. What about I come round tomorrow and sort it out? I'm a dab hand at electronics."

"It's really no problem."

"No, I only want the best for you, Trev. Did you catch me on the box?"

"A little. Impressive speech. Look, I've got to get some shopping now."

He didn't recall passing his mobile details on to Murdoch but like a television or radio, one could always choose to turn the technology off and ignore it.

Later, queuing at the veg stall, a couple of young men in Burberry caps began talking to the Bangladeshi man in front of Trevor.

"Hey, Abdul, what you want with all them onions? You starting a hot dog stall?"

"Yeah, I bet you won't sell pork sausages, eh?"

Trevor watched and waited, wondering if this was good-natured teasing of a known neighbour or another depressing outburst of intolerance. The pair followed the hurrying Asian for a few steps then stopped suddenly and begin flicking used matches at each other in a desultory fashion.

Salt of the earth or sodium poisoning?

That night Trevor dreamed that he died and ascended to Heaven. There was a posse of angels trying to drag little Kelly the spinal op girl within the pearly gates and only Trevor could save her. But first he had to correctly answer Saint Peter's multiple choice questionnaire.

"Please answer on a scale of one to seven. You see a mugger steal an old lady's purse and you give chase with some bystanders. You catch him up and two of your companions begin giving him a right pasting. Would you join in, one to seven...?"

He had a headache bordering on a migraine come Sunday morning. The television had reverted to the usual five terrestrial channels. He briefly tuned into 'Political Week', which featured an interview with an environmental activist campaigning against further encroachment on a protected area of woodland in the West Country. The woman could have been Susanne's twin sister; the resemblance was so striking. He even compared her with the snaps saved on his SIM card. Next time someone was leafleting on behalf of Pals of the Planet, he would be more than casually interested.

After the item was wound up, the anchor couple in the studio began a catty conversation for the benefit of their perceived demographic:

"Did you see her dress? How last year!"

"No, last century!"

"And those sandals? If people like this want ordinary people in the street to listen to their quotes green message, they ought to start dressing for the real world not airy fairy land."

Trevor switched off. It appeared that a return to free range eggs on wholemeal toast and a little spiritual reflection was out of the question when there were American teenage soaps, Big Mac and fries, and fashion self-victimisation to while away the day of rest.

"God, I'm thinking like my grandfather!" he muttered.

As if on cue, the doorbell sounded and there was Murdoch Celeste with his black-framed glasses, broad shoulders and slightly simian air, looking like most people's scary uncle.

"You don't mind if I just fix those leads, do you, son? Hey, are all these books yours? You read 'em all? I ain't got time for reading myself. Rather watch a DVD. Is that filter coffee? Bit too expensive for me and too much mucking about."

"It's no difficulty."

"Hey, Trevor, I can get you a German porn channel if you want. No subtitles but who needs 'em, eh? And they broadcast all day."

"I'm at work all day, Murdoch."

"Well, let me know... Missus doesn't like me watching it but you're on your own here, know what I mean...? There, that should do the trick. It's puzzling coz it's all right on my one."

Trevor put down his mug and plate of biscuits, asked, "You mean I'm getting everything through your receiver?"

"Yeah, I thought you understood that. Lots of people are hooked up to me. What do you reckon on the game this afternoon? Draw?"

"Probably nil-nil."

"You're a funny bloke. See you later."

The sun promised a dry day even if the underlying temperature was still a little chilly. Trevor took a long stroll around the park. This well maintained expanse of green was one of the reasons he'd chosen this branch of the tube line rather than going out west. The flower beds were pristine, if you ignored the occasional crisp packet, but some of the grassed areas had yet to recover from the wear and tear caused by a music festival held in the east side of the park last month.

Back home, Trevor caught all the goals on the BBC news. He was experimenting with ringtones and flicking through his final photos of Susanne when the phone bleeped.

"You're not watching," Murdoch accused.

"No, I'm not. Is that a problem?"

"Well, after all the work I put in it seems a little ungrateful."

"I pick and choose; I don't have the TV on for background. Uh, the microwave's beeping, I've got to go."

Trevor sat a long time thinking about the not so fine mess he'd stumbled into. At eleven, he unplugged everything from the mains and went to bed.

*

It was a week of temple pain and eyestrain. Monday was exhausting, Tuesday was tiring and Wednesday brought the local free paper through the door. Amid the tales of muggings and ads for tanning parlours, there was a double page spread on the councillor turned programme controller.

"TV – broadcasts, webcasts, Ceefax, and so forth," Murdoch had responded, "TV was the greatest invention of the twentieth century and the thing no one should ever be without. I cannot understand anybody who isn't hooked up or logged on. Without it, you'll just be so out of touch. You won't be able to carry on a conversation with people on the bus or the tube; during your lunch break, the chat's going to seem like a foreign language; and you're generally going to be so ill informed as to endanger yourself and maybe become a hazard to others."

Trevor felt that it was all some sort of coded message or weird threat directed mainly against him, but he wasn't sure what to do about it apart from keep all his information technology disconnected. What if the bloke started phoning or emailing him at work, though?

His mental fortitude faltered somewhat during sleep as he was plagued by recurring dreams in which he again took part in a quiz show with ridiculously easy questions. The prize at the end involved a curtain being rapidly drawn back to reveal a host of gold and silver angels who whisked him up towards the heavens. As they ascended, he realised that some of the spirits had cameras for faces or sported sunglasses that turned into screens showing endless images of himself. Part of his mind said, "At least you're not falling." And then he started to fall... but woke well before he hit the ground. To his left, however, lay the crumpled carcass of Little Kelly, her corpse resting awkwardly upon an oversize cheque for several hundred thousand pounds.

In the morning, there was a large note pinned to his inner door – not even the block's shared entrance, but his inner door. It read, "Thanks for nothing!" in red script on cardboard.

Her hippie chick clothes and captivating perfume gave her away. He stepped up gently behind her and delicately tapped on her shoulder.

"Fancy seeing you here," Susanne smiled.

"How've you been? I've missed you."

"Sure you have, Trevor." She frowned, creating facial lines to dispel the myth of Galatea. "You don't look too good," she stated. "Bleary-eyed and – here, let me feel." Her fingers probed the skin of his forehead with surprising sensitivity for a heart-breaking witch. "If you keep working too hard, you'll give yourself a brain tumour," she concluded merrily.

"It's just worry about you," he whispered.

"You've got to move on, Trevor. Talking of which – here's my cab. See ya."

The imprint of her soft fingers faded rapidly on the way home, leaving behind only a permanently lingering cranial pain.

He was in so much discomfort at work that he could no longer concentrate on even a minimal level. With a promise to book a doctor's appointment, Trevor made his weary way home early in the afternoon. Two youths were waiting on the pavement outside his block's main door. "I'm gonna get mugged," he thought, "or forced to contribute to some fund for the Krays' grandchildren. Did the brothers even have children?"

As he reached them, the two delinquents began a street charade to block his path, speaking in catchphrases and MTV slang, most of which went over his head. After some sixty seconds, they took a little bow like true performers then proffered their baseball caps for largesse.

Except, "See what you're missing," the taller one said.

There was a small screen inside the hat. It was a staring glass eye, unblinking, certain to win the war of nerves and force him to switch back on.

Salt of the earth clogging and blocking the arteries.

Although he'd escaped relatively unscathed, the slight adrenaline rush left him cold and shivery. The flat felt like a suddenly foreign habitat. Trevor was sure Murdoch was watching him, maybe on one of a bank of screens like in the police CCTV control room. He threw a blanket over the TV, although he suspected Murdoch might have rigged up some sort of spy camera elsewhere in the flat during his several visits.

Trevor stayed awake much of the night, huddled in a duvet. He rose once to glance out of the window. He was sure he saw one of the satellite dishes move and that it wasn't mere fancy. As he pulled the curtain, it came loose and clattered down by his bare ankles. He rigged up a makeshift barrier with a shirt and an old jacket, returned to sleep for maybe an hour or two. He couldn't face work so called in sick. As he put the phone down, it rang again.

Murdoch, of course.

"Trev, I'm sorry you're feeling under the weather, old son. You're getting yourself worked up unnecessarily. It's just an entertainment system. Everybody wants it. I can do you a top of the range home cinema system half the list price."

"I don't want it," Trevor whispered, determined to stand up to the geezer, even from a position of being slumped on the sofa. "A previous neighbour had one and I had to listen to explosion films every night while my walls shook. You're so into good neighbourliness, Murdoch, how can you justify such intrusion?"

"Your neighbours don't bother 'cause they're watching an action film on their own system, idiot!"

"Look I can't spend the day on the phone, I've brought some work home that I've got to get on with so if you'll excuse me..."

"There's no point in making up stories –"

Trevor cut him off, thinking that he'd probably bugged the phone, too. At about one-thirty, he decided it was safe to make a dash to the shops for some nosh. He hoped he wouldn't meet any of the local posse at this time of day.

Back home, he noticed the blanket had fallen off the telly. He didn't bother picking it up – maybe some sort of static charge would continue to disturb it. At just after nine o'clock, he cracked and switched it on. Each channel was broadcasting the very same test transmission he'd seen previously, with Murdoch offering his Arthur C. Clarke style future technology predictions. Somewhat relieved, though not sure why, Trevor turned it off. He intended to make it to work tomorrow.

In his next dream, he was collected by the quiz show angels. They wore TV monitor sunglasses. Two removed theirs and revealed themselves to be Murdoch's truanting cronies from yesterday.

His dizzying headache had become a permanent fixture. The sun was streaming in through the uncurtained window: photons, UV rays and transmissions from the local Lucifer.

As he bent to wash his face in the basin, he was aware of a sudden new protuberance above his right temple. He couldn't see it in the dishonest mirror but to his unsteady fingers, it felt like some sort of receiver or mini dish.

"Feels like I'm turning into a Teletubby!" he groaned and wanted to laugh. But suddenly his eyes misted over and, blink as he might, the face in the mirror became Murdoch Celeste's.

He stumbled out of the bathroom. Where the calendar had hung by the wall mounted telephone, he now had a flat screen showing a selection of shopping channels. He could press the red, yellow, green or blue buttons and scroll through the menu for everything he might require to be delivered. Quality, convenience and value, without question.

The clock in the kitchen displayed the weather in case he felt like leaving the flat at any unlikely stage. His friends from the next street had been active in the lounge, too. There was now a ceiling panel to remind him of the appeal donation hotline number for little Kelly. Maybe he could spare another tenner or a score. The three main wall screens all offered *The Murdoch Gardening Half Hour*. It was nice to fantasise, even if he wouldn't be planting any seeds or pulling up weeds. He had to admit the residents' champion had done a really good job, although he detected the lovely Maureen's hand in the improved décor and overall layout of his home.

Grade your satisfaction from one for 'low' to seven for 'complete'.

He was glad they had kept the back wall clear because the sofa made a lovely, comfy place to lie and lap up all that was best in local home entertainment. Today and everyday.

Definitely seven.

NINE VIEWS OF THE LIGHT OF THE WORLD

1

In universal terms, light is a measure of distance. Heat loss is a measure of age. Space is an apparently expanding absence.

2

Time travel was invented in September 1848 when seven Englishmen formed a brotherhood to rewrite medieval history and give it a rosy, chivalrous glow it surely never possessed in reality. One of these so-called Pre-Raphaelites made a journey even further back, concerning himself with strictly Biblical subjects. Travelling to Palestine for added authenticity, William Holman Hunt tethered a symbolic scapegoat on the shores of the Dead Sea. Wilderness or not, today's animal rights activists would be up in arms.

3

Hunt's painting *The Light of the World* is symbolic of Jesus knocking on the door of the soul. He is crowned with thorns and barefoot but is wearing a richly embroidered royal cloak. The bright, lunar halo behind Christ's head is a lambent counterpoint to the light emanating from the loosely held lantern in The Saviour's left hand. His eyes have an imploring, doe-like quality. The picture itself is cut into the shape of a door. Let Him in.

4

The sun is the true light of the world: a coalescing cloud of waste matter from the Big Bang become a thermo-nuclear time bomb ultimately responsible for the maintenance and sustenance of all life on this, the most favoured of all its worlds. And He saw that it was good. Morning and evening, the first day.

5

In the art of pigment and pencil, size really is everything. Accustomed to student wall posters and the glossy sheen of modern reprographic techniques, seeing the 'real thing' can sometimes be a disappointment. Dali... Hokusai... your works are dwarfed by their replications. The swans have all become elephantine; Mount Fuji has been sold to a time-share holiday firm.

6

Still I remain enamoured of the Pre-Raphaelite conception of feminine beauty. I am in love with the russet maidens burning brown Autumn leaves and the drowned Shakespearean heroine only serves to inspire necr-Ophelia. Beyond all these, however, is the ubiquitous Jane Morris, the muse of the movement and mother of five children. The official line, which nobody nowadays swallows, is that she stayed faithful to her gifted husband Socialist William despite the attentions of a coterie of admirers. She remained Dante Gabriel Rossetti's subject even after relations were broken off. He casts her mythologically, attired in silks and flimsy cottons, blue-grey eyes ever serious, long wavy dark hair an extended halo. I have a black and white postcard which suggests she was less full-bodied than traditionally depicted. I prefer her my way.

The Radical Feminist Faction will admonish me for such thoughts. I should not speculate beyond the veil and the Doctor Marten boot. They will crucify me. At the very least I will be exiled from the community estate for forty days, returning barefoot and penniless with only a dim torch to light my way. Doe-eyed, I shall knock on the door of their conscience. Let me in, let me in.

7

What we think of as Victorianism should really be called Albertism. Before her marriage, the then princess was a partygoer accustomed to high jinks and late nights. In true Gothic manner, her husband's influence lingered on long after he had made a bed among the lilies. The Victorian obsession for dark rooms over-cluttered with furnishings can be seen as a physical manifestation of the blackly dressed queen closing down her personal parameters to a box full of memories.

In this context, William Holman Hunt, with his light of the world, his scapegoat and his errant hireling shepherd, seems the archetypal painter of his age. Never art for art's sake, his work is overloaded with symbolism: deliberate detail that reveals the true nature of the characters but only allows *that* one particular reading. It lacks the ambiguities usually associated with greatness.

As the street market trader would say, "Lovely engravings! Ten for half a crown! Every picture tells a story!"

8

Yesterday's provocative art is today's product placement. What once had the power to shock or inspire is now charged with the task of selling something other than itself. The crumbs from the wealthy patrons have been replaced by the drip-feed from the multi-nationals.

In Islam it is not permitted to represent the physical form of either God or the Prophet Muhammad. However, devotional art is the very foundation of Western civilisation. Our energies have long been focused on looking back, re-interpreting.

Our first evidence of Man/Woman The Artist is the cave paintings at Lascaux and other places which show people figuratively attempting to come to terms with both the objective world and their own inner feelings.

Even your friendly neighbourhood atheist with his technological crutches and his theoretical certainties is engaged in the process of looking back. The *COBE* spectrographs of the echoes of the Big Bang paradoxically reveal our insignificance and yet contend that we're smart enough to understand the how and why of what we're doing here.

Take me back to your first recollection. Let there be light.

9

I read in one of the Sunday supplements that dating agencies, evening classes and even Internet chat rooms were passé: the way to meet the woman of your dreams – educated, articulate, liberal, blah blah – was to frequent art galleries. Across the street from the Holman Gallery the Church notice-boards proclaimed in day-glo colours, 'Christ is the Light of the World' and 'Jesus Saves'. Beneath the latter some wag had added the graffiti, "But Rooney nets the rebound".

Sustained by visions of encountering a latter-day Jane Morris or Elizabeth Siddal, I took both guidebook and courage in hand as I lingered overlong by blobs and abstractions. The female visitors wore deliberate mismatches of primary coloured or pseudo-ethnic clothes, sported experimental hairstyles or suffered jewellery piercing in unusual parts of the face. Mistakenly, I made my few moves in the Special Exhibition Hall. Against a backdrop of monochrome, muscle-bound torsos lovingly photographed by an American gay rights activist I must have seemed a paltry specimen of manhood with my thinning hair, chain store tie and scuffed white trainers.

Reputedly Jane Morris stayed faithful to William despite the attentions of a coterie of admirers.

In the gift shop I purchased another two dozen postcards – Impressionists and Surrealists – to add to the hundreds already cluttering up the bottom of my wardrobe.

My only recent diary entry reads, "Everything is familiar. No painting has really moved anybody since Picasso's *Guernica*. Art is dead."

THE SHORT AND THE LONG OF IT

It had never been my intention to become part of a secret society. I just sort of fell into it as part of a romantic quest after the enigmatic Lola Preston. Which wasn't even her real name. Layer upon layer of see-through subterfuge.

"We simply can't keep excusing ourselves and blaming the Yadrill for everything that's gone wrong over the past five years," were the first words she ever said to me. Hardly Shakespeare or Christina Rossetti, I know, but at least she was treating me as an intellectual near-equal, which was rare faint praise since Queen Beatrice came to power.

Five and a half years, I muttered to myself but kept this unattractive strain of pedantry inaudible. Instead I offered, "You're so right: it's time we all grew up and took some responsibility."

She laughed, "Are you always this self-deprecating?"

"Meaning…? Oh, my height. I'm only six inches shorter than average, you know."

"And are there compensations elsewhere?" she twinkled.

"Let me buy you a drink and we can start the exploration," I answered.

I had ten crowns in my pocket. If I eked out my half of lager, I could treat her to two more glasses of Chianti. As long as she didn't want pepper crisps. Or a taxi home.

If I wanted to see her again then my best bet would be to spend Saturday night at the Pennywhistle Pictures and Poetry meeting. My emotions were torn as Juliet Brahms was giving a two-hour piano recital that same evening from Liberation Hall which would be broadcast live in its entirety on the Baroquephione. I was even twelfth on the ticket returns list to maybe attend the actual concert. Juliet had lately re-incorporated her early material such as "Stay Silent through the Years" back into her hypnotic set and now I was likely to miss it. However, Juliet was a distant star whereas lovely Lola Preston was at least close to my current sphere. Girlishly tall but full-bodied, sporting dark trousers and a floaty floral top, Lola was modern womanhood personified. Intelligent, independent and, I hoped, unencumbered.

I was thirty minutes early. A pensionable gentleman, even shorter than I am, made a fuss about unlocking the door and then cajoled me into putting my name down to read something from the floor. In truth, the only item which sprang to mind was a piece that had garnered a school prize many revolutions ago. I commenced a frantic mental rehearsal whilst the small hall gradually filled with young men sporting shocking haircuts and women of all ages wearing mismatched arrays of incongruous garments.

At last Lola arrived, long black locks coiled into a snake sculpture on the crown of her head – like a princess frequenting a nightclub – and star-shaped tears drawn in subtle make-up around her eyes. Enchanting. She leant over my seat to kiss me and her full breasts pushed the air out of my rib cage. Then she sat down next to a good-looking young man. His pernickety appearance offered the one crumb of hope – that he might be fastidiously gay – but the likelihood was that this was her proper boyfriend, my love rival, the consort and keyholder.

I had expected the art show to consist of tedious still lives of cut flowers and bowls of oranges; instead, the paintings were riotously abstract and vibrant, blocks and splodges literally dripping off the paper and filling the air with the smell of newly decorated municipal buildings. My best friend Dreyfus – tattooist, part-time graffiti villain, and all round Yadrill-sceptic – would have been well impressed.

Likewise, my assumptions were overturned during the poetry readings. I had a slew of soliloquies along the lines of, "This is a poem about my cat that died". I was glad to get my callow offering out of the way early doors because the more accomplished readers offered intense cogitation upon the true nature of the alien visitation and aching suggestions of aspirational access to alternate realities. Dreyfus would have called it a "head trip" and, as I sipped a rusty glass of red wine during the interval, I began to wish I'd approached the meeting on a full stomach.

"You don't have to stay for the second half," Lola whispered wetly in my ear. "It gets a little...political."

"I'd like to grab a bite to eat but it can wait. Are you staying?"

"Of course. I'm presenting a proposal for temporal transcendence."

"I'd love to hear it. Are there any crackers lurking nearby?"

I must have been well absorbed in the text on my suspicion machine even though the download seemed to have frozen partway through the word constellation. Certainly I wasn't aware of Dreyfus' approach until he plonked a glowing sphere next to my console.

"Whoa – hey, what'ya doing? Say, how are you, Dreyf? An' what's this?"

"Slow down, Hoff. This is the new executive toy – alien balls. Some sort of new plasto-metal alloy synthesised from the lining of the Yadrill spaceship."

"I thought you didn't believe in their visit?"

"I don't. This is probably the same material as Queen Bea's impenetrable knickers."

I let the blasphemy pass. Dreyfus looked smarter than usual: hair and beard trimmed to neat shortness and his fresh white shirt bearing a cryptic logo shaped like the ringed planet Saturn. I tossed the gift in my hand like a crafty spin bowler. It felt very finely grooved, like a worn-down phonodisc; it smelled of freshly minted copper.

"And don't worry, it won't interfere with the magnetics of your sus machine. Although it looks like you need to crank it again."

"What exactly are you doing in the office, Dreyfus? Security's been pretty tight lately."

"Oh, I've got a new day job. My, ah, artwork has always been nocturnal. So, too, the tattooing. People mostly want a rose saying, 'Mum" or an arrow on their arm proclaiming, "Walk This Way" after they've quaffed their fill of beer and mother's ruin. I'm running errands for these people now."

I took his card, squinted past the favourable stars and planets, and read aloud, "'Pluto's Paninis. Cappuccino at your Console'. You're selling coffee?"

"It's good commission. Don't laugh."

"I'm not, mate. I'd like a double espresso and a sticky bun. But what about all that stuff you wrote about Starbuck's sucking the lifeblood out of the working class?"

"Different persona, pal. Those curlicues nearly got me into a gallery long before that chancer Banksy."

"Nearly got you into the royal dungeon, more like. Anyway, will five crowns be enough? I'm parched."

"I dream of a world so different from ours.

    I draw its buildings scraping clouds.

    For just one moment I'm allowed

    This glimpse of Earth alternate."

I went to sit down again but Lola grabbed me in a bear hug. Although her arms rarely did more than carry a beaded handbag, she was surprisingly strong. Her firm nipples strained against the tight fabric of her blouse and their proximity excited me. But when I sat down again my thoughts and emotions were spinning.

Lola squeezed just my hand and thigh for the next five minutes whilst the other poets and philosophers said their stuff. Meanwhile, I struggled with the classic male two brains dilemma. My head brain told me that I was a fraud and I'd only written this doggerel to impress the ladies; my trouser brain told me that nobody would get badly hurt by my ingenuity and that in a few blissful hours I would be sharing a duvet with this full-bodied goddess.

Trouser brain found me at eleven o'clock blowing out the meeting hall candles then standing in the cold November air watching my breath coalesce into plumes whilst Lola argued with the taxi driver who didn't want to travel so far south this time of night. Initially, anyway. When Lola grabbed his horsewhip and tapped it intimidatingly against her firm thigh just the once, he meekly acquiesced.

We pulled the blinds in the carriage and commenced some lively horseplay. Arriving at her over-furnished apartment, I barely had time to register the Indian throws and the shelves of books with titles such as, "The Yadrill – People Just Like Us" before we were entwined on the shag pile.

Later, she brought me tea and toast with thick-cut marmalade. She switched on the baroquephone at a comfortable nocturnal volume. They were repeating Juliet Brahms' piano recital from a fortnight ago. Could life get any more blissful?

"You need to be gone by eight," Lola mumbled sheepishly. "I don't want a scene with Stephen."

Dreyfus wiped an exasperation of tasteless white froth off his upper lip and said, "So this Stephen is still on the scene because he's the scientific brain behind everything?"

"That's the long and short of it," I answered.

He snickered. "You really ought to stop using that idiom, Hoffman, you know." He finished his drink. "Seems to me," he continued, "that this Lola is not only manipulating your secret society but is playing you and Stephen for dupes. You need to stand up and be a man."

"Ha ha with your quips. Listen, Drey, can you come along to a meeting with me?"

"I don't do poetry."

"There's art as well."

"Hoffman, I don't buy this Yadrill story. Or the alternate world stuff. We've got one life to live in this material world. And I'm expected back on shift."

"Some mate you turned out to be," I muttered.

"Hey, come on, the coffee and cakes are free. All right, Hoff, I'll think it over. I'll leave a message on the walls. Look out for it."

Like cryptic spray can squiggles ever helped anybody!

It was the letter I'd been ignoring for ages. Now red-stamped and re-delivered.

"Your conscription is enclosed."

Previously, I had been too high up n the department to warrant a spell of royal service. Now my main hope was that I was not tall enough. I would practise slouching in my stockinged feet. They must be pretty desperate if they're trying to enlist wimps like me.

The letter spoke of the glorious defence Queen Beatrice's brave women and men would mount against the next Yadrill invasion. Whenever it came.

Sure, there had been a few casualties last time but that was surely due to mishap rather than malice. Why the sabre rattling?

"A distraction, like I said on the night we met," Lola affirmed. "All those plebs marching up and down with their 'anti' placards – they've got the wrong enemy."

"I may not be able to wriggle out of it this time."

"Become a conscientious objector."

"I would do if I could spell the term. And stay off their locatorscope for the next ten years."

"I'll see if I can pull a few strings, dear."

She ripped up the summons; burnt it on a candle, envelope and all.

We stumbled along the gangplank, awaiting the attention of the indolent cashiers controlling the Yadrill exhibition. There were twelve of us from The Secret Other World Society, so we could qualify for a group discount even though Lola had a season ticket and could simply waltz in and out whenever she chose to. My erstwhile rival, suave but sulky Stephen, stood at the back of our line scribbling cryptic formulae with a leaky fountain pen onto recycled cartridge paper.

At the entrance, we were all thoroughly frisked for the usual array of illegal religious icons, decorative weapons and imported cutlery. I registered Stephen's annoyance at having to temporarily relinquish a polished pair of alien balls. He kept all his writing equipment, however. Must have convinced then that he was a journalist.

It was a case of look, don't touch. Nothing interactive. Here's some sparkling Yadrill fabric behind a glass case. Here's what might have been a tool, weapon or communicator. Behind reinforced glass. And this next room features a cine film on an endless loop: The Amazon Wing of the Royal Guard rescues the crushed aliens; the visiting humanoids are formally introduced to the expectant court of Queen Beatrice. Requisite protocol carefully observed: look, don't touch.

I sneezed suddenly. One of the female guards had her pistol out and pointed in my direction in world record time. This world.

"Just a reaction to my perfume, ladies," Lola placated, and she was probably right. "Or maybe they never bother to dust properly," she whispered *sotto voce* to Caroline, the woman who wrote dense sonnets about breaking through, complete with Latin equations.

Outside, Lola switched into full maternal mode by adjusting my slightly rumpled clothes and giving me a swift peck on the cheek. As I longed to be wrapped up in her soft skin, once more I felt the urge to sneeze. This time I successfully suppressed it.

"Hoffman, my little lover," she crooned, "try not to draw attention to us like that again. Although the authorities will probably have us down as a right bunch of incompetents now. So, folks, what have we learned?"

"I've got tons of ideas," smirked Stephen. "If any of you would like to come back to the lab to help –"

"Get on with it on your own, Stephen. That's your role," Lola interrupted. "Now, my feeling is that the key may lie in the silver cape. We need someone small and supple to go in and filch it..."

I didn't need to be Galileo to know that the eyes of the Poetic Inquisition were all firmly fixed on *this* recently acquired satellite.

Dreyfus sat on my decaying sofa casually juggling one-handed with a trio of alien balls. Persistence of vision made his dexterity with the spheres give them the impression of a mobile pawnbroker's sign.

"Can you give that a rest, Dreyf? It's quite distracting."

He laughed. "I thought you were going to ask if I'd ever dropped one. A ball, that is."

"And?"

"They don't break, Not under household conditions, anyway. But that doesn't make them extraterrestrial. The whole Yadrill business is a sham. I knew one of the actors in the cine clip. Man, he was hot; I wish he'd get back in touch."

"It's unlike you to pine."

"Fair enough. What's this Stephen like?"

"A geek. Hetero. Although if you could convert him, that would leave me a clear path to Lola."

"Just how many favours do you need, Hoff?"

"A whole new world full. Did you read that book I filched?"

He sipped at his lager, wrinkled his nose, brushed fluff off his trousers and finally answered, "Sure. The art was primitive and as for the poetry… Coleridge on cheap medication."

"They sincerely believe in an alternate Earth. One with a more advanced technology than ours. It's the place the Yadrill came from."

"But why are you helping them? It can't just be because of your feelings for this strapping woman Lola."

"It can. For the last time, will you help me with the distraction?"

"So you can steal the golden fleece? Why not? Lead the Queen's bitches a merry dance. There's just one problem."

I sighed, "What's that?"

"Didn't you hear the forecast on the baroquephone? Torrential rain for tomorrow evening. Like a bloody monsoon."

"So you're a fair weather revolutionary now?"

"Just saying. Guerrilla graffiti is not much use if it runs in the street."

I wanted to reply, "You can say that again," but kept my own counsel.

"The Yadrill were not alien."

- "The Yadrill were so human."

"The Yadrill are not to blame."

- "Their Earth is not the same."

"To reach across to their city -"

- "Is the purpose of our society."

It was call and response time at the Battersea Doggerel Home but I was spared the task of learning all the shout backs. Oh no, they had better plans for me. Stripped right down to goose-pimpled bare flesh, I was now about to be body-oiled for greater sinuousness and flexibility. As Lola's fingers helped massage the ointment into my pores, I had just the briefest concern that I might get aroused and embarrass myself in front of this arty crowd. I needn't have worried. As it turned out, such public exposure made me shrink into myself like a shy flower dragged away from the sheltering wall. In all my years of shortness, I had never felt so vertically challenged.

They armed with a geologist's hammer. Instead of allowing me a pair of lycra pants in which to tuck the tool, that know-it-all Stephen strapped it to my wrist with an over-tight twist of rope.

He gave me a brotherly wink and announced, "Show time!"

Dreyfus was the star performer. Even though he initially made fun of my unclothed state.

"You know I've never fancied you, Hoff," he quipped. "This just confirms it."

Even though the rainfall – more dreary Peak District precipitation than Indian monsoon – was not conducive to the unsubtle art of street tagging. Even though he was not and never would be part of our gang.

"Hey, you bovines!" he called to the guards. "Take a look at what I've written about your precious Queen Bea."

He drew two of the Amazons away immediately, their pistols cocked, their heels clattering on the cobbles. Stephen and Lola, with their chloroform hankies, saw off the other two armed harpies without a noticeable struggle. Which left me the bone-crunching, breath-expelling task of squeezing through the access hatch next to the tradesmen's door. Have I built up everybody else's role in this escapade and downplayed my own part? Maybe so. I was less focused on the prize and more concerned with painful abrasions and the ever-present possibility of emasculating myself should I get my angles of entry and exit somewhat awry.

I wanted to linger in this museum of mendacity, this actualised sleight of hand designed to distract the downtrodden populace from the true nature of the Yadrill's intrusion and to mask the ruling clique's subtle oppression by distraction. I was a true convert now – so much so that I was mentally quoting a recent speech by my love rival Stephen. Which was slightly worrying.

Four hefty taps – one in each corner – brought the protective glass tinkling and tickling around my toes. I had expected the cloak to weigh half a ton, like a swathe of chain mail, but the fabric was light and almost fluid to the touch. I pondered briefly whether to nick some other artefacts but told myself to stay on task. Just this once if never again.

I had one moment of blood-freezing panic. As Caroline took the Yadrill cape out of my hands and I was still on the other side of the hatch, I wondered if I was going to be callously sacrificed to the cause. But then Lola's strong arms were reaching up and helping me to clamber back through into the cold drizzle of freedom.

"Oh, look at the state of you, dear," she whispered.

"Be my nursemaid," I whimpered.

"It will be my pleasure, boy," she beamed.

We were only partway through the ritual when the first stone hit the window. I say 'we' but I still felt like something of an outsider as battery and wire wizard Stephen pulled all the strings. My long-term prospects didn't look good; now my short-term security might also be under threat.

Stephen had rigged up some sort of glass bowl which played pictures of the Yadrill's version of Earth. A baroquephone with a cine system pretty much covers it.

"That's not a parallel Earth," I warned, "that's clearly the future. Look at those balloon backpacks and hovering carriages. And everywhere is made of metal."

"The Yadrill are more technologically advanced," he agreed. "I can't wait to meet them."

"But you haven't even got any weapons. You'll be creamed."

Lola stroked my arm, gave me her most luscious smile. "We come in peace," she stated, without the slightest trace of irony.

Caroline was mid-soliloquy but could hardly be heard above the shouts from outside and the unmelodic pounding at the downstairs door.

"Skip the poetry!" my darling declared.

"But, Lola, this is a moment in history –"

"We'll all be history if we hang around much longer. Quick, Stephen, increase the power."

The cloak that I'd lost so many skin cells in acquiring had been spread ceremoniously over the floor and Stephen had placed an alien ball at each corner, with a couple extra along the longer sides for good measure. He gave each of these a violent twist and, whereas before they had glowed golden and hummed slightly, now they took on the incandescence of an exploding star and screamed like an unattended steam whistle on a train at Queen Mary Junction.

"Everybody aboard the transmat!" Lola shouted. "Squeeze up, folks. Hoffman – are you coming?"

Her be-ringed fingers reached out to me across space… time… dimensions undiscovered until now. I hesitated.

Then suddenly they were no longer there. The shocked air rushed to fill the vacuum. There were fists on my back and cries of, "Kill the Yadrill-loving scum!" from the stairwell.

But the sudden implosion ripped away walls, floors, ceiling and my attackers and I tumbled into a bruised, confused, brick and plaster dusted rabble on the street below. I tried to cough the debris out of my throat but it hurt my chest even to breathe. My left leg felt like it had taken a whack from an Amazon's night-stick.

There were soldiers and mobile apothecaries everywhere. I could smell blood and gunpowder. The cacophony of groans and shouted orders seemed strangely distant.

It was too much effort to keep my eyelids apart.

Surrender.

I fell in love with my nurse.

Prostrate and slightly delirious in a charity hospital bed, what red-blooded man would do otherwise? She had an unusually small face with a squashed nose at its centre but her eyes were kind, her fingers clever and her long red curls reminded me achingly of the unattainable Juliet Brahms.

Juliet herself, so Dreyfus informed me, had lately been arrested for putting subliminal pro-Yadrill rhythms in her wayward piano concertos. It sounded like a stitch-up to me. Juliet was far too a-wayward with the fairies to involve herself in anti-government propaganda.

Which left my erstwhile best friend and his sometimes consort, the immaculately dressed deputy commissioner of police. I opened my eyes a fraction once during visiting hours and caught the pair of them bickering like an old married couple.

Could I ever forgive Dreyfus his lust-fuelled betrayal? I wanted to shout recriminations and lob a barrel load of guilt at his handsome visage; but most days I could hardly stay awake more than a minute at a time. Yet when I drifted into slumber, I kept catapulting back into the fateful moment when that pocket of reality stretched, expanded and then collapsed like a bursting balloon and Lola and her cohorts left this mortal plane.

The scent from the flowers by the bed reminded me of her. The nurse's gentle touch reminded me of her. The murmur of voices in the next corridor or down on the street reminded me of her florid poetry.

"Sleep, Hoffman," Sister Juliet whispered.

"The Royal Court has agreed not to press charges," Dreyfus chirped from the chair next to the bed.

"A new life awaits us in the world beyond," sang a soft, feminine voice in my memory.

One morning I woke up and felt completely better. Aware that this was probably an overdose of adrenaline and would soon pass, I rose slowly and carefully. I used the chamber pot beneath my cot, placing a dry towel over the steaming yellow liquid. I dressed quickly. For a moment, I thought of asking my guardian angel of the past two weeks to accompany me on this escape. Maybe it went against some sort of professional code; maybe I'd call for her later.

It was evening but there was no one about in this part of the city.

Suddenly the sky lit up with fire and explosion like it was a royal celebration. I thought I made out an airborne craft, saucer shaped, hurtling towards the Palace of Justice. Cannon fire burst out from the battlements and the UFO – hostile aggressor or Lola-inspired rescuer – exploded into a million pieces.

The flash must have confused my senses. All around the walls were covered in fresh graffiti, all welcoming the liberating Yadrill army and signed at each corner with Dreyfus' tag. Who was double-crossing whom?

Debris was falling from the shattered sky. Having not walked for a fortnight, I was finding it difficult to gain adequate shelter.

"Hey, Shorty, over here!"

For a moment I truly believed it was the piano siren herself, the goddess Juliet Brahms, calling me to a recessed doorway. But no, it was my nurse, Georgina as I now must call her, rescuing me yet again.

I hobbled into her arms. She couldn't have been more than four foot ten. But strong... capable.

"You and me have a bright future," she promised and, on cue, mile distant missiles detonated in the sky behind us. It was clearly a good omen. "Just promise to give up the poetry," she added.

"Must I?"

"All right, for a while at least. Come on, let's go to your apartment. It's the far side from the fighting and we can listen to reports on the baroquephone."

"I've got coffee… wine… gin."

She winked. "Nice one, big boy. Now you're talking my language."

A shell exploded maybe half a mile distant. "We need to move before the conflict reaches us."

"Sure thing, big boy. Any port in a firestorm."

Given the extreme circumstances, I let that last remark pass. From an open window ahead of us, jaunty harpsichord music played. The explosions to our rear might signify a personal new dawn or terminal sunset. Only time would tell.

SLOW PLANES

For just how long could they keep this glorified, stylised, over-sized metal arrowhead in the air travelling at so few miles per hour? Gary looked at his watch again. He'd set it to Glasgow Independent Time when the plane had taken off, which was three or four hours ago depending on one's punctiliousness, but he was sure they hadn't even hovered over Coventry yet. This new top secret aviation fuel promised to make the airways of the Common Isles the most carbon negative in the world but journey times had seemingly regressed to those of the Victorian era. The extra hours had allowed the botoxed stewardesses to indulge in a camper-than-thou safety semaphore before offering a seemingly endless selection of gloop, stodge and tepidity whilst the latest CGI thriller flickered mutely on the seat screens.

Gary tried to cop a look out of the too small window. His neighbour fidgeted crossly, curling his arm over his laptop to obscure the data.

"What you doing, pal?" the guy grunted.

"Just looking to see where we are," Gary answered.

"Some town full of immigrants, just like any other. It's a concrete Sahara down there. Refugees in white tents as far as the eye can see. Satisfied?"

Gary nodded, tight-lipped, and reconnected his headphones. The brawny hero was battling with a giant, winged Cyclops. Blood from previous victims dripped copiously from the monster's maw; its foot-long talons slashed perilously close to our champion's flesh. He was armed only with a long, sharpened stick like a lead-free pencil.

"Stab the beast in its eye," Gary sub-vocalised. It was so obvious a child could have guessed it.

The plane inched forwards through the softly resistant air. Five minutes later, the monster was dead and our victorious avatar stumbled on to his next task.

Sheila had been off the scene for several days now, not even answering her mobile. It was maybe an hour's walk to her flat. The route was reasonably pleasant during daylight – if you ignored the noise from low-flying aircraft, the stench from perennially blocked drains and the shifty looks from petrol snatch groups. Give the convincing appearance of being a pedestrian and these latter wouldn't bother you, went received wisdom. Apart from the usual ingrained habits of dissing your clothes, posture or manhood as you strolled past; spitting carefully just behind your back as you retreated.

Today there was a gaggle of them leaning casually against the semi-abandoned vehicles lining the road – hunters posing for cameraphone photos with their close to extinction trophies. Further up the street, around about number 52 or 54, another urban menace prowled around the bin bags and containers: a hit squad from the council's recycling team clocking up beer cans, coke bottles, discarded copies of *The Sun* and *The Advertiser* and the meagre fortnightly landfill allowance. Sheila lived at number 46. Maybe she was off their itinerary on this occasion.

The curtains were all drawn and the downstairs flat emanated an air of unoccupancy. I rang the buzzer three times with lengthy pauses in between. As if I had willed her back into existence, the door opened a crack and there she was with bed hair and a ragged dressing gown that had once been red towelling but had now faded to the land of grey and pink.

"Oh hi, Stuart," she mumbled. "Have you come to collect your robe?" she added, casually fingering the butter-stained left sleeve.

"I'd forgotten about it till now," I answered.

Within, she still had shelves of kitsch ceramics and stacks of magazines around the chairs – fashion, antiques, a dash of poetry.

"Why the Blitz spirit?" I asked, gesturing at the windows.

"Keeps the heat in, apparently. Some days I have to choose between starvation and hypothermia. I lost that temp job and Ebay's been unnaturally quiet."

I perched on the less dusty end of her beige sofa. "My mother used to put up clingfilm in the colder months to stop the draughts. I could get you some at the corner shop and have it all up with sellotape in about an hour."

"That's kind, Stu. Maybe later. Or another time."

She'd unfastened her dressing gown. Underneath she was wearing good quality cotton pyjamas sporting an elephant motif. The loose jiggle of her breasts against the fabric suggested she was not wearing a bra. I catalogued the information with the casual insouciance of a previous lover. She saw through me with knowing female intelligence.

"Didn't take you long to think about sex," she muttered.

"I was concerned for your welfare. Honest."

"Sure, that's a good line. The doctor does his rounds."

As she pulled down the grey bottoms, I caught a sweaty smell like she hadn't washed down there for two or three days. Or weeks. Then she was skipping to the bedroom, her white arse a ship of hope on troubled seas.

It was at least as good as old times and, lying wrapped together afterwards under a thin duvet, I couldn't see any reason or need to explain any of this to Kelly. Her space in my life remained uncertain for now and for the foreseeable.

"I'm out of tea and coffee," Sheila whispered. "It's so depressing. There's a little bit of fruit squash in the fridge."

"Water will be fine."

"Listen, Stu, if you want a wash, can you boil a kettle? It's more cost effective."

"Are you sending me on my way?"

"Not at all. Just being Miss Housewife. Hey, when I'm freezing here at midnight I'll have this half hour of warmth to dwell on at least."

The annoying guy in the window seat was squirming a little and surreptitiously rubbing his belly beneath his striped shirt as if placating a fidgety child below the fabric. He looked like he needed to either vomit or defecate but couldn't decide which.

"If you'll excuse me, pal," he muttered, rising and pushing insistently against Gary's knees.

Yet he couldn't have been in that much of a rush as he stopped to chat up the airhostess lurking angelically halfway down the aisle. She had lustrous chestnut hair, neatly tied back but promising a loose waterfall once in the sanctuary of her hotel room. She had beautiful skin – evident when she was serving the entrée or pointing out the emergency exits. Gary couldn't understand why she felt the need to plaster so much terracotta foundation onto her cheeks and forehead. But he was wasting valuable viewing time by dreaming of Shahanara…

The ground seemed unusually close, the roofs of the occasional skyscrapers rather proximate. And beyond the wingtip, other aircraft, not at all distant, as if this were a passenger plane version of the Red Arrows, and yet not entirely in formation but slightly haphazard, like traffic on an aerial equivalent of the M25

"Hey, that's my seat and I paid good cash for it!"

"Oh, right, sorry."

Shuffling out then in again, Gary wondered whether he should say something about what he'd observed, maybe seek some clarification from his erstwhile companion who seemed to have, if not the complete answers, then at least a handle on everything.

The man pulled the shade down to obscure the porthole as if closing the lid on potential discussion.

"Airline food," he muttered. "It makes the Macs and PFC seem like haute cuisine. It's all reconstituted, see? And you know from what."

Gary wasn't one hundred percent certain and put the man's moaning down to gastric hyperbolism.

I didn't really want to see Kelly, at least not just yet. I'd spun her some line about us needing to talk things over but that was just so that she would buzz me through the downstairs intercom. My real aim was the communal chute on the back staircase. No sorting out plastics and glass for recyclables, no CCTV checking who was dumping what. Just shove it down the gaping maw and let it land in somebody else's in-tray. I'd come with pockets full of crap as well as two carrier bags. Sweet release.

"Is it really cold enough for a coat?" Kelly asked.

I shrugged, waited while she made herself thin and let me enter her ninth floor eyrie. A forlorn pair of socks, suspiciously masculine and navy, perched on a wooden drier adrift in a sea of yesterday clutter. Two or three trips to the chute would have done the trick. I'd have been happy to help.

"I've only got instant," she announced, topping up a mug of warm brown liquid with an overabundance of semi-skimmed.

"At least your lift's working today," I offered.

"Yeah. Bang goes the fitness regime. Although I'm not sleeping so maybe I'll burn up the calories that way. Too much aircraft noise. They seem to be flying so low these days they'll soon be using the Central Line."

"Won't improve the service any."

She smiled, stroked my hand that wasn't holding on to the milky coffee. "I'm seeing someone," she whispered. "It's all happened rather quickly and it was certainly unplanned. We – I'd like to see how things work out."

"That's OK," I answered. Then, squeezing her soft white fingers and smooth turquoise rings, I added, "Kel, I'm delighted for you. It's good that you're moving on."

She laughed, wrinkling her nose stud. "I thought you might have, you know, come round… wanting a get back together shag or something."

"Are you offering?"

"Same old Stuart," she smiled. "My hands are quite clean and nimble," she added.

Later she told me how worried she was about her dear old granddad who'd retired to the seaside for some peace and quiet but whose pride and joy vintage car had been vandalised for its couple of litres of unleaded.

"Let's hope one of the suckers lit up a cigarette straightaway and burnt his mouth off," I stated.

"That's just an urban myth," she replied.

I shrugged. "Might have been true the first time."

Sometimes I felt that somebody had cracked London open like an eggshell and then pushed half into the future and half into the past. Did all major world cities suffer this temporal mishmash? The fuel shortages had provoked a return to the horse-drawn days and many of the high streets smelt of carelessly packed cargoes of wet flour and not yet ripe carrots, but mostly of sticky, cloying manure. However, the skies were crowded with planes running on the new green fuel *Super-Slo*. And that's how they went: super slow, like winged dodgems against a cerulean canvas.

John had offered me some work cash in hand if I took a little package from A to B. It wasn't drugs, he assured me. Probably gems or maybe the jewelled crystals of the third millennium world: computer chips. The trick to traversing the streets was to look as uninteresting as possible and if you were *carrying* then to give the impression that anything you held was as worthless as dry rusk or yesterday's change of undergarments. Don't look at the petrol gangs with their siphons and their skeleton keys and their gasoline grins.

If I could get this over with early maybe I could splash the cash at the local Turkish off licence and treat Sheila to more food and drink than she'd had in a week. Kelly need never know. Or care.

Somebody grabbed my arm and I spun around, one fist at the ready and the other holding my prize.

"Hey, guy, you're littering," said the first of the men in the yellow safety jackets.

"Like how? Where?" I asked.

His pal produced a wad of chewing gum half in its waxed wrapper.

I shook my head at the council clowns. "Go ahead, boys, try and lay this nonsense on me in front of a peeler. How about I do a breath test?"

The taller of the two looked like he fancied furthering the row and would maybe smear me with spearmint to justify his accusation. But he saw my eyes clocking his ID badge and slowly backed off, placing his fake evidence back inside his jacket for another victim later in the day.

"Fucking shitter litter picker!" I shouted. But not till I was fifty yards away.

The cliché beautiful airhostess Shahanara was back with another tray full of insipid drinks, gratis.

"They do it just to keep you in your seat," the guy to Gary's right remarked; but he took a tumbler nonetheless.

Gary offered his best smile to the heavenly trolley dolly, hoping his earnest sincerity might impress where the Armani-suited businessman had fallen short. Like he'd had much success down on terra firma…

"Yeah, I heard that story, too," he told his companion after a brief gulp and a puzzled pause. "But surely air rage is a thing of the past."

"That's what they'd like you to believe. Just you wait and see."

Honestly, this bloke and his conspiracies! And still hogging the window seat. Gary finished his drink, some sort of juice made from tropical fruit torn too soon off the vine but left too long in a tepid storeroom. It was horrible. But free.

The cameras at the rail station only faced one way and local residents had sussed out a segment of the alley and the overgrown embankment where they could dump unwanted furniture without being observed. The dilapidated three-person sofa was now stained and rain sodden, smelling of wet fabric and rusty springs. So who would be the third person on the settee? A child? A dog? A live-in lover?

Kelly had split with her new feller and gone back to her mother's for an indefinite stay. Maybe she was on Facebook or Past Life right now chasing down a host of childhood sweethearts. And I was back around Sheila's poverty-stricken neighbourhood yet again. I hoped she didn't feel I was exploiting her in any way by turning up unexpectedly like a low-rent guardian angel with a bag full of booze and groceries. Someone had to help counter her agoraphobia.

A train rattled past, headed for somewhere beyond the thinly stretched green belt. Even its moderate speed was so much faster than the flock of planes cluttering up the sky and appearing to hardly move from minute to minute.

Someone had humorously written to the BBC to complain that their suntan this summer was dappled with aircraft outlines.

There was activity at the north end of her street: black clothed security guards sporting stun guns and surrounding a pair of flashily dressed youths presumably caught sticky-handed and guilty-mouthed siphoning petrol from a parked car. The plastic tubing and jerrycan at their feet offered conclusive circumstantial evidence.

I walked on, doing that urban survival thing of pretending not to look.

But I had to look when I reached Sheila's house because there was a uniformed policeman standing sentry outside her door.

"It's quite simple," said the guy next to Gary, "the technology's existed for ages. It's just a matter of applying it."

Gary was still unsure of the man's name. He'd seen a 'T' and full stop on the seat plan. Terry? Trevor? He settled on 'Thomas'.

"I remember studying flight at school," Gary answered. "All about birds and the curvature of the wing and dipping a flap at the back."

"Ah yes, the aileron. The Wright Brothers used it when they flew for a quarter of a minute. We've come a long way in not much more than a hundred years. The breakthrough has been to achieve a forward thrust versus air resistance balance. We've permanently opened the air corridor."

He was busily scribbling biro diagrams on a thick white linen napkin. Gary squinted at the design revelation.

"I'm not one hundred percent sure of what you're driving at," he admitted.

Thomas shook his mousy haired head, muttered something about the modern education system before replying at normal volume: "Endless flight. Once you get started you can just keep on going forever, though at a fairly minimal speed."

Gary's jaw dropped. He reached for his seat buckle but Thomas restrained him. Where was the brown paper bag to calm his panic? He took several rapid breaths, more aware than ever of the food smells and slight tang of sweat and *closeness* of the re-circulated air enclosed by the fuselage.

"You mean," he croaked, "that we're never going to land?"

Thomas smiled like a lizard before it jets out its tongue. "Quite likely," he replied. "Get used to it."

*

I walked past once. I walked past twice. On the third occasion the copper called me over with a cheery, "Can I help you, sir?" straight out of a heart-warming 1950s Brit flick.

"I've come to see Sheila but…"

"Ah, that would be Miss Fielding," he answered.

I refrained from making the age-old playground quip about dropped catches and nodded silently before asking, "Is she in some sort of trouble?"

"You could say that, sir," he replied, already operating his shoulder walkie-talkie with a clean-shaven jab of his granite chin.

Almost before I could blink, I was being handcuffed like a litter lout and manhandled into the back seat of a high-speed saloon car stinking of sweat and Red Bull. All my protestations were met with a blanket refusal to divulge any further information until we reached the station.

Where they freed my wrists and set me down in Interview Room B. I didn't even rate first class treatment for my apparent misdemeanour. Still, this was the half-hour for the good cop to do his turn and I was offered coffee and wafer biscuits before the detective sergeant came to the point.

"I'm sorry to be the one to break it to you, Mr Nelson," he began, "but your friend Sheila passed away three days ago."

"Sheila, dead! No way. She was a bit anorexic but – no, it can't be!"

"Neighbourhood Patrol alerted us, sir. I accompanied the bod – er, Ms Fielding to the morgue."

My drink tasted like ditch water and the biscuits were as stale and hard as an Egyptian cartouche. I didn't want to shed any tears in front of a big, burly DS but they would come out sooner or later.

When I could speak sensibly, I asked, "Am I being held on suspicion of something? You know, that old euphemism of helping you with your enquiries."

"This is not a murder investigation, Mr Nelson; the autopsy was clear on that point. But we have a few loose ends we want to tie up before we close the case."

"What am I supposed to tell you? We'd known each other on and off since secondary school. I'm devastated."

It was hard to believe that a man with such a full face and healthy moustache could produce such a thin, snake-like smile. "We're fairly sure the lady's death was due to natural causes," he stated, "but the examination revealed some intoxicants in her stomach and, uh, we believe she'd had sexual intercourse quite recently." I didn't like the direction this was going. He continued, "So that we can complete that area of our enquiries, we'd like you to produce a semen sample for analysis."

"What? Can't you just take a fingerprint or something? You've just told me that my oldest friend is dead and now you want me to go off to the toilet and wank into a bucket like some randy farmhand."

"A test tube will be quite sufficient, Mr Nelson, but yes, that's the short and long of it. If you co-operate, we could get the stuff down to the lab and have this part of the investigation wrapped up in an hour or so. Look, I've got some magazines in the bottom drawer to, uh, get you stimulated."

He handed me a pristine copy of *Big Muthas* along with a slightly dog-eared *Asian Babes*. I tried not to think of Sheila at all, going instead for mental pictures of women in uniform – airhostesses, nurses and a fleeting glimpse of a pretty WPC out on the front desk, unpinning her blonde hair and stepping out of her black skirt to leave only flat shoes and a bullet proof vest…

I was seen by the same detective sergeant as before. Unusual consistency for British bureaucracy. He had a printed sheet of A4 in front of him with my name and mugshot at the top. I thought I'd kept my nose clean all these years and told him as much.

"Let's start from the most recent, Mr Nelson. You are confirmed as the last person to have sex with Miss Fielding. But that's not what killed her."

"And I'm supposed to find that reassuring," I muttered.

Just how was I expected to feel, really? Bereft, heartbroken and angry. Or guilty – like my fumbling affections had somehow been the last straw for Sheila's frail constitution? If I ever got back with Kelly – an 'if' about as tall as Canary Wharf – there was going to be some extraordinary explaining to do.

"– Recycling bin failed closure notice," the DS continued and I realised he'd been listing my apparent crimes and misdemeanours for a full minute now.

"Hey, that was thrown out on appeal!" I interrupted.

"Good for you, Mr Nelson." He wrinkled his nose and added, "We've also found a DNA match for the McKechnie art and gold bullion theft."

I performed a quick mental calculation then said, "I don't see how that can be. I was nine at the time. I wouldn't have made much of a getaway driver and the kickback from a sawn-off shotgun would've knocked me over."

"Hmm, yes, it was a nasty case. Still unsolved. Are you sure you weren't involved?"

"I never missed a day at junior school. Why don't you check *those* records?"

He tapped a code into his PC, scribbled down a response with a chewed-up biro. My mistake, I recognised now, was to have ever co-operated in the first place. Once they got you inside the Bureau, they'd never fully let you go again. Even now, some forensic fink was probably trying to tie me in with the Kennedy Assassination, the Whitechapel Murders and the mystery of the *Marie Celeste*.

Now he was Mr Nice Cop all over again. "We're still holding on to Miss Fielding's effects as evidence," he stated, "but I'm sure that will all be dealt with in a couple more days. Why don't you see about arranging a funeral service? I'll put you in touch with one of our social workers."

In truth, I had little input with the arrangements for Sheila's funeral. Her parents – estranged from my late friend for at least the latter third of her cruelly truncated life – turned up and took everything in hand. Despite the exorbitant cost, they arranged for a plot burial and, although I wasn't required to say any words aloud, I did get to crumble some soil onto her casket and mumble a stifled prayer to a God I'd long since stopped believing in. If only Ma and Pa had been so generous and attentive during Sheila's breathing days then just maybe…

Two undertakers stood guard with night-sticks by the trio of limousines. Grave robbing was a crime confined to antiquity but a street gang seeking to siphon off petrol from an unattended hearse was a very real danger within the memorial gardens. I turned my attention back to the ministrations of the vicar, his dull words mostly inaudible against the roaring aeroplane engines cruising sluggishly overhead. I'd thought I might break down with a few tears or else rail angrily at the uncaring world; instead, I simply felt numb. And a little cold in my best dark jacket beneath the occluded sky.

Back at the reception in a room above *The Faded Rose*, I sipped sweet sherry and palmed a couple of ham sandwiches into my coat pocket for the hungry evening.

"So, Stuart," asked Sheila's mother in a fake accent modelled on Radio Four but undercut by alcohol, "what are your immediate plans?"

"I'm making deliv – I'm a pedestrian courier," I replied. "Still working most days despite the recession." I didn't add that I was due back at the local nick in twenty-four hours to answer bizarre and incriminating questions about a blag that had happened whilst I was doing a school project on floating and sinking, little knowing that science would seemingly deem one guilty by genetics so many years down the line. I remembered my manners enough to ask: "And you?"

"We think we need a holiday after all this," she stated airily.

"But by boat," her husband added. "Certainly not jet."

This seemed to amuse them greatly. Grief does funny things to people. I mentally rehearsed my acceptable alibi: I wasn't there, I was playing 'On it' with Saj and Rahim, I was too young to see over the steering wheel or squeeze the trigger.

I drained my glass, bade goodbye. Adieu. Farewell Sheila and Co.

Gary remembered reading something about the perils of long-haul flights. What was it called? Deep vein thrombosis. Caused by sitting still for long periods. Could you get it on a little hop to Scotland? Was that a twinge of cramp in his right leg or something more serious?

There was a short queue for the conveniences.

"Get used to it," smiled the guy in front.

"What's beyond that curtain?" Gary asked. "First class?"

"Callisthenics. A small but neatly equipped gym. You're going to want to get your name down for it."

"Not really my scene. I prefer a bit of tennis or Frisbee."

"You'll sign up soon if only to take your mind off the recycled food. Oh, here we go, my turn on the dumpster."

At last Kelly was answering the phone to me. But she sounded far away: obviously, that was the case physically; but the emotional distance felt almost Siberian.

"I'm surprised they let you out on bail," she muttered. "That McKechnie case sounds horrible even by modern standards."

"It had nothing to do with me, I was a kid at primary school at the time. The DNA link is down to their messy procedures."

"They still printed your name and picture in the papers. I gave them that Ballard FC one where you had a little starter beard. And they got your name wrong, Stuart. They spelt it '*ew*'."

"I told you they were idiots. Nicking people who haven't closed their bin lids properly while the real villains and murderers –" I broke off, feigned a cough, looked at the handset – wondering if it was new enough to have GPS tracking. I'd contacted Kelly because I was a mess of grief, confusion, guilt and anxiety but I'd neglected to consider that she might have worries and issues of her own. And that the law would be bugging her phone to build up a convincing case against me for a crime that happened whilst I was practising my seven times table and writing a story where I pretended to be Prince Caspian.

"Stuart? Stuart, have you finished your rant? I've got stuff to do. Listen, you should probably go away for a few days and maybe we'll talk later."

Sure – in an interrogation room or during visiting hours at Belmarsh. Then again, maybe she was being genuine. I said goodbye but didn't cut the call. I waited in vain for the spy click to follow. Instead, my mobile simply buzzed and flashed a low battery warning.

During his absence, the stewardess had refilled Gary's plastic cup with another indeterminate tasteless beverage. He squeezed awkwardly back into his seat. Thomas was checking the window: other aircraft processing in synchronised formation, buildings barely skimmed by the plane's stately progress.

"I thought all your endless flight talk was a wind-up but now I feel like I've been left out of the loop," Gary stated.

"Meaning what?"

"Everybody else seems convinced and quite comfortable with the notion of us being in flight for days, weeks, maybe longer. I just thought it was a cheap ride to Glasgow. How are they doing it, Tom? Why are they doing it?"

"Because they can. Because it's cheaper to keep a whole bunch of people aboard a slow jet eating their own recycled shit than trying to house them down on the ground."

"Won't we run out of consumables? Like air?"

"They'll just open the vent. Settle down and get used to it. At least we're not as badly off as the cyclone and famine refugees."

"Honestly, though, Thomas, are we ever going to land?"

"Maybe one day when the Eco-Fuel runs out. In the meantime: tuck in, watch the movie, get some kip. Dream of Shahanara. Her shift finishes soon and she's got her own cabin. I've got an invite."

Lord of the air or exiled from the earth? Free from worldly care, as joyous as the birds; or banished from home and held away by an invisible force field?

The rage was building inside him, looking for an outlet. But that would be the worst possible course of action and might lead to summary justice without appeal or parachute.

Close your eyes. Relax. Drink the recycled piss coffee. Push away thoughts of rebellion. For now.

The clerk looked at the details on my credit card, checked the information against a hit list on his screen, handed the piece of plastic back to me with a smile. Stuart, not Stewart. APR was up around 35% but when you can't stump up the cash…

"Slo-Jet to Glasgow it is then, sir. Departs eighteen-fifteen."

"Good. Just how slow are these planes?"

"Estimated flight time varies between thirty-six and forty-eight hours."

"What? A Victorian horse and carriage would be quicker."

"They may be coming back, sir. Ecologically quite sound. Now, if you'll excuse me…"

I had enough change in my pocket to purchase a watery cappuccino from the vending machine. The drink was lukewarm. I treated myself to extra sprinkles and went to stand by the observation window. The take-off runway was continuously busy and away to the north stretched a sky train of slow aeroplanes, moving gracefully and without apparent effort like an aerial armada of giant metal swans.

Some errant kid bored by waiting crashed into my right leg and I spilt a little brown liquid on my sleeve. His laissez faire parents were nowhere to be seen. I dried myself off and went to stare at the information boards. I'd heard the public bar rumour that these aircraft were a humane way of thinning the burgeoning community on the ground, creating a mini self-sustaining ecosystem to keep the population surplus airborne and out of our hair. The fact that every arrival was indicated as being 'Delayed until further notice' gave some credence to this water cooler conspiracy theory.

Boarding Gate 13… Passengers please make their way to… Final call for…

There was my flight. Better pick up my grip bag, dump the cardboard cup and make my way to my planned departure.

WAR HAVEN

War throws up its own mythologies. Christmas Day football in the Somme, trenches for goalposts. Angels and fiery crosses in the sky above the battlefield. A labyrinth of white painted stucco walls, a grinning terrorist or freedom fighter at every corner. Shoot or shake hands? Duck or destroy? You have point two of a second to decide, starting… NOW!

In the midst of war we wish for peace. There is a legendary place whispered about after dark and mentioned in despatches from many a cold, eye-rubbing sentry duty. There are several extant speculations regarding its true nature.

For Tony, it was 'That bar that never closes.' Lights, laughter, a warm yeasty smell pulling us towards it.

Steve-O's vision was of a 'twenty-four hour twilit whorehouse.' Soft flesh, smooth silk, sputtering candles and the ancient rhythm of irregular suction.

Ambrose, good old Ambrose, pictured the secret oasis as a 'health spa' and this received plenty of raucous laughs and slaps on the back.

My expectations were already pretty well formed but I kept my own counsel.

Private Daniel Fanthorpe, your first and foremost duty in this conflict is to survive.

For your second choice, you have selected the task of discovering the fabled war haven.

Soldier, go seek!

Sergeant Scruton fixed us all with a steely look and stated, "I want no more talk about a war haven. We're here to fight, for as long and as much as it takes. The world's going to hell in a handbasket and we're the only saps who might pull the boat round so it rights itself. The only real haven is death and although we don't fear it, we ain't gonna seek it."

Yes, sir; but as soon as he'd gone we were back to the bored barrack-room when's the next battle conjecture.

Ambrose whistled. "Hey, that man can sure mix his metaphors," he commented.

"Should've been a preacher," I suggested.

"But he's right in a way," Steve-O countered. "I mean, everywhere you go there's conflict. War's like blood – it keeps dripping endlessly and filters into every gap, flooding it."

"Man, you shoulda been the preacher!" Ambrose responded.

I smiled but I wasn't so sure of his simile. Where I came from was a peaceful seaside town in which even Friday and Saturday nights passed without major incidents. So what was I doing here?

I remembered my father taking me to the memorial stone in St Ann's churchyard and being fascinated that so many men sought to influence the inimical world beyond our safe streets and houses. And here I was following in his size ten footsteps.

Maybe that "You have to go away in order to come back and find the old home town" cliché was true. But who really buys that?

Perhaps I wanted too much to emulate my late father. Though I grew taller and easily achieved better school results, I could never quite replicate his straight arrow military bearing. I remained in awe of him even when things turned bitter between my two parents, even when the tobacco addiction and the sour spirits brought his days to an early conclusion. You still salute a general even when he's out of his head on painkillers in some rundown NHS hospital.

Father could be a little rambling at times; other days he'd tease and joke with me in that typically masculine way which always left me pondering what was honesty and what was fakery. In his later days, he spent much of his time on a sun lounger, surrounded by cigarette butts and clutching a TV listings magazine like a shield against advancing mortality. He'd once enjoyed a fruitful five years playing the London FTSE and ensuring Mother would receive a decent divorce settlement. Now his main occupation seemed to be deciding whether to watch a film, chat show or obscure sports round up as an alternative to nicotine exacerbated insomnia. And reminiscences, always dredged-up memories, mostly of boyhood crushes and an enigmatic string of conquests from his soldier days. Was he testing my loyalty to my mother in some warped way? If only I could trust their validity.

"This woman, Danny, I was besotted with her. This was before your Ma got her claws into me. But where it all happened, now that's a more difficult question."

"I don't understand, Dad."

"Have you ever gone scouting in the woods and found a beautiful clearing or a brilliant place for a den? So you go home and tell your friends about it but you can never find the spot again."

"I thought you hadn't bothered to read my school prize story!"

"Of course I did, son, just didn't want to be too effusive with the praise. You've read *Alice in Wonderland*, I take it."

"Kids' stuff!"

"Not at all. Still, that's another discussion. Alice was a real girl, you know. But she never found the rabbit hole again. There are… special places only a privileged few ever get to."

"Like heaven?"

He smiled through his moustache. "I was thinking more of Camelot. Avalon. Shangri-La. There are people, too, that you meet once and spend your whole span trying to rediscover."

"And… this woman was like that? You've been chasing her or seeking her all these years?"

He tapped his head. "Only in here, son. I guess I got too lazy for anything else. No real harm done, eh?"

A quick-fire burst of sordid though half-formed images of a neighbour's daughter who went to the Catholic Girls' School briefly filled my mind and made my gangly legs wobble even in a seated position. I nodded silent assent. Sons aping fathers all the way back to Adam; or all the way back to the apes…

"Hey, Danny, be a good lad and fetch us a brew, eh?"

They issued us with new combat zone maps today. I don't know why they bother. Sketchy details in the bottom left corner and blank white spaces everywhere else. My forebears used to worry about going into No Man's Land; despite the advances in surveillance techniques and killing technology, this crack battalion of modern fighting men seems destined for Nowheresville.

It only added to the after-hours rumour and conjecture. Even the typically bellicose sergeant admitted that intelligence and front-line support ought to have done a little better.

For once I couldn't remain purse-lipped. "I don't get it, Sarge. Are we supposed to despatch the enemy or fill in the gaps on these poxy maps?"

"Yeah," Ambrose added, "what are the top brass keeping from us? Radiation? Contamination? Is this some sort of experimental zone?"

He tensed but wouldn't be drawn. Finally melting a little under our combined gaze, he offered, "Gentlemen, it is not our role to understand or perceive the whole picture. Security, you know. Which reminds me, the colonel is worried for your health and sanity. He's heard reports that the enemy has some new chemical, which may induce strange dreams. You're to take this tablet to prevent incapacitating delusions."

Later, Ambrose twisted the pill in his large brown hand and pondered, "Probably won't do anything for you. Just chalk or something."

"Nah, it's good gear, this," Steve-O declared, ostentatiously washing his down with a slug of blended whisky. "My brother gets them – he's on a psychiatric ward."

I used the general laughter to slip mine past my ear lobe and down my collar. It was a soldier's duty to stay alert and fully aware at all times.

I'd warmed to Ambrose more than anybody else in my platoon. Blessed with the physique of a semi-pro boxer, he was a comforting, bear-like presence in a dugout or when crammed shoulder to shoulder behind a temporary barricade. He could be a bit intense at times, though, within his frequent references to biblical geography. Or, as he liked to put it, "We're trespassing in holy places."

"Holy hell-holes, more like," I answered. "Anyway, Armageddon's biblical, so where does that leave us?"

He smiled. "You're quite a scholar, Danny, for a lowly private. Where's your church?"

"I… don't worship formally," I replied. I wondered if he'd caught me instinctively touching my head and heart.

"You ought to," he continued. "Gives everything a greater meaning. That's important. But this –" He held the latest issue order paper aloft. "People have lived here for millennia. You'd think HQ would have a mountain of data to bombard us with, not this half-baked, half-empty nonsense."

Steve-O stirred in the far corner of the tent. "They say the Garden of Eden was somewhere around these parts," he offered. "Same site as several other mythical heavens on earth. All in the mind, if you ask me."

I watched the wave of anger ripple across Ambrose's face. Composed again, he stated, "There's only the one true paradise to be regained, my friend. Fighting won't take us there, though."

"So why enlist?" I asked him.

"Maybe for the fighting *alone*. It's just one step along a rocky path."

Steve-O propped himself up on an unsteady elbow. "Are you two evangelists going to leave off saving the world until morning? Some of us want to get some kip before Judgement Day, you know."

"That's fair enough," Ambrose answered. "You certainly won't be getting much rest from the avenging angels."

I tensed but he was grinning and already settling down in his sleeping bag.

I dreamt of flaming crosses, winged statues coming to life, fig trees and world encircling serpents. Then an all-pervasive white light. Whose name was bone-aching morning.

I lost track of how far I wandered. And for how long. Scurrying like a rodent to escape the confusion of smoke and shells, I let my legs carry me further and further from the relevant action and well into the countryside designated blank on our combat maps. The largely featureless, arid scrubland was occasionally broken by the odd copse, each of which I approached with as much stealth and suspicion as my fatigued body and mind could muster. Still I saw no one and no sign either of recent human habitation.

The blanket grey sky offered no help to my broken inner compass and I veered more towards AWOL than MIA. The sweat of flight had long dried onto the inside of my uniform and although it wasn't a cold day, I felt alternately fevered and chilled.

Gradually the landscape revealed lusher touches of green interspersed with flashes of yellow and red. Untrammelled grass tickled my ankles; unexpected beds of delicate blooms made me detour to avoid crushing their texture and just discernible fragrance. I shifted the weight of my pack, held my gun more loosely – first in one hand then the other. Here were some trees, fuller developed than previously, thicker trunked and heavier canopied. Now, more flowers half-familiar from the temperate climate of home. A slight incline, then down again into a gentle hollow. To my left were rows of staked peas and carefully tilled square patches of soil erupting with vegetable leaves.

Someone lived here! In the middle of this wilderness: an oasis, a haven…

This was the delusion I'd been warned about. At any moment a picturesque little cottage would materialise and my deep fugue would be complete.

"You must be tired," she said. "Come inside, I've been waiting for you."

*

"I've just got word from home. My next door neighbour's signed up for the other side."

"There's a bad apple in every barrel, Dan."

"The thing is, he's not a bad apple at all. He's not a religious extremist or political activist or anything other than your ordinary, regular guy."

"Maybe you only know the, uh, surface. There's lots goes on behind the curtains."

"Sure, but… I just feel there's all this side-taking and enforced enmity. Smaller and smaller cliques. We'll be fighting soon because that group of guys wears a different aftershave. The world's unravelling, Ambrose."

But tonight it's quiet and peaceful with only our voices and a few nocturnal insects bothering the desert stillness. Maybe we are close to the haven. Just on the edge, even…

"Get some kip, man, or you'll be shooting at your own side tomorrow. The Battle of Body Odour? You crack me up, guy."

"You must rest."

"I can't. I've got to report back for duty."

"You're in no fit state."

"I'll be the judge of that. Besides, what on earth are you doing here? This is a declared unsafe zone."

"It's safe enough for me."

"Ignorance never prevented bullets or bombs. I'm sorry, that sounded harsh. I just don't wish you any harm. Come back with me, I'm sure my CO can arrange safe passage."

"I know more about your manly conflicts than you give me credit for. Besides, you're not going anywhere."

"Meaning?"

"Take a look at your left leg, just below your hip."

I realise that much of my lower half has felt numb for some time. I roll down the light cotton sheet. She's made an able job of applying a field dressing and left the rest of me naked from the waist down. I'm not at all embarrassed but modestly replace the coverlet after a few seconds.

Her soft white hands are stroking my crew cut and my cheeks. "My poor brave soldier boy," she mutters. Then: "You must be hungry."

"Starving," I smile. "How ever did you guess?"

This is the strangest place. I never see, hear or smell gunfire, missiles, explosions or debris. Most days there is barely a breeze… and this only carries the tang of ripening fruit trees or the scent of damp flowers after the light nocturnal rain. We are – apparently – surrounded on all sides by rolling hills, generally fallow fields and non-threatening trees.

Phaedra – "Call me Faye, don't burden me with so much Greek mythology baggage" – keeps a few farm and domestic animals after a laissez faire fashion. I've yet to compile an accurate inventory and, still unsteady and a long way from sprightly, I've yet to explore the full limits of her domain.

From the east window I can see her fetching water from the stream. It may seem cool and pure but untreated liquids are always dangerous, often fatal. Still, we'll be drinking it at dinner this evening.

I want to believe this is the mythical haven. A bubble of redemption… or a cruel delusion? I take another sip. Maybe this is the only real action and I'm being offered drops of comfort before I expire on the battlefield; or perhaps I'm hooked up to an intravenous drip in some god-forsaken third world casualty unit. This is the long fugue prefiguring and preceding death. I hope I see the white tunnel soon.

Who knows what's real and what's illusion in this capsule? Faye's daylight skin is that alabaster cliché in its whiteness and perfection but as her nightdress rides up under the drowsy moonlight I see strange shadows and movements upon the epidermal surface as if the scenes of a great drama are being projected upon it. But by whom and from where?

Sleepless, I rise and head for the room of secrets. It's locked, as ever. One night she'll forget; one night I'll be within. It wasn't just Eve and Pandora who brought disaster down upon mankind by their inquisitiveness. All you scientists, thinkers and rationalists – stand and take a bow. And then duck low to avoid the bullets, bats and infections.

In the morning I hang around the kitchen, getting in her way as she prepares bread and a sponge cake to celebrate… nothing in particular. Our diet is largely vegetarian and homegrown but she's not milling her own flour so where is she purchasing it from? The fridge freezer, the electric lights, the surveillance equipment that is so indicative of the modern age – but who laid the hidden power cables and how does she pay the bills? Of course, I should ask her outright but her standard response – born of care and kindness – is to place a soft, stopping finger on my parched lips.

I check on the chickens, laze through the olive grove and wonder idly whether we could both ride Samuel the donkey to town for new supplies this afternoon.

I believe I'm now close to the limit of her demesne. Not that the horizon suggests much beyond a somewhat featureless, undulating, dry landscape framed by a watercolour sky.

I notice evidence of recent digging some few yards off. I still habitually carry a Swiss army knife and hope it's up to the investigative work required. So I'm very soon scraping and scrabbling and when the blade snaps I'm reduced to bare hands like a desperate archaeologist in the Valley of the Kings or a deranged pirate with a stolen map of Treasure Island.

At last I uncover a silk scarf Faye wore on my second night in this haven. Concealed within its folds is my army issue wristwatch, believed lost on manoeuvres weeks ago. It's definitely mine – there's a strip of red tape on the back reminding of the time differential for Greenwich and it's in my handwriting.

And they're buried together here as a containing spell. Entwining us together for my protection and our shared future.

Do I dare disturb the bubble universe?

I can hear her calling to come eat, drink, live off the milk and honey of this wonderland. So I restore order… for now.

I banged fists with Ambrose and wished him luck. "Action at last," he grinned. Below his surface level of smiling gentle giant I discerned the blood lust of a Herculean warrior or an Old Testament prophet. He would survive in any age.

"Take care, you guys," Steve-o advised. "My dad used to say the afterlife always arrives just when you're not expecting it."

"And on that cheery note!" I responded.

"Gentlemen," Sergeant Scruton harrumphed. "Stay aware and stay alive today. Let's go give the enemy hell. And remember I'm right behind you."

Sure, I thought, about five miles or so back in the safety tent.

Once more into the breach with blood and sinew... and blood... and blood...

The days pass slowly and dreamily here. Even the grey skies wait patiently until the sleeping hours before delivering their rounds of soft wet bullets in an irregular fusillade against the cottage roof. Faye breathes gently beside me. One night, I carefully disentangle her smooth arms and tiptoe down to the small back room where she'd set up all her monitoring and surveillance equipment. Just this once, it's open. I gaze somewhat uncomprehendingly at the images and bright text statistics for maybe an hour before I feel her warm hands on my shoulders and she guides me back to bed. The chatter of the wide world seems unreal and irrelevant to me here. As the sun rises again over the backyard and the chickens scratch and cluck I pray again to a god I don't truly believe in: Let this bubble last, keep us safe together.

In the tired morning, she says "Well, you've seen it all now, it's not much to keep us safe but it does. And it's lasted through the generations, with the occasional technological improvement."

I close my eyes and picture her clad in animal skins, Diana the Huntress on a hillside or in the branches of a tall tree, maintaining watch, keeping the conflicts of mere mortal men at bay.

She brushes stray hair away from her face, wipes her eyes with a delicate hand, mutters, "Why is there so little good in the world today? This farm, this smallholding used to be bigger, once it covered much of the world. My sisters, my female ancestors they all had their own places..."

"At least you've still got this," I offer.

"I'm going for a walk."

As I watch her leave, I briefly run with a horrible fantasy that she doesn't return and I somehow inherit her mantle, her strange role in this quasi-world. The thought of such responsibility is too much to bear so I lamely attempt to follow her.

Some fifty yards beyond the lemon grove, I encounter a too familiar figure.

"Soldier, you're supposed to salute a superior officer!" he barks.

"This is not a field of conflict, sergeant; you don't have authority here."

"You were never de-mobbed, son. You're still in uniform to my eyes, you'll do as I say."

In the still daylight air I think I can just discern the slight implosion of bubbles popping. Or are my thoughts too fanciful – as ever? Never mind self-preservation, I must stop him reaching Faye.

"Where's your combat jacket, private?"

"Stolen, sarge, *sir*. Follow me and we'll get them back."

I haven't run in a while and the leg wound is still killing me but this is survival and I have a good lead as we reach the trees and I'm praying to a god or a goodness or a goddess that my suppositions are upheld… And I stop, clutching the thin trunks, gasping for breath.

He can see me but he can't reach me. I watch him bang against an invisible barrier worthy of our top military installations. Oh, but he's smart, old Scruton: he doesn't spend too long pounding the force field with angry fists but instead starts circumnavigating its extent, looking for possible breaches. As I step backward through the grove I believe he can no longer see me and I'm certain he can't approach the farm or the cottage. Yet.

I don't say anything to Faye because I believe she already knows about the sergeant and all the other threats encircling us. I am curious, though, to her response. How many barriers of thorns and wonderwalls will we require to keep Scruton and his kind at bay? We have lived in an idyll maintained by matrilineal magic mixed with modern surveillance and constant vigilance. As the conflict draws closer, maybe we need to erect white picket fences whose planks stretch immeasurably up to the sky or whose very plainness confuses, disorients and despatches would be desecrators.

I take pencils and paper to a grassy spot where a withered fig tree offers some little support and shade. Usually I can only draw from direct observation but today I produce a sketch of a crowd at a railway station, something I vaguely remember from a historical documentary. Soldiers emerge from flung-open wooden doors to ecstatic joy and relief from the waiting women. But look at this face in the corner, the war widow tasting the grim defeat of victory.

"Grim defeat of victory?" Phaedra comments. "You're both the artist and the poet today. Anyway, it's not all handsome fighting men coming home to doe-eyed maidens, you know. Have you never heard of the Amazons? Or the fighting women of Kalamadora? They painted their bare breasts with swirls of pink and purple to confuse the aim of their attackers."

"You're making that up. Faye, how old are you?"

"A little older than you. A little older than I seem."

"And who are you?"

"I'm who you want me to be. I'm who you've been looking for."

I turn my attention back to my drawing, absorbing myself with details for a minute or so. When I look up she's still there.

"Why are you thinking of leaving?" she asks. She takes my numb silence for assent and continues, "This is the only place to be; you're safe here and you want for nothing. The outside world can't get us because we're always aware and *ahead* of it."

"But I'm from what you call the outside world. It's my duty to go back, to try to change it for the better. To end the war."

"You'll never end the war."

When next I glance up, she's headed back to the cottage. I leave my drawing on the dry ground. And I still haven't asked her what we should do about the sergeant poking around the outskirts, the snake attempting to slither into the garden.

It's a cloudy night with a hint of welcome rain. I'd wished for moonlight but we make do with candles as we make love by an unshaded window. Afterwards, the gradual fall of her breathing tells me Faye sleeps. I stare into the dimness.

Oh Man, always looking gift horses in the mouth and searching in the shrubbery for earthworms and dog shit. Faye ought to be enough… except I still feel the need to be with other people. No, it's more altruistic than that – I want other people to share in my good fortune; in the knowledge that there is an escape, there is an alternative to the constant conflict.

In the morning she says, "I've taken care of things."

"Meaning?"

"I don't like intruders. Only guests."

It takes me nearly an hour to gauge the depth of her antipathy: about thirty centimetres' depth of disturbed soil not far from where I recovered my wristwatch. I dutifully check for signs of life about the late sergeant. Cause of death? Too early to determine. But I can fetch a spade and make a better job of his shallow grave; so I do.

Everybody mentioned on the war memorial back at home died on active service in a foreign country. In many cases there's no accompanying body or pile of bones to grant physicality to the distant memory. And who's to say their sacrificial lives were of more worth than a shopkeeper's stay at home existence?

We perished so as to keep the monarch on the throne, the landlord in Parliament and the banks in profit.

I can see the cosy roof of the cottage but not the bedroom window from this side.

I begin doing something that is against all my training and good sense – I start walking backwards away from the house as if retracing my steps in a reversed film. There is no telltale lurch or pop as I retreat from the nucleus but one moment it's there and the next… I can no longer discern it.

I breathe deeply against ensuing panic, take a couple of steps forward, even daring to close my eyes as if to conjure the memory. To evoke… or erase.

Desperate now, I realise the cottage has disappeared. Or else my angle of approach is blocked or wrong… and will always remain so.

I walked for the longest time, leaving the rain of bullets behind me. The ground here had only a slight inclination. It almost looked tended, cultivated… in these killing fields? Ridiculous thought.

Night fell but I didn't stop for more than a minute or so. Miraculously, my water bottle was still half-full and I discovered a couple of energy bars in the lining of my flak jacket. A little squashed but edible.

Morning came and my pace had slowed but from somewhere deep within I dredged up the stamina to keep going. Here was a road. Paved, if a little potholed. Street signs in English. Unknown but phonetically plausible place names. Suggestions of houses… Actual houses… Safe streets leading to a square decorated with bunting in red, white and blue. A buzz of expectation ran through the crowd. I glanced behind me and saw half-familiar comrades from my battalion just a few steps to the rear. As I faced forward again, I spotted banners proclaiming 'Peace' hung from the gabled rooftops like Thursday's washing.

In a trice the parade became a joyous throng and I was embraced by men and women alike, offered celebratory bottles, cheering words, welcoming arms…

For a second I caught the eye of a willowy young woman at the edge of the mob. I tried to force my way towards her but the press of the gathering was too great. I took a swig from a proffered wine bottle, turned to kiss an excited young factory girl full on the lips and gave myself up to the pleasure of the moment.

SHIRTS

Kevin preferred things the way they were nowadays. At least as far as shopping for food was concerned. His personal life was the pits but the *New Honesty* supermarket made him realise how, in the past, he'd been conned by adverts and labels.

He had grown to love these pristine magnolia walls whose plainness was occasionally broken by flattering portraits of The Widow.

No music, no muzak, even the tills beeped silently. So here, plainly labelled with the name of the product and with the ingredients listed in clear, legible type were all the things he might require over the succeeding few days: filter coffee, milk, ready meals, bread, half fat cheddar, dried fruit, healthy yoghurts. A bit heavy on the dairy products, but…

Catriona had taught him how to make biscuits. He was holding a bag of plain white flour – plain white bag with the product name written clearly but nothing else – when a whisper washed through the shop like a tidal wave flooding and filling all the valleys and crevices.

"The Shirts are coming!"

He quickly took his basket to the checkout. The operator scanned the items hastily, almost dropping a bottle of detergent which, although designed to cleanse, could have made a nasty mess. The girl was quite pretty in an unmade-up, slightly severe way. As Kevin retrieved his swipe card, she locked her till and scampered nervously off towards the staff room.

Kevin saw the gang of Shirts as he walked calmly home. They were at the top of his street where it crossed the main thoroughfare, sweeping sylph-like past the post box and assorted street furniture. They weren't currently headed his way. He jangled his key fob in his right hand, let himself into his block, and relaxed.

Once he'd put all the items away carefully, Kevin sat and checked the news texts on his screen. The colours were primary school bright even though he'd spent half an hour yesterday trying to tone down their brilliance. If only the stories were as pleasant and life affirming. He wondered if he'd left anything behind in the sudden rush to clear the aisles and pay for everything. But the only thing likely to be abandoned was his life with Catriona. Unless he could retrieve the situation this one last time tonight.

They finished the final dregs of his wine, carefully shared between two glasses, red and dry but not at all musty.

At last he had to ask her, "Why are you chasing that… that existence? It's an irreversible transformation, you know, for… for fifteen minutes of fabric!"

"Very amusing, I'm sure. I need to do something, be somebody. What's wrong with wanting good things, Kev?"

"Nothing in itself but... I just feel you've been swayed by their rhetoric."

"You've been reading too many social theory books. Too much leisure time, if you ask me. Listen, honey, all I'm after is a better life."

Her soft fingers were on his lightly downed forearm. He felt like grabbing her wrist with impatience…love... desperation.

"But, Cat, this obsession with new technology is killing the planet."

"Screw the planet! If it dies, I won't be around to care, I'll be long gone; so let's live for today."

"Even now things are being irrevocably damaged and we'll all pay for it in our lifetime."

"So what? I want my life to mean something."

"To mean something how? To be a record of how much you consumed?"

"Are you saying I'm fat? Fuck you, I'm a size 10."

The front door rattled so hard he was convinced she'd split the beech wood.

The Saturday morning airwaves were the usual ethereal battleground between the Jammers of Commerce and the local debuggers. Kevin couldn't get a signal on his mobile and the dial-up on the broadband kept freezing. He thought he might have better luck at the library; he had a book and a couple of disks to return anyway. He'd take the long route and cast an eye over the good quality fruit and knock-off goods at the weekend street market.

The diamond screen at the edge of the safe area was up and functioning again. A clone crew had worked through the night and removed all the carefully applied black paint that had temporarily obscured its sales pitch. Now the board expounded the dubious joys of Kool Cola in pulsing, neon glory. Kevin had preferred, politically and aesthetically, the previous incarnation and how it had glowed *darkly* in the nocturnal landscape.

He tried to put a positive spin on his split with Catriona. Without the coupled requirements, the day was open to him. He could get a ticket to a sporting event or a show; maybe hang around up town where all sorts of sociable types liked to mingle uneasily.

Instead, he was at home in the superficially cluttered desert of his first floor flat reading an old detective novel when he heard the commotion in the street outside. He could only get a partial view from his lounge, so watched from the communal hall and stairs area.

The Shirts were becoming more cocky by the day. He strained his eyes against the dusty glass but he didn't recognise any of their number. He wondered if The Netters had set up again down on Story Street. But The Widow had banned this activity until she reasserted block control. Kevin loved to see The Netters at work, scooping up the rampaging Shirts like they were so many spawn crazed salmon headed upstream into an inevitable trap. It was the only way of dealing with a whole phalanx of Shirts – apart from the obvious alternative of running away to a safe bolt hole as quickly as possible.

The intruders moved on and out. The street gradually refilled with people discarding their rubbish, walking their dogs or polishing the tainted chrome on their assorted vehicles.

Kevin wished fervently that his habitation – indeed, his whole life – were not so patently positioned upon the front line.

There was a summons to visit The Widow. Her abode was located somewhere in the centre of the local neighbourhood. Entrance required at least three security checks at deadlocked corridors and Kevin had never managed to pin down her particular flat with absolute certainty. Doubtless that was the point.

Her room was always cloaked in semi-darkness, with the only illumination coming from a dusty skylight. The acrid fug was nigh on impenetrable on cloudy days and, even at the height of summer, one's eyes took minutes to adjust to the gloom – by which time dismissal was imminent.

Kevin could just about make out a tough looking male nurse over to the left. Nutrition tubes snaked this way and that. Piercing eyes burned behind a black veil. It was pointless to question how a seemingly disabled, middle-aged woman wielded so much power.

"Why have you split up with Catriona?" the sibilant voice demanded.

"She wanted things I couldn't offer her, Madame Hosseini," Kevin replied at last.

"She's history," hissed The Widow. "Stay focused on the now."

A firm hand was guiding him out of her parlour back through the labyrinth to the outside world. Rain bounced off the cracked, cheap wooden windowsills and the fungi-encrusted pavement. His phone bleeped with a text message reminding him that his credit was critically low. He shook his head at his apparent good fortune – The Widow did not take kindly to electronic interruptions to her carefully considered sermons.

Kevin set off early for work on Monday, not because of the need to get a seat on the train but in the hope of clocking off early and devoting the extra hour to a considered plea to Cat. Boil it down to bones and it would be etched: "Come back to me. I'm sorry." As his left hand tapped and checked figures against the flickering screen, his right siding digits scribbled in crabbed code on a notepad: opening lines, conciliatory gestures, ways to circumvent the wishes of The Widow and yet still not be cast as a traitor to the cause.

On his way back from the *New Honesty* shop, he was confronted by a solo Shirt. Initially taken aback to encounter one unusually on its own, Kevin stood his ground and placed his light bag of groceries on a clean bit of pavement.

Stalemate. Ten seconds. Twenty seconds.

At last, "Go on, try your tricks," Kevin provoked.

Almost immediately, the Shirt began its merry dance of confusion around Kevin's personal space. A blur of imprinted fabric blurting out threats and imprecations, "Join us! Don't resist us! Ours is the right way!"

Unarmed but stoically calm, Kevin poised one palm to repel and the other hand to chop in pale imitation of a martial arts master. With a brief, successful flurry, he reduced the transformed wretch to a twisted, motionless rag at his feet. It had been a person once; now it was a matrix of thought impressions, memories and metamorphosed desires preserved on electronic elastane. It would likely recover and bother the world again but for the moment it was non-functioning.

"You should burn it, mate," said a male voice at his shoulder.

"I thought they were fireproof these days."

"Not against one of these," the stranger snickered. "Look – it's a super-oxy torch."

"You see to it, pal," Kevin suggested, walking away, feeling the sweat under his arms and atop his thighs turning icy and uncomfortable.

Why did reinforcements always turn up too late for the actual battle?

*

"Are you still going through with it?"

"Yes, Kev. It's a better life than the shit one we're living now."

"It's not a *proper* life, Cat."

"Listen, stay in your greyness. Gaze out on empty walls, dog shit pavements and scrawny little rowan tress. I want more. I'll have more."

"Cat… I still love you. It's not too late to change your mind."

"That's sweet, Kevin, but I think it'll be you who comes round to my way of thinking eventually. Until then, goodbye."

Kevin's boss asked the whole workforce to stay 'an hour or two later' until all the data was collated. Several of his colleagues groaned at being delayed in their regular decampment to the local pubs. Kevin felt the offer of a later start tomorrow in lieu was not really of any personal value but kept his silence.

Returning home some time after nine, Kevin wondered whether Catriona was right in her impassioned description of his current life as humdrum and monochrome. Somehow the neighbourhood maintained its fragile immunity to the acquisitive, consumerist ideals of the outside world which encroached regularly and seemingly inexorably. Ancient laws of criminal trespass and the still not fully tested Edict of First Offence preserved the capsule for now.

The present remained an intermittent struggle; the future a cloth of uncertainty.

All the houses he passed had their low-level lights on behind thick curtains. The occasional blue glow from a screen broke the monotony just a little. Some might be taking in The Widow's latest pronouncement if her personal channel had beaten off the external jammers. But most people would be watching the holiday and property shows: entrancing fantasies about places they would never know or own.

It had lately rained, rendering the pavement darker than usual and making the mixed human, canine and leaf litter soggy and slippery.

He became aware of noise and action up ahead and slightly towards the east. He hurried for a few steps but then slowed warily like a character in a forgotten fable.

A man he recognised, as both a local councillor and a confidant of Madame Hosseini, was striding back and forth with an industrial sized tape measure. Behind him, and only half as active, the super-sized image of a foreign footballer – loved and loathed in equal measure – played out a looped advert for Sporty Kicks.

"The bastards!" the amateur surveyor was complaining. "Shoving their lifestyle commercials down our throats and onto our preserve. Look, they've encroached again another eighteen inches – which is, what, about fifty centimetres of land grab –"

"Hey, granddad!" a kid of fifteen interrupted from a few feet away. "Are we legal?"

"Certainly," the councillor smiled. "Fire away, boys!"

As he ducked clear, the crowd released a volley of stones and half-bricks at the live screen. Bulbs and tubes fizzed and exploded in a brief but exciting display, Guy Fawkes Night updated for the third millennium. The screen was shattered into thousands of fragments, glass cuboids much prized locally as footpath adornments or markers for flower borders. Some residents also kept these square marbles as makeshift ammunition for home-made weapons of dubious purpose.

A few random sparks added their belated coda to the thrilling, crystalline percussion of the smashed hoarding. Too soon the show was over and it was time to think about rustling up some survival nourishment back at his cold, half-empty flat.

The morning newspaper carried another variant on the conundrum of the Law of First Offence. A speeding driver headed inexorably towards a pedestrianised, children's play area had been shot dead at the wheel by a marksman on the thirteenth floor of a local high rise. So who had broken the rules first – the boy racer or the sharpshooter? What if the latter legally owned the weapon and claimed a level of familial self-defence? What about if the auto nutter had also stolen the vehicle he was driving so perilously?

The centre pages promised an *Exclusive Exposé of The Widow's Lair*. In truth, the grainy photos and sensationalist reportage didn't do justice to her personal charisma and the way one felt when in her presence that she knew everything and reached controlling tentacles into most aspects of one's life. The benevolent matriarch: on the side of the angels; the kittens, birds and spiders; dear old Mother Nature.

Kevin usually left his paper on the train seat for another passenger to enjoy but today he decided to dispose of this calculated and troubling misinformation in the first convenient litter bin. And maybe drop a lit match or two in on top.

*

The shelves and open topped containers in the *New Honesty* supermarket were uncommonly bright today. A lorry covered in plain tarpaulin had delivered a plethora of fresh produce late the previous night. Kevin took several detours past the fruit corner, gratefully inhaling the heady aroma of still green bananas, wax smooth apples, and the beetroots, plums and strawberries promising to stain the finger in varied, vivid shades of red.

His favourite cashier was on duty. Her line was one person longer than the others were but he didn't mind the wait. Close up, he could tell that she was five to eight years his junior: not an insurmountable age gap. Maybe he'd try and get to know her better. Then again, she probably already boasted a local boyfriend with scary tattoos, a big dog and fierce political views.

"Jane," proclaimed her name tag.

"Kevin," he whispered, retrieving his card and offering the lightest of handshakes.

"You always queue here," she announced.

"Thanks for noticing," he mumbled.

He hadn't prepared any further lines so he let his words evaporate into the comparative silence. At last they exchanged smiles and he grabbed his carriers and sauntered towards the exit.

I should've said, "I always will" or "Let's meet up later" he told himself during the walk through the scruffy car park. Still, perhaps the door was open for next time…

His thoughts were interrupted by the sudden wailing and converging of two sets of sirens about a hundred yards ahead. Seconds later he was aware of a helicopter chittering directly overhead. From this angle, he couldn't tell whether it was police, military or air ambulance. He hurried forward, planning to decant his groceries at his flat and then rush to the site of the emergency. Instead, he found himself rapidly caught up in an exponentially increasing street crowd moving like a flash flood to its inexorable destination: the central block where –

"It's The Widow," somebody shouted, "she's been taken ill!"

The news flickered through the assembly like an electrical charge, gaining voltage, becoming a shrieked certainty that Madame Hosseini was dead, had been murdered by government agents, and had already ascended to heaven to marshal an army of avenging angels.

At last, the two ambulances began to make their halting progress back along the narrow streets. The Widow's erstwhile minders tried to clear a path but couldn't prevent several emotional onlookers flinging themselves against the side of the vehicle, keening and wailing like castrated dogs.

Kevin suspected The Widow – or her corpse – would actually be airlifted to hospital and that the ground vehicles were a distraction. The crowd was slowly clearing, many intent on expressing their grief through random acts of destruction and violence against commercial property. The neon display board had not yet been replaced so they would seek vengeance further afield. Kevin remained in situ until the chuck-chuck of rotor blades became apparent above the looting and lamenting.

She wasn't quite dead yet. He could feel her psychic tendrils touching and activating his brain cells, reminding him to stay strong and keep the faith, whatever the future threw at him.

He'd lost one bag of shopping in the melee. Mere consumables of no importance at this moment of history. As people departed like haphazard firecrackers, Kevin tried to gain access for one final time to The Widow's stuffy lair. A couple of tasty geezers barred his attempted entrance with only minimum force.

As he wandered home disconsolately, pickling at the slightly squashed seedless grapes in his remaining carrier, Kevin called to mind the tubes, wires, sensors and harnesses that had kept Madame Hosseini alive and in control. It was, he reflected, a miracle that she'd lasted this long.

So here they came, focused on an unprepared victim, circling around him in a flurry like sharks around a human bait ball. There were five or six Shirts in the gang and one solitary target. Technology advances but the bullying law of the jungle remains constant; tested and proven by a long, bloody history.

Most of the Shirts gleamed whitely, their long arms rotoring in hypnotic rhythm, encircling, entrapping. The young guy caught in their electronic whirlpool slumped to his knees and appeared already done for but Kevin rushed forward to help nevertheless. No one could afford to be an innocent bystander in this civil war of attrition. It was Us versus Them.

And no use calling the police to try to keep order. Internet chat professed solemn certainty that underneath their uniform, the police were just Shirts, too.

Two of the attackers detached themselves from the main group and barred Kevin's way whilst the other four Shirts conjured out the man's essence. Kevin jabbed and parried but these assailants were experienced, calculating, transformed beings.

Except the one now entering the fray. Imprinted onto a button free, glowing and lightly buzzing, unusually short sleeved abomination was a face he recognised as Catriona's. Probably on her first murder rampage – or 'recruitment mission' as their apologists styled it – and keen to impress with her commitment to her new creed. She bobbed and reared in front of him, a phantom on fabric, an enhanced existence down a path unforeseen by evolution. She taunted, smiled, hummed… and her accomplices manoeuvred next to her, closing the rescue gap.

It was over. The Shirts swirled together over the dead resident; the whirring of their hidden propulsion became an insectile keening like a dying wasp… amplified. The Catriona chemise briefly detached itself from the departing group, hovered in front of Kevin and casually mouthed,

"You're next."

Kevin's boss put up several obstacles to him attending The Widow's funeral. These clustered into variations on the following theme: "She's a neighbour, not a relation. You didn't really know her." Or: "You'll have to take a day's unpaid annual leave, although we're so stretched I don't want to lose you." Or else: "You can watch all the important bits on telly this evening."

Heartless, callous bastard! Ripe Shirt material when the encroachment finally reached the west end of town.

Kevin stationed himself near the *New Honesty* car park, hoping surreptitiously that some good might emerge from the day and he might bump into Jane, the cheerful checkout girl. He wondered whether he'd recognise her out of uniform.

At last, a tolling bell announced the imminent arrival of the funeral procession. The lone campanologist was succeeded by four sable horses in black hoods and sparkling brasses. The beautifully turned out beasts were pulling an open carriage carrying a closed coffin. As the sombre charabanc passed, Kevin found himself forced out into the road by the mourners to right and left and rear of him. This seemingly spontaneous wave of grief settled into a ragtag crocodile line behind the official conveyance. The number of followers increased at every corner. He was jostled and buffeted from side to side and soon completely lost sight of the lead vehicle.

About fifteen minutes into the march, he formed the impression that the casket had been turned off into a side road and that the mourning crowd had gathered its own momentum. Some of the younger men close by sported extra-strength nylon nets at their waists, as if disciples of Theseus. One of the urban fishermen coiled the material expectantly around his rough fingers, sensing the proximity of Shirts and other enemies.

An independent post-mortem had offered conclusive proof that Madame Hosseini had died of natural causes, not foul play or poisoning. Medical evidence didn't seem to matter much to the increasingly angry mob. They knew who was really to blame for The Widow's sudden demise and vengeance would be swift, if random.

As they neared the edge of the so-called safe zone, the crowd's fracturing became obvious. Some people armed themselves with stones, half-bricks and non-recycled glass bottles. A few charged forwards uncaringly.

The whole business marked an undignified end to a solemn, potentially historic occasion. The hacks would be putting their inevitable, antipathetic spin on events in tonight's newscasts and tomorrow's tabloids. They'd all be wearing the hats of the falsely righteous.

Kevin let the wilder elements breeze past him in search of skulking Shirts, crass commercialism and any other foes who crossed their paths.

How long could it all continue? Skirmish, battle, loss, reclamation… an unending array of minor milestones and setbacks in a marathon that might last for decades. Fashion victims and victims of fashion at each other's throats and collars, day after deadly day.

There were neither Shirts nor friends waiting for him back at his poorly heated flat. He threw his coat on the back of the sofa, collapsed as if robbed of all essence, switched on the rolling news channel and waited to be told exactly what to think.

FUTURE CITIES

Grandfather was an inventor. He conformed to all the usual stereotypes – pipe smoking, tweed jacket, owlish eyebrows, brilliant but forgetful. Every family should possess such an erratic, dynamic character. Straight out of *Oz* or *Chitty Chitty Bang Bang*. I knew and recognised his value at the time even though as a kid my grasp of science was as shaky as an earthworm's understanding of space travel.

Funny little rockets and helicopters and other magnificent, micro flying-machines. Along with contained explosions in his back garden, leaving telltale scorch marks against the wooden fence boards. Incorrigibly old-fashioned, he'd claim that he made less mess than Grandma's failed experiments with a recipe for a new Victoria sponge.

I should have spent more time there. He was rubbish at sports, no doubt deliberately so, and this was a boon to my fragile male ego: I could bowl him out at cricket, beat him in penalty shoot-out, overtake his wheezing body in any decent sprint. I should have gone round every late afternoon with my school bag and let him help me rattle through my homework in fifteen minutes and then let him explain a few more of the mysteries of the universe with his star charts, mildewed encyclopaedia and bent out of shape slide-rule. But there were cartoons on the TV, mates just down the road with a cheap plastic football, and negligible but time-consuming chores like washing the breakfast dishes as soon as I got home. So it was the occasional Sunday or spare hours during the summer holidays. Moments grabbed but missed opportunities, too. Depends on how you read it.

Boys' stuff. Taking traditional roles, my younger sister Judith tended to cling to Grandma's apron and spend her spare time cross-stitching. Whereas I was glad of, though sporadically embarrassed by, Grandpa's copious gifts.

Which abruptly ceased the day the government sequestered his services at gunpoint from an unmarked sedan.

Bossy, know-it-all Judith says to me nowadays, "Why do you see our childhood as some sort of endless summer and Grandpa as the paragon of virtue?"

"What do you mean?" I bluster down the phone, wondering if the dodgy mobile reception has somehow distorted the words emanating from her poky rural retreat.

"I'll tell you another time. I'm breaking up here, Will."

How can two people share so many of the same experiences only to put entirely different slants on their content? It's all about perception, I suppose. As Mother was fond of telling me when I pushed overcooked cabbage carefully to one side of my plate, what seemed a plain meal to me would be a feast for an orphan from a war-torn African republic.

Put it in the tupperware and mail it in the morning then, Mother.

A sweeping vista of towers and spires, curved against the desert wind, reaching hundreds of metres into the blue sky. Buildings of metal and plexiglass spread across the surface like a futuristic ants' nest. All is silver, white, semi-transparent – gleaming -reflective in the sun's renewed heat. Ergonomic curves, rounded walls, everything designed with a painterly flourish. Small black vehicles scurry constantly through tubeways or jump nimbly from sloping rooftop to flat landing bay. These are all semi-automatic drone carriers, part of a computer regulated maintenance and repair system keeping the city clean, sparkling, and at maximum operating efficiency.

But one starts to question the apparent absence of people. Here is the beehive, where are the bees…?

Having achieved perfection for their mass dwelling, the humans have retreated into their somno-shells deep within the bowels of this ultimate city. Drip-fed, mostly still, maintained for millennia if necessary – these advanced descendants of modern homo sapiens still live with the one abiding wish:

To dream.

They required his help with defence developments at a specialised facility somewhere off the coast of Scotland. We couldn't go and visit him; perhaps he'd be granted leave soon to return to us.

To my knowledge, he never was.

They took away his notebooks, his technical drawings, several models and prototypes that they liked the look of. Anything that might be important in the hot, cold or lukewarm war against the Ruskies / the Chinese / the Republicans / the rogue states of the Middle East. They made a thorough examination of a remote control car he'd constructed for me as a Christmas present. Eventually they let me keep it: it was just a toy, not a weapon or a shield.

Even in those days I was prone to pre-sentiment and possessed enough foresight to carefully secrete his most intriguing gift. There was a little depression round the back of the sycamore tree which dominated the rear of our back garden. I wrapped the item in two Tesco carrier bags to protect it from the slightly damp soil, scrubbed the evidence out of my fingernails with an old toothbrush. Even the very name of the bequest made clear that this was something special and wondrous strange.

It was a futurescope.

My now grown-up sister Judith is on the phone again giving me grief. It's all a deflection for her own failures but it gets under my skin in the way only siblings know how to achieve.

"Will, Grandpa wasn't Albert Einstein, he was a petty criminal making a few extra quid handling stolen goods. That's why he kept that ratty old shed."

"You just haven't got a clue," I bark back. "It's all a smokescreen. He was taken away to do defence work – against his wishes. The so-called trial never actually took place. The government paid the newspapers to print the verdict… of a case that never happened."

"Take your rosy fucking spectacles off, Will! What about the schoolgirl photos? They're not a conspiracy theory – Grandma saw them with her own eyes. Including the one of the girl masturbating. She told me."

It's an apparent aspect of my Grandfather that I've never quite been able to come to terms with. Sure he came from sexually repressed times but I've never been able to disprove that this affable old buffer with his pipe and slippers and crazy gadgets didn't actually sneak across the unkempt playing fields with his Polaroid Instamatic attempting to catch the local under-age sirens *deshabillé* or even *in flagrante*. It was a long step further than Charles Dodgson ever went.

"They always accuse people of sex crimes when they want to discredit them," I shout back. "Look at Winston Smith."

Who was fictional. Judith snorts. I can picture her sneery nostrils wrinkling and her viperish tongue preparing to spit more venom. "Talking of which," she says, "are you still seeing that Sandra?"

"Of course."

"She's no good for you. She needs to lose a lot of weight."

"So do most women in the western world apart from Posh Spice. It's not your business."

"Just trying to look after my big bro'."

"Interfere, more like. Call me when you've something useful to say. Not before."

"Step right up if you'd like to ride."

"The shuttle for Vega Four will depart in fifteen – oh one five – micro-revs."

"Can passengers please remember to disconnect their jet packs when entering the terminal building?"

This is the technological future. This is the spaceport that makes Cape Canaveral seem like a random pile of bricks in a nursery. This is practical astronomy on a galactic scale.

Wormholes are our friends. We enter and exit and, although reconstituted, we are not changed. One may experience some slight turbulence and even a touch of nausea: be assured, these sensations will soon pass. Travel time to all parts of this rich Milky Way is measured in mere days in the old calendar. Everything here runs smoothly and is geared to make your journey pleasant and memorable. There have been neither accidents nor fatalities in well over a hundred macro-revs.

Earth is not the centre of the universe but the invention and application of the Blink Drive has put us at the hub of the new siblinghood. Every flight *in* brings creatures with green or grey skin; tentacles, suckers, compound eyes; breathers of unusual gases; jelloids and invertebrates; giants and palm size travellers. Aliens. Visitors. Friends.

The longed-for intellectual and emotional miracle has occurred. As we explore further into the cosmos so our altruism and open-mindedness have increased exponentially. By getting to know, accept and, indeed, admire so many other species from the stars we have finally stepped away from the infighting and self-loathing that so dogged our two million year history. By embracing others we have learned to love ourselves.

To help achieve all this we have terra-formed Terra itself. Much of the moveable landmass of the northern hemisphere is now given over to our great gateway city. See the peaceful hardware gleam! Ranks of rockets destined for the skies. Gantries, service areas, luxurious chrome and glass accommodation. When one tires of the bustle, why not take a hover-plane ride to a coastal resort? Watch the crop robots and the ore droids keeping up production levels for the benefit of humankind and all our extraterrestrial allies.

The one great city is the last great city. Geared for arrival and departure. Take your seats. Countdown starts…NOW!

"You know what a telescope is, don't you? And a microscope and periscope. Do you children still play with kaleidoscopes?"

"Miss Clarke's class made them last term. They didn't stick properly and there was broken mirrors and bits of coloured plastic everywhere. Judith says that's seven years of bad luck."

He smiled through his neat moustache and beard. He smelt of a newly opened pouch of tobacco but there was an egg stain just below the collar of his plain white shirt.

"Scopa – to see. Latin, of course," Grandpa mused. "What I've made here, William, is a futurescope."

Already schooled in classic science fiction films, I expected something resembling early forms of television or radar: a deep, cumbersome cuboid with a grey-green screen featuring swirls and wavy lines which might eventually resolve themselves into a message from beyond. Instead, the contraption was more like a one-piece diving mask with a pair of binoculars stuck onto the glass.

"How does it work?" I croaked.

"How do you think it works?" he snapped back.

He tightened the straps slightly, asked a couple of times whether the weight was OK on my still growing skull. I realised after a while that I had instinctively closed my eyes against a possible lurch over the pain threshold. With his toothpastey, "Well?" ringing in my unobstructed ears, I cautiously opened my eyelids.

To a vista straight from the cover of my favourite Arthur C. Clarke book. A city in a bubble spread before me in all its Technicolor glory. Heli-ships hovered; minuscule passengers disembarked from monorails; others ascended floorless elevators to sun-kissed roof terraces to eat golden fruit or relax beneath the shade of palm trees not seen this size since the Cretaceous.

"It's amazing," I said, carefully disengaging.

The present seemed unremittingly grey and dull after such a vision and not simply because of the dreary weekend rainfall tumbling past his workshop window.

"It's still a prototype," he stated, packing it conscientiously in half-popped bubble wrap. "I'm hoping to build on some controls soon so that it will take the viewer to other times and places."

"It's wonderful. I'd really like to look through it again soon."

"You will, boy. This is my crowning glory but… there's those who would take it away from me." He picked at some barely visible fluff on his waistcoat. "Or change its purpose. Mediocre stuff like seeing their own death or finding out who wins next year's FA Cup Final."

I had the presence of mind not to mention that this latter information would delight and enthral me if he could make it available.

He clapped me on the back rather harder than I would have wished and pronounced, "You and me don't bother with the individual, though, do we? We care about species survival. Man the explorer, ever onwards and upwards!"

I think I avoided his gaze at that point, knowing even then that I'd never get much further than a steady job in suburbia coupled with two weeks in Spain every summer. So much for the spaceships, the star shine and the galactic pioneer corps. Too busy making ends meet and seeking an uneasy truce in the family wars. And trying to hold onto Sandra against the bitter artillery of my spiteful sister.

No time in this life to be a spaceman.

I was spending too long lately in The Fisherman's Arms. The creek had long dried up and his hairy limbs offered little comfort but the evenings were warm in the pub garden and this was the bench where Sandra and I had celebrated her promotion. Now there was just me sitting here.

The woman at the next table asked me for a light. I obliged. Her shoulder-length hair was dyed with more subtlety than the hennaed handmaidens who generally frequented this bar. She indicated that her wineglass was virtually empty. I returned with a half bottle of Riesling.

She was a couple of years older than me, a local girl who'd been away for some years but had lately returned.

"Between jobs," she smiled. "And what did you say your surname was?"

"I didn't. It's Dickinson."

She spluttered a little, gazed at me quizzically through a veil of mascara. "I was at Mary Magdalene School for Waywards – well, that's what we called it. St. Trinian's with a big dose of sex. I think I knew your grandfather. The guy with the Polaroid."

"That's him," I mumbled, checking my coat for my car keys.

"Hey, don't go," she said, grabbing my arm. "It wasn't his fault. We led him on big time. He just took the rap." She stubbed out her Silk Cut, continued, "We were a bunch of little sluts experimenting with booze, pills, boys… each other. All the old duffer did was take a few pictures. And we really twisted his arm to get those. It was a big kerfuffle out of nothing."

"He suffered. His reputation never recovered. The world lost a scientific genius."

"Shit, I'm well sorry about that. We were too young to know the consequences – of the photos or anything else really. Half my friends were pregnant at fourteen."

"Am I supposed to see this as therapy? If so, for me or for you?"

"I've kept a lot of my uniform. It's a bit of a squeeze but being unbuttoned is half the fun. Are you sober enough to drive?"

"I'm always sober enough to drive."

The tie was the pink and blue stripes of Mary Magdalene but the rest of her gear – navy pleated skirt, short-sleeved blouse, knee-high white socks – was all far too new and probably came from Ebay or School Disco Dot Com. As she knelt down to suck me off I kept thinking of Britney Spears in *that* video. I wasn't proud of my thoughts or my actions. I came like a loose petrol pump nevertheless.

When I got home I found that my wallet was fifty pounds lighter. Streetwise tongue, moist lips, butterfly fingers: it was a winning combination.

Though still obviously a city, this is also the semi-pastoral idyll long pictured and dreamt of by poets, painters and philosophers. We have partly patterned the layout on a mythical version of Venice. Everywhere is linked by water and walkways. There are softly splashing fountains around every corner; the air is fragrant with the fresh smell of apples, lemons, figs and olives; most habitations look out over pleasant courtyards ripe for relaxing and mingling with one's neighbours.

New concepts are abroad. No property is privately owned anymore. Sleep where you wish. Move on after a few days. Since the advent of Lux energy our needs are easily catered for. There is no work or labour as conceived in the olden times. Except for within the arts.

Plays and shows spontaneously spring up almost anywhere: unannounced, unrehearsed, sometimes *unseen*. They have their moment in the controlled sunlight and then they are gone to memory. Let the musician play for your ears only: a gentle ode in pentatonic mode. Let the costumier festoon you with garments so fine that you forget you are wearing them. Let it not matter what you wear or whether you wear. Stand still and muse awhile on the uncharted extent of this jewel of the future. There, now your portrait is done. Hang it in the alcove tonight. Take it with you when you move on tomorrow or leave it behind as a facial footprint; it matters not.

Tonight we are gathering a small crowd to go up onto the roof and observe the stars. Remember when we stretched out to try and conquer? Remember how it was before we realised that we should not seek paradise but make it, right here and now at home? No, you're probably too young. But come and count the astral blessings, anyway, if you will.

No more hunger, no more war, no more lack of shelter. No cold or swelter. We could explore all our days and never be tired of, nor ever reach the limit of, this metropolis where one can say "I love you" simply by touching hands.

I love you, too.

Grandma was safely buried in this plot – I had overseen all the funeral arrangements some ten years ago – but Grandpa's fate was slightly less certain. The Ministry had solemnly reported his demise and arranged a cremation before any relatives could be scrambled into action. They sent us an urn by special motorcycle courier but, frankly, it could have been anybody's ashes inside the container. We arranged for it to be placed by Grandma's side, like a canoptic jar in ancient Egypt packed full of vital organs.

This was a quiet spot in the lately sprawling-out village. Down the hill the lightning conductor on the church spire twinkled in the thin sunlight. Graves closer to the building dated back more than two hundred years. From this elevation I could see all three of the pubs that were within walking distance; also, the mini-mart with its volunteer staff and erratic opening hours. All the houses – thatch roofed cottages, converted barns, new red brick developments – sported satellite dishes like the whole area was listening out for a message from the heavens. In truth, TV and mobile reception was somewhat variable round these parts.

And here came a welcome sight – dainty, painted feet in brand new Birkenstocks. She wore a floaty, long-sleeved top to prevent her soft arms from burning and I caught a hint of the perfume I'd bought her last Christmas.

"I thought I'd find you here," Sandra said.

"You know how much I think about Grandpa," I mumbled.

"Most men revere their fathers."

"He didn't stay around long enough for me to make a choice."

"Shall we get a drink, Will? Have a chat? It's past opening time."

"Sure. Let's do The Buxom Wench. It was always my favourite."

I still have the futurescope. It's been around the country with me – university, postgrad, jobs up North and in the Midlands, even stuffed into a guitar case during my brief spell busking and playing coin in the hat gigs on the near continent. The device is somewhat the worse for wear and I suspect that at some stage it was accidentally damaged, perhaps rendered almost inoperable. How else to explain its static display?

Grandpa made it quite clear that the machine would not divulge one's individual fate. Sandra is back living with me; but for how long this time? That mostly depends how we stand up to the snooping and sniping of my spiteful sister and her hapless husband who live just two hundred yards down the road. We can grow a higher hedge out the front; we can buy our groceries five miles away; or we can hold hands, link arms and step together bravely in the face of Judith's narrow-minded, parochial hostility. Not all of us get our worldview from crappy tabloids and GMTV.

I want to look beyond. I want to see the sights I saw as a young boy. I put the contraption to my eyes, blink, hope for change, but it's the same old same old.

Broken cities. Death, decay and devastation. Are there one hundred corpses piled on that corner or one hundred thousand? The air stinks yellow. Already the last of the tall buildings are starting to crumble. The dams and the sea walls need repair; maybe they are already beyond it and soon the polluted waters will come rushing in to reclaim this territory. Radioactive leftovers glow like forgotten dinners in a microwave. The wind roars and the detritus – mineral and once-organic – moves in a maelstrom. But no plants grow and nothing animal moves of its own accord. Even the war machines are immobile now, rusting...

This is the only future I'm ever shown now by Grandpa's Wellsian invention. I can't find the energy or belief to doubt its veracity. Which means I must concentrate on the now, the next minute, maybe the close-by happy years I shall spend with Sandra before the whole planet goes tits up.

I long to be shown again the heli-ships, the domes, the spacecraft docking in orbit, the pale pink skyscapes and the rings around Saturn. Instead the picture is frozen onto post-apocalyptic Earth – a vision, a prediction, an inevitability.

All promises have been broken. The taste of tomorrow is regret.

TODAY WE WERE ASTRONAUTS

Almost the first thing Harold did when the wind eased a little was to dispose of Evans. This had to be undertaken at night when David was asleep, or at least safely locked away from all ills inside his bedroom on the first floor of Macaverty Head lighthouse. Sprightly and focused throughout the horrendous journey here, Evans had succumbed suddenly to the effects of the Moon Plague. Harold had seen so much death these past months and had been unable to shield his young son from the horror that had gripped the country. Even so, small mercies and all that…

Evans had driven the armoured truck, second in line behind Harold's emergency supply lorry. His shotgun was occasionally visible poking out of a concealed slot in the darkened, strengthened windows. He was their eyes in the rear, dealing with any lingering resistance to their progress, their mission to maintain and preserve an outpost of the old order. Harold was sure David could hear the gunfire above the groan of the engine but still played a straight bat to all enquiries.

"Daddy, what happened to those men in the road?"

"We had to leave them behind, son. They, uh, someone will be along to help them in a day or two."

A division of labour: Harold, you keep on driving with your kid and your slowly sickening wife beside you, just make sure you get us there. Evans – no, Leslie, let's humanise him with a Christian name – you do the dirty work out of sight except in the grubby wing mirror.

And now after two frantic days setting up and securing this research outpost, Jennifer also was fading fast in the cloying, warm fug of her quarters, with a drip in her arm helping to temporarily preserve her existence, though not much of a life. And Leslie Evans had so abruptly slumped from the constitution of an ox to the condition of a carcass.

Dragged over the scrubby grass of the headland to the very edge of the recently rain-lashed cliff.

"I'm sorry I can't offer you a decent burial, my friend," Harold muttered over his exhaustion. "The sea will have to do."

With a final effort, Harold manoeuvred his colleague's body so that the head and shoulders were dangling over a precipice. Mindful of his own safety, he pushed the corpse's legs through an arc that caused the late Leslie Evans to teeter and then plunge into tonight's wild water. Harold muttered a quick prayer half-remembered from some TV drama or other.

The Moon Plague had reportedly killed everybody within a six to ten mile radius. It was just exhaustion and fancy that had Harold imagining he could hear a choir carried on the wind as he consigned his dead companion's bones and flesh to their wild, grey grave.

The Mind Blocks were chattering, going over the same old ground. What was their purpose? They never seemed to have anything new to offer.

And I'm charged with maintaining the wittering existence of these arrogant brain patterns, Harold mused. I'm just the night watchman or the zookeeper.

– Suppose we caused a disaster that could have been averted. Humankind has become so powerful that, with a little foresight and willingness, we can prevent disasters almost as easily as we can cause them. Except we didn't really know what sort of disaster we were causing.

– Suppose they called a war and nobody came? My late father told me that everyone used to wear that slogan on a badge or a T-shirt when he was a young man. These days we have several ways of running wars which don't involve calling a multitude of young men to come and sacrifice their lives for the greater glory. We can arrange for all the killing to be done by remote.

– Suppose you thought you were harming the world in one way and were prepared for that but the damage you and your notional enemy actually caused caught you off guard and somewhat under-prepared.

– Notional enemy? The fighting, the aggression, the brainwashing, the exertion of control, the land grabs – we're all much of a muchness in this.

– And yet, and yet… there was still time to make some plans, to preserve some of the what and the who of our culture and leave a cadre of brave fools to stand guard.

– The fallacy of this is that a disaster, any disaster, punctures the prevailing order and the wound never properly heals. Yes we can all start again but why would those who'd stayed outside, away from the bunkers and the sealed laboratories, allow the useless leaders to waltz back in and say thanks guys, we'll take over again now? The little Indian kid sewing clothes for a pound a week; the tea or coffee picker being ripped off by the multi-national companies; the illegal immigrant gypsy whore selling her body for a takeaway meal and a flop in a broom cupboard – all the wretched and deprived are going to have some radical ideas about the new world order, the *next* world order even. Behead the king! Guillotine the aristocrats! Vive le revolution! Bring on the next dictatorship!

*

David had broken his thoughtful silence to yell, "It's a lighthouse! It's really a lighthouse!"

The adults smiled at his excitement. Macaverty Head didn't quite match up to the red and white barber pole storybook vision; rather its grey painted stone solidity stood as a reassuring standard against an uncertain sky. The outbuildings were slightly battered but fixable, useable.

Once the generator had coughed into life, they had begun an exploration of the interior with its mix of spiral staircases, access ladders and general paucity of windows for such a lofty building. David had rediscovered his childish joie de vivre at the prospect of staying in such a romantic habitation. Harold admired the boy's ability to compartmentalise, forget... maybe. Jennifer helped with what little she could manage; Evans attended to the electrics, the unloading and the transferring of the clone copies of the Mind Blocks into the main drive. Let these saved brain patterns recommence their pondering upon the purpose of life, the nature of the damaged universe and possible courses to combat and overcome – perhaps even cure – the dreadful disease.

After nightfall, with everyone safely quartered and as comfortable as could be expected, Harold had risen and made his way to the outdoor platform at the very top of the tower, braving the rising breeze next to the dormant, unlit giant bulb that had once warned sailors and attracted suicidal lovers. It was natural to fancy that one could feel a few ghosts in a location that had previously housed a laird's folly and a long since de-consecrated monastery. Macaverty Head had always meant something and now it was to be an outpost of knowledge, research, preservation – linked to the remains of the civilised world through the fraying strands of the World Wide Web.

The place held a dual history of being at once a beacon of hope but also a flame to the moths. Its bright beam had warned ships away from the rocks but the modern shallow hulled vessels plied their trade elsewhere these past decades. The light had called to the community in times of stress. The smugglers had used the old tower as a landmark and braved the stones and squalls and sharp precipices in order to unload their counterfeit and their booty. Harold had heard a tall fable that at one time there had been a lynching near here and the local priest or priestess was hung from the light itself. He or she had been the leader of an outlawed Moon cult.

The Moon and the lighthouse – both calling, both misused or disused, both attractive and attracting. Both leading to death.

*

It's too obviously tempting to see a lighthouse as a phallic symbol: Man's firm, upright seeding of the headland. So, maybe as much as it's a beacon of hope spreading its illumination all around with a metronomic pass, it's also a brave attempt to use a stone finger to point the way to heaven. An *optical* Tower of Babel.

Save our souls from shipwrecks. Warn us of the killing rocks. Become the focal point of our small, disparate community. Serve as a sanctuary.

Time moves on and buildings change their function or fall into disuse. Memories fade but legends linger. The winds batter this tall monument to ingenious construction and the will to ensure survival.

But we do not place our lighthouses in busy streets, shrouded by coal-fired power stations, shops and high rise blocks. Before the building comes the need. Not everywhere has the requirement; not everywhere has the resonance. Upon this bleak cliff, there was previously a cairn and prior to that a sacred place marked by even the earliest mapmakers.

Preceding humankind and its warped spirituality, the tectonic plates drifted and the mountains rose and fell. In a climate even warmer than our own, the plesiosaurs gambolled in the waves and cared not for the rocky outcrops and granite hazards hanging above their fishing grounds.

Yet this was always an area… a locale… a power node.

Harold knew this was just the latest in a series of 'manly' talks with his son, none of which he'd either expected or desired. But the world and its thin patterning of human civilisation had changed so much since the onset of the Moon Plague that the 'Be strong, be brave, be a survivor' mantra had become a nightly event.

He had cooked the last of their fresh food in pans over a couple of Primus stoves and set a cartoon with zany antics and uplifting music playing on a computer in the background.

"Daddy, has Mr Evans left us?"

"Yes, he… had some other business to attend to, David."

"He was nice. He was going to help me with my numbers and stuff… like Mummy used to."

"Yes, it's going to be hard with just the three of us, especially while Mummy has to sleep. Listen, David, you can play in the rooms I said but you really mustn't touch anything if I say you mustn't. Deal?"

"Mummy's going to die, isn't she?"

Dissolving now, needing comforting arms, calm words, reassurance and promises... white lies...

"She's going to be asleep for a little while. We must be gentle with her. I'm still hoping a doctor will reach us soon. She'll hold on till then."

As he wiped the boy's tears with a disposable tissue, Harold felt overwhelmed again by the changed responsibilities. Just a couple of years ago he'd stood at the apparent apex of his life: his son David cute and wide-eyed in his fresh school uniform; his wife Jennifer healthy and beautiful, about to resume her career in pharmaceuticals; his own promotion and raised security clearance bringing greater remuneration and the opportunity of seeking a bigger house with an enclosed back garden and lockable garage and other middle class aspirations for the nuclear family...

David pulled away from him suddenly.

"Daddy, I can hear the angels! They're coming for Mummy!"

He muted the PC, strained his ears in search of the heavenly chorus, began flicking switches and swooshing the infrared mouse.

"David, stop emoting! It's just some radio interference. Some show to cheer people up. Look, if you're worried, go and sit with Mummy for a while. But be very still and quiet."

The boy scampered away from his half-finished meal to his more than half-departed parent. Harold cleared up in a desultory fashion. He'd heard the ghostly choir too.

Harold's Notebook:

Macaverty Head is new to both David and my delicate, dying darling Jennifer.

The place was once a lighthouse – a single glance from a hundred yards away would confirm that – but it hasn't been active in that capacity for many, many years. Along with its sturdy outbuildings, it is the last house standing on this remote headland. There has been some subsidence over the decades but the tides have turned the other way now. I holidayed here when I was a kid. Something about character building in the bleak North wind; or else, we couldn't afford the Algarve or even Majorca that year.

I remember my father going the half a mile or more inland to the pub, which is now just rubble; and mother buying overpriced packets of tea bags and slightly stale cakes from the general store attached to the post office. All gone now in the climactic disruption. The previous occupant – Nic, Vic, the handwriting is barely legible – left a florid notice saying that for a time you could watch the angry waves spit and snarl salty saliva over the debris. Now the rise and fall of the tide is so uncertain.

So the sea's a bit troubled? Big deal! He won't have seen the real effects of the Moon Plague, the pandemic wiping out swathes of humans and higher mammals across the globe. The Judgement from Space punishing us for two million years of wrongs.

My wife is so much sicker than me, even with the occasional good spells. Why the hell are we entrusted with this preservation job? We've all of us come here to die.

The latest emails had spoken of Congealed Clouds bringing a new strain of the Moon Plague to rain down its abhorrence upon the last people. If Harold, David and Jennifer didn't venture out for a few days… weeks… years, would they be safe?

But two of them were outside playing what the boy called 'Pine Ears', although the father was actually checking the security of this haven. Automated in the nineteen fifties, decommissioned in the nineties, declared an off-limits government installation at the century's turn, Macaverty Head had seen a brief spell of hectic activity – fence erection, CCTV placement, stockpiles of fuel and food – about a year before the global disaster. Had someone high up known what was going to happen and already made contingency plans to preserve Western culture at this and other far outposts?

From ground level, the lighthouse was like an accusing finger pointing at the sky declaring, "That's where all your trouble comes from." Visible for miles distant, it drew locals and visitors alike with the power of a magnet amidst iron filings. A rogue German aeroplane had fired at its stone façade during the Second World War. Macaverty Head was not to be so chipped and dissed: the pilot crashed into a thicket below the headland and was left hanging from his harness by the friendly farmhands.

This once luminous minaret called all manner of people, like a Statue of Liberty without the stylised torch or the hopeful aura.

It stood on the site of a shocking massacre hundreds of years ago. Less a beacon and more a memorial marker. You could put the place in the hands of the Coastguard and Fisheries, the Ministry of Defence or the Coalition for Continued Survival… no matter. Macaverty Head the building, Macaverty Head the location had too much history, too much resonant and accumulated power to be overly affected by Man's squabbles.

Come inside and be protected from harm in this blunt instrument against the combined affray of meteorology and errant technology.

Enter at your own risk.

"Daddy, I want to go home."

"David, we can't go home, you know that."

"But I hate this place. It's cold and spooky."

"It's a lighthouse, Davie. Thick stone keeps the wind out. I think it's quite warm."

"There's ghosts and Jesus and stuff, Dad."

"What do you mean? Have you actually seen anything, heard anything?"

The young blue eyes were welling up, cheeks reddening. Harold realised he was being too hard on the boy. He spread his arms, welcomed the kid for a manly hug. He was surprised David could even remember home -by which he surely meant their old townhouse with its half lawn, half patio round the back where the sun sometimes shone. When the effects of the lunar damage and the subsequent Moon Plague were first suspected, Harold had been called into the initial safety of the government compound with the concession of being able to bring 'spouse or equivalent and closest next of kin.' As the unlucky 'outsiders' died in their droves, the ruling cartel had made a policy shift to disperse resources and survival stations on the basis that, with more outposts, statistical chances of survival were much higher. He had volunteered for this lonely, crumb-of-hope mission for the simple reason that Jennifer had already contracted the disease even though she was a few days away from visible signs. Better to take their chances in the wilds of the North East Coast than be separated by the enforced segregation of quarantine laws.

"When I was a kid," Harold whispered, "we had a few difficult months when my father was out of work. We had to leave somewhere I really loved. I had a favourite apple tree. The apples were sour, what few the tree ever produced, but I had a rope and a swing and I could play pirates on sunny days. I never got over leaving. But I'd rather have you and Mummy. Shall we go and say hello to her? Very quietly."

"OK, Daddy. But can we play pirates later?"

*

Harold's Notebook:

I've set David the task of recording his day as a lasting record from a young and innocent perspective. If only I could apply such qualities to my own existence.

At school, despite my high grades in science, I'd always wanted to be a historian. From about the age of fourteen, I blagged my way onto local walks and river cruises, helping out with the commentary, the anecdotes and the provision of tea. The course was set. But I got side-tracked after a confusing series of university entrance interviews and found myself involved in what came to be known as the *Mind Block* programme. "We're going to tablet knowledge so that the great minds live on and keep creating even after the body dies," was the professor's summation. It sounded like some crazed cross between *Frankenstein* and Philip K. Dick but they were offering me a bursary that would keep even a drink-sodden student clear of debt. I was in… for good.

Technology was racing ahead and I became a minor player as brain patterns and thought processes were imprinted onto modified chips. Eventually we could transfer the whole consciousness; people's essences, their souls, if you like. Sitting here with their voices and random thoughts threatening a power surge from the generators at any moment, I can't quite decide whether their combined wisdom is truly at work to save and reclaim our great civilisation or if I'm simply in charge of a decaying, schizophrenic library of the electronic cerebellum.

Each memory module contains lives and speaks to me just the same way as, in ancient times, a god might have spoken from the bush or the pulpit; or a ghost from the very walls. Yesterday's superstition becomes tomorrow's science.

Jennifer had rallied slightly and was awake briefly.

"It's just the final ray of sunshine before the slide into the dark," she whispered.

"Don't say that. You're strong. You're going to pull through."

"I'm not, Harold, and you know it. This is my chance to say a proper goodbye. Where's David?"

"Doing some lessons on the computer. Geography, I think."

"He won't need it. We've come to this haunted lighthouse to die, all three of us. Four of us, I mean. Where's Evans?"

"He… uh, he had to leave us."

She gripped his cold hand with all the strength she could muster. "We can't survive much longer. Soon it will be just you and David and the ghosts of shipwrecked sailors. God, what have we come to! We should do something romantic like make a suicide pact."

"Don't talk like that, darling. Whatever happens to either or both of us, we must do what we can to give Davie a chance. Now, is there anything you need?"

She managed a hollow laugh and for a moment he glimpsed again the goddess he'd first spoken to at the Graduate Careers conference more than a decade earlier. Green eyes, oval face framed by soft brown hair, warm and welcoming nature and altruistic heart. Now her eyes were all-washed-out white and she could hardly raise her hand –

"You've done a brilliant job with the IV drip, H. I can't get to the toilet. I need a bedpan and then… if you fix me up with a catheter, will you ever fancy me again?"

"I'll adore you in this life and throughout the next."

"You big soft teddy bear." Her lips brushed his forehead. They were dry like brittle leaves. "Let me see David," she whispered.

David's diary:

Daddy wants me to keep this diary for something he calls 'posterity'. I don't no what it meant so I looked it up. Something about the future or your bottom. I think he means the future.

Daddy has to work. I no that. But I don't see him all day till tea time. Can't he have a day off or some ink?

And Mummy just lies their. I no she's ill but I wish she would talk or something. I don't think she's getting better even tho she's been their days. Daddy says the – hang on, look it up – journey made her tired. But she could be getting better now.

I'm cold. I'm hungry. Not starvers but bored with same old tin food and not even coke or tango. I'm bored. I try to do the sums and the reading off the computer and then go and play and pretend. Daddy dusent mind if I make a mess in the bedroom or the play room and thas cool. But I miss my firends, I mean friends.

I no he reads this. But as Johnny says, "Wos the worst that can happen?"

*

"O Lord, my shepherd,
Protecteth me.
Within thy bosom
Thy warm, round stones,
My hearth, my prison."

It was no spiritual he'd ever heard but seemed somehow pertinent to the persecution and siege. He could no longer pass it off as stray radio waves. The ghostly choir was louder every night. He could even discern whole lines of lyrics. The tune haunted him through the day: music to whistle while you work. Where would it all end? How much louder, how much more prevalent, how *present* would the voices become?

He re-programmed part of the brain tray to deal with the issue. How do you exorcise ghosts in the twenty-first century? How come there's still a necessity in these days of science and technology?

– Give them what they need to be at rest.

How am I supposed to know?

– Ward them off with spells, incantations or lengthy quotes from the Good Book.

They are the ones quoting the Bible!

– Break the bread of the holy sacrament, sprinkle it around the dwelling along with copious draughts of holy water.

We've barely got enough to drink; we're not even washing ourselves or our clothes. There's nothing holy about what little water we have left.

And sometimes, with the wind harmonising their heavenly hymn, he believed they were actually singing, "*Harold*, my shepherd."

David was having a major sulk, a succession of "why?" and "why not?" enquiries posed with the childish whine of a spoilt brat. When could he eat fresh food and bananas, when could he get attention rather than being on his own all day? He wanted to see his friends at school, he wanted to quit doing sums and reading, he wanted to jump on Mummy's bed. Christ, son, we all wanted those things! Harold was torn between the desire to be comforting and the need to maintain discipline and order. Survival was surely about self-control. Die tomorrow from indulgence today.

He locked David temporarily in the boat hut. There were some biscuits and water bottles in there and he could piss in a pot if he needed to, just stay out of my hair, I've got work to do that doesn't involve your tantrums.

The sky this morning was pale blue in all directions and Harold could appreciate the stark beauty of Macaverty Head and its surroundings. Early records had the place as a religious retreat until the community had been swept off the face of the Earth one desperate, stormy night. Today the sea still wasn't behaving itself but otherwise he was catapulted back to his own childhood memory of holidaying in the nearby camp site and taking invigorating walks up the slope to admire the view amidst the alternate encumbrances of sea-spray wind or sun-called midges. His parents had been the 'outdoor types' until the Moon Plague did for them along with ninety-nine percent of the rest of humanity. How strange the way the past repeats and influences or interferes with the present.

So here he was back again on an ill thought through desperate mission that even Odysseus might find uninviting.

All was quiet back at the boat shed. Let David stew for a little longer, he had work to do. The greater good above personal indulgence. Always. Perhaps.

Harold's Notebook:

It's a difficult balance to strike: I have to ensure David's safety and well being but I can't be with him every waking moment or else I'd never get my tasks completed. And the world would… Well, part of me doesn't care too much about the world, what had it done for me and my offspring?

There are plenty of educational programs for him to complete, projects for him to research. Even at a similar, tender age, I had been very independent and self-motivated and my son has inherited that part of my character. From his mother – or maybe from Granddad, a moderately successful playwright and theatre director, the talent having skipped a generation – comes a lively interest in the internal life, a capacity for make-believe. He knows where he is allowed to go and what he is allowed to do; beyond that, the lighthouse and outbuildings are his mental playground. In the absence of other primary school age children, his only real option is to invent and pretend. Occasionally, I partake; mostly I leave him to it.

I should offer him more, guide him as only a father can. But we'd been through that intense male bonding business just to get here. We need to re-establish our own characters a little.

And one day, maybe very soon or at best only in the medium term, I will succumb to the after-effects of the Moon Plague and David will have to do what he can entirely on his own. Perhaps on his own not just on this bleak headland but within the whole area… the country… the world.

I've muted the response screens and I'm going to take a walk down to the locked stores, seek out a treat to take to the boy. I wonder what he's been studying or playing at this morning.

Every old building, every ancient human habitation has its ghostly presence and the Macaverty Head lighthouse is no different to the Tower of London or St John Ignatius' Abbey.

Ah, the lighthouse at Macaverty Head. A warning and guide through the rocks and rubble where a medieval village met its fate beneath the angry waves of the riled sea. That outcrop there is believed to be the remains of the church spire. The manor house lays scattered into wayward rubble. We lost a whole segment of cliff and half a dozen permanent habitations during that two-day storm. Lean-tos, encampments and their poverty stricken inhabitants, too, all gone, washed away, mourned, half-forgotten.

For a while there was only a blazing beacon here on the hilltop to warn away passing ships from the curse of Macaverty Head and its rock-strewn narrows. A campaign underpinned by a mixture of fiery sermons, misplaced guilt and local taxation raised the funds for a blinking cylinder to stand as both warning and memorial. Heady days of yore before the lighthouse was fully automated; then decommissioned. The whole area being declared off the beaten, wave tossed track for anything more important than a couple of local, semi-legal fishing boats.

Celebrate its surreptitious history: For a time, its very obviousness and cautioning aspect meant that it called to those somewhat outside the law. Lovers met on the perilous rocks beneath its gaze. Pray it's a dry night, Morag. Aye, with barely a breeze, Hamish, and we shall meet yonder where our parents can find us not.

Beneath its gaze, small-time smugglers unloaded their booty and counterfeit goods, daring Excise Men to negotiate the deadly waters in pursuit. Speculative maps of the best channels through the killing sea changed hands for good coinage in the local tavern.

There was many a slip 'twixt land and ship: errant suitors who missed this and every remaining rendezvous with fair maid; bringers of booty and treasure who misjudged the distances in the flickering floodlight and went down with their punctured craft.

It's not just the gulls and gannets who cry from beyond the almost bare granite face visible to the rain-lashed east. Listen carefully and you'll hear human cries of woe in the subtext: those who set off and never arrived, those who arrived on the outcrop but not in the hale and healthy condition necessary for continuance of life. Those who simply disappeared below the wrathful water. Their spirits haunt this building. Their memory lingers, however misty. They don't expect redemption or demand fearful attention; they simply remind visitors and residents that they are still there, though they would certainly have chosen not to be, never to be.

David's diary:

I know Daddy is busy with all his work and things. I'm trying to be a good boy and stay out of his way. He gives me stuff like school work and some of it's easy but some of it I need to ask him but I can't go and get him coz he needs to work.

He's told me I can sit with Mummy. He said he trusts me to be very good and quiet. I love Mummy so much but she's been ill for so many times and I sit with her and tell her stuff but she don't talk back and then I don't know what to tell her now. So it's quite quiet. Have I got them spellings right? My friend Johnny used to mix them up and teacher used to shake her head and make her brown hair go all floppy.

I miss Miss Humble and Johnny and Ashraf and Leroy and Mohammed and all my other friends. I often say that they are here and I talk to them and we play some games. Sometimes we just play that it's school and I do my lessons – the ones Daddy gave me, not Miss Humble's – and then it's playtime and I tell Ashraf he's on it or we stand around the climbing frame or play football with a tennis ball.

I can kick the ball against the wall and kick it back about a hundred times without missing. And it's hard with no friends there really. And in my big coat coz it's windy and a bit rainy.

And maybe Daddy will play with me tomorrow.

*

The alarms had been tripped. Harold set them to 'Mute', swivelled the joystick, panning through the camera settings. The intruder had parked a 4 X 4 with blacked-out windows down by the five-bar gate cutting off the approach road. Perhaps spotting the camera activity, the driver stepped out of the vehicle and stood in full view. Harold nodded to himself, checked that David was safely engaged with his schoolwork, grabbed his rifle and set off to greet the visitor.

Up close, the man bore slight signs of the Moon Plague malaise. His naturally fair skin seemed a little too ghostly pale; standing up clearly tired him and he was already leaning wearily against his powerful car.

"Victor Trenchant," the newcomer stated, passing across his ID card for Harold to swipe with his pen scanner. "Vic, to my friends. Although they're... not here now."

"Why have you come?"

"I was here before. Didn't you see my notes?"

"You reclaiming possession?"

"Nah. Not yet, anyhow. Just a courtesy call. The government – or what's left of it – has to be seen to be doing something."

Harold frowned, answered, "I've posted everything I've got online, emailed all the answers the brains offer."

"People – survivors and hangers-on – don't trust technology much these days."

"Science is the only thing that will bring us the answer."

Victor shrugged then replied, "Knowledge is a double-edged sword. Or a bipartite apple."

"Sure, or Eve gave Adam the wrong fruit from the fig tree. You'd better come in. I've got tinned meat, beans, soup... Have you got any fresh food with you?"

" I can't help you there, mate. No one's got the long-term commitment to plant and nurture anything anymore. We'll soon be out of stores and oil across the globe. It'll be like a Biblical famine. Are you on your own here, Harold?"

"No... my wife's quite unwell but there's my son, David. He's eight years old. He seems to be immune at the moment."

"Lucky boy! You must be really proud."

"I am. But I'm shit scared, too, that one day soon he'll have to get by on his own. Anyhow, let's get up to the house. David could do with the stimulation of another person to talk to. If he doesn't get too shy."

*

"There's no milk, of course," Harold stated.

"That's OK, I've always taken my coffee black," Victor replied.

Harold blew on his heated drink. "It's so strange to be back here, what, twenty five years or so since I visited as a kid. I remember my grandfather telling me ghost stories about this place."

"Sure, the siege of the heretics of Christ. Biggest crime story ever in these parts. Guaranteed to spook the tourists. If only ancient tragedies were all we had on our plate."

Harold placed his mug down on the sideboard, asked, "What did you see on the way, Vic?"

"Dead people. Loose sheep. Vehicles all over the place. Not a single living soul."

"We're never going to get it back, are we?" Victor didn't reply. Harold continued, "Do you want some dried fruit or nuts? Vitamin tablets?"

Victor strode over to the porthole shaped window. "Sometimes I think I'll just take a whole bottle of happy pills and let it all go. But we've got to keep going. That's what Man does. Besides, you've got your son to think about."

"And Jennifer."

Victor wouldn't catch his eye. "Sure, your wife as well," he muttered, "proper little Garden of Eden. I'd better not stay too long or I'll be the snake in the garden of Macaverty Head." Then, with sudden intensity, "I'm sure you can hold on here in this windswept outpost, Harold. A lighthouse was always a beacon of hope. Even a disused one."

Evening. Victor cleaned his hands fastidiously with a disposable airline wipe. "Thanks for the grub," he muttered. "By the way, I've reconfigured David's educational programs. There's a whole load of Web-based material still available."

"I thought it had mostly crashed," Harold answered.

"No: there's a lot that's in stasis. Never updated but still accessible."

"He was quite a solitary boy even before the Moon Plague hit. He's going through a real fantasy play phase. I join in when I can but it's exhausting. Pirates, astronauts and similar make-believe adventures."

"You're holding up well, Harold."

"Am I?" He sipped at his instant coffee – bitter, dark and lukewarm. "Davie's full of questions which I try to answer as truthfully as possible. But I feel like I'm preparing him to be the last man on Earth."

Victor slowly unwrapped a second picnic packet of long-life biscuits, dunked one in his drink and replied, "There are pockets of survivors here and there. One day they'll link up and forge a new society, so – why are you waving your hand like that?"

"Those voices again. The choristers. Can't you hear them?"

Victor pursed his lips, twitched an ear, shook his slightly shaggy head. "Nah. Not that I disbelieve you. Then again, in this wind with the climactic disruption and the Mind Blocks chattering in the other room... well, one might hear almost anything."

Harold picked up the two mugs and stood them in the sink. He would wash them when he could spare the water. "I thought you might be coming to tell me to go out and find fit survivors of child-bearing age and start up a new colony here," he stated.

"Very John Wyndham," Victor commented. "That may be my next task. I just follow the orders from on high."

Harold wiped his hands on his already grubby trousers and said, "That's all I've been doing, too. That booster shot they gave me, though, it's only warding off the symptoms. It's not a cure. Me, you... we're both starting to succumb. Evans has gone already and Jennifer is... very sick... close to the end. We're not really in any fit state to start a new Garden of Eden."

"Maybe not. Still, there's always David. He seems to be in rude health. Let's pray he stays that way."

Harold nodded, whispered, "That's what keeps me going, pal."

Morning. Victor was getting ready to go. He shook hands with Harold and muttered something about going off to do the Law's work.

"Let's hope we can maintain the rule of law," Harold concurred. "That's the only thing holding society together."

Victor gave him a beatific look, zipped up his jacket then mussed David's hair in an affectionate way. He smiled and said, "Look after the boy. He's the hope for the future. Kids like David will save Humankind."

"Don't put so much pressure on the poor lad," Harold answered. "We're just trying to survive till the summer."

"Have some faith – in yourself and others," Victor commented as he unlocked his armoured car.

The wind was gentler today and last night's pounding rain had ceased. The father and son stood awhile watching the deserter. Soon even the speck of his vehicle was no longer discernible in the distance. Even at this habitually bleak time of year there should have been more than the handful of scraggly sheep grazing on the scrubby hill; there should have been gannets and gulls circling raucously in the grey sky. Three years ago, migrating birds had brought a brief outbreak of bird flu; people had volleyed back something much worse. So now, Mother Nature offered only a weak sun pushing at the drab clouds and the damaged Moon hanging in the east – diurnal and accusing.

Harold took the kid indoors and began the morning search for symptoms. Anything silvery, unnaturally shiny or hinting of leprosy, eczema or related conditions about the skin, any milkiness around the eyes... David was clear but not clean. Harold himself had the disease at a vestigial level and tried not to peer too closely in the mirror. Keep up the pretence and you might just fool yourself into thinking that, since the antibiotic booster the General had administered back in Edinburgh, you were slowly recovering like one in a thousand, one in ten thousand, one in a million…

"We need to wash today, Davie boy. Can't have you becoming too crusty and full of scabies. I'm sure there's enough rain collected in the water butt."

"Daddy, I hate baths."

"That's because I've let you go too long without a good soak, sonny boy. We'll stand you up and use a flannel – you won't get too wet."

"Then will you play pirates or astronauts with me?"

"Sure, for an hour or so. Deal?"

"Deal."

Where were all the psychoanalysts and the therapists in the world when you finally needed them? Where had all the overpaid shrinks gone? Gone to Moon Plague, every one.

Jesting aside, it was clear to Harold that even if he were just about keeping his shit together, the long-term effects on young David were likely to be catastrophic and would manifest at some point in the future. That which remained of such a suspicious prospect. He wished he could spend more time with the boy, indulge in the age-old father and son male bonding rituals, ground him in the necessary mind set for long-term survival. But his tasks here at Macaverty Head meant he had to leave the youngster to his own devices for much of the day.

If only Jennifer hadn't become so sick. Between the pair of them they could have protected David against every sling and arrow, every virus and psychosis. But she lay still in the locked third bedroom of the annex, a sleeping beauty not a Mrs Rochester, and, worry upon worry, Harold wished he and David could simply spend all day by her bedside; and hope and pray for her eventual recovery.

They were in the kitchen area with its bare boards and rain-lashed windows. At least they closed securely and, if you put on an extra jumper, you didn't feel the cold too much. Harold was reluctant to try and light the wood stove in this part of the complex. Therefore, it was a cold supper this evening: vitamin tablets, dry long-life crisp bread, bottled water and… sardines.

"I've taken the bones out, David, but chew the fish carefully just in case. It's Sunday tomorrow – maybe we'll treat ourselves to salmon, eh?"

"I like sardines, Daddy."

"Even the tomato sauce? You're a good lad. What did you play this afternoon?"

"Arty – er, Arctic explorering. Me and Jacko had to hide from a polar bear. You mustn't kill them, they ain't many left."

"That's true… sadly." Harold wiped ketchup from his lips, pulled a tiny white bone out from between his teeth.

"Daddy?"

"Yeah?"

"I heard the church singing again. Do you think…?"

"Now, David, I've told you that ghosts are just stories… like you and your polar bear."

"But…"

"Listen, David, I'm running so much electronic equipment inside the lighthouse that I'm bound to pick up old radio signals and all sorts of interference. You probably heard some BBC broadcast that's been bouncing around the ether for a couple of years. All right?"

"OK, but I knew what they were singing."

"You must have heard the song at school. Mr James probably played it in assembly. Everyone knows a few hymns and spirituals and the like."

With that sudden change of focus peculiar to the under-nines, David asked, "Daddy, is there any tinned custard?"

"All right, but it doesn't really go. Don't make yourself sick."

Whatever you do…

*

David's diary:

Today we were astronauts. Daddy used some old car board boxes and we painted the helmets. We stuck an old rapping off a packet over the face and it made every think go yellowish. It was so cool! We bounced around like we was on the moon. Before the moon got damage. I wanted to play this game for ages but Daddy was too busy but today he said ok and it was brill. I want to be a astronaut when I grow up and go out in space and on rockets and go moon and make it all better. I no I ull have to train and that and it ull be hard and take a few years but is what I want and Daddy says go for your dream.

So we bounced around and made re pears – no, that's repairs – to our space ship and our space station and we put on voices to be earth and… mission control, no red line for spelling mistakes now – and we saw the stars and rocks in space and dug up stuff on the moon and kept the whole game going for the ages. It's the best day I had hear and I didn't think about Mummy tell later when I went and toll her all about it. She didn't say nothing but I no she heard. I just wish we could all free play the game.

"Daddy, I'm scared."

"There's nothing to be scared of, David."

Except the present. And the future. And the legacy of the recent past: Humankind's constant meddling with nature and the repercussions that this time were inescapable and possibly insurmountable. Man must have his toys and must be at liberty to deploy them, if not inside the hearth and home then out in the back yard of the lunar surface. We have shifted our satellite in its orbit: we have broken its pristine beauty and silvery sheen into rubble and a dust cloud clogging up our atmosphere with subtle poison. Some have suggested that certain unscrupulous governments and cartels used the coming of the cloud to unleash their own biological weapons against their hated neighbours and rivals. Likely true but unproven: the net result was the same, as first thousands and then millions upon millions succumbed to the debilitating effects of the Moon Plague.

With the changed gravitational relationship came the environmental disasters: the European tsunami, the increased tectonic plate activity, the desert scorch across the temperate zones, the crop failures, the wobbling of Earth's axis, the religious crises, the breakdown… The truth is that we can never get back to how things were before and that if a few pockets of civilised people do manage to survive, the best we can hope for is to preserve a little of our knowledge and culture and hope that the rest may one day be re-discovered.

The Moon Plague has left the air unfit to breathe and the water not safe to drink but we had to do it anyway and hang the consequences. The future was the next five minutes or twenty-four hours. To greater or lesser degrees, we were all infected.

David, my boy, you have every right to be scared.

"Shall we play a game of something? Ludo, snakes and ladders, cards…?"

"I'd like that, Daddy. Bagsy I get the blue counters."

How long since he had a bath or a shower? There was always the option of the water butt, which had collected plenty of recent rain, but the lack of proper sanitation facilities was yet another irritation grinding them down. He and David flushed the chemical toilet once, maybe twice a day. It was no way to live in the twenty-first century.

What was the use of his pathetic mission here? Running the Mind Blocks with the wisdom of the age and the great brains imprinted into digital code hadn't yet saved anybody from the ravages of the Moon Plague. And just how many humans were left to rebuild and repopulate this ravaged Earth anyhow? Maybe we should all make our peace with God / Nature / or the universe and admit that we messed up our short span and should never have been given so much leeway in the first place.

He had seen so much death and desperation. As much as a survivor of the Somme, the Black Death and the *Titanic* rolled into one. And just what psychological scarring must David be shielding with his invented games of imaginary adventures?

And then there were the voices echoing ghostly inside his head and around the walls… but not registering on any recording equipment or empirical basis.

"Our Lord, my light,
Through darkness unending,
In broken skies,
Thy beacon shining,
My faith unbending."

But he had no faith, no belief in anything other than simple survival from one twenty-four-hours to the next.

*

A flag is an affront. So says any self-determining nation that didn't plant that particular pole in that particular surface.

We came in peace for all mankind. But not all mankind is at peace, far from it and not all of mankind feels you have the right to represent them. An old target, the stylised conflict of the age of the space race, suddenly became a field of conflict, a ball of rock worth squabbling about, a significant goal again. If you can build rockets to wipe out your neighbours' towns, ports and bus stations, you can build rockets to shatter the dust bowls on poor Luna. The technology is largely the same, it's only a matter of scale.

A sudden boom in sales of telescopes, a sudden rash of nocturnal and diurnal sky watchers. Look, I can see the damage from here.

We couldn't quite bring ourselves to kill one another properly down here on Earth, so we played it out on the less than neutral ground of our ancient satellite, thinking we had suitably externalised all our anger and acquisitiveness and one-upmanship. Oh so wrong.

The reflective silver sphere was more than just a mirror for all our hopes, our aggression and our lunacy. All our religions and spiritual beliefs had taught us that whatever we do in this life will eventually come back to haunt us. So the Moon shall take her revenge for such mistreatment and we shall suffer her unpredictable wrath. Had we not been sufficiently warned by her twenty-eight day moods?

Unpredictable tides. A wobbling in *our* orbit. Chunks crashing towards us, testing the accuracy of our fabled missiles and the efficacy of our response. And worse – a disease, a malaise, not immediately explicable by modern medicine, but effective nonetheless. Revenge is sweet, revenge is cold. Space is not sweet but it is definitely cold. And increasingly empty. What lies above shall be mirrored below. And who shall survive the Moon Plague?

"Goodbye, Jennifer."

No matter how inevitable a tragedy, it still rips at the heart. David would wonder why he couldn't gaze upon his mother's sickly, somnolent form before bedtime but Harold would make some facile excuse about tiredness or disarray. For now. Perhaps tomorrow they'd face the truth of the McClair family being reduced to the purely masculine. Then there was the question of what to do with her body. Perhaps he would seek a suitably giving patch of soil to demarcate as a final resting place. He would not be hurling Jenny over the cliff in a panic, like he'd done with Evans' corpse, nor would he attempt a do-it-yourself cremation. Doubtless, there were tools here to dig the sod.

He locked the door from the outside, kept David busy all evening with an impromptu English, maths and geography test. Geography? Some of the mountains and rivers might be unchanged but many of the capital cities were no more than concrete cemeteries.

The ghostly singing was back. The unquiet congregation who'd sought sanctuary within these very rounded walls only to become the victims of violent religious persecution. The locals had suppressed their story for a few decades but ultimately the murderous stain showed through all the coats of whitewash.

A lighthouse ought to be defendable. You had the traditional siege advantages of height and three hundred and sixty degrees vision. But the sect had pledged their allegiance to non-violence and a spirituality more akin to certain Eastern beliefs, with a concentration on sexual enlightenment, food deprivation and the occasional assistance of illicit roots and herbs. No wonder the local Protestants had so taken against them.

And yet all their songs were recognisably from the Christian tradition. He could see David's lips whispering along with some familiar phrase or other. Perhaps they would become accustomed to this eerie serenade.

Maybe the voices actually were angels, come to comfort and collect…

"OK, David, what's the longest river in the world?"

But the answer was surely the river of tears. Ready to flood and engulf at any moment.

It was another wild night with the restless sea smashing into the rocks on what passed for the beach. The wind had been incessant for almost the entirety of the past two days and the nocturnal sky was wild with clouds scudding against the cliffs and each other. Where they clashed, they sparked off electrical discharges – flashes of light, thuds of thunder, a localised warning of meteorological apocalypse. And again, Harold thought he could hear the hymns of the old religious sect who'd sought sanctuary here but been trapped in deadly siege. The story told that they had no weapons other than their faith.

Their spirit apparently lingered on whilst their murderers lay in the crumbled graves of the decayed churchyard. What was left of it.

What are they trying to tell me? Are they even here or am I just conjuring up an expectation?

The CCTV cameras showed nothing. He consulted the Mind Blocks. With steadfast scientific bent, they ordered him to go out and check the equipment. In this weather?

But there was surely movement over there on the curve of the headland, apparitions gathering in the spectral evening poorly lit by occasional lightning and the reflected silver nuggets of a cracked moon.

They were coming to take him.

They were coming to save him.

They weren't coming at all, just Harold losing his grip.

Harold had kept David with him for almost the whole day. Keep him occupied, don't mention Jennifer, somehow we'll get through the next few minutes, hours… days. Initially the boy had been fascinated by the array of drives and monitors running the encryption of the preserved brain patterns of so many scientists, artists and renaissance men. Their chatter and conjecture was supposed to help Harold, David and everyone else survive, keep in touch with the other outposts and pockets of humanity. But to Harold's jaded ears all they seemed to do was bemoan their lot or demand things from him that he couldn't give and that were entirely inappropriate. He'd taken to calling them *The Wailing Wall*. He'd lately kept the speakers mostly on mute.

For all the high hopes and the hands across the ether, his world was narrowing and, despite today's surprisingly clement weather, Harold felt he was losing touch with the world. He had a truckload of oil, generators and supplies of wood; and the lighthouse itself, despite being cold stone, was thick walled and insulated quite well against the stormy spells. There was dried food, tinned food, bottled water. Between them, he and David could hold out doing the government's work in this bleak, promised land till the summer at least. But then what?

"Daddy, what's 'without form and void'?"

"It means there was nothing at all, David. Why are you reading the Bible?"

"Mr Victor gave it to me."

He held his hand out gently and David reluctantly handed over the book. The print was a little dense for Harold's liking. Along with a few Greek myths and philosophical tracts, this tome was the root of Western culture and, even in his short time at school, David would have heard the odd quotation at Christmas and Easter. Even so…

"Listen, son, if you want to read about Jesus or Noah, we'll get something up on the computer with simpler language."

"Mr Victor said I should try and read the orig- proper version."

"He's not my boss and he's not your boss, Davie. And he's not here now."

It was time to undertake the daily trudge to the scrubby patch of hedgerow that Harold had denoted as the outdoor latrine. The wind was ripping through his jacket and the granite-faced clouds were starting to empty their own bladders. Gazing back at the sixty-foot lighthouse and the battered buildings adjoining its southern side, he wondered how much longer they could sustain themselves in this bleak promised land. He'd heard the voices again last night yet there was surely no one else around for miles. Electronic interference, then? Or a stone-held memory of previous occupants of this hopeless bolt hole?

His watch told him it was early afternoon although it was hard to believe with such a louring sky and daylight with the quality of gloom. Whilst he waited for David to relieve himself, he performed a cursory examination of his wrists and forearms. He needed a long bath or shower, that was for sure, rather than a quick rub with airline style hand wipes. He couldn't determine any new signs of Moon Plague, no leprosic silvering of the skin, so that was a small mercy. For now. During the early days following the unleashing of the disease everyone had carelessly or unknowingly breathed the tainted air and drank the unsafe water – and hang the consequences. The future became the next five minutes or twenty-four hours. It was highly likely that at some level, every single person was infected. Even David.

"I can't go, Daddy. Just a little wee-wee."

"OK, son. But we can't come out again today. It will be raining cats and dogs soon."

"I'd like that!" David beamed.

He shared a smile with the boy at the idiomatic image. Anything was conceivable in these post-apocalyptic days.

As they hurried back to the shelter of Macaverty Head, he briefly recalled a few books he'd read during a brief flirtation with science fiction as a student. The last man on Earth tales often dealt with the difficulty of obtaining decent food from the abandoned supermarkets but no one ever dealt with bowel issues. All that tinned or re-hydrated mush sloshing around, giving you debilitating stomach cramps…

And was he now the last *man* on Earth? Had Victor made it back to base? Was there really anybody at the other end of the satellite-relayed communications? Could you count the Mind Blocks as being truly alive?

He squeezed David's gloved hand and – to a muttered "Yuk!" and screwed up face like the remnant of the Moon – told the kid, "Raisins and prunes for you tomorrow morning, my boy."

The Moon Plague had hit just as hard here as everywhere else. Human and animal corpses littered the roads and hedgerows. They'd driven as courteously and courageously as they could but even so had occasionally brushed an outstretched limb or appendage. After a while they no longer thought of them as the recently living but merely obstacles like building debris after an earthquake or arboreal hazards after a hurricane and flood.

"O Lord, our shepherd,
Bring life and resurrection."

Some thirty miles earlier, a lone supplicant had begged help, succour, rescue… but he was clearly close to the last throes of the space-borne disease and they drove on despite his clutching hands, the rocks he launched and the painful cries for help.

So where had all these survivors sprung from?

"Save us for heaven,
Through thy holy son."

Go away, I can't help you! You don't get me or David!

If you really exist, head inland and loot the abandoned supermarkets for supplies and shelter!

If you don't exist, get out of my head! I don't believe in ghosts, spirits, haunting, the whole supernatural caboodle!

Launching his voice from the lighthouse gantry: "I deny you!"

A silvering of the skin.
The epidermis takes on a slightly luminous sheen before beginning to flake and dry.
Lethargy, oh lethargy!
Today I have no energy.

Some stronger spells as my appetite waxes but then inevitably wanes.
I want to return to the place I call home,
Orbit around Mother's solidity,
Reflect her glory with the shiny membrane that once lived and breathed,
But is now merely my shroud.
Lethargy, oh lethargy!
I'm robbed of all my energy.
No strength: I am broken though I hang on still.
My influence once strong but now uncertain
Give me no food,
No air,
No water
I want to rebel and blame those who brought me to this state,
But I barely have the strength to whimper.
Leave me to my protracted death
In peace.

"O Lord, our shepherd"
The shepherds are all dead; the flock is running free.
"Salvation is at hand."
No, you are bringing death, destruction, the final nail in humanity's coffin.

"Through your holy son."
He's my boy, get away from him!

Harold knelt down in front of the boy and mustered as much manly earnestness as he could.

"Listen, David, we are in a bit of danger but we've got to be strong. The voices you've heard – the hymns and suchlike – they belong to some people who want to take over the lighthouse and hurt us. They think they've found God but really it's just a new strain of the disease. Do you understand?" A mute nod. Deeply frightened eyes. "OK," Harold continued, "now if I tell you to throw some rocks at these people, I'm not asking you to be naughty. We have the right to protect ourselves. Always."

The inevitable question. Harold looked away for a few moments to compose a plausible response. At last:

"Mummy's still very ill, David. She'll stay locked in her room where no one can get to her. But we've got to fight... like pirates or astronauts. All right?"

So while his attention had been on the daily domestic ritual of feeding and educating his precious son and on running and overseeing the Mind Block program that was going to preserve Humankind and reclaim the Earth – Yeah, right! – Harold had temporarily taken his eyes off the bigger picture. All the half-dead and dying survivors of the Moon Plague must have massed over the weeks in the nooks and crannies of the cliff top, the hardy trees and hedges dotting the incline, and the bolt holes of the wrecked and wind blasted buildings way down in the village.

David has hardly spoken during the preceding three days. Only mortal fear has loosened his lips now.

You consult the modern oracles but their Delphic vision is self-referential... obscured... patently useless.

How secure are your outbuildings? And the lighthouse itself?

Because you knew they were coming. You heard them all along. The singing, the chanting, the rejoicing.

The expectation of a better life.

"Daddy, they're outside!"

"Stay strong, David. Keep your place at the window. Keep your eyes open."

"Daddy, they're trying to get in."

"It's OK, son, everything's locked and bolted."

Just how many were there? Such a mass of bodies circling the lighthouse, giving him vertigo, making him feel like he was about to fall into their spectral morass, give up the battle... No! He must hold on.

"Daddy, they're singing a song I know from school. Can you hear it? Daddy, ghosts don't sing."

Misplaced anger flavoured with fear: "They can talk, for God's sake!" And pass through walls?

Evening and this time they were massing with intent, ready to claim – or even reclaim – this ravaged scrap of land. He'd fired a couple of warning shots above their distant heads but to no avail. This rifle was a long-range weapon, slow to load, wayward at close quarters. And Harold had had his fill of killing in order to survive.

"Daddy?" David's whisper broke his doomed watch. "Daddy, you know when King Herod wanted to kill baby Jesus? Well, they ran away to Egypt."

"Egypt's a long way from here, son."

And there's not really anywhere left to run away to. The last inevitable stop is high up in Macaverty Head lighthouse. This is the end of the Earth.

The constant background of chanted spirituals must be getting to the boy, reawakening memories from school lessons and assemblies. But the female member of this holy family was already dead and even in the original story did anyone know or care what happened to Joseph the father and protector?

The enemy was approaching. He loosed off a brief volley of bullets, taking down at least two of the diseased disciples. They were running now, a multi-headed beast of united voices joined in a violent song of praise:

"Kill the unbeliever!

Restore to us

The Lord's pure order."

There was no further point holding this window position. The key battleground had shifted to the locked and barricaded front door of Macaverty Head.

Punch a ghost and your hand might go right through their spectral ectoplasm.

Push, shove, hold fast to your Alamo.

Feel resistant bone and muscle. No phantoms, these, but flesh and blood. Disease-ridden in many instances, shining phosphorescent silver like the Moon of memory. But still strong enough to keep attacking, pressing up the spiral staircase into this last chance panic room on the second floor of the lighthouse. They were ragged adversaries, to be sure, and their faces and flesh carried the mark of the

Moon Plague; but they showed no apparent weakness. And there were so many of them; however hard you fight, there seem to be too many of them.

Hands pinned Harold's arms painfully behind his back; a scything kick took his resistant legs out from under him and he fell awkwardly to his knees. Worse, two men and one woman had grabbed David. The boy was scared into silence, trying to catch his father's eye for the slightest flicker of hope.

Pandora's Box was dark and empty.

A trio of combatants abased themselves briefly, offering a wordless prayer, then created a space for the grand entrance of their leader.

Victor.

Thank God for that! He would sort out this tragic misunderstanding.

Victor threw back his ceremonial cape and proclaimed, "The judgement is at hand. The broken Moon looks on. Those who breathe, those who believe, shall follow the new creed."

"What is this mystical nonsense, Victor? People brought this damnation down upon ourselves."

"Be silent, heathen. Your function is over as, sadly, is the dead modern Madonna. But no matter, for it is written that the meek shall inherit the Earth. The survivors. The new people. We have come to claim the saviour whose rebirth has long been promised."

"Take me!" Harold screamed. "Just leave David alone!"

"We don't require you and the other assassins of scripture. Science has failed us; your science has brought us death. We don't need so-called empirical knowledge, we just need faith."

The last word echoed around the cramped stone walls. Some of the disciples began humming the nocturnal spiritual but Victor's raised right hand silenced them.

Through bruised lips, Harold answered, "Your religion exported slavery, death and disease across whole continents. Science is the only answer to the challenges of the present and the future."

Victor smiled. "We know our future, we are sure of salvation now. The boy child of the Virgin will grow and lead us all to Paradise."

Harold struggled against his captors, momentarily freeing one arm and attaining a half-standing position. "This is utter nonsense!" he yelled. "Jennifer was not a virgin; David was conceived normally. Your Holy Spirit is... just a fairy tale!"

Victor turned his attention towards the holy boy and said softly, "David you will grow up to be an astronaut and you will lead us to the Moon and to Heaven. Come away with us now. I shall mentor you until... it is time."

"Daddy, I don't want to go!"

"David, stay strong. I will rescue you. Even from beyond the grave, I'll come –"

The blow to the back of his head was brief, brutal and almost instantly fatal. As Harold slumped for the last time, he saw silver – behind his eyes; at the edges of his vision; on his afflicted hands, fingers and forearms…

The boy was encircled. Victor spoke again, "You must consider today as your coming of age. The mission begins now, David. Leave this shabby existence behind you, special one. Destiny awaits you."

As the ragtag band quit the lighthouse, their prophet gave whispered instructions to disconnect the generators and set fire to the ancient stone building. Even if Macaverty Head itself wasn't completely razed to the ground, the burnt out black tower itself would serve as warning and reminder enough to any recalcitrant heretics hereabouts.

The twittering electronic voices of the great thinkers who had brought Mankind to this parlous state would be silenced.

The wind would carry abroad only the mob's joyously renewed songs of praise as they sought their twisted, unattainable vision of Paradise.

Allen is a stalwart of the independent press scene and is well known as a writer, editor and commentator. His debut story "Dead to the World" (1982) has been reprinted on six different occasions, including a translation into Spanish. His first novel was the highly acclaimed "The Planet Suite" (TTA Press, 1997), described by Brian w. Aldiss as "The course for the future."

Since the turn of the millennium, Allen has had two previous collections of his shorter fiction published - "Somnambulists" (Elastic Press, 2004), short-listed for the British Fantasy Society award; and "Urban Fantastic" (Crowswing, 2006). "Once and Future Cities" is the third distinct collection of his unique stories.

Allen was short-listed for the BFS award for his non-fiction collection "Days of the Dodo" (Dodo London Press, 2006). As an editor, he won the BFS award for "Best Anthology" with "The Elastic Book Of Numbers" (Elastic Press, 2005). He has also edited "Subtle Edens" for Elastic Press (2008) and is currently compiling "Catastrophia", an anthology of catastrophe fiction due from PS in 2010.

Check out Allen's web site at www.allenashley.com

Contact Allen at allen@allenashley.com